Convertible Counterpoint

Music scholars who are acquainted with the *Convertible Counterpoint* o   ...o..o..c.. ᴛa-neiev consider it the greatest work ever written in its field. As a textbook on composition it has *the* high recommendation, of such authorities as Dr. Serge Koussevitzky, Serge Rachmaninoff, Leopold Godowsky, Moritz Rosenthal, Gregor Piatigorsky, Lazare Saminsky, Alexander Siloti, Nicholas Orloff.

Every history of modern music mentions the Taneiev *Counterpoint,* every serious scholar has heard of it; yet the riches opened up by Taneiev 's principles and methods have until now been available only to those who have a knowledge of the Russian language. The appearance of the text in English is a landmark in musical education, for by placing within the reach of American and British composers and students material that heretofore has been accessible only to their Russian contemporaries, it supplies a lack that has long been felt among students of contrapuntal theory.

This book reveals possibilities for the art of composition that up to the present have been but vaguely realized or actually unknown. For the study of counterpoint is here put on a basis of pure mathematics, and the Taneiev method opens up an enormous range of resources, hitherto untouched because of the lack of that adequate approach which only mathematics can provide.

In the Preface to his work, Taneiev states his aims as follows:

"In studying the difficult and involved treatment of counterpoint, especially double counterpoint, as presented in the textbooks of ancient and modem theorists, I encountered various obstacles that seemed to result: from faulty classifications, too many useless rules and not enough essential rules. The system expounded in the present work appears to me to be simpler, more accurate and more accessible, as the result of applying the processes of elementary algebra to contrapuntal combinations, and by restating certain essential rules in terms of the conventional symbols of mathematics. This enabled me to take into consideration a far greater mass of relevant facts, and to bring them under the control of a comparatively small number of general principles."

Assuming knowledge of simple counterpoint on the part of the student, Taneiev proceeds to develop on an algebraic basis a theory of complex counterpoint. The mathematical system clears up a number of difficult points that in other counterpoint texts are either slurred over or not mentioned at all, but which occur in composition. Far from resulting in "mathematical" music, the Taneiev approach to Counterpoint actually releases, and stimulates the imagination, pointing the way to endless possibilities that otherwise would never have been conceived. That this was true of Taneiev's own original work is attested by Rimsky-Korsakov, who wrote: "It would seem that his method ought to result in a dry and academic composition, devoid of the shadow of an inspiration, in really, however, his *Oresteia* proved quite the reverse—for all its strict premeditation, the opera was striking in its wealth of beauty and expressiveness."

Taneiev deals exhaustively with twenty-three ways of writing double counterpoint, not by endless lists of rules and exceptions, but by algebraic equations that eliminate all trial-and-error methods and give positive results. He also treats of triple counterpoint at intervals other than the octave—something that virtually no other writer on counterpoint has done. Though applying, according to the title, to the strict style of the Polyphonic Period, the principles of *Convertible Counterpoint*—as Taneiev himself points out—can be extended to the free style of later times and to the modernism of today and of the future. The study and mastery of the Taneiev system will result in a command over the resources of composition that can be obtained in no other way, for, by the application of Taneiev 's method, an inventory of what is still untried in counterpoint would run into astronomical figures. Although an advanced work. *Convertible Counterpoint* may be successfully attempted as soon as the principles of two-voiced mixed counterpoint have been grasped.

Serge Ivanovitch Taneiev

CONVERTIBLE COUNTERPOINT
In The Strict Style

Translated by G. ACKLEY BROWER
Introduction by SERGE KOUSSEVITZKY

BOSTON
Branden Publishing Company, Inc.
Originally Bruce Humphries Publishers

Printed in the United States of America

Library of congress Catalog Card No. 61-10738

ISBN 10: 0828321841
ISBN 13:: 9780828321846
Paperback edition

BOSTON
www.brandenbooks.com
Branden Publishing Company, Inc.
(Originally Bruce Humphries Publishers)
PO Box 812094
Wellesley MA 02482

TO THE MEMORY OF

HERMAN AUGUSTOVITCH LAROCHE

(1845 – 1904)

INTRODUCTION

This translation of my late friend's labor of twenty years opens up to the English-speaking world one of the greatest musical treatises ever written, yet one that the barrier of language has denied far too long to countless students and composers whose careers might have been forwarded by it. If anyone ever raised the question as to what author commanded the most comprehensive and ready knowledge of counterpoint through the ages I believe none other than Taneiev could be named, because this work is the synthesis of two centuries of study and learning in the realm of counterpoint.

Serge Ivanovitch was one of the most extraordinary intellectuals of the many to which Russia has given birth. In addition to music he acquired a really deep knowledge of natural science, sociology and philosophy. Russia's artists and thinkers sought him out all through his life—even flocking to visit him in the poor dwelling of his last years. Tschaikowsky, fifteen years his senior, would submit to criticism from this pupil of his which he would tolerate from no one else. Rimsky-Korsakow, with all his technical brilliance, felt like a student musician in the presence of Taneiev, and admitted it.

This great treatise was published in Moscow in 1909. Since I practised composition in my early career I fairly devoured the book and urged on many others the advantage of doing likewise. When I had to devote most of my time to my career as a double-bass virtuoso, and later when my activities emphasized conducting to the detriment of composing, I found that Taneiev's *Counterpoint* was an invaluable asset on innumerable occasions in working out interpretation of orchestral scores—especially those of Bach, Handel and Brahms.

In Moscow we lived in the same neighborhood and frequently called on one another. We had long, interesting talks, and he amazed me by the boldness of his ideas; often in the field of musical interpretation he was daring to the point of radicalism. I recall when I was preparing for the first time to conduct Beethoven's Ninth Symphony that I used to go to Taneiev with the score. His conception was so striking and free from established traditions that even I, revolutionarily inclined, did not dare to accept it.

I knew him, of course, as one of Russia's formost pianists—although unknown to America. I have never heard the Fourth Concerto of Beethoven given a more brilliant and vivid performance; free and logical at the same time.

And I knew him also as a composer of unique qualities. So much was he the master of contrapuntal theory and not its slave, that his music concealed his immense technique in its application. This is particularly true of his only opera, *Oresteia*, his chamber music, and especially his cantata *On the Reading of a Psalm*.

It was my privilege to introduce this masterpiece to the public in two different ways. Taneiev in his last years was much reduced from lifelong affluence, and was living in a primitive dwelling with not even running water. In the beginning of 1913 he told me how he wished to compose a cantata which would require two years of intense work, but that he could not even dream of doing it because he must make a living—giving lessons and so forth. I immediately offered to give him the sum he needed, and to publish the cantata in my publishing house, *Editions Russe de Musique*, which, by coincidence, had been founded the year his book appeared. The sum he mentioned was ridiculously small even for those days. All he needed, he said, was 3000 roubles—equivalent to $1500—for two years of life! This may well give an idea of how modestly he lived, but he positively refused a higher offer.

7

In two years the cantata was completed and I placed it on my program in both Moscow and Petrograd. It was indeed a masterpiece—a great and noble work. When I conducted two performances in each city in April, 1915, it was declared by all competent judges to be the finest work Taneiev had produced. I have never seen Serge Ivanovitch as happy as at these performances of his cantata. Later in the month he caugh a severe cold at the funeral services for Scribin, and this produced a heart complication which caused his death on June 19, 1915.

The enlightment on musical structure, the mental stimulus, in Taneiev's book are of far-reaching service. As counterpoint is presented by Serge Ivanovitch the reader finds himself, like the author, making of it not so much the analysis of a process as a habit of thought, a second thought, a second nature, which leads on to the creation of beauty—flawless in its form and proportions.

SERGE KOUSSEVITZKY

TRANSLATOR'S PREFACE

The works of Serge Ivanovitch Taneiev (1856-1915), both musical and literary, seem to be little known outside of his native country, though recent years have witnessed an increased interest in the labors of one who as composer, theorist, concert pianist, critic, and teacher, became one of the outstanding figures in the musical life of Russia and who is now gaining the wider recognition that he deserves. Taneiev's compositions must speak for themselves; the present purpose is neither to attempt a critical estimate of them nor to give a biographical sketch of their composer, but to introduce to teachers and students of composition his work on advanced counterpoint.

It is difficult to discuss this book in terms of restraint. Since the fourteenth century, or earlier, many books on music theory have appeared. Amid a mass of indifferent writings and others of considerable value but not outstanding there are a few that have made history; one of the greatest was the *Dodechachordon* of Glearanus, another was the *Gradus ad Parnassum* of Josph Fux. Not without good reason has Lazare Saminsky referred to *Convertible Counterpoint* as "having the same meaning for musical science that Newton's *Principia* has for cosmology." It may be said without reservation that the student has at hand the greatest work on counterpoint ever written. It is a book that will reveal possibilities for the art of composition that have hitherto been but vaguely realized or actually unknown. Though applying, according to the title, only to the strict style of the Polyphonic Period, its principles, as the author himself says, may be extended to the free style of later times and to the modernism of today and of the future. To study and master its contents will give the student a command over the resources of composition that can be obtained in no other way. The variety of subjects in it, the thoroughness and clearness with which they are presented, their logical arrangement, the examples illustrating the text, and above all the astounding originality of the author's thought—all this makes this a work compared to which other books on counterpoint seem elementary.

From this it may be inferred that *Convertible Counterpoint* is not a beginner's text, yet its study may be undertaken sooner than might be expected. The author says (in §175) that the exercises he suggests should start as soon as three-voice counterpoint can be satisfactorily managed, and that thereafter simple and convertible counterpoint should be studied concurrently. To this I would add that there seems to be no reason why the exercises in two voices should not be successfully attempted as soon as two-voice mixed counterpoint (i.e. both voices in the fifth species) has been studied. The student should then be well able to cope with the simpler of the fascinating problems set by Taneiev in the earlier chapters of Parts One and Two, though the more difficult ones will require skill in the manipulation of from three to six voices.

The first thing that is likely to surprise the reader who may think that this is "just another book on counterpoint" is the proposition advanced by the author in his Preface—that the study of counterpoint is here put on a mathematical basis—algebra in fact. Yet this is quite in accordance with present-day tendencies, and the fact that Taneiev thought about it as far back as 1870 shows that he is a pioneer in a field of research that now includes several prominent names in the musical world. But the student may be assured that he is not expected to know more than the fundamentals of algebra; of this more will be said presently. Taneiev's method opens up an enormous extent of untried resources, heretofore inaccessible because of the lack of an adequate approach—and only mathematics can provide it. Let no one get the idea that such an approach will stifle the imagination and yield the unwelcome result of writing music that sounds mathematical. The effect of Taneiev's method is quite the opposite; it releases the imagination, pointing the way to endless possibilities that otherwise would never have been thought of. Here a few statistics may be enlightening, as showing how inadequately a vast subject has hitherto been treated.

Referring to eighteen standard texts that claim to teach double counterpoint[1], I find that while all of them deal with double counterpoint at the octave (or two octaves), none mentions double counterpoint at the fifth, only three at the sixth, two at the seventh, six at the ninth, seven at the eleventh, all except two at the tenth and the twelfth, six at the thirteenth and five at the fourteenth. Two of them deal with double counterpoint only at the octave. Several speak disparagingly of double counterpoint at intervals other than the octave, tenth, and twelfth. Not one mentions a use of combined themes that is found in Bach but which can be classified as neither simple nor double counterpoint. Put together, these texts provide for only nine ways of writing counterpoint in which the interval-relationship could be changed; Taneiev deals exhaustively with twenty-three, not by giving endless lists of rules and exceptions but by equations in simple algebra that eliminate all trial-and-error methods and that give positive results. All of them are practicable in the strict style, not to mention the free. Furthermore, none of these texts deals with triple counterpoint at any interval other than the octave, and one of them (Jadassohn) definitely states that such a thing is impossible. Taneiev shows how it is done

Of the authors cited in the first footnote and who could be expected to know about Taneiev's work only one, George Conus, mentions him. Conus' book *A Course in Modal Counterpoint*[2] refers briefly to double counterpoint at the octave, tenth, and twelfth, but he gives credit to Taneiev as having written the only complete treatise on the subject. After all, the sources upon which Taneiev's work is based were available to many who came before him, to his contemporaries, and to all who came after, and the fact that no one took full advantage of them certainly justifies the remark made in § 279 about certain theorists being exposed to "grave suspicions."

Nearly all these texts confuse the issue by treating double counterpoint at the tenth and the twelfth and duplication in imperfect consonances as belonging to the same category, whereas they do not. Again, the changes possible in the time-entrances of two or more melodies, called in this book the horizontal shift, are ignored in all texts except Taneiev's, though some authors call attention to this interesting phenomenon in occasional quotations from Bach. But none of them throw the faintest light upon how it is done. Finally, the principles of duplicated counterpoint and the horizontal shift combined with other varieties of counterpoint in both two and three voices leave one amazed at the enormous scope of the subject. An inventory of what is still untried in counterpoint would, by the application of Taneiev's methods, run almost into astronomical figures.

Now as to algebra: the amount needed is very small—only a knowledge of the meanings of positive and negative as appiled to numbers and letters; the special meanings of the signs $+$, $-$, $<$ and $>$, the principles of addition and subtraction; the transposition of terms in equations, and the rules for the removal of parentheses. Three hours spent with any algebra textbook should be enough for the most complicated of Taneiev's problems.

---

[1]The authors consulted were: Bandini, Bridge, Cherubini, Conus, Dubois, Goetschius, Haupt, Jadassohn, Jeppesen, Kitson, Krohn, Marquard, Morris, Prout, Richter, Riemann, Spalding, and Stohr; by no means exhaustive of the literature on the subject but, I think, a fair cross-section.

[2]In Russian; it is published by the Soviet Government.

A few additions of my own are in footnotes or at the ends of chapters. The musical quotations have been verified—a necessary measure as the original edition contains many misprints. On the last page of the original is the word *konyetz,* which I have omitted, as this book was not "the end" but was followed by a sequel dealing with the canon, doing this difficult style of composition what the present work does for convertible counterpoint—puts the study on a scientific basis.

I am indebted to several whose interest, advice, and information are in no small measure responsible for the appearance in English of the monumental work of Taneiev. First to be mentioned in Lazare Saminsky, who, about twenty years ago, told me of Taneiev's book and how radically different and superior it was to other texts. Without his description of the book and his enthusiastic recommendation of it I might never have known about it. Next are the obligations I owe to Alexander Siloti and Nicholas Orloff, both pupils of Taneiev whose reminiscences of their teacher were of the greatest interest. From Serge Rachmaninoff, Leopold Godowsky, Moritz Rosenthal, and Gregor Piatigorski I have received encouragement in a project that I entered upon with some doubts as to its interest to a publisher but none as to its value. Dr. Serge Koussevitzky, whose activities in the musical life of America were too well known to need further comment, contributed an Introduction. From books I have got valuable help from the *Memoirs of Taneiev,* by Leonid Sabaniev, and from the second volume of the *History of Music in Russia,* a symposium on Taneiev, published in Moscow.

Tha manager of Bruce Humphries, Mr. Edmund R. Brown, and the members of the editorial and production staff have solved most successfully the peculiar mechanical problems that the printing of such a complicated text involves—the first of its kind to be done in English.

G. ACKLEY BROWER

AUTHOR'S PREFACE

In studying the difficult and involved treatment of counterpoint—especially double counterpoint—as presented in the textbooks of ancient and modern theorists, I encountered various obstacles that seemed to result from faulty classifications, too many useless rules and not enough essential rules.

The system expounded in the present work appears to me to be simpler, more accurate and more accessible, as the result of applying the processes of elementary algebra to contrapuntal combinations, and by restating certain essential rules in terms of the conventional symbols of mathematics. This enabled me to take into consideration a far greater number of relevant facts, and to bring them under control of a comparatively small number of general principles.

For many years I have used separate parts of this theory in my classes in counterpoint at the Moscow Conservatory, and I have tried to simplify the treatment at those places where experience has shown that difficulties were encountered by students.

The present book is an exposition, of the utmost comprehensiveness, of convertible counterpoint in the strict style. In using it as a textbook the teacher should select, from amid the detailed development of the subject, what is most necessary for the student.

I have dedicated this book to the memory of H. A. Laroche, whose articles (especially *Thoughts on Musical Education in Russia*) have had a profound influence on the trend of my musical activities.

SERGE TANEIEV

Klin, July 1, 1906

PART ONE

VERTICAL-SHIFTING COUNTERPOINT

DIVISION A

TWO-VOICE VERTICAL-SHIFTING COUNTERPOINT

Chapter

13

CONTENTS

DIVISION D

THREE-VOICE HORIZONTAL-SHIFTING AND DOUBLE-SHIFTING COUNTERPOINT

INTRODUCTION

The art of counterpoint has passed through two eras: that of the strict style, which attained its highest development in the sixteenth century (Palestrina and Orlando Lasso), and the period of the free style, of which the crowning achievements are found in the works of Bach and Handel. The differences between the contrapuntal writing of these two eras are to be found both in the nature of the melodies themselves and in the character of the harmonies formed by these melodies in combination.

Strict counterpoint, developed on the basis of the so-called ecclesiastical modes, was a pre-eminently vocal style that had not been exposed to the kind of influence that instrumental music later exerted; antedating such influence, it attained to complete self-fulfilment. Strict counterpoint excludes everything that presents difficulty to voices singing without instrumental accompaniment. Melodies in the strict style show evidences of their origin in the chants of the Catholic Church — they exhibit many characteristics of these early canticles. They are strictly diatonic, are written in the ecclesiastical modes, and in them are no. progressions of intervals that are difficult of intonation, such as sevenths, ninths, augmented or diminished intervals, etc

The basis of multi-voice counterpoint of the strict style is of course the two-voice texture. Two-voice counterpoint is subject to the rules governing the progression of intervals, these being employed in a way that for the normal hearing is the most simple and natural. A knowledge of the rules of simple counterpoint in the strict style is essential in order to understand the present work. though this is not the place to explain them. In strict writing the rules of two-voice counterpoint apply also to more intricate polyphony. With a few exceptions it is observable that in a multi-voice combination each voice together with every other forms correct two-voice counterpoint; that multi-voice counterpoint is an association of several two-voice combinations, as a result of which is obtained a series of varied consonant and dissonant harmonies, foreign to contemporary harmony and often sounding strange to us. Although isolated harmonies may be classified under the heads of certain chords, the term "harmony," in the sense in which it is used in the music of today, is not applicable to the old contrapuntal style. Harmony of the strict style is not subordinated to the requirements of our modern tonal system, in which a series of chords is grouped around a central tonic chord: a system that in the course of a composition allows the tonic to be shifted (modulation), and groups all secondary tonalities around the principal key, besides which the tonality of one division influences those of others, from the beginning of a piece to its conclusion.

In the harmony of the strict style there is no such dependence of some parts upon others, or of what may be called harmonic action at a distance. Only in the perfect cadence, where as a result of the ascent of the leading-tone to the tonic the gravitation of dominant to tonic harmony is temporarily brought about, can be seen the embryo of our present tonal system. Aside from such cadences the strict style does not present a series of harmonies that are unified in this sense; key-continuity may be entirely absent, and any chord may follow any other, on a strictly diatonic basis.

In music of the Polyphonic Period — essentially vocal — coherence was provided for first of all by a text. But besides the text———an external factor not belonging to the domain of music — the works of the period possessed another — purely musical

17

— resource, by which composition took on coherence and unity; a resource all the more valuable inasmuch as harmony did not as yet possess the unifying power that it subsequently acquired. This was imitation: the recurrence of a melody in one voice immediately after its presentation in another. The result of this use of a single melody that appeared in different voices was to distribute the thematic material equally among all of them, giving to the whole a high degree of coherence. An imitating melody often entered before the preceding melody had closed, and then did not end until still another imitation had begun, a process that served to knit still closer the contrapuntal texture.

For two or more centuries the working-out of imitative forms in the strict style received much attention from composers. There arose many different phases of this device; imitations on a given voice and without it, canonic imitation, imitation in contrary motion, augmentation, diminution — forms that in the course of time culminated in the highest contrapuntal form of all — the fugue. From the introducing of one melody in all voices it was natural to take a further step and apply the same process to two melodies at once; hence double imitation, double canon, double fugue. At this transference to different voices of two melodies simultaneously the question must have come up as to the possibility of changing their relationship at the successive recurrences, and thereby from an original combination to obtain another, the derivative. Thus the origin of complex counterpoint, i.e. the obtaining of derivative combinations, also came in the era of the strict style.

In multi-voice music melodic and harmonic elements are subject to the influences of the time and to the nationality and individuality of composers. But the forms of imitation, canon and complex counterpoint — either as actualities or as possibilities — are universally valid; they are independent of such conditions, capable of entering into the plan of any harmonic system and adaptable to any melodic idiom. The idea is prevalent that the old contrapuntalists of the Flemish Schools exhausted the resources of imitation, especially as regards the canonic forms, but in reality they worked out completely only a few of them; the rest received only incidental treatment or were not touched upon at all. The outstanding merit of the Flemish composers was that they invented these forms and from them developed a flexible and efficient system of technical procedure.

Arising in the era of the strict style, these forms survived without material change until the end of the seventeenth and the beginning of the eighteenth century, when under the powerful influence of instrumental music they were enriched by acquisitions which up to that time had constituted mere technical virtuosity; also by harmonic, figurative and other elements that in the preceding era had been absent. This free counterpoint of the time of Bach and Handel, essentially the same as our own, was sharply distinguished from the counterpoint of former times, and its subsequent development naturally contained its own elements. The new counterpoint was not based on the ecclesiastical modes but upon the present major-minor tonal system. Not only in instrumental but also in vocal melody progressions are found that are difficult of intonation for voices and which were unconditionally forbidden in the strict style, such as leaps of sevenths and of augmented and diminished intervals, figuration based on dissonant chords, chromatics and other resources unknown to the older order.

The harmony of the free style is no less sharply distinguished from that of the preceding era. The free style enables entire groups of harmonies to be consolidated into one organic whole and then by means of modulation to dissect this whole into factors that are tonally interdependent. This characteristic, absent in the former harmony, provided the conditions for the development of the free forms of instrumental music that appeared at the end of the eighteenth and during the first half of the nineteenth century. This new tonal system made possible the writing of works of large dimensions that possessed all the qualities of effective structural style and that did not have to be reinforced by texts or by imitative forms *per se*, but contained within themselves the necessity for the latter. By degrees this system widened and deepened and its spreading circle embraced newer and newer resources and laws governing the relations between remote harmonies. Such were the broad horizons opened up for harmony; the creative activity of Beethoven then appears, and he, by a further expansion of the modulatory plans as they stood at the end of the eighteenth century, showed how much variety of key-relationship a composition could exhibit, both in its larger and smaller aspects.

Superseding the ecclesiastical modes, this tonal system was in turn affected by a new one that tended to endanger key-sense by the substitution of a chromatic for a diatonic basis; this led to a transformation of musical form. Applying the principle that by the use of chromatic progression any chord may follow any other, and pushing it too far, is likely to compromise key-relationship and to exclude those factors by which the smaller units of form are grouped and amalgamated into one organic whole. Neither did the harmony of the strict style, in which any chord could follow any other, though on a diatonic basis, exhibit the characteristics of tonality and form as now understood. The new harmony, as it now stands and which Fetis called "omnitonal," is inimical to the logic of tonality and form; the chief difference between the old and the new is that the diatonic basis is replaced by the chromatic. Omnitonal harmony, though adding to the resources of composition, at the same time lacks the virility characteristic of the diatonic method. To remain for a time in one key, as opposed to more or less rapid modulation, the contrasts afforded by passing gradually to a new key, with a return to the principal key——all this, by contributing to the clearness of long movements and enabling the listener to comprehend their forms, has little by little disappeared from music since the time of Beethoven and far more rapidly since the beginning of the twentieth century.* The result has been the production of small works and a general decline in the art of composition. Unity of construction appears with less and less frequency. Works are written not as consistent organisms but as formless masses of mechanically associated parts, any of which might be replaced by others.

As for the music of today, the harmony that has gradually lost its virility would be greatly benefited by the strength that the contrapuntal forms can infuse. Beethoven, who in his later works reverted to the technical methods of the old contrapuntalists, sets the best example for composers of the future. The music of today is essentially contrapuntal. Not only in large orchestral works, where the abundance of independent parts often results in obscurity, or in opera, where leitmotifs are worked out contrapuntally, but even in pieces of insignificant dimensions, can counterpoint be employed to the greatest advantage. The study of free counterpoint is therefore indispensable for the technical training of composers, but because of its melodic and harmonic intricacy it cannot be studied first. The foundation must be laid by counterpoint of the strict style, more accessible because of its simplicity. The preliminary steps as regards shifting counterpoint is the subject of the present work.

The term "complex" is used for that kind of counterpoint in which an original combination of melodies yields one or more derivatives. The term does not refer to the

---

*The original reads: ". . . has little by little disappeared from contemporary music," but as this was written in 1906 it can hardly be considered a violation of the author's thought to bring the statement up to date.—Tr.

complexity that results from the union of many voices, nor to the complexity of their melodic or rhythmic features. The essential mark of complex counterpoint is the possibility of obtaining from an original combination of melodies a new one, the derivative.

Complex counterpoint is divided into categories according to the methods by which derivative combinations are obtained. The principal methods are: (1) the shifting of voices; (2) duplications in imperfect consonances, and (3) transmutation; hence the three aspects of complex counterpoint: (1) shifted, (2) duplicated, (3) metamorphosed.

(A) Shifting Counterpoint

A derivative is obtained by shifting the voices. The following classification exhausts all possible shifts:

(1) Vertical shifting———upward or downward———hence vertical-shifting counterpoint:

In the third example, the upper voice is shifted underneath and the lower voice above, a special case of the vertical shift known as "double counterpoint."

(2) Horizontal shifting, in which the time-intervals between the entries of the voices are changed, hence horizontal-shifting counterpoint:

(3) Vertical and horizontal shifting together, hence double-shifting counterpoint:

In this work double-shifting counterpoint is included in the divisions devoted to horizontal-shifting and is explained parallel with it, as the methods of writing both are similar.

The subdivisions of shifting counterpoint are therefore:

Shifting counterpoint (a derivative from the shifting of voices):
(1) Vertical-shifting (upward or downward);
(2) Horizontal-shifting (changing relation-
    ship between entries);
(3) Double-shifting (the combination of the
    two preceding).

(B) Duplicated Counterpoint
A derivative combination is obtained by duplicating one or more voices in imperfect
consonances. Therefore the number of voices in the derivative combination is increased: at the duplication of one voice, to three; at the duplication of two voices, to four:

An original three-voice combination yields derivatives of four, five, or six voices,
according to how many voices of the original are duplicated. Examples will be found
in Chapter XV.

The connection of this counterpoint with the vertical-shifting counterpoint is obvious:
each duplication is nothing but the vertical transference of a voice at an interval equal
to an imperfect consonance. Therefore the study of counterpoint admitting of duplications is included in the divisions dealing with vertical-shifting counterpoint.

Of the various phases emunerated of complex counterpoint, forming the contents of
the present work, the detailed treatment of double counterpoint is of the utmost value
in music theory. It is of practical importance both in connection with counterpoint admitting of duplication and with certain cases of multi-voice vertical-shifting counterpoint, for instance in triple and quadruple counterpoint, especially at the octave. In
theoretical literature little reference is found to any aspects of vertical-shifting counterpoint other than double, and still less to horizontal-shifting counterpoint, the study of
which, as a special department of shifting counterpoint,. is here presented for the first
time.

(C) Metamorphosed Counterpoint
The derivative is obtained by a process of transmutation. By metamorphosis is meant
such a change of the original combination as would correspond to its reflection in a
mirror——this is also known as "mirror counterpoint." To avoid ambiguous terminology

"metamorphosis" will be used only in this sense, and will not refer to the shifting of voices in double counterpoint. Since metamorphosed counterpoint does not enter into the plan of the present work it will not be considered further.

The statement has been made that the transference of voices is a characteristic of shifting counterpoint. The changes that this counterpoint makes in a melody amount only to its transference vertically to other degrees or horizontally to other measures or parts of measures. Every other change, such as metamorphosis, augmentation, diminution, made simultaneously with shifting, places the given combination beyond the scope of convertible counterpoint, and shifting ceases to be a vital characteristic.

Another feature of complex counterpoint remains to be mentioned: the existence of rules in relation to its various subdivisions and to simple counterpoint. The study of the latter, in either the strict or the free style, is that of a system of rules to which every union of voices must conform. In complex counterpoint the same rules apply to both original and derivative combinations. The significance of the rules of complex counterpoint is that if they are ignored in the original combination the derivative will show progressions that violate the rules of simple counterpoint. The mutual relations of the aspects of complex counterpoint and their relations to simple may be illustrated symbolically by the accompanying diagram, where the large circle represents the domain of simple counterpoint, and the small intersecting circles, with the portions of their areas coinciding, the various aspects of complex counterpoint.

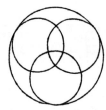

From this diagram it is clear that the combinations used in complex counterpoint must also belong to the domain of the simple, but not vica versa; portions of what is permitted in simple counterpoint are found outside of the circles that represent the various aspects of complex. The intersections of the circles show that certain phases of complex counterpoint may be combined, as was illustrated in the examples given.

This work is divided into two parts; the first deals with vertical-shifting counterpoint and with counterpoint admitting of duplications; the second with horizontal-shifting and double-shifting counterpoint. Each part consists of two divisions, one devoted to two-voice counterpoint, the other to three-voice. The investigations are limited to two or three voices. More than these are found only as the result of duplications; they are given at the end of the first and second divisions of Part One, where duplications are found using a larger number of voices, up to six inclusive.

PART ONE

DIVISION A

TWO-VOICE VERTICAL-SHIFTING COUNTERPOINT

Nissuna humana investigatione si po dimandare vera scientia, s'essa non passa per le mattematiche dimostrationi.

Leonardo da Vinci
Libro di pittura, Parte prima, § 1

PART ONE

VERTICAL-SHIFTING COUNTERPOINT

DIVISION A

TWO-VOICE VERTICAL-SHIFTING COUNTERPOINT

CHAPTER I

INTERVALS

The Notation of Intervals

§ 1. The subject of the study of vertical-shifting counterpoint consists of an investigation of those combinations from which derivatives are obtained by means of shifting the voices upward or downward. Such alterations in the relative positions of the voices are effected by changing the intervals that are formed by these voices in combination. For the analysis of these changes the best method is that of mathematics, by which the quantitative differences in the sizes of intervals are expressed in figures; mathematical operations are derived therefrom. For this purpose it will be necessary to employ a more accurate method of indicating intervals than that in general use. This new method, used in the present work, consists in taking the interval between two adjacent scale-degrees, i.e. a second, as the unit. The interval is then indicated by a figure showing the number of these units that it contains. The unison is indicated by O, since in it this quantity is equal to zero.

Therefore each interval is represented by a figure that is 1 less than its usual numerical designation: a third by 2, a fourth by 3, etc.

Addition and Subtraction; Negative Intervals

§ 2. By indicating intervals according to this method processes of addition and subtraction become possible. An interval may be added to another, either up or down. In the former case the upper voice is shifted upward, in the latter the lower voice downward. In both cases one voice moves away from the other. For example, a fifth added to a fourth---

gives an octave, an interval equal to the sum of the terms: 3 + 4 = 7. Addition is also
possible both up and down at the same time; here the result is the sum of three terms:

$$4 + 3 + 2 = 9$$

Other combinations of the same terms yield the same result; the order in which they
are taken does not affect the total:

etc.

§ 3. The reverse process, subtraction, causes the voices to approach, i.e. the higher
voice is shifted downward or the lower voice upward, or both. For example, subtracting
a third from an octave leaves a sixth:

$$7 - 2 = 5$$

If the subtracted interval equals the value of the first interval the result is 0, i.e. a
unison:

$$4 - 4 = 0$$

If the subtracted interval is greater than the value of the first interval the result is
a negative quantity:

$$4 - 5 = -1$$

§ 4. A negative quantity therefore refers to an interval of which the lowest tone belongs to the upper voice and the highest tone to the lower voice. These intervals are
termed negative. The same mathematical processes may be applied to them as to positive intervals.

§ 5. It is possible to regard the addition and subtraction of intervals in the algebraic
sense; i.e. to consider both processes as addition, in which the amounts concerned may
be either positive or negative quantities. Results so obtained are algebraic. The sum
of two or more positive numbers is only a special case.

§ 6. The order in which the terms are taken does not affect the total. Therefore when
the two voices shift simultaneously it will be found more convenient to add their algebraic values all at once, not to add each item in turn to the given interval. Suppose that
the given interval is a fourth and that one of the voices shifts -9 and the other $+1$. The
sum of these quantities is -8. Adding -8 to the value of the interval 3 gives
$3 + (-8) = -6$, i.e. a negative sixth.

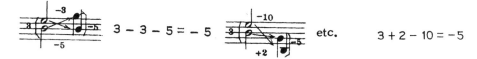

If other shifts are substituted of which the algebraic sums are the same the result remains unchanged:

3 − 3 − 5 = − 5   etc.   3 + 2 − 10 = −5

Compound Intervals

§ 7. If an interval contained within the octave limits is increased by one or more octaves an interval is obtained that is termed compound, in relation to the first.

To separate the voices forming an interval by an octave, add 7 to its absolute value:

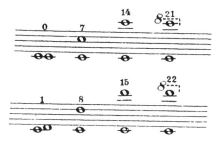

etc.

etc.

To separate the voices two octaves, add 14 to the absolute value of the interval; for three octaves add 21, etc., in multiples of 7:

§ 8. The following table is a list of simple and compound intervals within the limits of four octaves:

Unison	0	7	14	21
Second	1	8	15	22
Third	2	9	16	23
Fourth	3	10	17	24
Fifth	4	11	18	25
Sixth	5	12	19	26
Seventh	6	13	20	27

§ 9. To find what interval within the octave limits corresponds to a given compound interval, divide the latter by 7. The remainder will be the desired interval and the quotient will indicate by how many octaves the voices are separated. Suppose that the given interval is 30. Dividing this by 7 gives 4 as a quotient, with 2 as a remainder. The desired interval is therefore a third, and the voices in the given interval are separated by four octaves in addition to the third.

§ 10. The propositions following are based on what has been established. Considering each voice separately, the vertical shift in one direction is a positive operation, in the reverse direction a negative operation. The voice for which the upward shift is regarded as a positive operation will be termed upper, first, and indicated by the roman numeral I; that for which the positive operation is the downward shift will be termed lower, second, and indicated by the roman numeral II.

The positive and negative shifts of the voices may be represented by this diagram:

$$+ \qquad -$$

$$\text{I} \qquad \text{II}$$

$$- \qquad +$$

When the voices are arranged in the order $\frac{\text{I}}{\text{II}}$ the intervals formed by their union are positive; in the order $\frac{\text{II}}{\text{I}}$ they are negative.

If two voices forming an interval a shift by intervals of which the algrebraic sum is $\pm s$, then from a is obtained $a + (\pm s)$ (§ 6). The same result is obtained if one voice shifts at $\pm s$ and the other remains stationary, s being the algebraic designation for the interval by which the voice is shifted up or down.

Successive Series of Intervals;
Division into Two Groups: ^{1}int. and ^{2}int.

§ 11. Intervals may be put in a successive series, such that from the unison (0) positive intervals are ranged on one side, negative on the other. In the following series the consonances are in bold-face figures, with p. or *imp.* added, for perfect or imperfect.

Positive and negative intervals are divided into two groups; (1) intervals that appear in three forms: perfect, augmented, diminished; and (2) intervals that appear in four forms: major, minor, augmented, diminished. The first group consists of 0, 3, 4, 7 and the corresponding intervals beyond the octave. The second group consists of 1, 2, 5, 6 and their compounds. Intervals of the first group are indicated ^{1}int., those of the second group ^{2}int.

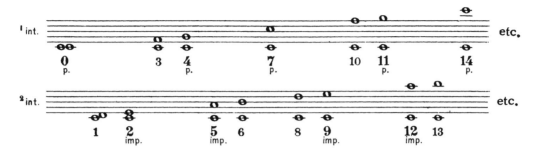

The first group includes the perfect consonances, the second group the imperfect.

Obs. These groups of intervals have other characteristics. For example, each ¹int., counted upward from the first degree of the major scale, is identical in size to the same interval counted downward; both intervals are perfect:

On the contrary, the quality of each ²int. is changed; under the same conditions; those counted upward are major, those downward, minor:

Also notice that the first four notes of the harmonic series include all the perfect intervals of the first group; the fifth note forms one of the intervals of the second group from each of the preceding notes:

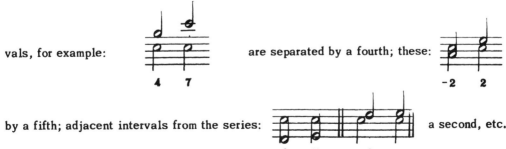

§ 12. The distance between two given intervals in the successive series is determined by the interval at which one voice is shifted, the other remaining stationary, a process required in order that from a given interval another may be derived. There intervals, for example: are separated by a fourth; these: by a fifth; adjacent intervals from the series: a second, etc.

§ 13. If a positive interval (termed here *a*) is added to a given interval, the interval obtained will lie in the successive series to the right of the given interval at the distance indicated by *a*. If a negative interval, -*a*, is added, the interval obtained will be will be found to the left of the given interval at the distance -*a*. For example, adding a positive sixth to a third gives an octave (2 + 5 = 7), lying a sixth to the right of the

third:    Conversely, adding a negative sixth to a third gives a negative

fourth (2 −5 = −3), lying a sixth to the left of the third:

Order of Intervals in the Successive Series

§ 14. It is desirable to dwell at some length on certain peculiarities in the order of intervals of the successive series which will be referred to later on.

(1) The perfect and imperfect consonances alternate, in both directions.

(2) Two consonances are adjacent, 4 and 5, but not two dissonances. (Here the possibility is not considered whereby a consonance can be changed to a dissonance by chromatic alteration.) Thus the fifth and sixth have a dissonance on one side only; all the other consonances have dissonances on both sides.

(3) On both sides of each dissonance is found a consonance, one of which is perfect, the other imperfect.

(4) Of two consonances found at equal distances, right or left, from a dissonance, one will always be perfect, the other imperfect; e.g.:

§ 15. In the following the consonances only are taken from the successive series:

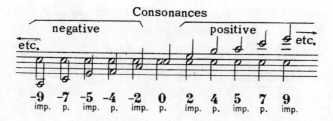

The calculation of the distance between positive consonances only or negative only proceeds as follows:

(1) Two consonances of the same group (i.e. both perfect or both imperfect) are separated from each other by a [1]int.

(2) Consonances of different groups (i.e. one perfect, the other imperfect) are separated from each other by a ^{1}int. For example, consonance 2 (imp.) is separated from consonance 5 (imp.) by 3 (= ^{1}int.); consonance −7 (p.) is separated from −11 (p.) by 4 (= ^{1}int.). Conversely, consonance −5 (imp.) is separated from −7 (p.) by 2 (= ^{2}int.); consonance −4 (p.) from −9 (imp.) by 5 (= ^{2}int.), etc.

§ 16. Exceptions to the foregoing statements are not found as long as positive consonances only or negative only are compared. But in comparing positive consonances with negative the following sole exception is encountered:

Two fifths, negative and positive (thus corresponding to a compound interval) are separated from each other by a ninth (or at an interval larger than a ninth by an octave, or two octaves, etc.). Since the ninth is a ^{2}int. the case represents an exception to what was stated in § 15, (1).

With these exceptions the statements in the preceding section relative to the distances between consonances of the same group and those of different groups apply also to all cases where one interval is positive and the other negative.

§ 17. Proceeding to dissonances:

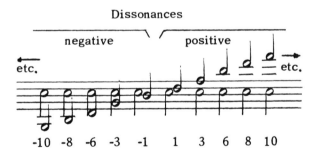

First the distance is to be measured between positive dissonances only or negative only.

(1) The second and its compounds (1, 8, 15 etc.) are separated from one another by a ^{1}int.:

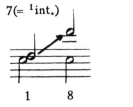

(2) The other dissonances—the fourth, seventh and their compounds (3, 6, 10, 13, etc.)—are also separated by a ¹int.:

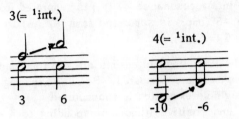

(3) The second and its compounds are separated from the other dissonances by a ²int.:

§ 18. Next to be considered are the mixed cases where one dissonance is positive and the other negative. Here the statements in § 17 regarding dissonances are presented in reverse order:

(1) The second and its compounds are separated from one another by a ²int.:

(2) The other dissonances (3, 6, 10 etc.) also are separated from one another by a ²int.:

(3) The second and its compounds are separated from every other dissonance under the same conditions (that one interval is positive, the other negative), by a ¹int.:

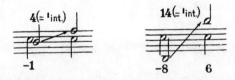

§ 19. If under one successive series of intervals is placed another so that a new interval a comes directly below O (unison) in the upper series, then each interval in the lower series will be equal to the algebraic sum of the interval above it $+ a$. Let m equal any interval in the upper series and n the interval in the lower series directly underneath m; then $m + a = n$. In the following—

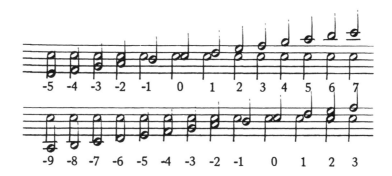

under O in the upper series is placed $a = -4$. Taking for example 7 in the upper series, $m = 7$, and adding -4 gives below it $n = 3$ $(7 - 4 = 3)$.

Such comparison of two series of intervals is necessary in working out exercises in vertical-shifting counterpoint.

CHAPTER II

THE VERTICAL SHIFTING OF CONTRAPUNTALLY COMBINED VOICES;

THE SHIFTS; INDEX OF VERTICAL-SHIFTING COUNTERPOINT

Notation of the Vertical Shift: v, vv. Formulas
for Original and Derivative Combinations

§ 20. In the preceding chapter the shifting of the voices forming separate intervals was investigated. The present subject is the shifting of the contrapuntal union of melodies. To show that two voices form correct counterpoint the Roman numerals indicating the voices (melodies) will be used, united by the plus sign: I + II. Each voice in the derivative combination is indicated by the same figure that it had in the original. I + II is the formula for the original combination.

Obs.—The sign +, used as indicated, refers to addition as meaning a combination of voices (two-voice addition, multi-voice, etc.), and is to be taken in this sense only when employed in connection with the roman numerals for the voices.

§ 21. The letter v, for "vertical" (plural vv) refers to the vertical shift of a voice, and is placed to the right and slightly above the roman numeral corresponding to this voice. The number indicating the direction and interval of the shift is united to v by the sign of equality. For example, the expression $I^{v=5}$ means that the upper voice shifts a sixth upward; $I^{v=-2} + II^{v=-7}$ indicates a shift of the upper voice a third downward, the lower an octave upward; the sign + means that the voices so shifted form correct counterpoint.

Such an expression, indicating shifts of the voices united by the sign +, is the formula of the derivative combination. Formulas for derivative combinations may differ, but that of the original can only be I + II.

§ 22. When a voice remains unshifted neither the letter v nor $v=0$ need be associated with its Roman numeral. Therefore the expression $I + II^{v=1}$ and $I^{v=0} + II^{v=1}$ are synonymous, both meaning that the upper voice remains in place but that the lower is shifted a second downward.

The Shifts

§ 23. The relationship of melodies in the derivative combination may present one of the following three cases:

(1) The Direct Shift. — In this the melodies retain their relative positions; the upper voice stays above, the lower underneath, though they may approach each other or recede (Ex. 1). This shift may be illustrated by the diagram:

Orig.   Deriv.

I ———————— I   The symbol for the direct shift is: ⊐⊏

II ———————— II

Ex. 1

(2) The Inverse Shift. — Here the melodies change their relative positions; the upper

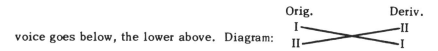

voice goes below, the lower above. Diagram:

Symbol: ⊃⊂   This shift is what is commonly known as "double counterpoint,", but it is only a special case of the vertical shift.

Ex. 2

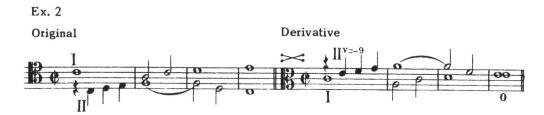

The final consonance in this example is the unison (0); in the derivative combination it can occur in either the direct or the inverse shift.

(3) The Mixed Shift. — This is partly direct, partly inverse:

Ex. 3

Relations of Original to Derivative Intervals

§ 24. The combination of melodies I + II forms a series of intervals: $a, b, c, d, \ldots\ldots n.$ If one of the voices shifts at $\pm s$, that is, takes for the derivative formula $I^{v=\pm s} + II$ or $I + II^{v=\pm s}$ (§ 21), then a new series of intervals is obtained: $a + (\pm s), b + (\pm s), c + (\pm s), \ldots\ldots n.$ (§ 10). For example, the original combination of Ex. 1 represents the series of intervals: 4, 7, 6, 5, 4, 2, 3, 4.

Original (Ex. 1)

Its first derivative is I + II $^{v=3}$. Adding 3 to each original interval gives the intervals of the derivative combination.

Intervals of the original combination:	4	7	6	5	4	2	3	4
	+3	+3	+3	+3	+3	+3	+3	+3
Intervals of the Derivative combination:	7	10	9	8	7	5	6	7

In the successive series (§ 11) each of these derivative intervals lies from its own original at a fourth to the right (§ 13). In the same way a series of intervals could be obtained for the second derivative, I $^{v=-2}$ + II, by adding −2 to each interval of the original.

In Ex. 2 the series of intervals for the original combination is: 7, 6, 5, 2, 3, 7, 9.

Derivative formula: I + II $^{v=-9}$. Adding −9 to each interval of the original combination gives a series of negative intervals, each of which lies from its own original in the successive series at a tenth to the left (§ 13), and showing that the shift is inverse.

Intervals of the original combination:	7	6	5	2	4	5	7	9
	−9	−9	−9	−9	−9	−9	−9	−9
Intervals of the derivative combination:	−2	−3	−4	−7	−5	−4	−2	0

§ 25. From the definition of the shifts it follows that at the direct shift the derivative intervals take the same signs as those of the original, and at the inverse shift the opposite signs.

Index of Vertical-Shifting Counterpoint (Jv)

§ 26. To obtain the result of the simultaneous shifting of two voices it is necessary to add to each interval the algebraic sum of the quantities indicating the shifting of either or both voices, i.e. the algebraic sum of their vv (§ 10). This rule is of general application, since the idea of algebraic sums includes those cases where one of the voices has $v=0$, that is, remains stationary.

§ 27. The algebraic sum vv of two voices contrapuntally united is termed the index of vertical-shifting counterpoint, and is indicated by Jv (plural JJv), J standing for "index" and v for "vertical shift." In distinction to the sign v, referring to the individual voice (§ 21), the sign Jv can refer only to the combination of two voices.

§ 28. To indicate that a given shift of voices applies at a certain index, the formula of the derivative combination will be put in parentheses and after it Jv; e.g. $(I^v = -2 + II^v = -7)$ $Jv = -9$. When the formula of the original combination is presented in a similar manner it will mean that the voices admit of a shift at the index indicated; e.g. $(I + II)$ $Jv = 2$, $(I + II)$ $Jv = -2$, etc. If one and the same combination admits of shifts at two or more indices their respective figures are placed after the sign of equality and are separated by commas. For instance, Ex. 1 admits of two shifts: at $Jv = 3$ and at $Jv = -2$; this is indicated: $(I + II)$ $Jv = 3, -2$. Such a Jv, referring to a single original but stating the conditions of two or more indices, is termed a compound index. A compound index may be double, triple etc., according to how many indices are united in it (this has no reference to double or triple counterpoint). A compound index is always printed in the singular: Jv, but if several indices are to be considered that refer to different original combinations the sign is printed in the plural: JJv. If, for example, it is required to list the indices that correspond to perfect consonances, the expression will read: $JJv = \pm 3, \pm 4$ etc., equivalent to $Jv = 3$, $Jv = -3$, $Jv = 4$, $Jv = -4$ etc.

§ 29. Shifts of voices I + II at a given index may be replaced by other shifts that give as a result the same series of derivative intervals if the algebraic sum of these shifts remains without change (§ 26). A derivative combination will therefore be reproduced on other degrees. In this way one and the same index can generate various shifts of voices and therefore can belong to different formulas of the derivative combination.

§ 30. It is possible to get a derivative combination in which one voice remains unshifted. In this case the other voice must take: $v = Jv$. This follows from the fact that the index is equal to the algebraic sum vv of both voices (§ 26).

The Formula m + Jv = n; Inferences Therefrom

§ 31. Adding the value of the index to an interval of the original combination gives the corresponding interval of the derivative (§§ 26–7). Indicating the original interval by m and its derivative by n, the relationship is expressed by the equation $m + Jv = n$.

§ 32. From this equation it follows that—

(1) If $m = 0$, then $n = Jv$; i.e. from the unison is obtained an interval in the derivative equal to the value of the index.

(2) If m and Jv are equal but have opposite signs, then from $m = Jv$ is obtained $n = 0$; i.e. from an interval equal to the index but having the opposite sign is obtained a unison in the derivative combination.

(3) Since at the inverse shift $m + (-Jv) = -n$ (§ 25), then $n + (-Jv) = -m$; i.e. in double counterpoint, from the derivative intervals are obtained intervals equal to the original. At $Jv = -7$, for example, from a fourth is obtained a fifth in the derivative $(3 - 7 = -4)$, and from a fifth a fourth $(4 - 7 = -3)$. At $Jv = -9$ from a third is obtained an octave $(2 - 9 = -7)$, and from an octave a third $(7 - 9 = -2)$ etc.

§ 33. Comparing the formula $m + Jv = n$ with the statements in §§ 12 and 30 the conclusion is that in the successive series of intervals (§ 11) a derivative interval lies from an original at an interval equal to Jv. If Jv is positive this distance will be to the right; if negative, to the left (§ 13).

Conditions of the Shifts

§ 34. The index (Jv) may be of positive value, of negative value, or may equal zero. The conditions under which Jv yields the direct, the inverse, or the mixed shift are next to be investigated. From the equation $m + Jv = n$ and what was stated in § 25 it follows that—

(1) If m and Jv are both positive or negative the shift is direct.

(2) If one of the quantities m or Jv is positive and the other negative either the direct or the inverse shift is possible, depending on the value of the intervals in the original combination relative to the value of Jv, namely:

(a) At m with absolute value greater than Jv the shift is direct.

(b) At m with absolute value less than Jv the shift is inverse.

§ 35. From the fact that in the derivative combination the unison (0) may be found in either the direct or the inverse shift, the conditions of the shifts can be stated as follows:

(1) If $m > Jv$, then with like signs for m and Jv the shift is direct.

(2) If $m < Jv$, then with like signs for m and Jv the shift is inverse.

§ 36. These principles for the shifts apply without exception to all cases, whether the intervals of the original combination are positive or negative. But since in practice it is advisable not to cross the voices but to use only positive intervals in the original combination, the rules for the shifts applying to the latter may be formulated thus:

(1) At a positive Jv the shift is always direct.

(2) At a negative Jv the shift may be direct, inverse, or mixed. Condition of the direct shift: $m > Jv$ (§ 35, [1]); of the inverse shift: $m > Jv$ (§ 35, [2]). The union in the same original of these and other conditions forms the mixed shift (§ 23, [3]).

Limiting Intervals; Their Signs ($<$, $>$)

§ 37. A successive series of original intervals for a positive index (giving always the direct shift, § 36, [1]), starts with 0:

§ 38. A successive series of original intervals for a negative Jv, in order to yield the direct shift, must start with an interval equal to the absolute value of Jv. Therefore, at the direct shift, an interval equal to the absolute value of the index is the limiting interval for approaching voices of the original combination; it is indicated by the sign $<$. At $Jv = -2$, for example, the voice must not approach closer than a third:

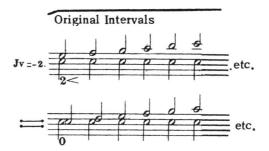

at $Jv = -3$, not closer than a fourth, etc.

§ 39. A successive series of original intervals for a negative Jv, in order to yield the inverse shift, must start with 0 and end with a positive interval equal to the absolute value of Jv, showing in this case the limiting interval for receding voices; it is indicated by the sign $>$. For example, at $Jv = -7$ (double counterpoint at the octave) the voices must not recede from each other by more than an octave:

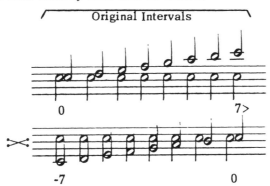

at $Jv = -11$ (double counterpoint at the twelfth), by not more than a twelfth:

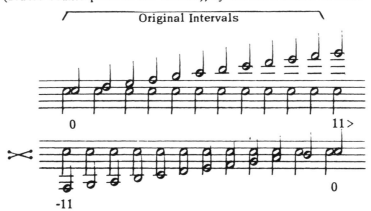

Obs.—Limiting intervals for receding voices are necessary only for indices giving the inverse shift. For others the series of original intervals can be continued to the right as far as required.

§ 40. If in an original combination at a negative index are taken intervals some of which are less than the absolute value of Jv and some greater, the result is the mixed shift (§23,[3]). Cf. Ex. 3, written at $Jv = -7$. In the second measure, where in the original the voices exceed the limits of an octave, the shift is direct.

Signs for the Shifts. $(<, >, <>, \gtrless)$

§ 41. To indicate the shift of a negative Jv the same signs are used as for the limiting intervals; they are placed after the figure for the index. The sign of the limiting interval for approaching voices $(<)$ will be used for the direct shift; that for the limiting interval for receding voices $(>)$ for the inverse shift. Placed in succession $(<>)$ the signs will refer to the mixed shift. For example, $Jv = -5<$ means that this index gives the direct shift, i.e. that the series of original intervals relevant to it starts with a sixth; the limiting interval for approaching voices is also shown: $5<$. The expression $Jv = -5>$ means that the index gives the inverse shift and that the series of original intervals, while starting with a unison, ends with a sixth; the limiting interval for receding voices is indicated by $5>$. $Jv = -5<>$ indicates the mixed shift, i.e. the presence of both the preceding cases, more or less in alternation. When one sign is placed above the other $(\gtrless)$ they refer to two negative indices of identical value but with different shifts. Therefore, $JJv = -4\lessgtr$ serves for two expressions: $Jv = -4<$ and $Jv = -4>$.

§ 42. For positive JJv it is not necessary either to indicate or to establish distance limits for the voices.

Jv Equal to Zero

§ 43. The positive and negative indices have been considered; the index equal to zero (§ 20) remains to be mentioned. This Jv, like all the others, can denote different shifts of the voices; for example $(I^{v=9} + II^{v=-9})\ Jv = 0$; $(I^{v=-3} + II^{v=3})\ Jv = 0$, etc. The result of such shifts is to yield a series of intervals identical in value to those of the original.

§ 44. It is possible to regard every recurrence of a two-voice combination on the same degrees or its removal to other degrees as a shift at $Jv = 0$. The rules of simple counterpoint are the rules of $Jv = 0$, and therefore simple counterpoint can be understood as a special case of the vertical shift.

§ 45. The important idea implied by the use of the symbol Jv simplifies the study of vertical-shifting counterpoint; it yields numerous possibilities of voice-shifting with a comparatively small number of indices.

CHAPTER III

THE GROUPING OF INDICES

List of Indices

§ 46. The indices of which the conditions are presently to be examined correspond to intervals of the successive series taken within the limits of three octaves. In the following list they accordingly fall into three groups, with seven indices in each group. Beginning with $Jv = 0$ the positive indices proceed to the right up to nearly an octave; the negative indices down to the left to two octaves. Shifts of negative indices are indicated by their proper signs (§ 41).

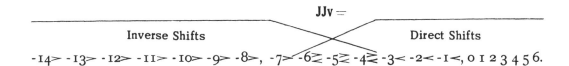

§ 47. The positive indices end with $Jv = 6$ for the reason that to continue to $Jv = 7$ would merely shift a voice of the original combination an octave higher:

Ex. 4

It is obvious that anything conforming to the conditions of simple counterpoint (i.e. a combination at $Jv = 0$) would also be correct for $Jv = 7$, so this index does not require special rules. Similarly, to separate a derivative combination at $Jv = 1$ gives a derivative at $Jv = 8$:

Ex. 5

A combination at $Jv = 2$ will serve equally well for $Jv = 9$, one at $Jv = 3$ for $Jv = 10$; the same relation holds between $Jv = 4$ and $Jv = 11$, etc. It is therefore unnecessary to formulate rules for positive indices equal to compound intervals; those equal to the corresponding simple intervals can be used instead.

41

§ 48. Proceeding to negative indices: those of the values $-1{<}$, $-2{<}$ and $-3{<}$ will always refer to the direct shift, because those of the same values for the inverse shift would result in limiting the movements of the voices to too narrow a range (§ 38). For the same reason it is advisable to regard −4, −5 and −6 as indices also applying to the direct shift, though these values also admit of the inverse shift. In the former case they are indicated $-4{<}$, $-5{<}$, $-6{<}$; in the latter $-4{>}$, $-5{>}$, $-6{>}$ (§ 41).

§ 49. The next three indices $-4{>}$, $-5{>}$, $-6{>}$ begin the series of shifts in double counterpoint; the fifth, sixth and seventh. The indices beyond them to the left, beginning with $Jv = -7$ and continuing to $Jv = -13$ inclusive, are regarded as inverse shifts (double counterpoint at the octave, ninth, tenth etc.). Only exceptionally will they be treated as direct, in which case they will take the sign ${<}$.

§ 50. One index remains: $Jv = -14$, but neither this nor the ones beyond ($Jv = -15$, $Jv = -16$ etc.) require special study. Any combination written at $Jv = -7$ can be shifted at $Jv = -14$, since here the derivative is only separated an octave as compared to the derivative at $Jv = -7$; similarly with a shift at $Jv = -21$, where the voices are separated two octaves. The same applies to a shift at $Jv = -8$, also possible at $Jv = -15$ and $Jv = -22$ etc. Therefore by double counterpoint at the octave will be understood not only $Jv = -7$ but also $Jv = -14$ and $Jv = -21$; by double counterpoint at the tenth, $JJv = -9$, −16, −25 etc. (cf. table, § 6).

The only difference between these cases concerns their limiting intervals, which always are equal to the absolute value of the index (§ 38). Thus, at $Jv = -14$ the voices may be separated by two octaves, but at $Jv = -7$ by not more than one.

Columns of Indices

§ 51. The indices listed in § 46 presented three series of figures, seven in each. Putting these series in numerical order, one underneath another, gives the seven columns below. Four of these, shaded, contain indices corresponding to intervals of the second group (^{2}int.). The other columns, unshaded, contain indices corresponding to intervals of the first group (^{1}int.).

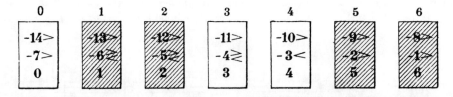

These columns, except the first, are numbered; each reference number corresponds to the figure of its lowest Jv. The first column to the left is not counted, it will be referred to as the zero column. It contains $Jv = 0$, i.e. the index of simple and not one of vertical-shifting counterpoint (§ 44). The upper index in this column, $Jv = -14$, represents the same double counterpoint at the octave as does the middle index, $Jv = -7$, hence it is not necessary to discuss it further as a distinct index. The only essential index in this column is $Jv = -7$. Therefore the zero column will often be referred to in an incomplete form, restricted to the middle index.

§ 52. In these seven columns are placed the indices corresponding to the intervals of the successive series, taken in a range of three octaves; the positive indices within the limits of one octave, the negative of two. If more indices are needed to indicate an octave extension on either side, each column will contain four indices instead of three; for an extension of two octaves each will have five indices, etc. Therefore the value of any index determines its place in one of the seven columns. But, as already stated, for practical purposes three indices in each column are enough.

§ 53. It is not difficult to remember the indices contained in each column. The lowest indices are all positive, each of them corresponds to the number of the given column. The middle and upper indices are all negative and may be easily learned if attention is paid to the following relations:

(1) The sum of the absolute values of the lowest and middle indices in each column is 7.

(2) The sum of the absolute values of the lowest and upper indices is 14.

(3) The difference between the absolute values of the upper and middle indices is 7.

Octave Relationship of JJv

§ 54. The lowest Jv of each column corresponds to a positive interval within the limits of an octave; the middle Jv to a negative interval, also within an octave, and the upper Jv to a negative interval beyond the octave limit. If −7 is added to the lower Jv the middle one is obtained; if −7 is added to the middle Jv (or −14 to the lower) the upper Jv of the same column is obtained. Therefore if in a combination I + II one of the voices remains in place while the other shifts in conformity to each of the three JJv of a given column, shifts of the melody will result, to the same degrees though in other octaves. All three indices of the same column are thus in an octave relationship. This is clearly shown in the following table, using the indices of the third column:

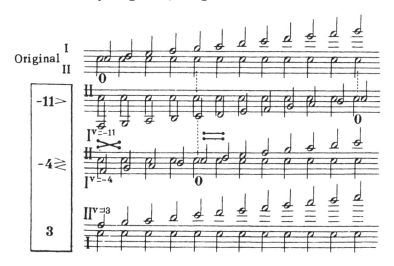

§ 55. In each column the lower Jv has the direct shift, the upper the inverse shift. Of the middle numbers, three: $-6\gtreqless$, $-5\gtreqless$ and $-4\gtreqless$ have both the direct and the inverse shift, and three: $-3<$, $-2<$ and $-1<$ have the direct shift only (§ 46).

§ 56. If a derivative is written at a middle Jv and one of the two voices of the derivative is separated an octave, a derivative is obtained at an outer Jv of the same shift as the middle Jv.

Take for example the table in § 54. Writing a combination at $Jv = -4<$ (i.e. with the direct shift) and separating a voice of the derivative an octave gives another derivative at $Jv = 3$, i.e. at the lowest Jv of the same column, also a direct shift. Taking a derivative at $Jv = -4>$, i.e. at the Jv giving the inverse shift, and separaring a voice an octave, gives a derivative at $Jv = -11$, the highest Jv of the same column and also an inverse shift. Similarly, a derivative at $Jv = -5<$, separated an octave, yields another at a Jv in its own column: $Jv = 2$; one at $Jv = -5>$ in the same way a derivative at $Jv = -12$. The same relation holds bewteen $Jv = -6<$ and $Jv = 1$; $Jv = -6>$ and $Jv = -13$, etc.

In general, every combination written at a middle Jv yields a valid derivative at each outer Jv of the same column and with the shift indicated. But the contrary is not necessarily true; writing at an outer Jv may be unsuitable for shifts at the middle, as will be seen later (§ 72).

§ 57. The statement was made in § 51 that the unshaded columns contained JJv corresponding to intervals of the first group (^{1}int.), and those shaded, JJv corresponding to intervals of the second group (^{2}int.). On this fact is based a division of indices into two groups that has great importance for the whole study of vertical-shifting counterpoint. In the first group are JJv corresponding to the ^{1}ints. (i.e. those in columns 3, 4 and the zero column). In the second group are JJv corresponding to the ^{2}ints. (i.e. columns 1, 2 5 and 6). When it is necessary to refer the characteristics of a given Jv to either of these groups, use will be made of the indications ^1Jv and ^2Jv.

Grouping of the Columns in Pairs

§ 58. In the following table six columns (1-6) are grouped in pairs; the zero column is isolated. In each pair of columns the sum of the lowest indices equals 7, and each lowest index is of the same value as the middle index in the other column of the same pair, but with the opposite sign; the lowest Jv is positive, the middle Jv negative. The zero column is unrelated and cannot pair with any of the others.

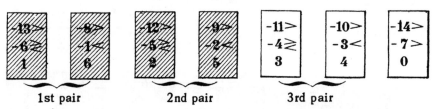

<table>
<tr><td>1st pair</td><td>2nd pair</td><td>3rd pair</td></tr>
</table>

§ 59. The ^1JJv in the zero column correspond to perfect consonances; in the third pair of columns some JJv correspond to perfect consonances, others to dissonances of the first group. The ^2JJv in the first pair of columns correspond to dissonances of the second pair to consonances of this group, i.e. imperfect.

§ 60. Classifying the JJv in this way into two groups, arranging them in columns showing the octave relationship, and then combining the columns in pairs that bring the indices in logical order—all this facilitates their study and recall.

Determination of the Value of an Original
Interval and of the Index

§ 61. Reference to the formula $m + Jv = n$ (§ 31) shows that a derivative interval (n) is equal to an original interval (m) to which Jv has been added; i.e. the equation constitutes a definition of what the two other quantities m and Jv are equal to. Taking—

(a) $m = n - Jv = n + (-Jv)$
(b) $Jv = n - m = n + (-m)$

i.e. (a) the original interval (m) equals the derivative interval (n) plus Jv taken with the opposite sign; (b) Jv equals the derivative interval (n) plus the original interval (m) taken with the opposite sign.

§ 62. This will be illustrated by two examples determining the value of the original interval (m) according to the derivative (n) and Jv (equation (a), § 61).

(1) From what interval is obtained a derivative tenth at $Jv = 4$? Since Jv is positive and has the direct shift, the derivative tenth (9) is also positive. Adding to it the index with the opposite sign (equation (a), § 61) gives: $9 - 4 = 5$. Therefore at $Jv = 4$ a derivative tenth is obtained from a sixth.

(2) From what interval at $Jv = -11$ is obtained a derivative ninth? Since $Jv = -11$ has the inverse shift (§ 49) a derivative ninth is negative (-8). Adding to this quantity (according to the same equation) the index taken with the opposite sign gives: $-8 + 11 = 3$, i.e. a derivative ninth is obtained from a fourth.

§ 63. Considering now the determination of Jv according to an original and a derivative interval (equation (b), § 61); given the original and derivative combination shown in Ex. 6, at what Jv is the shift?

Ex. 6

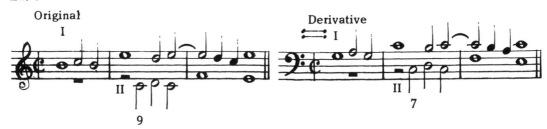

It would be possible to determine Jv by indicating the shifts of both voices and taking the algebraic sum of these shifts (§ 27), but it is shorter to make use of equation (b), § 61. Take one of the intervals of the derivative, for example the octave that appears at the entry of the second voice. Since the shift is direct this octave (7) is positive. At the corresponding place in the original is a tenth (9). Adding with the opposite sign to the derivative octave gives: $Jv = 7 - 9 = -2$.

§ 64. To determine Jv according to the intervals of the original and the derivative (equation (b), § 61) is best in practice. This will be further illustrated by several examples from the works of Palestrina.

Given the original and derivative (Ex. 7), required to find the value of Jv. The shift is inverse. At the entry of the first voice $m = 2$, $n = -9$. Hence $Jv = -9 - 2 = -11$ (double counterpoint at the twelfth).

In Ex. 8 the derivative combination is accompanied by supplementary parts, these are printed in small notes.

Here the shift is inverse. At the entry of the second voice $m=2$, $n=5$. Hence $Jv=-5$ $-2=-7$ (double counterpoint at the octave).

In Ex. 9 the derivative is transferred to another part of the measure, otherwise it is similar to the preceding, with index of the same value, -7.

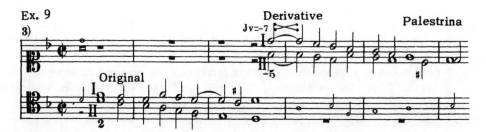

In Ex. 10 the first note of the second voice in the derivative is abbreviated to half its original value; this is often found, especially where imitation is present. Beginning with the second note the voice proceeds without further change.

The initial intervals are: $m = 7$, $n = 0$; $Jv = -7$ (double counterpoint at the octave). In the third measure of the original the voices cross, resulting in the intervals -2 and -1. Adding -7 gives -9 and -8 at the corresponding places in the derivative. The star indicates where shifting counterpoint passes into simple counterpoint.

In Ex. 11 the shift is inverse. Initial intervals: $m = 0$, $n = -4$; $Jv = -4 >$.

Ex.11

Allocation of the Melodies of the Derivative Combination According to Voice

§ 65. In the preceding examples the original combinations were worked out with two specific voices and the derivatives with two others. But it can also happen that a single voice-part can function in both combinations, for instance the soprano in the following example:

Ex.12

or even both voice-parts can function in both original and derivative:

Ex. 13

or finally, that the highest melody, though still remaining the highest, functions as a lower voice:

Ex. 14

The shift in the last example must be regarded as direct, notwithstanding the fact that at first glance it appears to be inverse. In general, by "voice" is to be understood a melody to be sung, and this sense is meant when referring to the shifting of voices. To avoid such an anomaly as Ex. 12 the original and derivative will be printed on separate staves, with the highest voice above and the lowest below; the nature of the shift will then be apparent. But the method by which both melodies are assigned to voice-parts remains uniform.

Intervals Determining Jv; Entrance Intervals

§ 66. In determining the index, initial intervals were adopted for *m* and *n*. It is understood that a progression of intervals will serve the same purpose. Sometimes an initial interval is altogether impossible for determining Jv, as for instance in fugues where the countersubject is delayed and a definite relation is established between it and the subject. At the tonal answer the initial motive of neither the subject nor the countersubject can be exactly reproduced. In such cases *m* and *n* must be taken at the place where all mutation in the voices has ceased.

§ 67. In fact, *m* and *n* may be taken as intervals between degrees not found simultaneously in both voices but at some distance apart. For example, at the entries of voices in stretto it is sometimes convenient to take for *m* and *n* the interval forming their initial notes. Such an interval will be termed an entrance interval. An entrance interval may be positive or negative; positive if it is above the first note in the upper (first) voice, or below the first note in the lower (second) voice:

It is negative if the situation is the reverse:

In vertical-shifting counterpoint, when comparing entrance intervals in the original and derivative combinations it is necessary to consider their directions. The signs of both intervals are the same when they are in the same direction; in different directions their signs are opposite. Consequently if the shift is direct the direction of the derivative interval is the same as that of the original; at the inverse shift it is opposite.

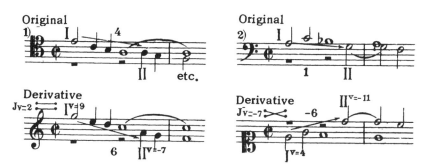

Here, according to original and derivative, the entrance intervals determine Jv by equation (1), § 61. In illustration (a) above, $Jv = -4 + 6 = 2$; in (b), $Jv = -1 - 6 = -7$.

Interchange of Original and Derivative combinations

§ 68. Ordinarily the combination that occurs first in a composition is regarded as the original, but it is possible to treat a later combination as the original and an earlier one as the derivative. Examining the nature of the alterations in the formula of the derivative and the value of the index when the original and derivative are interchanged, two cases are to be distinguished:

(1) Jv *has the Direct Shift.*—Taking the derivative for the original and vice versa it follows that in the formula of the derivative the sign v of each voice will change to the opposite. Therefore the sign also changes for the algebraic sum vv of both voices, i.e. the sign of the value for Jv. For example, the derivative formula $(I^{v=5} + II^{v=-2}) Jv = 3$, when derivative and original are exchanged, reverts to the formula $(I^{v=-5} + II^{v=2}) Jv = -3$. This will readily be seen in the following illustration:

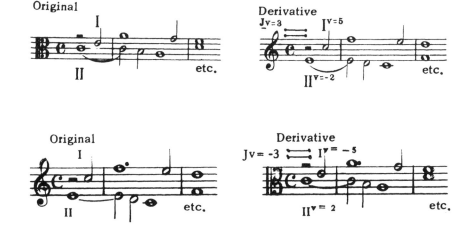

(2) *Jv has the Inverse Shift.*—If here the derivative is taken for the original and vice versa, in the derivative formula v of the first voice is transferred without change to the second voice, and v of the second voice to the first. Jv remains unchanged. The voice that previously was first now appears as second, and vice versa. For example, the derivative formula $(I^{v=-1} + II^{v=-6})$ $Jv = -7$, when original and derivative are exchanged, reverts to $(I^{v=-6} + II^{v=-1})$ $Jv = -7$.

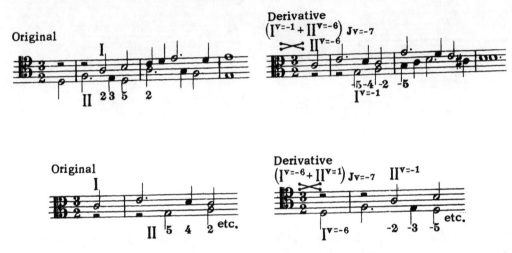

The Augmented Fourth and Diminished Fifth

§ 69. One and the same Jv may yield different shifts of voices (§ 29). When these shifts are made to various degrees of the diatonic scale the quality of certain melodic intervals may be changed; such alterations as major to minor or minor to major involve no irregularities.

But if instead of perfect intervals in a melodic progression augmented or diminished intervals should result one of the principal rules of simple counterpoint would be violated—such progressions are not allowed. The diatonic scale contains an augmented fourth (the so-called "tritone") and a diminished fifth, both formed by the fourth and seventh degrees of the Ionic or major scale. Melodic progressions of these intervals are forbidden in the strict style, and their use is limited in other ways that are doubtless familiar to the reader. The avoidance of these intervals in the derivative is possible, by means now to be described.

(1) Having in mind a definite shift of voices, it is possible to calculate beforehand which two degrees give an augmented fourth or a diminished fifth in the derivative. To do this, the two degrees forming the objectionable interval in the original are transferred, for the voice that shifts, at an interval equal to v of this voice, taken with the opposite sign, i.e. these degrees are transferred in the opposite direction. Having obtained the two degrees in this way, they must conform to all the limitations of the augmented fourth (or diminished fifth). It is well to choose shifts that will result in one of the voices either remaining in place or shifting an octave, in which case the precautions indicated

apply to only one voice. In Ex. 11, the derivative formula of which is $(I^{v=-7} + II^{v=3})$, the upper voice shifts an octave. Therefore the avoidance of a possible augmented fourth concerns only voice II, a contingency that may be provided for in advance. Taking the two notes forming the augmented fourth in the given key: 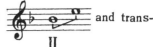 and trans-

ferring them in the direction opposite to that of the shift $II^{v=3}$, i.e. a fourth higher,

gives: 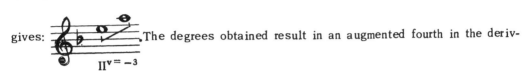 The degrees obtained result in an augmented fourth in the deriv-

ative, and to them must be applied all the conditions that in the strict style surround this interval.

(2) Another and more simple method consists in writing the original regardless as to whether or not an augmented fourth (or diminished fifth) will appear in the derivative, and when the problem is completed and the voices shifted, to make whatever correction is necessary for its removal. These corrections consist in altering an augmented fourth to a perfect fourth by raising the lower note or lowering the upper note by a chromatic half-step. The choice depends on the melodic or harmonic conditions that precede or follow.

(3) It is also possible to change the key signature of the derivative, getting a key resulting in the removal of the augmented fourth, then to transpose so that both combinations will be in tha same key.

In Ex. 15, a combination at $Jv = -9$, the shift $I^{v=-9}$ is written on the third staff. To get the derivative without putting it in the key specified involves these irregularities: the augmented fourth in the melody between the first and second measures, and the interval of the diminished fifth between the parts in the third measure.

Ex. 15

Supposing the signature to be one flat the errors mentioned are corrected but a new one appears: the leap of the diminished fifth in the lower voice between the third and fourth measures. Assuming a signature of two flats corrects this, but again a new fault appears—an augmented fourth formed by the extreme notes in the last three measures:

 But a signature of three flats yields a correct combination:

Here voice I enters with the first degree of the major scale and voice II with the third degree. Transposing this combination so that it agrees with the key of the original gives: $I^{v=-11} + II^{v=2}$:

It is sometimes impossible to get a key-signature that will remove all errors. In such cases select the most convenient signature and eliminate the remaining errors by one of the other methods.

CHAPTER IV

THE RULES OF SIMPLE COUNTERPOINT*

§ 70. In complex counterpoint both the original and derivative combinations must conform to the rules of simple counterpoint, which in no case may be infringed. These rules may be regarded as being of a prohibitory nature; they are not so much formulations of what can be done in a certain situation as they are statements of what not to do. Such, for instance, are the rules forbidding similar motion to a perfect consonance, the resolutions of the second to the unison, the seventh to the octave, etc. An interval may not be released from the limitations imposed on it by the rules of simple counterpoint, but to these limitations new ones may be added. To investigate the conditions under which a certain interval is used at a given Jv it is necessary to compare the limitations of this interval with those of its derivative. If according to the rules of simple counterpoint the derivative does not show limitations that exceed in strictness those of the original, the conditions governing the latter remains unchanged. But if the derivative interval, according to the rules of simple counterpoint, does show more limitations than the original, this excess must be added to the conditions of the original interval. The sum of these limitations constitutes the conditions under which an original interval may be used at a given Jv. All the rules of vertical-shifting counterpoint are to be interpreted in this sense.

Limitations Imposed on Intervals by the
Rules of Simple Counterpoint

§ 71. According to the scale of their limitations in simple counterpoint of the strict style, intervals are classified as imperfect consonances, perfect consonances, and dissonances.

(1) Imperfect and Perfect Consonances

§ 72. The Imperfect consonances have the greatest freedom. They are also the most satisfactory in effect, but because of this a certain monotony will result from their excessive use in parallel motion. Hence has arisen the rule in two-voice counterpoint that recommends the avoidance of a succession of parallel thirds or sixths that is too prolonged. Except for this, imperfect consonances are under no restrictions.

§ 73. The next degree of limitations refers to perfect consonances; the rules governing them fall into three groups: (1) limitations as to the moverments of the voices; (2) limitations regarding the proximity of similar perfect consonances, and (3) limitations based on the fact that perfect consonances, as compared to imperfect, sound harmonically empty.

§ 74. The first group of rules, limitations as to the movements of the voices, includes the following:

---

*A knowledge of the rules of simple counterpoint is assumed. They are here summarized for future reference.

(1) Similar motion to a perfect consonance is not allowed. Formulated in this way, the rule includes both parallel and hidden progressions, but it is relaxed as the number of voices is increased.

(2) Contrary motion from a perfect consonance to its compound, and vice versa, is forbidden:

4   11   11   4   7   0   0   7

Obs.—Frequent exceptions to this rule are found in multi-voice counterpoint, especially where fifths and twelfths are concerned:

Ex. 16   Palestrina

Ex. 17   Palestrina

Very infrequently such progressions are found in two-voice counterpoint:

Ex. 18   Palestrina

Contrary motion from a unison to an octave or vice versa is restricted to multi-voice writion, where it is allowed between the two lowest voices:

Ex. 19

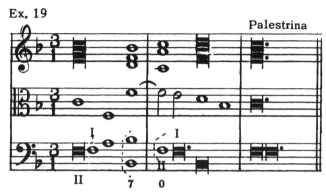

Palestrina

Such progressions are usually found in seven- and eight-voice textures, especially between the basses of the first and second choruses in a double chorus.

§ 75. The second group of rules consists of limitations regarding the proximity of similar perfect consonances. In the second species fifths and octaves are forbidden on the accented beats of adjacent measures:

and in the fourth species on the unaccented beats:

Obs. 1.—As regards the first of these rules, its strictness, as well as that of many other rules of two-voice counterpoint, is relaxed as the number of voices is increased. If in two-voice counterpoint infringements of it are sometimes, though seldom, found—

Ex. 20

Orlando Lasso

in multi-voice they are quite frequent:

In multi-voice textures such progressions are often found, but in two-voice counterpoint they are best avoided altogether.

Obs. 2.—In the fourth species, fifths on accented beats are not forbidden:

However, the composers of the era of the strict style did not consider it impractical, in the fourth species, to write fifths also on the unaccented beats:

Such progressions must be considered as very exceptional.

§ 76. The third and last group of conditions also refers to perfect consonances; they consist of limitations based on the fact that these consonances, as compared with the imperfect, sound empty. The result of this is the requirement that in two-voice counterpoint perfect consonances should alternate with imperfect, whenever possible. The most empty-sounding of all, the unison, is especially limited. With the exception of the first interval and the last the unison on accented beats is to be avoided, and it should not progress by similar motion to any interval following.*

(2) Dissonances; (a) Passing and Auxiliary; (b) Suspensions

§ 77. The most stringent limitations apply to dissonances. It is necessary to dwell at some length on the distinctions presented by the conditions under which passing and auxiliary dissonances and tied dissonances (suspensions) are used.

§ 78. These distinctions refer, first of all, to the location that the dissonances occupy in the measure. Suspensions are placed on the accented or comparatively strong beats; passing notes and auxiliary notes on the weak beats or parts of beats. For instance, in $\frac{2}{2}$ time a passing note (but not an auxiliary note) may occur on the third quarter, which is unaccented:

Similarly, in $\frac{4}{2}$ time passing notes of the values of quarters may occur on the second or fourth beats (third or seventh quarters):

Passing notes should not be longer than halves, auxiliary notes longer than quarters. Such cases as are illustrated in Exs. 30–31, where this rule is not observed, are very exceptional.

---

*Cf. Bellermann, "Der Contrapunkt," 4-te Aufl., s. 159. [The reference reads: "Der Sprung vom Einklang in ein anderen konsonierendes Intervall in gerader Bewegung ist im zweistimmigen Satz nicht gut, und daher möglichst zu vermeiden." —Tr.]

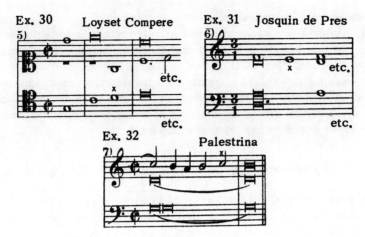

§ 79. The second difference between passing and auxiliary dissonances and tied dissonances is that the two former are not restricted as to direction; they are equally correct when the movement of a voice is by step upward or downward. On the contrary, prepared suspensions must resolve by moving the dissonant note one step downward—the strict style does not allow resolutions from below upward. Therefore the movement of suspended notes (dissonances) is restricted as to direction.

§ 80. The last and most important difference consists in the fact that the conditions of the correct use of passing and auxiliary notes are implied by their designations. When a dissonance satisfies the definition of either, the use of it is correct. The only exception is that auxiliary notes should not be taken from the unison:

Obs. 1.—Some theorists, Richter for instance, consider progressions incorrect in which a passing note approaches too closely to a sustained note in another voice, and forbids stepwise movement into the unison:

But such an interdiction is not in accordance with the practice of composers of the era of the strict style. In their works such instances as shown in Ex. 33 are frequent (cf. also Ex. 10, measure 3; Ex. 11, m. 2, two lower voices, and Ex. 28).

Obs. 2.—A passing note in the strict style is not to be regarded as a passing note to a chord, but to whatever note with which it forms a dissonance. Other voices may be free to take notes consonant with each of the other notes forming the dissonance:

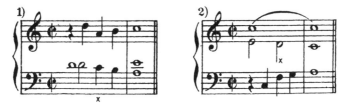

Progressions such as the following are characteristic of the strict style:

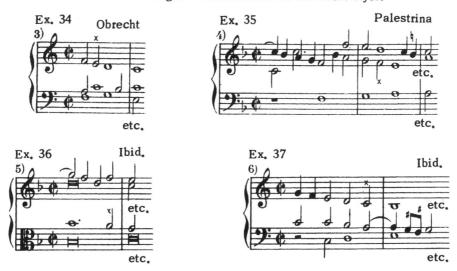

Resolution of Tied Dissonances; The Dissonant Note

§ 81. A tied dissonance represents delayed movement. Not all the conditions of its correct use enter into the definition of it. In the successive series of intervals (§ 11) each dissonance has a consonance on both sides (§ 14,[3]) of which one is perfect, the other imperfect (the fifth will always be regarded as a consonance, inasmuch as a diminished fifth may be altered to a perfect fifth). If one of the voices forming a dissonance is prepared and leads to the step below (§ 79) a resolution of the dissonance to an adjacent consonance is effected. All such voice-leadings are included in the idea of "resolution" but not all of these resolutions are valid. Considerations of euphony preclude the resolution of a dissonance to a note already present in another voice, such as the resolutions of the second to the unison and the seventh to the octave. With these exceptions the following list applies to both positive and negative intervals:

§ 82. In two-voice counterpoint the foregoing rule admits of no exceptions within the limits of an octave. But the first dissonance beyond the octave, the ninth, is an exception. The ninth may be a dissonance, and may resolve to a note appearing in the good

other voice, i.e. to an octave: 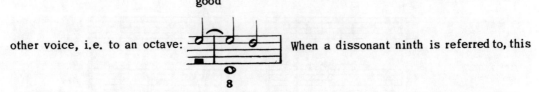 When a dissonant ninth is referred to, this

particular case is to be understood. On the other hand, a ninth, as a compound interval derived from a second, resolves the same as the latter, i.e. one degree downward, and in this case a ninth is referred to as a second. The difference between a second and a ninth consists in the fact that a second may be a dissonance only when below, while a ninth may be a dissonance either above or below. All the other compound dissonances resolve in the same way as the corresponding intervals within the octave limits. Hence it follows that every two-voice combination may without restriction be expanded by an octave (§ 47). But the reverse is not always true; to contract two voices by an octave, even though they are not less than an octave apart, may eliminate a ninth if it is a dissonance above. At the contraction of the voice it reverts to a second, which is not admissable as a higher dissonance.

The Fourth and Ninth in Multi-Voice Counterpoint

§ 83. There are two intervals of which the use in multi-voice counterpoint is to be distinguished from their use in two-voice: the fourth and the ninth. The fourth, when it occurs between an upper and an inner voice, or between two inner voices, may be released from its limitations and regarded as a consonance,* and used according to the rules for imperfect consonances, for example in the parallel movement of first inversions. In this case it does not lose its consonant character, even when the other voices form dissonant harmony, for example:

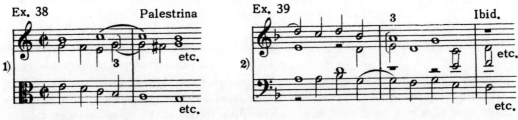

---

*Of course, the strict style allows between these voices also the augmented fourth (and diminished fifth) without preparation, provided each note forming the interval is consonant with the bass, a condition that satisfies the requirements of the diminished triad in the first inversion. In the following illustration the diminished fifth is worthy of notice, as with the other voices it forms a dominant seventh:

Cristofero Morales

Generally speaking, in multi-voice counterpoint the fourth retains its dissonant character only in relation to the bass, in which case it is subject to the conditions of preparation and resolution and is governed by the rules of two-voice counterpoint. But even in relation to the bass the fourth may sometimes assume the functions of a consonant interval; more will be said about this in Chapter X.

While in multi-voice counterpoint the fourth may be released from the limitations of a dissonance, thereby is imposed a new limitation on the ninth resolving to the octave; it should not form a dissonance with an inner voice—only with the bass. If the number of voices is not less than four it is exceptionally allowed as a dissonance to the tenor.

§ 84. The dissonant note in a tied dissonance, as stated before, resolves one degree downward. Simple cases have been examined where the suspended note is followed immediately by the note of resolution. More complicated cases are those in which a consonant note taken by a downward leap (usually a fourth) is inserted between the suspended note and the note of resolution:

In two-voice counterpoint such resolutions sound harmonically full as applied to intervals 1 and 6, and rather empty as applied to 5 and 8. In Fux's classic work *Gradus ad Parnassum* (1725) this form of ornamental treatment is frequently illustrated. Composers of the era of the strict style often use it in multi-voice textures.

On the discretion of the teacher will depend to what extent these resolutions may be applied to problems. In two-voice counterpoint intended to form part of multi-voice, such cases may be left to broader considerations, and the application to 3 and 8 allowed.

Obs.—In general it is forbidden to double a dissonant note in multi-voice counterpoint, but an exception is sometimes found: a voice moving stepwise in notes of smaller value may, at an unaccented part of the measure, run into a brief doubling of the dissonant note:

The Free Note to a Tied Dissonance

§ 85. At the same time that a suspension (tied dissonance) is conforming to the conditions of preparation (§ 86) and resolution, the other note may be free; it has these characteristics:

(1) A free note may enter or progress either stepwise or by leap:

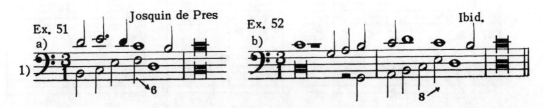

In Ex. 52 the voice taking the free note to the dissonance progresses simultaneously with the resolution to another note, a complex form of treatment which because of its importance is classified separately:

(2) The free note to a suspension may, just when the latter is resolved, progress to another note that is consonant with the note of resolution. In two-voice counterpoint this form of resolution is more applicable to seconds and sevenths than to fourths (especially fourths resolving to fifths) or ninths. The following examples from Zarlino's *Istitutioni harmoniche* show the application of it to 1, 6 and 3.

(3) A voice may enter on the free note to a dissonance after a rest:

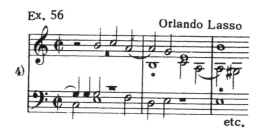

(4) Although the doubling of a dissonant note in multi-voice counterpoint is forbidden (cf. *Obs.*, § 84) the doubling of free notes is allowed if this does not involve some new difficulty, such as the incorrect resolution of a dissonance. For example, it is bad to double the free note to a ninth resolving to an octave:

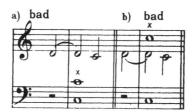

since here as the result of such doubling the upper and middle voices show: at (a) the bad progression of the second to the unison; at (b) the resolution, also bad, of the seventh to the octave. In all other cases the free note may be doubled without restriction:

In Ex. 58 the free note is doubled at the entry of the tenor:

(5) There remains to be mentioned that in cadences where the resolution of a sus-pension immediately precedes the conclusion of the cadence, the voice having the free note is often silent—it drops out at the actual moment of resolution. This is an idiom characteristic of the strict style and occurs only at the intermediate cadences during the course of a composition. At the final cadence, or at a cadence ending an important part or division, all the voices must participate. This silencing of voices is illustrated in Exs. 59–63.

The Preparation of Suspensions

§ 86. The suspensions (1 and 6) that resolve to imperfect consonances are not sub-ject to any limitations as regards their preparation; they may be prepared by any con-sonance, provided that no rule governing the melodic conduct of the voices is broken. But the dissonances that resolve to perfect consonances (3 to 4 and 8 to 7) are subject the to following rule: A dissonance that resolves to a perfect consonance can not be prepared by a consonance of the same value as that to which it resolves:

Obs. 1.—In multi-voice works progressions of fourths and fifths are often found:

Ex. 64

Obs. 2.—The complex forms of resolution mentioned in § 85, (2) allow the fifth as

preparation for the fourth, with the suspension in the lower voice:  But

the ninth, with the suspension in the upper voice, can not be prepared by the octave:

impossible

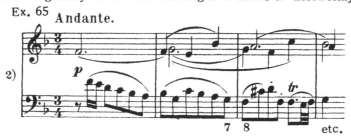 , so the foregoing rule holds. Such preparation of the ninth by the octave

is allowed in the free style, Ex. 65 illustrates this. It is from Recordare of Mozart's *Requiem,* and in the ingenuity of its voice-leading is a model of noteworthy perfection.

Ex. 65 Andante.

§ 87. In the strict style the relative duration of tied notes must be considered. For example, the note of preparation should not be shorter than the note to which it is tied. Both tied notes may be of equal value; the second may be half the value of the first but not one-quarter of the value. The following values for tied notes are unconditionally allowed:*

---

*Cf. Note at end of chapter. —Tr.

Symbols Indicating the Conditions of the Uses of Tied Intervals

§ 88. A suspension and its resolution one degree downward, in whatever rhythmical form is permissable in the strict style, will be indicated by a horizontal line placed above or below the interval figure, and will be called the tie-sign (or sign of syncopation). When placed above a figure the line will refer to voice I, when below to voice II. For example, $\overline{3}$ means the suspension of a fourth in the upper voice and its resolution one step downward:

The expression $\underline{1}$ means the dissonance and downward resolution of a second. Applied to negative intervals, $-\overline{3}$ for instance, the line above refers to voice I, i.e. to the voice which in fact is the lower.

Placed in parenthesis: (–) the sign will mean that the note to which it refers can not be used as a suspension. This enables the resolution of positive and negative seconds to be fully expressed thus: $\overset{(-)}{\underline{1}}$ and $-\underline{1}_{(-)}$. In both cases the signs – and (–) indicate that for seconds the resolution permitted is that to a third, but the resolution to a unison is not allowed. Applied to the suspension of the seventh the signs are $\underline{6}_{(-)}$ and $-\overline{6}^{(-)}$:

Fourths and ninths as suspensions are indicated by $\overline{3}$, $-\overline{3}$ and $\overline{8}$, $-\overline{8}$, abbreviated $\pm\overline{3}$ and $\pm\overline{8}$. The complex forms of resolution do not require special signs.

§ 89. From the foregoing it will be seen that negative intervals have the same tie-signs as positive intervals of equal value, but the position of the signs is reversed; the upper sign of a positive interval and the lower sign of a negative interval are the same, and vice versa.

§ 90. The following table, which should be thoroughly memorized, contains the signs indicating all the conditions under which suspensions are used in simple counterpoint of the strict style.

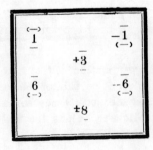

Beyond the ninth the compound intervals take the same tie-signs as the corresponding simple intervals; e.g. $\underline{10}$ has the same signs as $\overline{3}$, $\underline{13}$ the same as $\underline{6}_{(-)}$, $-\overline{13}$ the same as $-\overline{6}^{(-)}$.

If the context refers to a single tie-sign, either upper or lower, of a given interval, the other sign should be omitted. Thus, $\underline{3}$ denotes a fourth resolving to a fifth; $\overline{8}$ a ninth resolving to an octave, etc.

§ 91. It has been seen that the rules of complex counterpoint arise from the necessity of subordinating the rules of simple counterpoint not only to the requirements of the the original combination but also to those of the derivative (§ 70). Hence is shown the need of transferring to the original those limitations of the derivative that the rules of simple counterpoint would otherwise not impose upon it. They are applied not only to dissonances but also to consonances. For instance the expression $_c\underline{5}$ means that a sixth is to be treated as if it were a real suspension; that is, is to be used only on an accented beat, that the upper note is to be tied, and that it is to progress one degree downward (§ 88).

etc.

The expression $\overline{-4}$ means that a negative fifth is to be used only on an accented beat as a tied note of voice I (i.e. of the upper voice, in negative intervals found below):

It is understood that whatever limitations control intervals, they do not prevent the use of passing notes and auxiliary notes on unaccented beats.

§ 92. In illustrating the preceding, those cases were intentionally chosen in which the intervals concerned occupied the same positions as would a dissonance and its resolution, and in which the progressions were to two consonances, the fifth and the sixth. In the successive series ot intervals these are the only consonances that have dissonances on one side only (§14, [2]). All the other consonances have dissonances on both sides. Therefore if the progression is not to a fifth or a sixth any application of the tie-sign to a consonance will result in a progression to a dissonance, at the point corresponding to the resolution:

In this case the note that sounds the dissonance must be regarded as a passing-note, continuing in the same direction. Occurring as a quarter-note, it may be treated as an auxiliary:

As to the fact that a dissonance formed at the sign × may in its turn function as a suspension, more will be said in § 134.

§ 93. To indicate the dissonant note corresponding to the note of resolution—therefore either a passing or an auxiliary-note—the supplementary sign × will be used, its addition to a tie-sign meaning a tied note and its progression one degree downward. The expression $\underline{5}$ means that a sixth can not be taken as a tie on an accented beat on voice I, but that it may be taken as a tie in voice II on condition that the note corresponding to the note of resolution is either passing or auxiliary.

§ 94. Three signs are now available for indicating the conditions under which tied intervals are used. According to the scale of limitations their order is: −, −×, (−). The first of these, forbidding the free use of an interval on an accented beat, admits of its use as a tie in the voice to which the sign refers. The second, −×, adds a further restriction: the note corresponding to the note of resolution must be either passing or auxiliary (the other voice sustained—oblique motion). The third sign, (−) forbids altogether a tie applied to the note to which it refers, nor can such note be otherwise used as passing or auxiliary.

If a tie-sign applying to a given interval according to the rules of simple counterpoint is replaced by either of the signs indicating more strict conditions (−× or (−)), no relaxation of any rule of the strict style can ensue; the interval will only be placed under more stringent conditions as regards its use. But the substitution of a sign by one of lesser force in entirely inadmissable, for no interval may be released from the limitations imposed upon it by the rules of simple counterpoint.

"Translator's Note to" § 87

A commentary on the last sentence of this section and the illustration following it is necessary, for a point is involved that may cause needless difficulty if it is not cleared up. The author fails to make a distinction between the treatment of ties in $\frac{2}{2}$ time and those in $\frac{4}{4}$. All three of the illustrations at the end of § 87 are available in either $\frac{2}{2}$ or $\frac{4}{4}$ provided that the second note of the tie is not a dissonant; this is also true of the illustrations following in § 88. But if the second of two tied notes is a quarter-note it can be a tied dissonant in $\frac{4}{4}$ but not in $\frac{2}{2}$, for one of the most important rules governing the use of suspensions is that they shall resolve on a beat, not on a half-beat unless this is the second half of an unaccented part of the measure. The author is aware of this, for in the Observation preceding Exs. 88-90 he says that "it is very uncommon to find suspensions on the second and fourth beats," and in these examples the resolutions all come on a quarter-note, or second half of the second and fourth beats in $\frac{4}{2}$. Here the textbook rules and the practice of sixteenth-century composers are in agreement. In many of the examples written by the author he seems to have been in doubt as to what the time is: $\frac{2}{2}$, $\frac{4}{4}$, $\frac{4}{2}$, or $\frac{8}{4}$. All of which are represented by the signs C and ₵ in an utterly indiscriminate manner. The result is that resolutions are often found on a half-beat if the time is ₵, or on the full beat if it is C. The former is wrong unless this half-beat is the second half of an unaccented part of the measure; the latter right, according to the author's own statement just quoted, where, as in other places in the text, under the necessity of expressing his meaning with precision, he uses the figures, not the signs. The quotations from sixteenth-century composers have the resolutions on the beat, except in Exs. 88-90, where Taneiev calls attention to the irregularity.

In discarding the signs and using the figures instead I have only done what should have happened two hundred years ago. The sign for the "tempus perfectum," ◯, was long ago replaced by the more accurate figures $\frac{3}{2}$ and the modern equivalents $\frac{3}{4}$ and $\frac{3}{8}$, while for some unknown reason the signs for the "tempus imperfectum," ₵ and C were retained and to this day are responsible for much doubt as to how many beats in a measure are meant. Their continued use, instead of the figures $\frac{2}{2}$, $\frac{4}{4}$, or whatever is intended, is an unfortunate survival of the notation based on the old "mood, time, prolation" principles and that lacked bar-lines. Modern notation would gain in clarity and precision were the signs to be replaced by the figures (cf. H. Elliot Button, "System in Musical Notation [Novello]," Chapter I, especially page 6).

CHAPTER V

THE RULES OF VERTICAL-SHIFTING COUNTERPOINT; FIXED INTERVALS

§ 95. To prepare a table of rules for a given Jv a comparison must be made of the series of positive intervals in the original combination with the intervals on its derivative. The derivative intervals are obtained by adding to each original interval a value corresponding to that of the index (§ 31). The conditions governing the use of an original interval follow from a comparison of its limitations with those of its derivative at the given Jv (§ 70).

§ 96. Such comparison yields four possibilities:

(1) From a consonance is obtained a consonance;

(2) From a dissonance is obtained a dissonance.

Such intervals will be termed fixed.

(3) From a consonance is obtained a dissonance;

(4) From a dissonance is obtained a consonance.

These intervals will be termed variable. Each of the four cases will be examined in turn, beginning with the fixed consonances.

(1) Fixed Consonances

§ 97. Within the octave limits are four consonances (0, 2, 4, 5) and three dissonances (1, 3, 6). Therefore not all the consonances of a given Jv can coincide in the derivative combination with dissonances; every Jv has at least one fixed consonance. The following indices have only one fixed consonance (cf. table, § 108): $JJv = -10, -3<, 1$, and all JJv of the sixth column. On the contrary, the consonances are all fixed in $Jv = -2$ and in $Jv = -4>$. Between these extremes are found a number of fixed consonances from other JJv.

§ 98. Two tables will be prepared (§ 95): one for a ^1Jv (§ 57), for example, $Jv = -11$; another for a ^2Jv: $Jv = -9$. For this purpose is written out a series of original (positive) intervals from 0 to an interval equal to Jv inclusive (§ 38). Under the original intervals are placed their derivatives and under these a horizontal line. Below this line are written the original fixed consonances.

$^1Jv = -11>$												
	p.		imp.		p.	imp.		p.		imp.		p.
Original intervals:	0	I	2	3	4	5	6	7	8	9	10	11
	p.		imp.		p.		imp.	p.		imp.		p.
Derivative intervals at Jv = −11:	−11	−10	−9	−8	−7	−6	−5	−4	−3	−2	−1	0
Fixed consonances:	0		2		4			7		9		11

$^2Jv = -9>$										
	p.		imp.		p.	imp.		p.		imp.
Original intervals:	0	I	2	3	4	5	6	7	8	9
	imp.		p.		imp.	p.		imp.		p.
Derivative intervals at $^2Jv = -9$:	−9	−8	−7	−6	−5	−4	−3	−2	−1	0
Fixed consonances:	0		2		4	5		7		9

70

§ 99. Comparing these two tables it is seen that at an index of the first group (^1Jv) each consonance that is fixed yields a similar consonance in the derivative, i.e. perfect yields perfect and imperfect yields imperfect. On the contrary, at an index of the second group (^2Jv) from each fixed consonance is obtained another with the opposite quality: perfect yields imperfect and vice versa.

§ 100. Such a relation holds good between the fixed consonances of all indices of the first and second groups with the exception of $Jv = -8$. This can be verified by the General Table of Indices but the demonstration follows. In the successive series of intervals (§ 11) a ^{1}int. represents the distance between any two consonances of the same group, i.e. between two perfect or two imperfect consonances (§15,[1]), and a ^{2}int. the distance between any two consonances of different groups (§15,[2]). There is only one exception to this, the case of 4 and −4< (§ 16), in which two consonances of the same group are separated by 8, a ^{2}int. Since Jv is that interval in the successive series by which a derivative is separated from its original (§ 33), then at an index ^1Jv, i.e. $Jv = ^1$int., each fixed consonance and its derivative can only be consonances from one and the same group; at an index ^2Jv, i.e. $Jv = ^2$int. (except $Jv = -8$) they can only be consonances from different groups.

§ 101. The attribute of fixed consonances to which attention has been called allows the following broad generalization to be made regarding the entire series of rules for vertical-shifting counterpoint: *The imperfect consonances yielded by ^{2}JJv in the derivative must conform to the limitations of perfect consonances* (§§ 73-6).

§ 102. It is important, first of all, that an interval to be shifted at any index of the second group (^2Jv) shall not contain an instance of similar motion to an imperfect consonance, because in the derivative this will show up as similar motion to a perfect consonance. And since the latter progression is forbidden in the original by the rules of the strict style, it follows that similar motion at ^2JJv is altogether out of the question. However, the strictness of this condition as it applies to hidden progressions is relaxed as the number of voices is increased.

§ 103. Therefore, indices of the first group (^1JJv), as presenting the first cases of coinciding consonances (§ 100) are not subject to restrictions as to motion. But those of the second group (^2JJv), presenting the second, preclude the use of similar motion.

Obs.—It has been mentioned that $^2Jv = -8$ is an exception to the indices of the second group. While the fixed consonances of the other ^2JJv give intervals of opposite quality in the derivative, the only fixed interval of $^2Jv = -8$, a fifth, gives also a fifth in the derivative (4 − 8 = −4, § 31).

0	1	2	3	p. 4	5	6	7	8
−8	7	−6	−5	−4 p.	−4	−2	−1	0

4

But this fact does not admit of $Jv = -8$ being included in the indices that allow similar motion. Since the fifth is a perfect consonance, and the only fixed consonance that this Jv has, similar motion is rendered impossible. Therefore the rule stated—that ^2JJv do not admit of similar motion—holds good also for $^2Jv = -8$, so the rule has no exception. But it should be remembered that this rule is rigidly applied only to two—voice counterpoint. In multi-voice counterpoint its strictness is considerably relaxed, as a result of the use of hidden progressions.

§ 104. The first of the limitations imposed by the rules of the strict style on perfect consonances, forbidding similar motion to them, has been applied to the imperfect consonances of the second group. The next step is to apply to the perfect consonances of this group the remaining limitations of perfect consonances (§§ 74—6).

Applying limitation (2), § 74, gives this rule: *Contrary motion from a simple fixed consonance (either perfect or imperfect) to its compound, and vice versa, is forbidden.* The limitations in § 75 regarding the proximity of similar perfect consonances must be extended to include all fixed consonances of the indices of the second group. Finally, from the limitations in § 76 arises the requirement that in the original combination perfect and imperfect consonances should if possible be used more or less·in alternation. A preponderance of imperfect consonances in the original results in the derivative sounding empty, but inasmuch as supplementary voices are always available this requirement may be discounted somewhat.

§ 105. The only remaining limitations refer in particular to the unison (§ 76). Since at a positive Jv derivative unisons from positive intervals are not possible, these limitations can apply only to negative JJv, and refer to the intervals corresponding to the index. From this interval, as has been previously stated, is obtained a derivative unison (§32, [2]). Therefore, with the exception of the first and last sounds, an interval equal to a negative Jv can not be placed on an accented beat, though it may be used on unaccented beats, and when so used the voices must not progress to the next interval by similar motion. This rule applies also to all negative indices, both of the first and second groups.

Obs.—If the rule mentioned in *Obs.* 1 to § 80 is observed it will be necessary to forbid stepwise movement to an interval equal in value to a negative index.

§ 106. The student who has assimilated these rules can now undertake exercises with indices of both the first and second groups. On accented beats only fixed consonances should be used, and dissonances and variable consonances employed only as passing, or less often, auxiliary-notes.

§ 107. The table in § 108 consists of a list of the fixed consonances of all indices. In working out exercises those indices should be chosen that have enough fixed consonances to make study profitable—not less than three. With negative JJv the limiting interval of each index, always equal to it, must be taken into consideration. For negative JJv with the direct shift the limiting interval shows the distance to which the voices may approach (§ 38), at JJv with the inverse shift, the distance to which they may recede (§ 39). As to the order in which the exercises should be written, instructions are given in Chapter VIII, but before starting this work the present chapter must be thoroughly mastered.

§ 108. Table of Fixed Consonances

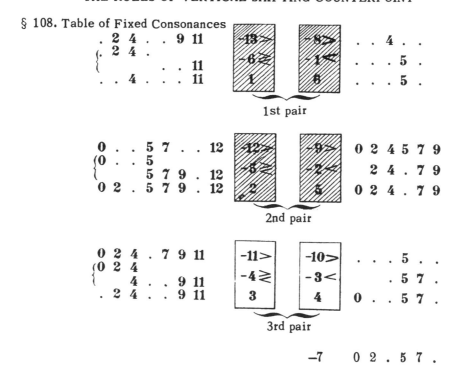

1st pair

2nd pair

3rd pair

$$-7 \qquad 0 \; 2 \; . \; 5 \; 7 \; .$$

Explanation of Table

To the right of each right-hand column of each pair and to the left of each left-hand column is placed the series of fixed consonances of its Jv. A dot occupying the place of a figure in the row of consonances means that this consonance of the corresponding Jv is variable. If a simple consonance is fixed its compound is also fixed. It would therefore be possible to restrict the list of fixed consonances to the octave limits, but for greater convenience in using the table the fixed consonances beyond the octave are also given. Consonances for JJv with the inverse shift are given from 0 to the interval equal in value to the index. For negative JJv with the direct shifts the consonances start from an interval equal to Jv and continue to the same limit as the upper row of intervals for the same column. Two series of figures are given for the middle Jv of each left-hand column, the upper series for the inverse shift, the lower for the direct shift.

§ 109. In the following examples showing the application of fixed consonances to JJv of both groups, those that have few fixed consonances are omitted. Thus, from ^1JJv is omitted $Jv = -10$; from ^2JJv of the first pair of columns only $Jv = -13$ is retained. In studying the examples the table in § 108 should be consulted. For limiting intervals v. §§ 38-9.

(A) Examples at ^1JJv

§ 110. Omitting $Jv = -10$ (§ 109) the remaining ^1JJv are taken in this order:

(1) $^1Jv = -11$, double counterpoint at the twelfth (cf. table in § 98).

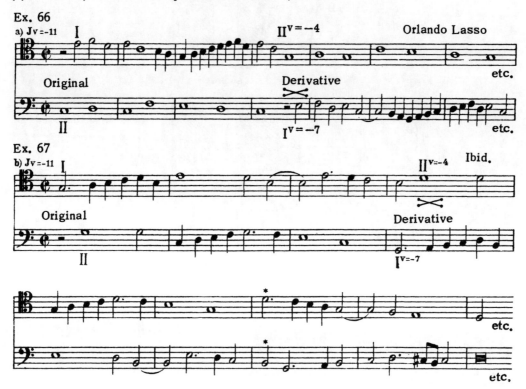

In each of these examples the first three measures present the original combination, the next three measures the derivative. In Ex. 67 the voices pass into simple counterpoint at the seventh measure. Cf. also Ex. 7 ($Jv = -11$).

(2) $^1Jv = -4>$, the middle Jv of the same column.

Cf. also Ex. 11 ($Jv = -4>$).

If, in a combination written at the middle index, a voice of the derivative is separated an octave, another derivative is obtained at an outer Jv of the same column (§ 56). Thus, Ex. 68 at $Jv = -4>$ may be shifted at $Jv = -11$.

The distance between the two clefs for I shows the Jv.

Ex. 69

3) $^{1}Jv = -4 <$ (The distance between the two clefs for I shows the Jv).

According to § 56 it is possible in this example to separate a voice of the derivative an octave, thus obtaining a derivative at the lower Jv of the same column, i.e. at $Jv = 3$. Because of the small number of fixed consonances that $Jv = -4 <$ has, while the one under it $Jv = 3$, has only two, also under the necessity of relinquishing animation and interest in voice-leading until suspensions can be used, combinations result that are musically rather meager.

Ex. 70

4) $^{1}Jv = 3$ Original

There is no need to cite separate examples for the middle and lower indices of the fourth column. If in Exs. 69 and 70, at $Jv = -4 <$ and $Jv = 3$, original and derivative are exchanged (§ 68,[1]), combinations result at $Jv = 4$ and $Jv = -3$, the lower and middle indices of the fourth column. In this way exercises in all essentials can be changed from the indices of any column to those of the other column of the same pair.

(5) $^{1}Jv = -7$, double counterpoint at the octave. There remains to give an example at this index from the zero column. In the free style double counterpoint at this interval is the most frequently used, but in the preceding era $Jv = -11$ (double counterpoint at the twelfth) was considered of greater importance.

Ex. 71

5) $^{1}Jv = -7$ $II^{v = -7}$

(B) Examples at ^2JJv

§ 111. Examples at ^2JJv (§ 108) are taken in this order:

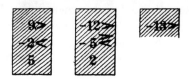

(1) $^2Jv = -9>$. At this index all the consonances are fixed (cf. table, § 98). This is the so-called double counterpoint at the tenth, and together with $Jv = -7$ and $Jv = -11$ forms a group of double counterpoints that in most textbooks exhausts the study of vertical-shifting counterpoint.

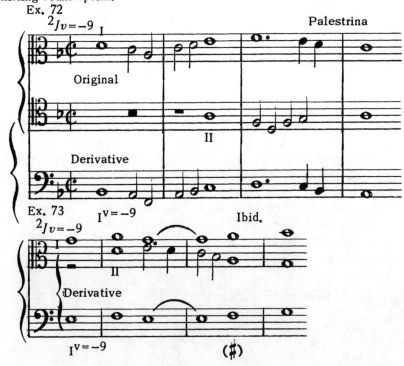

For further remarks on both examples *vide* § 119; also cf. Ex. 2. Ex. 74, in double counterpoint at the tenth, requires a shift at $Jv = -16$ (§ 50). In this example the voices are separated from each other by an interval greater than a twelfth. The limiting interval is 16> (§ 39).

*Taken from a four-voice combination.

Separating the derivative an octave (§ 56) gives a combination at the lower index of the same column ($Jv = 5$).

Ex. 76

Exchanging original and derivative in the last two examples ($Jv = -2$ and $Jv = 5$) gives combinations at $Jv = 2$ and $Jv = -5<$, indices from the other column of the same pair:

Ex. 77

(5) There remains a single index from the first pair of columns: $^{2}Jv = -13>$.

Ex. 78

§ 112. In concluding the discussion of fixed consonances, some special properties of two-voice vertical-shifting counterpoint must be mentioned; cases in which, suspensions being absent, there appear on accented beats only fixed consonances. These include:

(1) Combinations that may be shifted at two or more indices and—

(2) Combinations in which imperfect consonances may be duplicated.

Chapter X will be devoted to a detailed study of combinations in which all intervals, without exception, participate.

(1) Combinations Without Suspensions, Admitting of Shifts at
Two or More Indices

§ 113. At $^{2}Jv = 9$ all the consonances are fixed (§§ 98, 100). If a combination is written without suspensions, with consonances on the accented beats, that meets all the requirements of ^{2}JJv (non-use of similar motion etc.), and that does not exceed the limiting interval 9>, then whatever the consonances used and whatever their number, the combination will satisfy all the conditions of $Jv = -9$. Hence it follows that every combination from which suspensions are absent, and written at any index of the second group, can be shifted at $Jv = -9$. These shifts at two indices are called compound (double) indices (§ 28). For instance, in Exs. 75 and 76 the indices could be designated $^2Jv = -2, -9$ and $^2Jv = 5, -9$, respectively. The only obstacle to shifting at $Jv = -9$ would be that the separation of the voices might exceed the limiting interval -9. But this is easily overcome by separating a voice of the derivative an octave, taking $Jv = -16$ instead of $Jv = -9$. If in practice such shifts prove inconvenient because of the wide distance between the voices, they are still important from a theoretical standpoint, as confirming the fact that every combination (without suspensions) at an index of the second group will also yield a shift in double counterpoint at the tenth. Exs. 77 and 78 illustrate such cases of double indices: $^2Jv = -12, -16$ and $^2Jv = -13, -16$.

§ 114. The absence of suspensions has been stated as a characteristic of all ^2JJv, which includes $Jv = -9$, but this is provisional and must not be understood as preventing the use of every combination that contains a suspension. Certain shifts are possible with suspensions, but not all; some dissonances may render them impracticable, a matter that will be discussed in detail in Chapter IX.

§ 115. The attribute of ^2JJv under discussion is the result of a more general principle which may be formulated thus: *In a combination written at conditions that are more rigid than those of the given index the possibility of yielding a shift at this index is not relinquished.* In other words, the totality of rules for a given index must be understood as the minima limitations by which a combination is surrounded, in order that a shift may be made at this index. Whatever limitations are imposed in excess of the required index do not prevent a shift at this index. On the contrary, a combination that is released from whatever limitations the given index may have ceases to yield a valid shift.

§ 116. Guided by these considerations, it is not difficult to find a few cases where the given combination yields shifts at compound indices. For example, the fixed consonances of $Jv = -7$ and $Jv = 2$ are identical (cf. table, § 108). Since a combination written at $Jv = 2$ is subject to conditions more strict than those of $Jv = 7$ (because $Jv = 2$ belongs to the second group of indices, restricted as to movement), then any combination at $Jv = 2$ (without suspensions) can be freely shifted also at $Jv = -7$, if only the voices are not separated by more than the limiting interval, an octave. Even if they do exceed this limit a combination at $Jv = 2$ may still yield a valid shift in double counterpoint at the octave, not at $Jv = -7$ but at $Jv = -14$. At the same time $Jv = -2$ gives a shift at $Jv = -9$ (§ 113). Hence a combination at $Jv = 2$ may be designated by a triple index: $Jv = 2, -7, -9$ or $Jv = 2, -14, -16$ etc. It is clear that the opposite cannot be done, such as a combination written at $Jv = -7$ shifting at $Jv = -2$, since the admission of similar motion in the first of these gives an impossible shift at $Jv = 2$.

§ 117. Two rules ensue from the foregoing:

(1) A combination without suspensions, and containing similar motion, admits of shifts at those ^1JJv of which the fixed consonances include whatever consonances appear in the given combination. For example this combination—

containing similar motion, uses two consonances: 2 and 4. The ^1JJv that include 2 and 4 as fixed consonances are those from the third column: $Jv = 3$, $Jv = 4^>$ and $Jv = -11$ (cf. table, § 108). Therefore the combinations can be shifted at each of these ^1JJv:

Derivatives:

(2) If to a similar combination (without suspensions) is applied the limitations of ^2JJv it will admit of shifts at every index, both of this and of the first group, of which the fixed consonances include those in the given combination. For example this—

Original

includes the same two consonances as the preceding, but differs from it by the absence of similar motion. Therefore it can not only be shifted, like the preceding combination, at the ^1JJv of the third column, but also at all the other ^2JJv that include, as fixed consonances, the intervals 2 and 4. This concerns all ^2JJv from the fifth column and two from the first column: −13 and −6>. In this way the combination referred to yields shifts at a compound index that unites the conditions of eight JJv, namely: $JJv = -2<$, 3, −4<, 5, −6>, −9>, −11>, −13>.

Derivatives:

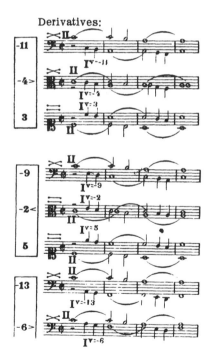

§ 118. If a combination is written at a middle index and a voice of the derivative is separated an octave there results a derivative at an extreme index of the same column from which the middle shift was made (§ 56). This was shown in the preceding illustration, where $Jv = -11$ was derived from $Jv = -4<$; $Jv = -5$ from $Jv = -2$; $Jv = -13$ from

$Jv = -6>$. Discarding the shifts that are only reproductions of others at the octave, there remain five different combinations. But this number of shifts is obtained at the expense of great restraint. By relinquishing similar motion the original consonances are cut to two at the most. In general, the number of derivative combinations that it is possible to obtain from an original is in inverse proportion to the musical resources employed in its composition. The more numerous the derivatives, the more monotonous the original from which they are obtained.

(2) Combinations Without Suspensions, Admitting the Duplication of Imperfect Consonances; Three-Voice Counterpoint

§ 119. Mention is still to be made as to a characteristic possessed by combinations (without suspensions) that belong to JJv corresponding to imperfect consonances, i.e. to the indices of the second pair of columns ($^2JJv = \pm2, \pm5, -9, -12$).

At each ^2Jv from the second pair of columns a derivative may be obtained that will be the execution of the original plus an additional shift of one of the voices. The result will be three-voice counterpoint in which two voices represent the duplication of one of the original voices in parallel imperfect consonances. Since the additional shift is possible in either voice, every such three-voice combination may appear in two forms. For example, $Jv = -9$ gives two three-voice combinations: $I + I^{v=-9} + II$ and $I + II + II^{v=-9}$. For brevity the added voice, doubling another, will be indicated by the letter d. Thus, $I^{d=-9}$ will replace $I + I^{d=-9}$; $II^{d=-9}$ instead of $II + II^{v=-9}$, etc.

Such three-voice counterpoint is most often the result of using $Jv = -9$, an index that yields parallel tenths in the outer voices. In parallel motion these consonances, rather than others, are the most euphonious. As has been often observed, all the consonances in $Jv = -9$ are fixed. Whatever consonances are taken, at the duplication $I^{d=-9} + II$ or $I + II^{d=-9}$, all three voices form a consonant union, as will be seen in this table:

In exactly the same way, at $d = Jv$ the fixed consonances of all the other JJv corresponding to imperfect consonances give a consonant union in three voices. Exs. 72 and 73, at $Jv = -9$, give two three-voice combinations:

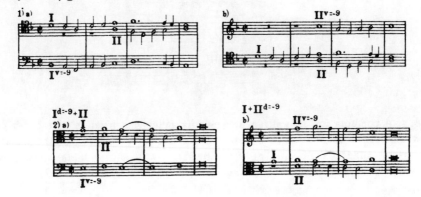

The same process may be applied to Exs. 75 and 76:

§ 120. If Jv refers to an index that has both the direct and the inverse shift, use will be made of the signs already known for indicating the necessary situations. For example, the expression $I + II^{d=-5<}$ means that the limit for the voices of the original combination is a sixth, consequently the direct shift; $I + II^{d=5>}$ means that a sixth is the separation limit, therefore the inverse shift. If in the last illustration the original and derivative are exchanged, the duplication would be indicated: (a) $I + II^{d=-5\times}$, (b) $I^{d=-5<} + II$.

§ 121. Furthermore, every three-voice combination without suspensions that is formed by the duplication of one of the voices is possible also, in three voices, by duplicating the other voice. In analysing the examples it may be useful to play them on the piano, duplicating first one voice and then the other.

§ 122. In accordance with the statements in § 113, any combination, at whatever ^2Jv (without suspensions and having fixed consonances on the accented beats), gives a shift at $Jv = -9$ (or $Jv = -16$). Also, a combination at $Jv = -9$, as an index of the second group, can be executed in three voices with the shifts $I^{v=-9}$ or $II^{v=-9}$ (§ 119). It follows that any combination at a ^2Jv from which suspensions are absent may be executed also at the duplication $I^{d=-9} + II$ and $I + II^{d=-9}$. And it is possible that a two-voice comination originally written at an index of the second group—corresponding to a dissonant interval, $^2Jv = -13$ for example—may be executed in three voices with either of these duplications. Two aspects of the original and derivative are here shown (cf. Ex. 78).

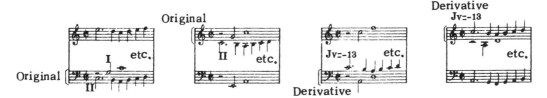

Playing the foregoing is inconvenient, due to the fact that the duplications in the originals are at $Jv = -16$ instead of at $Jv = -9$.

Obs.—Duplications have been dealt with only as far as they relate to the study of fixed consonances. Many more questions will arise as to duplications applied to tied intervals, dissonances and variable consonances; they will be discussed in Chapter X.

(2) Fixed Dissonances

§ 123. A dissonance in the original combination coinciding with a dissonance in the derivative is called fixed (§ 96). Their number varies with the different indices. For instance, all the dissonances in $Jv = -9$ and $Jv = -4>$ are fixed; all except one are fixed in $JJv = -11, -7, -5<, +2$ and 5. The indices of the sixth column and also these: -10, $-5>$, $-6<$, 1, have no fixed dissonances at all.

§ 124. To express the conditions under which a fixed dissonance may be used at a given index it is necessary to compare the original dissonance (m) with its derivative (n), the sign of one or the other indicating its use in simple counterpoint (§ 90). Next, the upper and lower signs must be compared with each other. If they are alike, or if the sign of the original dissonance indicates a higher degree in the scale of limitations than that of the derivative, then the sign of the original stands without change. If, with different signs, the highest degree in the scale of limitations is shown by the sign of the derivative dissonance, then the sign of the latter must be transferred to the original. In other words, the sign (–) at an original interval is always retained, but the sign – must be replaced by (–) in cases where the latter applies to the derivative interval. In this way the original takes over the surplus limitation which the derivative has as compared to it (§ 70), and thereby assumes the conditions necessary for its use in simple counterpoint.

§ 125. For example, at $Jv = -11$ the sign (–) must be substituted for the lower sign of the fixed dissonance $\overline{10}$, and must therefore appear as the lower sign of the derivative interval:

$$Jv = -11$$

$$m = \overline{10}$$

according to the rules
of simple counterpoint

$$n = \overline{\underset{(-)}{-1}}$$

Conditions of using original
at $Jv = -11$:

$$\underset{(-)}{\overline{10}}$$

Hence, in double counterpoint at the twelfth the lowest note of the interval considered cannot be used as a suspension, since in the derivative it would give the incorrect resolution of a second to a unison:

§ 126. In comparing the dissonance of the original and derivative it may happen that the original, already having the sign (–) for one voice, acquires the same sign also for the other voice. For instance at $Jv = 5$ a second, giving a seventh in the derivative $(1 + 5 = 6)$, takes the signs $\underset{(-)}{\overset{(-)}{1}}$, the result of comparing the two intervals $\overset{(-)}{1}$ and $\underset{(-)}{\overline{6}}$. An interval having the sign $(-)$ both above and below can not be used as a suspension, but only as a passing or an auxiliary-note.

§ 127. With the help of the table of dissonances (§ 90) it is easy to decide questions that relate to fixed dissonances; for example, at what indices is it impossible for a given dissonance to function as a suspension?

Suppose that this question arises concerning the second. A second $(\overset{(-)}{1})$ has the sign $(-)$ above. Its use in the capacity of a suspension would therefore be impossible in those cases where a dissonance in the derivative would result that has the same sign underneath. Taking these intervals from the table, and indicating by m an interval of the original combination, by n an interval from the derivative:

(a)

$$m = \overset{(-)}{1}$$

simple ctrp.

Conditions for original:

$$n = \underset{(-)}{-\overline{1}}$$
$$\underset{(-)}{\overset{(-)}{1}}$$

(b)

$$m = \overset{(-)}{1}$$

simple ctrp.

Conditions for original:

$$n = \underset{(-)}{\overline{6}}$$
$$\underset{(-)}{\overset{(-)}{1}}$$

It remains now to find the index according to original and derivative intervals. Using formula (2), § 61, the original interval is added to the derivative, taking the opposite sign, the result is the required index: $Jv = -2$ for case (a) above, and $Jv = 5$ for case (b). It is easy to find, in the same way, that, for example, a seventh can not be used as a suspension at $Jv = -5$ or at $Jv = -12$, etc.

§ 128. A table of intervals will be compiled for $^2Jv = -9$. The dissonances in the two upper rows are provided with their appropriate signs, according to the rules of simple counterpoint. Underneath the horizontal lines are the fixed dissonances (at this index all dissonances are fixed) and their signs indicated as explained in § 124.

$^2Jv = -9 >$

Original intervals:	0	$\overset{(-)}{1}$	2	$\underset{(-)}{\overline{3}}$	4	5	$\underset{(-)}{\overline{6}}$	7	$\overline{8}$	9
Derivative intervals:	−9	$\overline{-8}$	−7	$\overline{-6}$	−5	−4	$\overline{-3}$	−2	$\overline{-1}$	0
Fixed dissonances:		$\overset{(-)}{1}$		$\overset{(-)}{3}$			$\underset{(-)}{\overline{6}}$		$\underset{(-)}{\overline{8}}$	

Of the intervals in the bottom row $\overset{(-)}{1}$ and $\underset{(-)}{\overline{6}}$ retain their former signs, therefore the conditions of their use at $Jv = -9$ is the same as in simple counterpoint. But $\overset{(-)}{3}$ and $\underset{(-)}{\overline{8}}$ acquire new limitations, expressed by the sign $(-)$.

In any statement for the rules of a given index there is no need of enumerating those dissonances of which the signs remain the same as in simple counterpoint. Therefore the rule for suspensions at $Jv = -9$ is expressed by the figures $\overset{(-)}{3}$ and $\underset{(-)}{\overline{8}}$. Suspensions are used in Ex. 79. Before working out exercises one should get acquainted with the rules for the preparation of fixed dissonances (§§ 131–2).

§ 129. The dissonances are also fixed in $^1Jv = -4 >$:

$$
\begin{array}{ccccc}
0 & (\overline{1}) & 2 & \overline{3} & 4 \\
-4 & -\overline{3} & -2 & \underset{(-)}{-\overline{1}} & 0 \\
\hline
 & (\underset{}{\overline{1}}) & & \overline{3}) & \\
 & \underline{1} & & (\underline{3}) &
\end{array}
$$

The sign for the second is the same as in simple counterpoint. The fourth acquires a new sign for the lower voice: $\underset{(-)}{\overline{3}}$. Ex. 80 uses fixed dissonances at $Jv = -4 >$.

The remaining examples in this chapter are given without interval tables.

§ 130. (1) $^1Jv = -11 >$. Here the only fixed dissonance using conditions other than those applying in simple counterpoint is $\underset{(-)}{\overline{10}}$. Dissonance 6 is still excluded as it is variable.

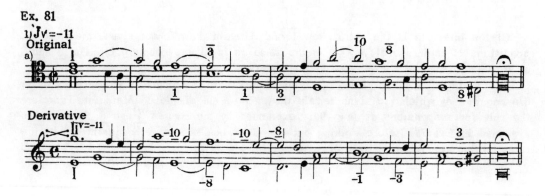

Ex. 82

(2) $^1Jv = -7>$. The use of the fixed dissonances (1, 6) is the same as in simple counterpoint. The variable dissonance 3 is for the present excluded from the available suspensions.

Ex. 86 shows a shift in double counterpoint at the octave, but at $Jv = -14>$ instead of at $Jv = -7>$, a case, therefore, of where the voices in the original are separated from each other by more than an octave (§ 48). The limiting interval is 14>.

(3) $^2Jv = 2$. The variable dissonance 3 is temporarily excluded. The conditions using the fixed dissonances are the same as in simple counterpoint.

Ex. 87

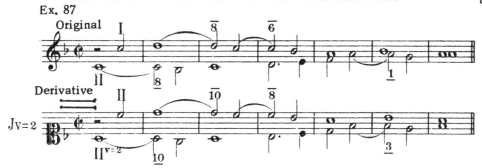

Exchanging original and derivative results in a shift at $Jv = -2$. At this index the variable dissonance 6 is temporarily excluded. The signs for the fixed dissonances are: $\overset{(-)}{\underset{-}{3}}, \overline{\underset{(-)}{8}}, \overline{\underset{-}{10}}.$

The Preparation of Fixed Dissonances

§ 131. According to the rules of simple counterpoint in the strict style a suspension that resolves to a perfect consonance cannot be prepared by an interval of the same value as that to which it resolves (§ 86). The suspensions resolving to perfect consonances are 3 and 8. Therefore the following preparations for these intervals are forbidden:

The rule forbidding such preparations in simple counterpoint may be formulated thus: In a suspension resolving to a perfect consonance the note against which the suspension is prepared can not progress diatonically downward to the note against which the suspension is sounded.

§ 132. At indices of the first group (^1JJv) the rules for the preparation of fixed consonances undergo no change from the rules of simple counterpoint, except the single requirement that the preparing consonance must be fixed. But for those of the second group (^2JJv) the restrictions of simple counterpoint as regards the use of perfect consonances must be applied also to the imperfect consonances. Therefore for ^2JJv the rule for the preparation of fixed dissonances may be stated as follows: At a ^2Jv the preparing fixed consonance can not be of the same value as the consonance to which the suspension resolves (the disengaged voice remaining stationary at the moment of resolution), furthermore, at a ^2Jv the note against which a suspension sounds can not be prepared by a note on the next higher degree.

CHAPTER VI

VARIABLE INTERVALS

(3) Variable Consonances

§ 133. Variable consonances are those that in the original combination coincide with dissonances in the derivative (§ 96). Since within the octave limits there is one more consonance than there are dissonances, the consonances of a given Jv can not all coincide with dissonances, i.e. can not all be variable; every Jv has at least one fixed consonance (§ 97). This is true of the indices of the sixth column and also of $JJv = -10$, $-6<$, 1; in all of these the consonances, with the exception of one, are variable (cf. table, § 108). The JJv that have no variable consonances at all are $JJv = -9$ and $-4>$. A number of variable consonances from other JJv are found between these extremes.

§ 134. A variable consonance must take over the limitations of the dissonance which it gives in the derivative combination (§ 70). If a note with the sign − progresses to a dissonance at the point where a resolution would normally occur, this dissonance must be treated as passing or auxiliary, and takes the supplementary sign × (§ 92).

For example, $Jv = -11$ has one variable consonance, 5. Adding to it the sign of the derivative gives 5̱. But to the lower sign must be added the supplementary sign, since the progression of the lower voice one degree downward gives the dissonance of a

seldom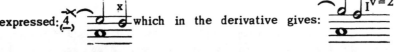 The conditions of using a sixth are expressed, therefore, by 5̱.

Similarly, at $Jv = 2$ the conditions of using the only variable consonance, the fifth, are

expressed: which in the derivative gives:

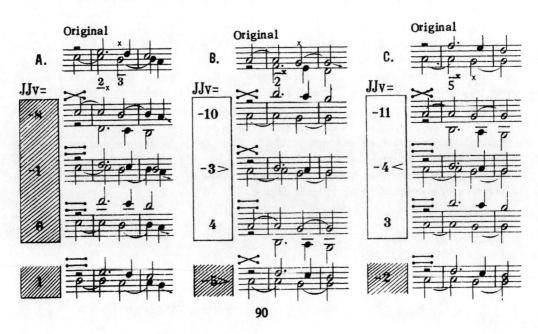

90

The sign × also has another meaning as shown above: If a consonance taking the sign −× is imperfect a dissonance is formed, to which the sign refers, at the moment of resolution; which in turn functions as a tied interval. As the beat on which it appears is comparatively strong, the dissonance resolves as though it were tied.

In § 161 will be shown the application of the sign × to ornamental forms of resolution (cf. also § 167).

Obs.—In compositions in the strict style written in $\frac{4}{2}$ time it is very uncommon to find suspensions on the second and fourth beats:

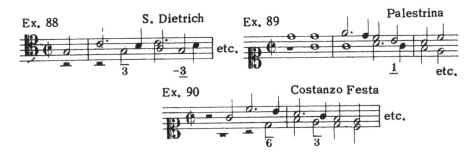

§ 135. The supplementary sign is not needed when the resolution of a variable consonance is to a fifth or a sixth. This happens when (a) the sign − is underneath the fifth (4): [musical example] and (b) when it is above the sixth (5̄): [musical example]

In all other cases the sign − for a variable consonance must always be accompanied by the supplementary sign.

§ 136. In the table to follow, the figures 4 and 5 in the two upper rows will take a short dotted line on whichever side the interval can not take the supplementary sign: 4, 5. In the second row of numbers this same sign will indicate the progression of a fifth to a sixth or a sixth to a fifth. Applied to negative intervals the sign is placed on the opposite side: −5 and −4 will refer to [musical example] and [musical example] respectively (§ 88).

The same sign will also apply to the compounds of the fifth and sixth, both positive: 11, 12 and negative: −12, −11. Examples:

a)   b)   c)   d)
$Jv = -11$ $Jv = 1$ $Jv = -7$ $Jv = -12$
       $m = 5$ $m = 5$ $m = 4$ $m = 4$
       $n = -6$ $n = 6$ $n = -3$ $n = -8$
       ——————   ——————   ——————   ——————
         5   5   4   4

The sixth at $Jv = -11$ (a) and the fifth at $Jv = -7$ (c) are the only variable consonances at these indices.

§ 137. With the exception of the cases mentioned, the fifths and sixths and their compounds, all other consonances that acquire the sign − from a derivative dissonance take also the supplementary sign ×.

$Jv=4$ $Jv=-8$ $Jv=-10$ $Jv=-4$

$m=2$	$m=7$	$m=2$	$m=7$
$n=\overline{6}$	$n=-\overline{1}$	$n=-\overline{8}$	$n=\overline{3}$
$\overline{2}^{\times}$	$\overline{7}^{\times}$	$\overline{2}^{\times}$	$\overline{7}^{\times}$

(4) Variable Dissonances

§ 138. The last cases of coinciding intervals in the original and derivative are the variable dissonances, i.e. dissonances that give consonances in the derivative (§ 96). The number of variable dissonances changes according to the JJv concerned. All are variable in the JJv of the sixth column, while in $Jv=-9$ and $Jv=-11$ every dissonance is fixed.

§ 139. At indices with the inverse shift the variable dissonances are equal in number to the variable consonances (this follows from § 32, [3]).

§ 140. When a derivative consonance is perfect it will be indicated by a small p. placed above the original dissonance. For example, at $Jv=3$ the second will be indicated: $\overset{(p)}{\underset{}{1}}$; at $Jv=-10$ the seventh: $\overset{p}{\underset{(-)}{6}}$ These and other intervals give a perfect fifth as a derivative consonance.

§ 141. Since no interval may be released from the limitations imposed on it by the rules of simple counterpoint (§ 94), a variable dissonance must retain its own signs. But in some cases the supplementary sign × must be added to the sign − . In fact, with the exception of the fifth and the sixth, the two consonances in the successive series having a dissonance on one side only, all the other consonances in the series have a dissonance on both sides (§ 14, [2]). Therefore, when a variable dissonance coincides with a consonance that has a dissonance on each side, the progression in the derivative, corresponding to the note of resolution, will be to one of these two dissonances (i.e. the original dissonance resolves to a variable consonance), and the sign × is indispensible.

(a)	(b)	(c)	(d)	(e)
$Jv=1$	$Jv=-1$	$Jv=-10$	$Jv=-13$	$Jv=6$
$m=\overset{(-)}{\underline{1}}$	$m=\overline{3}$	$m=\overline{3}$	$m=\overset{}{\underset{(-)}{6}}$	$m=\overline{8}$
$n=2$	$n=2$	$\overset{p}{n=-7}$	$\overset{p}{n=-7}$	$\overset{p}{n=14}$
$\overset{(-)}{\underset{-\times}{1}}$	$\overset{-\times}{\underset{-\times}{3}}$	$\overset{p\times}{\underset{-\times}{3}}$	$\overset{p\times}{\underset{(-)}{6}}$	$\overset{p\times}{\underset{-\times}{8}}$

When a variable consonance progresses to a fixed consonance at the moment of resolution the sign × is not needed. This is possible only in those cases where a dissonance and its resolution come on a fifth or a sixth, or on their compounds (4 and 5, −5 and −4, 11 and 12, −12 and −11; cf. § 156).

$Jv = 3$	$Jv = 2$	$Jv = -10$	$Jv = 4$
$m = \overset{(-)}{\underset{-}{1}}$	$m = \overline{\underset{-}{3}}$	$m = \overset{-}{\underset{(-)}{6}}$	$m = \overline{8}$
$n = \overset{p}{\underset{\cdots}{4}}$	$n = \overline{5}$	$n = \overset{p}{-4}$	$n = \overset{\cdots}{12}$
$\overset{p}{\underset{-}{\overset{(-)}{1}}}$	$\underset{-\times}{\overset{-}{3}}$	$\overset{p}{\underset{(-)}{6}}$	$\underset{-\times}{\overset{-}{8}}$

Obs.—It follows from the foregoing that all dissonances taking the sign -× are variable.

§ 142. Among the variable dissonances are some giving an imperfect consonance in the derivative, others perfect consonances (the latter indicated by p., § 140). A derivative imperfect consonance can not impose any new limitations on the conditions under which the original dissonance is used. On the contrary, a derivative perfect consonance may add its own limitations to these conditions (§ 73). Hence the following rule applies to dissonances taking the letter p.:

§ 143. Similar motion to a variable dissonance taking the letter p. is not allowed, for in the derivative it results in hidden consecutives or forbidden parallels. E.g. similar motion to a seventh:

Original

is inadmissable in two-voice counterpoint at any index where 6 takes the letter p., namely: at JJv of the first column and at $JJv = 5, -2, 10$

Derivatives

The parallel progression of dissonances taking the letter p. is unconditionally bad—

at $JJv = 1, -2$ and -10:

Derivatives
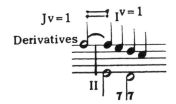

Obs.—The foregoing progression of parallel dissonances are found in simple counterpoint of the strict style, though seldom. Exs. 91 and 92 show the use of two fourths and two sevenths in parallel motion at the same time. In Ex. 92 notice the leap in the alto to a note consonant with the other voices.

Parallel seconds are occasionally tolerable, but their use is not to be recommended:

§ 144. It follows that the rule given in § 74, (2), applying to perfect consonances, is irrelevant as applied to variable dissonances, since dissonances in contary motion are not allowed, either within the octave limits or beyond.

§ 145. The restriction of perfect consonances concerning the proximity of intervals of the same size (§ 75) applies also to dissonances taking the letter *p*. However, this refers not so much to the case of such a variable dissonance used as a tie on an accented beat as it does to a dissonance taking the letter *p*. coming on an unaccented part of the measure as resolution of a variable consonance.

Concerning the first situation mentioned, in syncopated counterpoint perfect consonances of the same size may be found on the accented beats of successive measures, therefore the following cases are entirely admissable:

Here the seventh in the original, giving a perfect fifth in the derivative, can be freely used as a suspension on the accented beats of adjacent measures. But if the seventh appears on the weak parts of the measure a faulty succession of fifths will result in the derivative. For example, at *Jv* = 2:

These cases are closely related to the preparation of variable intervals, to be dealt with next.

The Preparation of Variable Intervals

§ 146. The object of the rules for the preparation of intervals in complex counterpoint is to prevent the appearance in the derivative of progressions that are forbidden by the rules of simple counterpoint (§ 70). These rules refer to the dissonances that resolve to perfect consonances ($\underline{3}$ and $\overline{8}$) and consist of statements to the effect that these dissonances cannot be prepared by perfect consonances equal in value to those to which they resolve (§ 86). In vertical-shifting counterpoint corresponding rules must be established that refer to all tied intervals. One rule for the preparation of fixed consonances was given in § 132. There are two more, referring to the preparation of variable intervals; they are:

Rule 1.—A variable consonance, of which the free note is approached by stepwise movement from above, can not be prepared by a dissonance taking the letter *p*. (i.e. *n*= perfect consonance). This rule eliminates such situations as these:

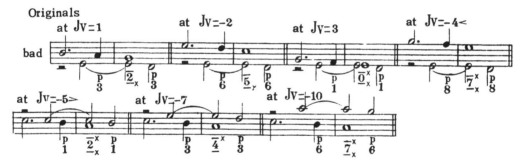

All these originals give the same bad derivative:

The following combinations give a bad preparation of the ninth in the derivative:

These originals also give the same faulty derivative:

Rule 2.—At ^2JJv a variable dissonance can not be prepared by a fixed consonance equal in size to that to which it resolves:

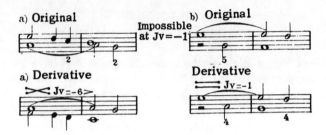

This rule does not apply to those cases where the preparation of a consonance gives a fourth; such fourths may become consonances by the addition of a supplementary voice below. In this way original (a) at $Jv = 1$ and original (b) at $Jv = 2$ are entirely admissable, as they give the following correct derivatives:

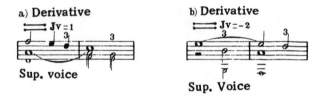

Obs.—These rules for the preparation of variable intervals must be strictly observed in all cases where, in the derivative, an octave is prepared by a ninth ($\bar{8}$). Likewise, where these rules prevent the appearance of $\underline{3}$, prepared by a fifth, a measure of their severity arises from the fact that in general such preparations are not allowed in simple counterpoint. It cannot be denied that the masters of the strict style indulged in progressions that later theorists were inclined to regard unfavorably (Ex. 64). In the future, when discussing complex forms of resolution, the rules for the preparation of variable intervals will to a certain extent lose their force (§ 162).

§ 147. As has been seen, cases breaking the rules of preparation occur only among those progressions where the free note to a tied interval is approached by stepwise movement from above. Therefore, no irregularities are encountered—

(1) When the tied interval is prepared by a fixed consonance that approaches the free note by a leap, as is seen in the following preparations of variable intervals:

Exchanging original and derivative (§ 68) illustrates the preparation of variable dissonances.

(2) When the tied interval is prepared by ascending stepwise movement to its free note:

Exchanging original and derivative again illustrates the preparation of variable dissonances.

Simplifications in Compiling Tables of Indices

§ 148. Before citing examples showing the application of variable intervals, some tables will be given that will result in important simplifications.

(a) Tables of Indices Giving the Inverse Shift

§ 149. A table for any index having the inverse shift consists of a series of original intervals beginning with 0 and ending with an interval equal to Jv. Such a series is divisible into two equal parts. If the index is an even number the division falls on the interval equal to one-half of the index value; this is called the central interval. For example:

$$Jv = -8: \quad 0 \quad 1 \quad 2 \quad 3 \quad 4 \quad 5 \quad 6 \quad 7 \quad 8 \quad \text{(central interval 4)}$$

$$Jv = -10: \quad 0 \quad 1 \quad 2 \quad 3 \quad 4 \quad 5 \quad 6 \quad 7 \quad 8 \quad 9 \quad 10 \quad \text{(central interval 5)}$$

If the index is an odd number the division occurs in the space between those two intervals of which the sum is equal to the absolute value of the index; e.g. for $Jv = -7$ these two intervals are 3 and 4:

$$Jv = -7: \quad 0 \quad 1 \quad 2 \quad 3 \quad : \quad 4 \quad 5 \quad 6 \quad 7$$

for $Jv = -9$ they are 4 and 5:

$$Jv = -9: \quad 0 \quad 1 \quad 2 \quad 3 \quad 4 \quad : \quad 5 \quad 6 \quad 7 \quad 8 \quad 9 \quad \text{etc.}$$

§ 150. According to the foregoing, a central interval is an original interval equal to one-half of an even-number index for the inverse shift. Since $m + Jv = n$ (§ 31) the central interval gives in the derivative a negative interval of the same value. For example, at $Jv = -8$, from the central interval 4 is obtained $n = -4$; at $Jv = -10$ the central interval 5 gives $n = -5$ etc. Therefore, whether the central interval is a consonance or a dissonance, it will appear in every case as a fixed interval.

If this interval is a consonance then it is a fixed consonance, free from the tie-sign. If a dissonance, the upper and lower signs are always the same, i.e. it appears either as $\overline{m}$ or $\overline{m}$. This results from the fact that the derivative interval will be a negative interval of the same value and with the same signs but in reversed positions, the upper sign below and the lower sign above (§ 89). Consequently if one sign of the central interval in the original series, according to the rules of simple counterpoint, is (−), its derivative interval has the same sign on the opposite side, the final result being that the original interval will take this sign on both sides: $\overline{m}$. If the central interval takes the sign − above and below the derivative will be the same, therefore the original retains its own signs: $\overline{m}$.*

§ 151. The sum of the two intervals lying next to the central interval and on either side of it is always equal to the absolute value of the index, since the division falls either on the central interval or in the space between the two nearest the center. This same quantity is also equal to the sum of every two intervals that lie at the same distance on either side of the center, i.e. the sum of the second interval to the right and the second to the left, of the third interval to the right and the third to the left, etc. In the following two series of original intervals (one for an even-numbered index, one for an odd) every two intervals of which the sum is equal to the absolute value of the index are connected by bracketed lines.

$$Jv = -8: \quad 0 \quad 1 \quad 2 \quad 3 \quad 4 \quad 5 \quad 6 \quad 7 \quad 8$$

$$Jv = -7: \quad 0 \quad 1 \quad 2 \quad 3 \mathbin{|} 4 \quad 5 \quad 6 \quad 7$$

Either of the two intervals connected by brackets (here referred to as a and b) may represent the derivative if taken with the minus sign: if $m = a$, then $n = -b$; if $m = b$, then $n = -a$ (§ 32, 3). And since a negative interval has the same tie-signs as the positive interval of the same value but with the positions of the signs reversed (§ 89), the following relation holds between the tie-signs of the original intervals:

At a negative index giving the inverse shift, any two original intervals of which the sum is equal to the absolute value of the index have the same tie-signs but in reversed positions: the upper sign of one interval is the same as the lower sign of the other, and vice versa. For example:

---

*The foregoing applies only to the central interval of an even-numbered index. Evidently the author did not consider it necessary to explain what happens in the case of an odd-numbered index for the inverse shift, but this works out in such an interesting way that the following is submitted as supplementary to the text:

A series of intervals for an odd-numbered index with the inverse shift gives two central intervals, of which the sum is equal to the absolute value of the index (§ 149). (1) If one central interval is a consonance and the other a dissonance they will always be a variable consonance and a variable dissonance. If the signs for one are different, the other will have the same two signs but in reversed positions. If the signs for one are the same the other will have the same two signs, though this occurs in only one index: $Jv = -5 <$. (2) If both central intervals are consonances both will be fixed; they will have the same signs but in reversed positions. This also occurs but once, in $Jv = -9 >$. —Tr.

$Jv = -11*$

(1)
Original: 5 6
(—)

according to the rules
of simple counterpoint

(—)
Derivative: −6 −5

Original at $Jv = -11$: (—) X
5 6
−X (—)

(2)
Original: (—) 10
1

according to the rules
of simple counterpoint

Derivative: −10 −1
(—)

Original at $Jv = -11$: (—)
1 10 etc.
(—)

No reference is here made to the sign p., but it must be placed above every dissonance that is bracketed with a perfect consonance (§ 140).

§ 152. This relationship of signs makes possible the compilation of tables for indices with the inverse shift. The first row in such a table consists of the left half of the original series (§ 151), including the central interval if the index is an even number. Under this, as second row, is placed the right half of the original series, but in reversed order and with all signs reversed. Below the horizontal line is the third row, beginning with 0 and ending with a number equal to the absolute value of the index. The derivation of the signs for the left half of this row has already been explained; those for the right half are derived from the left half, using the reciprocal relationship of signs previously referred to. The following tables for $Jv = -8$ and $Jv = -12$ illustrate the process:

1) $^2Jv = -8 >$.

p	(—)		—	p
0	1	2	3	4

—	p	(—)		p
−8	−7	−6	−5	−4

−X	p	(—)	−X			−X	−X	p X
0	1	2	3	4	5	6	7	8
−X	−X	−X			−X	(—)	(—)	−X

---

*It is of interest to note the fact that the use of variable intervals was unknown to Zarlino. In Chapter 56 of the "Istitutioni armoniche," speaking of double counterpoint at the twelfth, he gives a rule not to write sixths and sevenths: "Osservaremo di non porre la Desta nel principale; imperoche nella Replica non puo far consonanza." And further on: "Non porremo anco la Sincopa, nella quale se contenghi la Settima: perioche Replica non torne bene." In Zarlino's terminology "il Principale" refers to the original combination, "la Replica" to the derivative.

In this table the signs of each interval in the third row, counting from the center to the right, are the reverse of those at equal distances counting from the center to the left. The sum of any two intervals bracketed equals 8. Intervals 1 and 8 take the sign *p.*, they are bracketed with the perfect consonances 0 and 7.

For these examples *JJv* were selected that have the largest number of variable intervals. But in the exercises to follow, start with those that have the fewest, such as $Jv = -11$, $Jv = -7$ etc.

(b) Tables of Indices Giving the Direct Shift

§ 153. In compiling tables for indices with the direct shift it is impracticable to present any table complete—a portion from the beginning is enough. In these tables a series of original intervals begins at 0 for a positive *Jv*, and for a negative *Jv* at an interval equal to the index value. Either series may be continued as far as desired.

§ 154. Among the tables of indices with the direct shift, any two that have the same value, one positive and one negative, are closely related, and a study of their properties results in simplifying the conditions of a negative *Jv* as compared to those of a positive *Jv*, and vice versa. This will be illustrated by two tables, one for a positive *Jv*, the other for a negative *Jv* of the same value.

Jv= 1:

p 0	(→) 1	2	3	p 4	5	6	p 7	8 etc.
(→) 1	2	3	p 4	5	6	p 7	8	9

(→) 0 —x	(→) 1 —x	—x 2 —x	p 3 x —	4	5 (→)	p 6 x (→)	—x 7 —x	—x 8 x

Jv= —1:

(→) 1	2	3	p 4	5	6 (→)	p 7	8	9 etc.
p 0	(→) 1	2	3	p 4	5	6 (→)	p 7	8

p (→) 1 —x	(→) 2 —x	—x 3 —x	—x 4 —	5	6 (→)	—x 7 (→)	p 8 x —x	—x 9 —x

Comparing these tables, it will be seen that the two upper rows in one table are reproduced in the other, and that as a result of this coincidence the tie-signs of the intervals in the third row are the same for both tables; therefore, from the third row of one table can be formed the third row of the other, if, reversing all tie-signs, the figures for the derivative intervals (second row) of one table are used for the third row of the other. A combination written at one of these indices will serve equally well for the other if the original and derivative are exchanged (§ 68, 1).

Ex. 96

Obs.—In working out exercises, use can be made of the tables accompanying the examples in two-voice vertical-shifting counterpoint. The original intervals are arranged in three rows. The fixed consonances are in the middle row, with the dissonances and variable consonances in the top and bottom rows, the upper row containing only intervals with the signs — and × above, the lower row with the same signs below. An interval having either sign above and below appears twice, both in the upper and lower rows. Intervals having (–) as both upper and lower signs are omitted altogether. Presented in this way the tables are of special importance in the first exercises. They show at a glance what intervals are available, and the proper use, in each voice, of ties.

Distribution of Variable Dissonances

§ 155. Some variable dissonances give perfect consonances in the derivative, others imperfect. Sometimes met with in the same Jv, their distribution may have appeared quite fortuitous, but a strict order underlies the apparent disorder. The distribution of variable dissonances from any Jv can be expressed in one of two tables, called System A and System B. Those for $Jv = -1$ and $Jv = 1$ will serve as illustrations. The variable dissonances are listed in numerical order.

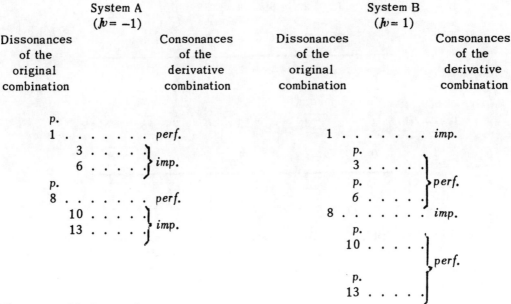

The same table in notations:

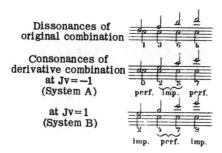

One system or the other includes the following general features: Intervals 1 and 8 (i.e. the second and its compound) give the consonances of one group; in System A perfect, in System B imperfect. Intervals 3, 6 and their compounds 10 and 13 also give in each system consonances of one group, but the opposite group of that to which 1 and 8 belong. In System A three intervals (3, 6, 10, 13) give imperfect consonances in the derivative, in System B, perfect consonances.

In the preceding table the indices took the direct shift. The next shows those for the inverse shift:

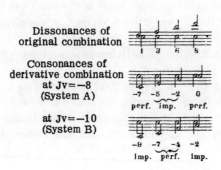

Those indices have been intentionally chosen in which all the dissonances are variable. But no matter how many variable dissonances a given index may have—if they are not less than two—they may always be arranged according to one of the two systems.

§ 156. It is not difficult to explain the reason for arranging the variable dissonances in this way. It has already been seen (§ 17) that the second and its compounds (1, 8, 15 etc.) are separated from one another by a ^{1}int. (referring here to the positive intervals of the original combination). Whichever of these dissonances appear as variable will infallibly give, in the derivative, consonances that belong all to one group, since only such consonances are separated from each other by a ^{1}int. (§15,[1]). It is exactly the same with the other dissonances: 3, 6 and their compounds, that are separated from each other by a ^{1}int. (§17,[2]). Therefore, since they are variable, they must likewise give derivative consonances also of one group.

Moreover, the dissonances of the series 1, 8, 15, etc. are separated from the dissonances of the other series (3,6, etc.) by a ^{2}int. (§17,[3]), consequently two dissonances from different groups must give consonances from different groups in the derivative, since only such consonances are separated from each other by a ^{2}int. (§15,[2]). In this way the distribution of variable intervals according to one of the two systems is shown to be the necessary result of the distance between the intervals in the successive series.

Because of this systematic order in the arrangement of variable dissonances it is sufficient to know the relation of one of them to an interval of the derivative—whether it gives a perfect or an imperfect consonance—in order to determine the group to which the derivative consonances of all other variable dissonances of a given index belong; in other words, to determine which of the two systems of distribution apply in a given case.

§ 157. The variable dissonances in $Jv = -1$ and $Jv = 1$ are those of two indices of equal value but of opposite signs; this is explained by the fact that in the successive series of intervals each dissonance has a consonance on each side, one of which is perfect, the other imperfect (§14,[3]). At $Jv = 1$ each dissonance gives in the derivative the next consonance to the right, and at $Jv = -1$ the next consonance to the left. Therefore the dissonance which at $Jv = -1$ gives a perfect consonance gives an imperfect consonance at $Jv = 1$ and vice versa; i.e. Systems A and B are interchanged.

If attention is directed to the fact that of the two consonances found at equal distances to the right and left of a dissonance, one is always perfect and the other imperfect (§ 14,[4]) it will be seen that everything referring to the distribution of variable dissonances at $Jv = -1$ and $Jv = 1$ applies also to all other indices of the same value but with different signs. Positive and negative indices of the same values always have their variable dissonances arranged according to either System A or System B.

§ 158. The distribution of variable dissonances according to the different indices is shown in the following table:

Order of JJv with Variable Dissonances

System A	System B
$Jv = -1$	$Jv = +1$
$JJv = \begin{cases} +2 \\ +3 \end{cases}$	$JJv = \begin{cases} --2 \\ -3 \end{cases}$
$JJv = \begin{cases} --4 \\ --5 \end{cases}$	$JJv = \begin{cases} +4 \\ +5 \end{cases}$
$JJv = \begin{cases} +6 \\ ....* \end{cases}$	$JJv = \begin{cases} ---6 \\ ---7 \end{cases}$

*Jv = 7 has no variable dissonances.

The tables could be continued, alternatihg positive and negative indices in the same way. $Jv = 9$, like $Jv = 7$, has no variable dissonances.

If from the foregoing lists the indices are selected that correspond to dissonant intervals the following table is obtained:

Order of JJv with Variable Dissonances
Corresponding to Dissonant Intervals

System A	System B
$Jv = -\ 1$	$Jv = +\ 1$
$JJv = \begin{cases} +\ 3 \\ +\ 6 \end{cases}$	$JJv = \begin{cases} -\ 3 \\ -\ 6 \end{cases}$
$Jv = -\ 8$	$Jv = +\ 8\,{}^{*)}$
$JJv = \begin{cases} +\ 10\,{}^{*)} \\ +\ 13\,{}^{*)} \end{cases}$	$JJv = \begin{cases} -\ 10 \\ -\ 13 \end{cases}$

Comparing this table with that in § 155 it will be seen that the arrangement of positive and negative indices is in exact agreement with the order of variable dissonances giving $n =$ perfect consonance and those of which $n =$ imperfect.

§ 159. With the investigation of variable intervals is ended the most essential part of the study of two-voice vertical-shifting counterpoint.

---

*Unusable.

CHAPTER VII

SUPPLEMENTARY RESOURCES

Ornamental Resolutions of Suspensions

§ 160. Ornamental resolutions of suspensions were mentioned in § 84 and in § 85, (2). In simple counterpoint they are applied only to suspensions; in vertical-shifting counterpoint both to suspensions and to tied variable consonances. At the sign (−) in the corresponding voice it is not possible to apply the ornamental forms of resolution. First to be considered are the forms involving the free note to a tied interval; these are used the most, especially in multi-voice counterpoint.

(A) The Free Note Progressing to a Consonance
at the Moment of Resolution

§ 161. Applied to vertical-shifting counterpoint, the rule given in § 85, (2) may be restated thus: The free note to a tied interval may, at the moment the latter is resolved, progress to another note which forms a fixed consonance with the note of resolution. For indices of the second group is added: At a ^2Jv the voice taking the free note can only continue upward one step. This prevents similar motion, forbidden at a ^2jv in two-voice counterpoint. Since the resolution of dissonant notes is the result of a voice moving one degree downward, the other voice, in order to avoid hidden consecutives, must progress in contrary motion.

At the sign −× the note of resolution can also take a fixed consonance. The note of resolution, to which the supplementary sign × refers, is in this case part of a consonant interval, and need not continue by stepwise movement in the same direction, as it would have to do were it a dissonance (§ 92).

In the following illustrations are shown these forms of resolution applied to the original dissonance. Above each is a list of the JJv at which the given dissonance takes the sign − without the supplementary sign. Below each illustration are listed the JJv at which the same dissonance takes the sign −×. The dissonances with this sign are all variable (cf. § 141).

Examples

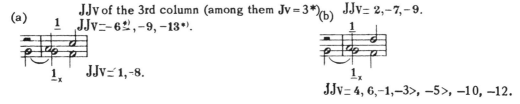

(a) JJv of the 3rd column (among them Jv = 3*) (b) JJv= 2, −7, −9.
    1   JJv= −6$^{\underline{\cdot})}$, −9, −13*).   1
            JJv= 1, −8.
                                              JJv= 4, 6, −1, −3>, −5>, −10, −12.

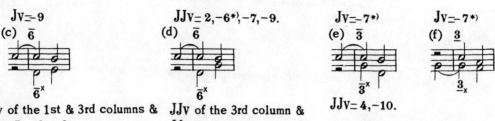

JJv of the 1st & 3rd columns &
JJv = 5, −2, −8.

JJv of the 3rd column &
JJv = 5, −2, −13.

JJv = 4, −10.

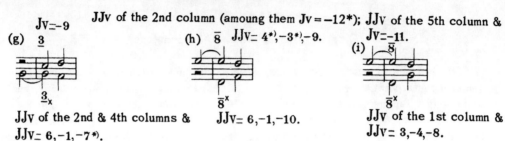

JJv of the 2nd & 4th columns &
JJv = 6, −1, −7*).

JJv = 6, −1, −10.

JJv of the 1st column &
JJv = 3, −4, −8.

It is not necessary to give illustrations for variable consonances, as the foregoing using dissonances will serve the same purpose. It is well to select, from the derivative combinations, an index that includes the required consonance, then to use this combination as the original and its original as derivative (§ 68). As to the application of these forms of resolution to multi-voice counterpoint, cf. § 213.

§ 162. In *Obs*. 2, § 86, it was stated that this form of resolution allows the preparation of a fourth by a fifth: It constitutes an exception to the rule of preparation previously given in § 86. Correspondingly, this ·exception is also allowed in vertical-shifting counterpoint. For example, this preparation of the fixed dissonance

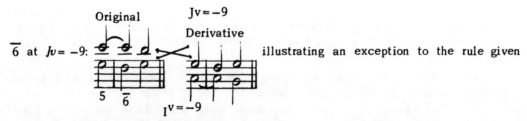

$\overline{6}$ at $Jv = -9$:   illustrating an exception to the rule given

in § 132, would be impossible if the free note did not return to the previous note at the moment of resolution. Exactly the same thing happens under the conditions by which the variable consonance $\underline{2}_x$ is prepared:

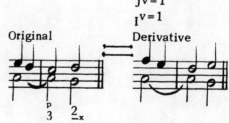

This is an exception to Rule 1, § 146.

---

*At this Jv the dissonance is variable.

(b) The Insertion of a Consonant Note Between a
Dissonance and its Resolution

§ 163. Another complex form of resolution, one of far greater importance in counterpoint than the preceding, consists in this: Between a suspension and its resolution is inserted, where the voice leaps downward, a note consonant with the free note (§ 84). In extending the application of this form to all tied intervals in vertical-shifting counterpoint, one requirement is necessary, referring to the voice in which the signs − or × occur: at the leap to the intermediate note, the latter must be a fixed consonance.

(1) Dissonances taking the sign −:

(a) Fixed
JJv = −9, −7, (2)   Jv = −9   (b) Variable

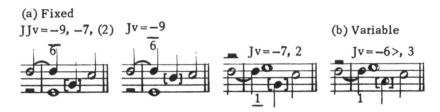

(2) Dissonances taking the sign −×. In a voice taking the sign −× this form of resolution can be applied in one of three ways:

(a) The note of resolution, to which the sign × refers, can change to a passing-note in the derivative. This is possible only when the leap from the tied note is a descending third:

JJv of the 1st & 3rd column & JJv = −8, −2, 5.

(b) If the note of resolution, to which the sign × refers, is a fixed consonance, both forms of complex resolution may be combined:

JJv of the 3rd column

(c) The note of resolution, to which the sign × refers, can function as the free note to a tied interval (cf. § 134):

JJv of the 3rd column & Jv = −8.

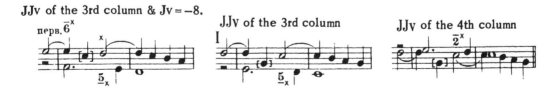

Illustrations showing the application of these forms of resolution to variable consonances may be obtained by the method described in § 161.

The Cambiata Figure

§ 164. The descending stepwise movement of a voice may be interrupted at a dissonance on the weak part of a beat, from which a leap of a third downward is made, to a consonance:

Such a dissonance, often found in the strict style, is called the nota cambiata. Following the leap the voice usually progresses one degree upward to a note of the same value, as shown in the preceding illustrations. However, cases are found where the notes concerned are of greater value than the nota cambiata, and even where, after the leap, there is no return at all to the absent degree.

Use of the nota cambiata in vertical-shifting counterpoint is usually on condition that the note to which the leap is made must be a fixed consonance:

A variable consonance may be used as a nota cambiata, in which case the preceding interval must be either a fixed consonance—

or a variable dissonance. The foregoing illustration shows the note to which the supplementary sign × refers. Examples of such cases can be formed from the illustrations in § 163, exchanging original and derivative.

The interval preceding the nota cambiata may be a prepared variable consonance, the prepared voice moving one degree downward to the nota cambiata:

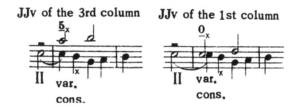

In a variable dissonance the note of resolution, indicated by the sign ×, may be treated as a nota cambiata, making a leap of a third downward to a fixed consonance. Examples may be formed from the foregoing illustrations, exchanging original and derivative.

Obs.—The nota cambiata is often found in the works of Russian composers:

§ 165. These complex forms of resolution and the nota cambiata will add freedom and variety to voice-leading; this applies especially to those indices that have few fixed consonances, and therefore present the greatest difficulties in the use of intervals.

§ 166. In the examples applying to Division A (Appendix A) are found all the complex forms of resolution—the nota cambiata etc. In writing exercises, study the examples according to whatever index is being worked at the time.

The Use of Notes Taking the Sign ×

§ 167. In the preceding chapters the various applications of the supplementary sign × were explained, but this information was necessarily scattered among different sections of the text. It is herewith summarized.

(1) The supplementary sign × is placed after the tie-sign, and means that the note following the one tied is a second lower, the voice descending one degree (in the original or in the derivative) to a note dissonant to the free note.

(2) It may indicate a dissonant passing or auxiliary note (§ 93).

(3) The note taking the sign may in turn act as the free note to a new tied interval (§ 134).

(4) The note indicated by the sign may take a fixed consonance, if no rule of voice-leading is thereby infringed (§ 161).

(5) The sign may indicate the nota cambiata (§ 164).

Negative Intervals in the Original Combination

§ 168. In stating the rules of vertical-shifting counterpoint it was assumed that the original combination formed a series of positive intervals, i.e. no crossing of voices was to be found in it. In this way needless complications were avoided that would have been inevitable had it been necessary to study combinations in which positive and negative intervals were intermingled. Moreover, for combinations intended for vertical shifting, the absence of voice-crossing is, generally speaking, advantageous. This condition enables the parts to be clearly distinguished by their melodic contours and they are easily recognized when shifts are made, especially in double counterpoint. Nevertheless these considerations are not sufficient to justify the complete removal of crossings from the original combination, as is insisted upon by some theorists. No composer of either the strict or the free style has felt obliged to observe such a condition (cf. *The Well-Tempered Clavichord*, Vol. I, Fugue 11, and Vol. II, Fugues 17 and 23, where the subject and counter-subject cross). Even in some cases, for instance in more or less extended imitation at close intervals such as the unison or second, crossing certainly contributes to freedom in voice-leading, and can be recommended for this purpose.

§ 169. In the tables of indices only positive intervals of the original combination were given, as there was no necessity for including negative intervals. To know the conditions in which a negative interval is used at a given index, regard the negative interval as positive, change the index to the opposite sign, and then use the interval according to the conditions of the index obtained. If the latter is positive and equal to a compound interval, substitute the index equal to the corresponding simple interval (§ 47).

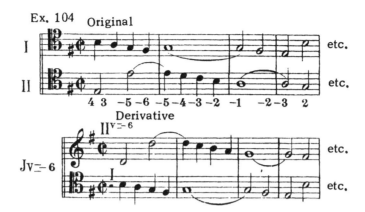

In this example at $Jv= -6$ all the intervals except the first two and the last are negative. Taking the positive index ($Jv= 6$) instead of the negative, and regarding the negative intervals as positive, the conditions of their use will be found in the table for this index.

In this example at $Jv= -11$:

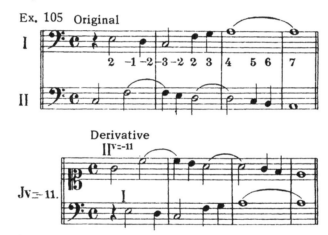

treat the negative intervals as positive and write according to $Jv= 4$, the substitute for $Jv= -11$ (§ 47).

§ 170. It follows that negative intervals in double counterpoint at the octave ($Jv = -7$) are written according to the rules of simple counterpoint. In fact, $Jv= 7$ must be substituted for $Jv= -7$, for at this index the derivative is nothing but the separation at the octave of the voices of the original (§ 47).

CHAPTER VIII

EXERCISES IN TWO-VOICE VERTICAL-SHIFTING COUNTERPOINT

§ 171. The study of convertible counterpoint should run parallel to that of simple counterpoint. In entering upon a course of exercises in two-voice simple counterpoint it is well to apply, from the start, the method of figuring intervals used in this book; this can be easily learned in two or three lessons. Passing to syncopated counterpoint (fourth species) learn what is said about suspensions in Chapter IV, beginning with § 81, and memorize the table in § 90.

§ 172. In two-voice problems on a cantus firmus written in simple counterpoint without any calculation for shifts, places are often found where a shift in double counterpoint at the octave is possible. It will be useful to pay special attention to such cases, and study the conditions under which such a shift may or may not be made.

§ 173. The first exercises in vertical-shifting counterpoint may begin after three-voice simple counterpoint has been studied, and before four-voice, if at this time the student has mastered the contents of the first four chapters of this book.

A good preparation for the study of vertical-shifting counterpoint is to work out exercises in two-voice mixed counterpoint,* under conditions in which suspensions and similar motion are absent. The dissonances in such problems appear only as passing or as auxiliary notes. It is very useful to be able to write counterpoint using only oblique and contrary motion, its importance consisting in the fact that the indices of the second group (^2JJv) do not admit of similar motion. Such exercises are unusual, but it is a study that should be mastered for its own sake in simple counterpoint, while for convertible counterpoint it is absolutely essential.

After this, when the student gets acquainted with the fixed consonances (Chapter V up to § 108 inclusive) the problems in double counterpoint at the tenth ($Jv=-9$) should be taken up, avoiding tied dissonances (Exs. 72, 73, 74). Similar motion still absent, these forms impose new restrictions (the limiting interval 9>) and the conditions given in §§ 104–5). Breaking with the long-established tradition—that the study of complex counterpoint should begin with double counterpoint at the octave—has some justification. From the very first exercises the student is trained to the strict and unaccustomed requirement that similar motion must be absent, and passing on to ^1JJv, where this motion is allowed, his work is facilitated and his technical resources increased. The overcoming of the next difficulty—not to use a variable consonance except as a passing note—is comparatively easy.

§ 174. After a sufficient number of exercises at $Jv=-9$ (without suspensions) next pass to the indices of the first group, especially to double counterpoint at the twelfth ($Jv=-11$) and continue the exercises in the order given in § 110. The indices with the direct shift may be passed over briefly, limited to some problems on each two indices of the same value but with opposite signs (§ 110). The division of indices of the first group begins with double counterpoint at the octave. To take double counterpoint at the twelfth before that at the octave is not customary, but in many ways this procedure is the more expedient. Aside from the fact that counterpoint at the twelfth was of primary

---

*The author refers here to two-voice florid counterpoint (fifth species) without a cantus firmus. —Tr.

112

importance in the era of the strict style (Zarlino, for example, in the chapter on double counterpoint in his *Institutioni armoniche,* passes on to double counterpoint at the tenth and does not mention counterpoint at the octave at all), to begin exercises at indices of the first group, with counterpoint at the twelfth, is better, because with the limiting interval 11> it offers greater freedom of voice-leading than does double counterpoint at the octave.

§ 175. In working out exercises first write the original combination. Time can be saved by using three staves, so that one voice remains in place on one staff, the other voices of the original and derivative combinations appearing on the other two. Next shift whichever voice will cause the fewest difficulties as regards augmented fourths and diminished fifths. To do this, previously read through mentally both voices concerned in the shift. Every place in the derivative where a rule of simple counterpoint is broken means that in the same place a rule of complex counterpoint is also broken. It is then necessary to be certain as to what the infringement is, and to make the necessary correction. Verification is simple, and the method is easily applied by the student who, in his approach to the study of complex counterpoint, must make free use of the resources of simple counterpoint.

§ 176. Passing to the indices of the second group (except $Jv = -9$, which has already been given), work out exercises in the order of indices given in § 111, Exs. 75 to 78. Exercises in shifts at several indices (§§ 113–18) and those in duplication of imperfect consonances (§§ 119–22) may best be deferred until later, taking up the former just before Chapter IX, the latter before Chapter X.

§ 177. Concurrent with the foregoing, study the uses of the fixed dissonances (§ 123 to the end of the Chapter) and the rules of preparation (§ 131). Returning to the first exercises at $Jv = -9$ (§ 128), work now with all the intervals of this index (in which all are fixed). After this, continue with exercises showing the application of the fixed dissonances to the other indices of this group, guided by the text as far as § 130 and Ex. 87, inclusive.

§ 178. Without interruption, take up Chapter VI on variable intervals and work exercises using all intervals without exception. In studying the examples in this chapter (review §§ 152 and 154), take those indices in which are found the greatest number of variable intervals and which therefore involve the most difficulties. But in writing the exercises begin with those indices that have the fewest variable intervals ($Jv = -11$, $Jv = -7$ etc.) and work up gradually to those that have the most.

§ 179. As regards the difficulty of these indices, especially of those having only one fixed consonance, i.e. $Jv = 1, -1, -6, -8, -10$, exercises using them should alternate with those at the easier indices. The abundance of conditions that surround the the· indices mentioned involves the disadvantage that the student is often uncritical of the melodic quality of his work, provided that it is done according to rule. The persistent use of some of these indices is bad in the long run, as they tend to militate against the esthetic side of the work. By alternating the difficult and easy indices the former will be mastered by imperceptible degrees, and instead of reacting unfavorably on the technique of the student will contribute to its development. Exercises at these indices may be played on the piano, though not without some inconvenience, due to the unusual fingering. Used in moderation they will assist in developing a virtuoso technic, but their excessive use will fatigue and injure the hand.

§ 180. In short, in a course of study in two-voice vertical-shifting counterpoint some indices may be omitted altogether or limited to only a small number of exercises. The student who is familiar with the applications to be found in the tables of signs will experience no difficulty in writing combinations also at those indices previously omitted. In class, teaching time can be saved by working out problems at the board, questioning the students at the same time. This will lighten the home work, especially as regards the more difficult problems, and will not retard the learning of the simpler ones. Exercises in complex counterpoint should run parallel with those in simple, and application should be made to the contrapuntal forms using imitation, such as the invention, figured choral, and fugue. However, this subject requires more detailed explanation than can be given here.

§ 181. In working out exercises at a given index study the example of the same index in Appendix A. In Chapter VII will be found the explanation of all uses of the complex forms of resolution and of the cambiata figure. As one gets familiar with the material it can be applied.

§ 182. In the first exercises the student will find it helpful to write out the tables for himself, as they are needed. For the exercises use can be made of the separate tables given with each example in Appendix A.

§ 183. Problems at easy indices having a comparatively large number of fixed consonances can be written on a cantus firmus. This is of advantage in studying the effect of tied intervals above and below a voice, according to which voice takes the cantus. But the same circumstances would lead to excessive difficulties with indices having few fixed consonances, so in such cases the use of a cantus is inadvisable.

§ 184. It is best to write the problems in two-voice mixed counterpoint, and in some to use imitation, the latter as a preparation for canonic imitation. Strict imitation throughout is not needed in order to illustrate the application of complex counterpoint. Canonic imitation at any index only requires that the original combination shall be given at a certain index.

An excellent study in indices with the inverse shift is to write two-voice infinite canons consisting of two divisions of equal length.* In such canons (except the infinite canon at the unison) the application on vertical-shifting counterpoint is a *conditio sine qua non*, the necessary result of the form itself. Exercises in two-voice canonic imitation are also valuable as a transition to the more difficult canonic forms. But they should not be attempted until considerable skill has been acquired in writing mixed counterpoint at all indices. Otherwise the restraint imposed might exert a harmful influence on voice-leading.

The practice acquired in writing two-voice vertical-shifting counterpoint gives the student the technique necessary for the various forms of multi-voice canons, and opens up abundant material for the application of counterpoint in general.

---

*Cf. "The Technique of Canon," Chapter II. —Tr.

CHAPTER IX

TWO-VOICE ORIGINAL COMBINATIONS GIVING MORE THAN ONE DERIVATIVE; COMPOUND INDICES

§ 185. In order for the original combination to yield two derivatives, each having its own Jv, the conditions of both JJv must be united. An index combining the conditions of two or more JJv referring to one original is called compound; it may be double, triple etc., according to how many indices are united in it (§ 28).

§ 186. In uniting indices into one compound index, the rule must be invariably followed that the fewest limitations are supersded by the most.

Double Indices

§ 187. Before stating the conditions under which the intervals of a compound index are used, it is necessary to define the groups to which they belong, and thereby to determine whether or not similar motion is allowed. In conforming to what was said in § 186 a compound index is a ^2Jv if one of the components belongs to the second group.

§ 188. Next is the question regarding the limiting distance between voices. Here no control is necessary if the combined JJv are both positive (§ 42). In all other cases one must be guided by the following rules:

(1) If of two JJv one is negative, its limiting interval is valid also for the combined (double) Jv.

(2) If both JJv are negative, and both give the direct shift, the limiting interval for approaching voices (§ 37) equals that of the index which has the greatest absolute value (§ 186). For example, in uniting the conditions of $Jv = -2$ and $Jv = -4<$ the limit for approaching voices is $4<$, that is, a fifth. This is indicated: $^2Jv = -2, -4 <$.

(3) If both JJv are negative, and both give the inverse shift, the limiting interval for receding voices equals that of the index which has the lowest absolute value (§ 186). For example, in uniting the conditions of $Jv = -7$ and $Jv = -11$ the limiting interval is $7>$; for $Jv = -9$ and $Jv = -12$ it is $9>$. The former is indicated: $^1Jv = -7>, -11$; the latter $^2Jv = -9>, -12$.

(4) If one of the JJv gives the direct shift and the other the inverse, the former defines the limit for approaching voices, the latter for receding voices. For example, in uniting the conditions of $Jv = -2$ and $Jv = -11$ the limiting intervals $2<$ and $11>$ are obtained; this is indicated: $^2Jv = -2<, -11>$.

§ 189. After deciding to what groups of indices the combined JJv belong, and having found the limiting distances between the voices, the conditions of using the intervals must now be expressed in signs; this is easily done (§ 124). Taking from the General Table of Indices the two series of intervals pertaining to the combined index, next compare each interval having the tie-sign with the same interval of the other Jv. If the latter interval also has the tie-sign it is necessary to compare separately the upper and lower signs of the two intervals, and to retain the sign that shows the greatest degree of limitation. In the absence of any signs for one of the intervals compared the signs for the other must be kept. If one of the intervals takes the sign p. this must also be retained in the final result.

115

Having found the rule for the individual Jv and made the comaprison between the various intervals of the original and derivative, resulting in the same rule for the combined index, next compare one and the same interval as functioning in the two different indices. First are united the limitations imposed on intervals in simple counterpoint of the strict style, then those by complex counterpoint.

§ 190. Suppose that the situation unites the conditions of $Jv = -7$ and $Jv = -11$. Then (§188,[3]) the corresponding double index will be indicated: $^1Jv = -7_>, -11$. Similar motion is allowed at a ^1Jv; the limiting interval is $7^>$. Now pass to the conditions of using the intervals, and from the General Table of Indices write in successive order the figures of the intervals applying to $Jv = -7$. Under them, from the same table, write the figures applying to $Jv = -11$, within the limit $7^>$, so that the figures of both series coincide in position. Then below the second row a horizontal line, and under this the sum of the conditions of the combined JJv.

Ex. 107

The next two examples, similar to the preceding, show combinations at two JJv with the inverse shift:

2nd Derivative

$Jv = -13$

In the next three examples one index has the direct shift, the other the inverse shift.

4) $^2Jv = 2, -7$

$$^2Jv = \quad 2: \qquad \overline{3}_{-x} \qquad \overset{-x}{\underset{(-)}{4}}$$

$$^1Jv = -7: \qquad \frac{\underset{p}{\underline{3}}_{-x}}{\underline{3}} \qquad \overset{-x}{\underline{4}}$$

$$^2Jv = 2, -7>: \qquad \frac{\underset{p}{\underline{3}}_{-x}}{\underline{3}_{-x}} \qquad \overset{-x}{\underset{(-)}{4}}$$

Ex. 110

5) $^2Jv = -2, -11$

$^2Jv = -2$: $\underset{}{(\overline{3})}$ $\overline{5}_x$ $\overset{p}{\underset{(-)}{\overline{6}}}_x$ $\underset{(-)}{\overline{8}}$

$^1Jv = -11$: $\overline{5}_x$ $\overset{-x}{\underline{6}}_{(-)}$ $\underset{(-)}{\overline{10}}$

$^2Jv = -2 <, -11 >$: $\underset{}{(\overline{3})}$ $\underset{(-)}{\overline{5}}_x$ $\overset{p}{\underset{(-)}{\overline{6}}}_x$ $\underset{(-)}{\overline{8}}$ $\underset{(-)}{\overline{10}}$

The interval $\overset{(-)}{\underset{(-)}{1}}$ is not included in this table, since it lies beyond the limit for approaching voices, $2<$.

Ex. 111

$^2Jv = -2 <, -11 >$
Original

1st Derivative

2nd Derivative

6) $^2Jv = 3, -8$.

	$^1Jv =$ 3:						

$^1Jv =$ 3: $\overset{-x}{\underset{-x}{0}}$ $\overline{3}_{(-)}$ $\overline{5}_{-x}$ $\overset{-x}{\underset{-x}{6}}$ $\overset{-x}{\underset{-x}{7}}$ $\overset{-x}{\underset{-x}{8}}$

$^2Jv = -8$: $\overset{-x}{\underset{-x}{0}}$ $\overset{p}{\underset{-x}{1}}$ $\overset{(-)}{\underset{-x}{2}}$ $\overset{-x}{\underset{(-)}{3}}$ $\overline{5}_{-x}$ $\overline{6}_{(-)}$ $\overset{-x}{\underset{(-)}{7}}$ $\overset{p}{\underset{-x}{8}}$

$^2Jv = 3, -8 >$: $\overset{-x}{\underset{-x}{0}}$ $\overset{p}{\underset{-x}{1}}$ $\overset{(-)}{\underset{-x}{2}}$ $\overset{-x}{\underset{(-)}{3}}$ $\overline{5}_{-x}$ $\overline{6}_{(-)}$ $\overset{-x}{\underset{(-)}{7}}$ $\overset{p}{\underset{-x}{8}}_x$

Ex. 112

Original.

1st Derivative

2nd Derivative

In the next example both indices have the direct shift. Since the limiting interval is 2< the preceding intervals 0 and 1 are omitted.

7) $^2Jv = -2<, 3$

$$^2Jv = -2: \quad \overline{\underset{(-)}{3}}^{(-)} \quad \overline{\underset{x}{5}} \quad \overset{p.x}{\underset{(-)}{6}} \quad \quad \quad \overset{}{\underset{(-)}{8}}$$

$$^1Jv = \ \ 3: \quad \overline{\underset{(-)}{3}} \quad \overline{\underset{x}{5}} \quad \overline{\underset{x}{6}}^{-x} \quad \overline{\underset{x}{7}}^{-x} \quad \overset{p.x}{\underset{}{8}}$$

Ex. 113

$$^2Jv = -2<, 3: \quad \overline{\underset{(-)}{3}}^{(-)} \quad \overline{\underset{x}{5}} \quad \overset{p.x}{\underset{(-)}{6}} \quad \overline{\underset{x}{7}}^{-x} \quad \overset{p.x}{\underset{(-)}{8}}$$

Original

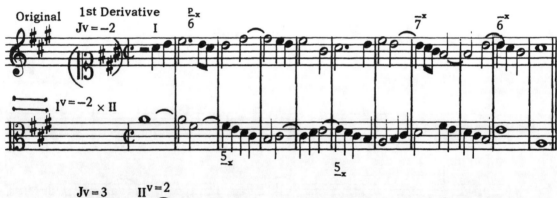

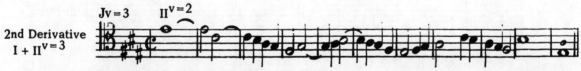

2nd Derivative
$I + II^{v} = 3$

Obs.—Stating all these situations in the form of mathematical symbols instead of words has the incontestible advantage that the study of complex counterpoint is thereby greatly simplified. The way in which almost insurmountable difficulties can be set up in the composition of such examples as the last four is well illustrated in Habert's book,* written according to the system of Simon Sechter.** He lists fifty-six separate cases of combinations in "double counterpoint," and for each of them detailed rules for the use of each interval; all this together with the examples occupying 155 pages in a book of 260 pages, not including the appendixes.

---

*Habert, "Die Lehre von dem doppelten und mehrfachen Kontrapunkt," Leipzig, 1899.

**Simon Sechter (1788-1867), theorist and composer, with whom Schubert had arranged to take

Triple Indices

§ 191. The method of indicating the union of two indices has been shown. In the same manner can also be expressed the conditions of a greater number. To compile a table for a triple index it is sufficient to take a table for a double index and indicate the process of adding the third index, for example:

$$^2Jv = -7, -9, -11.$$

$^2Jv = -9, -11:$	$\overset{(-)}{\underset{-x}{3}}$		$\overset{(-)}{\underset{(-)}{5}}$	$\overset{-x}{\underset{(-)}{6}}$	$\overset{-}{\underset{(-)}{8}}$ $\overset{-}{\underset{(-)}{10}}$
$^1Jv = -7:$	$\overset{p}{\underset{-}{3}}x$	$\overset{-x}{\underset{-}{4}}$			
$^2Jv = -7 >, -9, -11:$	$\overset{p}{\underset{-}{3}}$	$\overset{-x}{\underset{-}{4}}$	$\overset{(-)}{\underset{-x}{5}}$	$\overset{-x}{\underset{(-)}{6}}$	

§ 192. Another way to unite the conditions of three indices is as follows: Write the table of conditions for each index, and comparing separately the upper and lower signs for the same interval in the three rows, leave to the final result the signs that show the highest degree of limitations. For example:

$$^2Jv = 1, 3, 5.$$

	0	1	2	3	5	6	7	8	10
$Jv = 1:$	$\overset{(-)}{\underset{-x}{0}}$	$\overset{(-)}{\underset{-x}{1}}$	$\overset{-x}{\underset{-x}{2}}$	$\overset{p}{\underset{-}{3}}x$	$\overset{-}{\underset{(-)}{5}}$	$\overset{p}{\underset{(-)}{6}}x$	$\overset{-x}{\underset{-x}{7}}$	$\overset{-x}{\underset{-x}{8}}$	$\overset{p}{\underset{-}{10}}x$
$Jv = 3:$	$\overset{x}{\underset{-x}{0}}$			$\overset{-}{\underset{(-)}{3}}$	$\overset{-}{\underset{-x}{5}}$	$\overset{-x}{\underset{(-)}{6}}$	$\overset{-x}{\underset{-x}{7}}$	$\overset{p}{\underset{-}{8}}x$	
$Jv = 5:$		$\overset{(-)}{\underset{(-)}{1}}$			$\overset{-}{\underset{-x}{5}}$	$\overset{p}{\underset{(-)}{6}}x$		$\overset{-}{\underset{(-)}{8}}$	
$^2Jv = 1, 3, 5:$	$\overset{(-)}{\underset{-x}{0}}$	$\overset{(-)}{\underset{(-)}{1}}$	$\overset{-x}{\underset{-x}{2}}$	$\overset{p}{\underset{(-)}{3}}x$	$\overset{-}{\underset{(-)}{5}}$	$\overset{p}{\underset{(-)}{6}}x$	$\overset{-x}{\underset{-x}{7}}$	$\overset{p}{\underset{(-)}{8}}x$	$\overset{p}{\underline{10}}x$

To the conditions of a triple index may be added those of a fourth index, or a fifth, etc. But added constraint results as the number of indices is increased, and writing becomes more and more difficult.

The Polymorphous Index

§ 193. Here is encountered a problem that used to be of considerable interest to the old theorists—one even shrouded in secrecy—that of writing a two-voice combination that would yield all shifts without exception. This concerns polymorphous counterpoint, and the matter can easily be settled by applying the principles already learned. Uniting the conditions of all indices gives this table:

$$\widehat{\underset{(-)}{0}} \quad \widehat{\underset{(-)}{1}} \quad \widehat{\underset{(-)}{2}} \quad \widehat{\underset{(-)}{3}} \quad \widehat{\underset{(-)}{4}} \quad \widehat{\underset{(-)}{5}} \quad \widehat{\underset{(-)}{6}} \quad \widehat{\underset{(-)}{7}} \quad \widehat{\underset{(-)}{8}}$$

Obviously, to write counterpoint under such conditions is impossible, for there is not a single interval that can be placed on an accented beat. Therefore the question as to the possibility of polymorphous counterpoint in the strict style must be decided in the negative.

CHAPTER X

THE DUPLICATION OF IMPERFECT CONSONANCES
IN TWO-VOICE COMBINATIONS

§ 194. In concluding the treatment of fixed consonances in Chapter VI reference was made to a special characteristic of indices corresponding to imperfect consonances (indices of the second pair of columns: $^2JJv = \pm 2, \pm 5, -9$), consisting in the fact that they admit of the simultaneous execution of the original plus a shift of one of the voices at the given index, thus obtaining three-voice counterpoint in which two voices move in parallel imperfect consonances (§ 119). It remains to examine to what extent all tied intervals—dissonances and variable consonances—may be applied to duplicated voices. First of all will be studied the duplication of one voice (§§ 195-202 and §§ 209-12, three-voice counterpoint), then the simultaneous duplication of both voices (§§ 213-27, four-voice counterpoint).

I (A) The Duplication of One Voice Using Tied Intervals;
Two Derivatives; Two-Voice and Three-Voice

§ 195. In three-voice counterpoint resulting from the duplication of one of the voices in imperfect consonances (§ 110) three combinations are to be distinguished: (a) a two-voice original; (b) its derivative, also two-voice, consisting of a shift at an index corresponding to an imperfect consonance; and (c) a three-voice derivative, the result of the simultaneous execution of the original and a shift of one of the voices. As long as the accented beats are limited to certain fixed consonances the correctness of these two-voice combinations—original and derivative—guarantees the correctness also of the three-voice combinations obtained by executing them simultaneously. But when tied intervals are used they are changed by duplication. In this case, though each two-voice combination might be individually valid, showing correct two-voice counterpoint, this is insufficient in order that their simultaneous combination shall be equally correct. To secure this result it is necessary to be sure that the dissonance of a ninth ($\overline{8}$ or $-\underline{8}$) is not found between the upper and middle voices. According to a rule of simple counterpoint of the strict style, $\overline{8}$ may form a dissonance only with the lowest voice; as a suspension it constitutes the only superfluous limitation that multi-voice counterpoint offers as compared to two-voice (§ 83). For example, this original at $Jv = -9$:

gives this derivative but to execute

them simultaneously is impracticable, for the forbidden dissonance $\overline{8}$ appears, involving

the middle voice:

To prevent the possibility of $\overline{8}$ appearing between the upper and middle voices is the object of the rules presently to be given.

§ 196. Before passing to the statement of these rules, those cases will be considered in which the ninth will not be found at all between the upper and middle voices, consequently offering no obstacle for execution in three voices.

(1) When the upper and middle voices progress in parallel motion $\overline{8}$ obviously cannot appear, therefore such a three-voice combination is always correct. This refers to four cases of duplication:

$$I^{d=2}, I^{d=-2}, I^{d=5}, I^{d=-5<}.$$

Indicating each voice in detail gives the following expressions:

$$I^{v=2} + I + II, \quad I + I^{v=-2} + II, \quad I^{v=5} + I + II, \quad I + I^{v=-5} + II.$$

All the examples in Appendix A at these indices can be executed in three voices.

Obs.—Since combinations at these indices always give correct three-voice counterpoint when one voice is duplicated, the problem can be solved in reverse order, i.e. start with a three-voice combination, writing it in simple counterpoint with the highest voice duplicated in thirds or sixths. From this three-voice combination extract two of two voices, using one as the original and the other as the derivative.

(2) Every combination at $Jv = -5>$ can also be freely executed in three voices, since $5>$ shows the limiting interval for receding voices, whereby $\overline{8}$ is automatically eliminated. Such correct duplications are $I^{d=-5>} + II$ and $I + II^{d=-5>}$.

Ex. 13 in Appendix A (p. 312) can therefore be executed in three voices, as follows:

§ 197. Ending the duplications of which the correctness is provided for by the correctness of each of the two components, the next cases of duplication are those where the correctness of the two-voice combinations does not guarantee the absence of mistakes in the three-voice combination. The error, as stated before, is the appearance of $\overline{8}$ between the upper and middle voices, the prevention of which is the purpose of these rules. The two voices concerned may belong either to the original or to the two-voice derivative. In the first instance the rule refers to the original ninth, in the second to that m from which is obtained the derivative ninth. Hence the duplications about to be examined fall into two groups.

§ 198. *1st Group of Duplications.*—Here the upper and middle voices form the original combination, the lower voice duplicates one or the other. This group includes (a) the direct shift of voice II at a positive Jv, and (b) the inverse shift of voice I. Aside from the cases of duplication mentioned in § 196 where $d=5>$, the remaining ones are: (a) the direct shifts $II^{d=2}$, $II^{d=5}$; (b) the inverse shifts $I^{d=-9}$, $I^{d=-12}$. This group of duplications can be illustrated diagramatically:

(a) Direct Shifts	(b) Inverse Shifts
I ⎫ Original	I ⎫ Original
II ⎭ Combination	II ⎭ Combination
∀ II$^{v=a}$	∀ I$^{v=-a}$
a = 2 at a = 5.	a = —9 at a = —12.

The arrow goes from a voice of the original to the duplication of the same voice in the derivative.

Since in these diagrams the original combinations are formed by the upper and middle voices, in them the resolution of the ninth to the octave must be forbidden, consequently $\overset{\frown}{8}$ appears as a supplementary condition for the Jv of the original combination. It is understood, of course, that the lower sign belonging to the ninth of this Jv is retained, therefore in situations such as $II^{d=5}$ and $I^{d=-9}$, where this sign is $(-)$, the ninth must be excluded altogether from the available suspensions.

Based on this, Ex. 23 at $Jv=-9$ in Appendix A (p. 320) can be executed at $I^{d=-9}$ only as far as the seventh measure, in which $\overline{8}$ is found, making an incorrect three-voice combination.

A similar obstacle is encountered in the eleventh measure of No. 29 ($Jv=-12$), Appendix A.

§ 199. *2nd Group of Duplication.*—Here the upper and middle voices are those of a two-voice combination. This group includes both the direct and inverse shifts of voice II at a negative Jv. The duplications referring to this are: (a) with the direct shift, $II^{d=-2}$, $II^{d=-5^{<}}$. (Cf. what was said about $Jv=-5>$ in § 196). Expressed in diagrams:

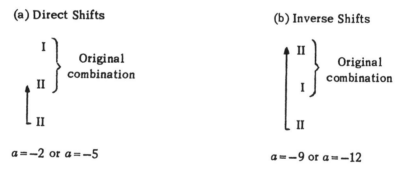

(a) Direct Shifts

$a=-2$ or $a=-5$

(b) Inverse Shifts

$a=-9$ or $a=-12$

Here the upper and middle voices appear as the voices of the derivative, therefore to prevent the appearance between them of a ninth resolving to an octave the interval in the original (a) from which the ninth was obtained must be reversed. To find m giving $n=8$ (or with the inverse shift $n=-8$), add the value of the index, taken with the opposite sign, to the interval of the derivative (n) (§ 61).

For an original interval found in this way the sign $(-)$ shows the conditions that must be added to those of the given index. Furthermore:

(1) If the derivative ninth is positive (i.e. if Jv has the direct shift, (a) in the preceding diagram), the sign $(-)$ must be placed above: $\overset{\longleftrightarrow}{m}$.

(2) If the derivative ninth is negative (i.e. if Jv has the inverse shift, (b) in the preceding diagram), the sign is placed below: m.

The lower sign of m with the direct shift and the upper with the inverse remains unchanged.

§ 200. The original interval from which is obtained a derivative ninth, together with the changes in its tie-signs, will be given for each index belonging to the second group of duplications.

(1) For indices with the direct shift $n= 8$ is obtained: at $Jv= -2$ from $m= 10$; at $Jv =-5<$ from $m= 13$. For these intervals the sign (−) above is obligatory, cf. § 199, (a). Since at $Jv= -5<$ the sign is already found below at $m= 13$ this interval is excluded from the available suspensions ($\overset{\text{p}}{\underset{(-)}{13}}$).

(2) For indices with the inverse shift $n= -8$ is obtained: at $Jv= -9$ from $m= 1$; at $Jv= -12$ from $m= 4$. When these intervals are duplicated they take the sign − below, cf. § 199, (b). Since the second, according to the rules of simple counterpoint, has already the sign (−) above $\overset{(-)}{1}$, at $Jv= -9$ it is excluded as a suspension: $\underset{(-)}{\overset{(-)}{1}}$.

§ 201. In the following table for the first group of duplications (§ 198) is indicated the conditions under which as original ninth ($m= 8$) can be used; in the table for the second group (§ 199), the conditions using that m which gives a derivative ninth (§ 200).

Obs.—The duplications $I^{d=2}$, $I^{d=-2}$, $I^{d=5}$, $I^{d=-5<}$, $I^{d=-5>}$, $II^{d=-5>}$, do not require any change in the conditions of their corresponding indices (§ 196).

§ 202. In order for a combination at one of the upper indices of this pair of columns (at $Jv= -9$ or at $Jv= -12$) to get a reciprocal duplication both above and below a voice, it is necessary, in the conditions of either index, to insert the additional changes required by one or the other of the duplications. For example, if in the table of intervals for $Jv= -9$ are inserted $\underset{(-)}{\overset{(-)}{8}}$ and $\underset{(-)}{\overset{(-)}{1}}$, this combination will give both duplication: $I^{v=-9} + II$ and $I + II^{v=-9}$

Uniting the Conditions of Duplications with the Conditions of Every Jv

§ 203. By the methods given (Chapter IX) the conditions of any index may be united with the conditions of duplication at any imperfect consonance. The absence of similar motion in the original is a necessary requirement, since the indices corresponding to imperfect consonances are all those of the second group (^2JJv, § 59). If a duplication is required of an index of the second group, if, above all, it has few fixed consonances and is therefore hemmed in by many limitations, then the number of changes inserted into the conditions using the intervals may be very small. Probably the greatest advantage of this is that the limitations belonging to the final process in a duplication are already present in the initial conditions. This explains the fact, strange at first glance, that a combination written at one of the difficult indices, $Jv= ±1$, $±6$ etc., sometimes admits of a duplication of either voice at any imperfect consonance.

---

*In the first group of duplications the upper and middle voices form the original combination.

§ 204. It will be found that Ex. 1 at $Jv=-1$ in Appendix A, from beginning to end, may be executed in three voices at the duplications $I^{d=2}$ or $II^{d=2}$. The beginning of the second of these duplications is herewith quoted, as it presents more inconvenience as to the augmented fourth than the first.

(b)

What is the reason for such coincidence? Why does a two-voice combination, written with no thought of parallel thirds, nevertheless admits of them? The answer to these questions is obtained if the conditions of the duplication at $Jv=2$ ($II^{d=2}$) are united to those of $Jv=-1$, and their differences made clear. Add $\widehat{8}$, the condition of the duplication $II^{d=2}$, to the intervals of $Jv=2$ (§ 201), comparing them with the intervals of $Jv=-1$.

$Jv=-1$:	0	1	2	3	4	7	8
$II^{d=2}$:				3	4		8
Uniting these and other conditions:	0	1	2	3	4	7	8

Comparison of the third row of figures with the first shows that few changes had to be added to $Jv=-1$ as the result of annexing to it the conditions duplicating at $Jv=2$. The absence of ties below the fifth (4) and above the ninth (8) is sufficient in order that a combination at $Jv=-1$ shall admit of duplication in thirds: $II^{d=2}$. The lack of these ties in the previous illustration was what made the duplication practicable.

§ 205. Next will be shown to what extent the conditions of $Jv=-13$ must be supplemented in order to obtain a duplication at $Jv=-9$, namely: $I^{d=-9}$ and $II^{d=-9}$. According to the table in § 201, to the conditions of $Jv=-9$ must be added 1 and 8.

$^2Jv=-13$:	0			5	6	7	8	
$^2Jv=-9$ { $I^{d=-9}$:		1	3				8	
$II^{d=-9}$:								
	0	1	3	5	6	7	8	

Thus, $\widehat{1}$ $\widehat{3}$ $\widehat{8}$ are the changes that have to be incorporated into the conditions of $Jv=-13$ in order for a combination written at this index to admit of the duplication $I^{d=-9}$ and $II^{d=-9}$. In Ex. 31 at $Jv=-13$, Appendix A, the first three measures may be executed in three voices by duplication at the tenth, i.e. $II^{d=-9}$; but the second used as a suspension in the fourth measure, $\widehat{1}$, prevents its continuance in three voices (the illustration is transposed an octave lower):

128   CONVERTIBLE COUNTERPOINT

etc.

impossible

etc.

The derivative of this example (*v.* Ex. 32, p. 329) allows the duplication $I^{d=-2}$ up to the eighth measure, and $II^{d=-2}$ up to the fifth measure. The example at $Jv=-6$ (Ex. 15, p. 314) allows the duplication $I^{d=-2}$ up to the sixth measure.

§ 206. It is a very simple matter to unite the conditions of duplication at $Jv=-9$ with $Jv=-7$, i.e. with double counterpoint at the octave. Since the limiting interval is $7>$, 8 is excluded from the table of duplication at $Jv=-9$.

$$^2Jv=-9 \quad \begin{cases} I^{d=-9}: \\ II^{d=-9}: \end{cases}$$

To the conditions of $Jv=-7>$ is added: $\frac{(-)}{1}\frac{(P.)}{3}$ and the absence of similar motion.

§ 207. Because of the greater practical importance of double counterpoint at the twelfth, a table will also be given uniting its conditions with those of a duplication at $Jv=-9$.

It will have been observed from the last two tables that few changes were needed in the conditions of $Jv=-7$ or at $Jv=-11$ to enable them to take duplications at the tenth. Likewise, similar motion is forbidden, as it alters the conditions of these indices to such an extent that a combination written at $Jv=-7$ or at $Jv=-11$ is seldom found that would allow of imperfect consonances; at every point similar motion is frustrated.

§ 208. All possible cases of duplications may be united not only with any of the indices but among themselves in any permutations desired. For instance, the conditions of two-voice counterpoint can be deduced that will admit of shifts at two indices and a three-voice presentation besides; the rule of counterpoint can be found that will satisfy the conditions for duplicating various imperfect consonances—the sixth, tenth etc. The number of permutations may be so increased that nearly every three-voice combination will admit an interchange of voices and the transposition at the octave of one voice or another. To write counterpoint satisfying such requirements is less difficult with the use of fixed consonances; more difficult with dissonances and variable consonances from which tied intervals are excluded.

(B) The Duplication of One Voice Using Tied Intervals; One Derivative, Three-Voice

§ 209. In the preceding sections the combinations were discussed that have two derivatives: (a) in two voices at a given index; and (b) in three voices, resulting from the duplication of one of the voices in imperfect consonances. The present discussion will be limited to three-voice derivatives.

The necessity for avoiding $\overset{\curvearrowright}{8}$ (or $\underset{\curvearrowright}{-8}$) in relation to the upper and middle voices still applies (§§ 195-202). The three-voice derivatives now considered differ from the preceding cases only in the use of derivative fourths between the upper and middle voices. Appearing before in two-voice derivatives, fourths were subject to the limitations of dissonances; they are now released (3 and 10 instead of $\overline{3}$ and $\overline{10}$), and may be used according to the rules for perfect consonances (§ 83). An original consonance giving a derivative fourth, now consonant, is released from its former limitations and become a fixed consonance. Therefore the original dissonance, of which this consonance is the resolution, is released from the supplementary sign ×. Such are the situations that allow consonant fourths to be added to the conditions of a given index. In a three-voice combination resulting from the duplication of imperfect consonances, successive first inversions may be freely used:

and therefore similar motion may be added to combinations at ^2JJv.

Obs.—It should be understood that this releasing of fourths from their limitations is in no sense a requirement; that also in counterpoint of three or more voices the preparation and resolution of a dissonant fourth according to the rules of two-voice counterpoint is still valid. But, having obtained the status of a consonant interval, the fourth need not be prepared and may be used freely.

§ 210. In duplicating one of the two voices of the original combination at imperfect  consonances, a consonant fourth is found only in first inversions: since any attempt to include it in a triad in fundamental form would result in the omission of the third, with no imperfect consonance present: 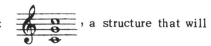 , a structure that will admit of no duplications.

§ 211. The results of legitimate duplications may be represented by this chord: . Here only the third or the sixth above the lowest voice may be duplicated.

A chord with such an arrangement of intervals admits of the following:

(1) At $II^{d=-2}$ from m= 5 (n= 5 − 2= 3, § 31).

(2) At $II^{d=-5}$ from m = 2 (n = 2 − 5 = −3).

In conformity with this, at $II^{d=-2}$, 5 is released from its limitations, and at $II^{d=-5}$ 2 Is released. Since each of these consonances reverts to a fixed consonance, the dissonances that resolve to them are released from the supplementary sign ×. At $II^{d=-2}$ the seventh is released from this sign, as the interval resolves to 5 ($\overline{6}$ instead of $\underset{(-)}{6}$), and at $II^{d=-5}$ the fourth reverts from $\underset{-x}{3}$ to $\underset{-x}{3}$.

§ 212. It would also be possible to examine the conditions presented by two other aspects of first inversions:  those found where compound consonances are used: $II^{d=-9}$ and $II^{d=-12}$. But this is unnecessary, because all instances of where fourths are released from their limitations are included in the following rule:

A derivative fourth changes to a consonant interval whenever the lower voice of the original combination is duplicated at the upper third or upper sixth, or their compounds. A duplication at the third is released from the limitations of the original sixth; at the sixth from those of the original third.

Both these intervals revert to fixed consonances, whereby the dissonances of which they are the resolutions are released from the supplementary sign above. It is such changes that must be inserted into the conditions of a given index. In the following example, where the duplication is $II^{d=-2}$:

Ex. 116   Josquin de Pres

the original combination shows a two-voice canonic imitation in the outer parts. In measure 6, where it is interrupted, is found an augmented second (between the lower voices), the use of which is uncommon in the strict style. It is an example of the free way in which dissonances were treated in the works of the Flemish composers who came before Palestrina.

II The Simultaneous Duplication of Two Voices; One Derivative, Four-Voice

§ 213. In concluding Division A is presented a study of the conditions under which a two-voice original will yield a four-voice derivative, involving therefore the simultaneous duplication at imperfect consonances of both voices. First will be considered the duplications in which suspensions are excluded from both the original and the derivative, later the duplications that use them.

(A) Duplications of Two Voices Without Suspensions

§ 214. When one of the voices is duplicated at the tenth ($d = -9$), from each original consonance is obtained a consonant three-voice harmony (§ 119). But when both voices are duplicated ($I^{d=-9} + II^{d=-9}$) not all the consonances will yield a consonant four-voice harmony. One of them, the sixth, gives the dissonance of a seventh (13) in the outer voices:

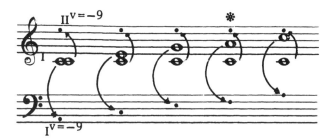

Therefore, if the sixth is excluded from the fixed consonances and the others from 0 to 9 are used, and counterpoint without suspensions written in conformity with the conditions of $Jv = -9$, such counterpoint will admit of the simultaneous duplication of both voices:

Ex. 117

§ 215. Returning to the dissonant harmony, it results from using the sixth. The outer voices form a compound seventh, 13. How does this dissonance originate? There are four voices, of which two constitute the original combination I + II. Every other union of voice I with voice II is a derivative; there are three of them:

$$\text{(a)} \quad (I^{v=-9} + II) \ Jv = -9;$$
$$\text{(b)} \quad (I + II^{v=-9}) \ Jv = -9;$$
$$\text{(c)} \quad (I^{v=-9} + II^{v=-9}) \ Jv = -18.$$

The first two combinations have $Jv = -9$, the third has $Jv = -18$, i.e. double counterpoint at the twelfth. The index of the third combination is always equal to the sum of the other two indices. The original combination must, therefore, satisfy the condition of the double index $Jv = -9 >, -18$ (§ 190). All the consonances of this index except 5 are fixed. Clearly, then, the dissonant interval 13 in the outer voices is the result of the shift $m = 5$ at $Jv = -18$, since $5 - 18 = -13$.

§ 216. Indicating the imperfect consonances that duplicate voice I by the letter a, and those that duplicate voice II by b, gives the following list of derivative combinations and their indices:

(a) $(I^{v\,=\,a} + II)\, Jv = a;$

(b) $(I + II^{v\,=\,b})\, Jv = b;$

(c) $(I^{v\,=\,a} + II^{v\,=\,b})\, Jv = a + b.$

Hence it appears that if vv of voices I and II are unequal, all three indices are different in value, therefore the original I + II must satisfy the conditions of the triple index $Jv = a,\ b,\ a + b.$

Furthermore, the supplementary conditions must be inserted into the conditions of this compound index, in view of the fact that a two-voice derivative is not independent two-voice counterpoint, but is only a constituent part of a multi-voice texture.

§ 217. In Ex. 118, a duplication at $I^{d\,=\,5} + II^{d\,=\,2}$, one of the consonances, the fifth, gives dissonant harmony at the duplication:  The other consonances give consonant harmony:

I   II

Excluding the fifth from the fixed consonances and using the rest, it is possible, by observing the limitations of ^2JJv, to write a two-voice combination that admits the above-mentioned conditions. The derivatives are:

(a) $(I^{v\,=\,5} + II)\, Jv = 5;$

(b) $(I + II^{v\,=\,2})\, Jv = 2;$

(c) $(I^{v\,=\,5} + II^{v\,=\,2})\, Jv = 7.$

The index of the third combination, $Jv = 7$, is rejected, since a derivative at this index would be nothing but the separation at an octave of the original (§ 47). The latter will have, therefore, the double index $Jv = 5,\ 2$. Since both indices are positive a limiting interval is not needed (§ 42).

§ 218. In a table for these indices must be inserted the following supplementary conditions, inasmuch as the two-voice combination to which the indices apply is not independent two-voice counterpoint, but enters into the structure of four-voice counterpoint.

When a derivative fourth (±3 or ±10) between the upper and middle voices or between the two middle voices is obtained from an original dissonance, it is released from the limitations acquired and becomes fixed. It is therefore allowable to include 5 among the fixed consonances of the double index $Jv = 5,\ 2$, listed in the preceding section, as it yields a consonant fourth.

Ex. 118

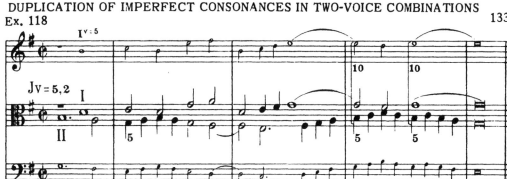

§ 219. The only chord resulting from the duplication of two voices in imperfect consonances and that also contains a consonant fourth is the first inversion with doubled third. It occurs in the following forms:

etc.

Since two first inversions with doubled third must not show parallel octaves—as would happen if all the voices moved parallel—successive parallel fourths, possible in three-voice counterpoint, are not allowed in four-voice. This is what distinguishes four-voice duplications from three-voice; therefore, at the simultaneous duplication of two voices the limitations of ^2JJv remain in force, and similar motion is impracticable.

§ 220. Since parallel fourths can not be used in the three upper voices (§ 219) these voices may appear in other octaves, i.e. may be shifted in double counterpoint at the octave (it must not be forgotten that this refers only to those cases of duplication where the accented beats take consonant harmony). Such shifts can be freely made as long as the lower voice remains the lower, i e. as long as a combination of the lower with any of the upper voices forms the direct shift. Otherwise, at the inverse shift of the bass and one of the other voices, the free use of a fifth would result in an unprepared fourth.

As long as the bass continues to remain the lowest voice, shifting the other voices at the octave can be freely done if an occasional crossing of the parts is not considered a disadvantage. The use of these other voices as bass would be possible only if they did not imply second inversions. For instance, the alto in Ex. 118 (voice I of the original combination) could not function as bass, since the notes indicated (***) are unprepared chord-fifths, which, if appearing in the lower voice, would give unprepared fourths:

The same applies to the tenor (voice II of the original)—it cannot appear in the role of bass since this is prevented by the triads in the second and third measures. On the contrary, no such obstacle is encountered in the upper voice, so it may function as bass. Therefore the following shifts are possible for Ex. 118:

(1) Bass remaining as lowest voice:

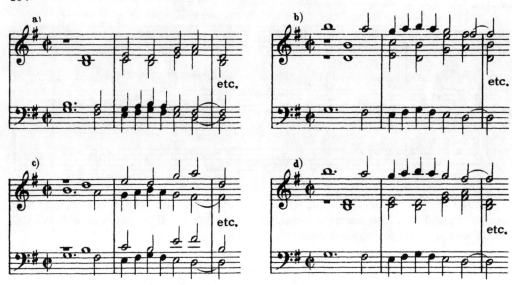

(2) The upper voice of the original functioning as bass:

(B) Duplication of Two Voices Using Suspensions

§ 221. To find the conditions under which both voices of the original may be duplicated simultaneously it is necessary (1) to compile a table of compound indices that
unites the conditions of three derivatives, and (2) to insert in this table the supplementary
conditions by which the use of fourths and ninths in multi-voice counterpoint differs from
their use in two-voice. The method of compiling tables of compound indices was given
in Chapter IX. Fourths and ninths require further explanation.

§ 222. The appearance of $\overline{8}$ (or $-\underline{8}$) should be prevented in all those two-voice combinations that do not include the bass voice. If the original (I + II) is such a combination
$\left(\frac{-}{8}\right)$ will appear as a supplementary condition in the table of compound indices. As to the

derivative combinations in which the bass is not concerned, it is necessary to find what equals m, given $n = 8$ if the shift is direct, or $n = -8$ if the shift is inverse. In the former instance the supplementary conditions show $\underset{\smile}{m}$, in the latter, $\overset{\frown}{m}$ ($\S\S$ 199-201). This supplementary condition is also inserted in the table of compound indices.

$\S$ 223. A consonant fourth (± 3 or ± 10) may occur only in those two-voice combinations that do not include the bass voice. First of all, from such combinations can be eliminated any original that forms independent two-voice counterpoint, for such a combination can not contain unprepared fourths. If in a combination where the bass voice does not participate n equals ± 3 (or ± 10), derived from m, and if at the same time m is a fixed consonance in each of the other derivatives, then m is released from the limitations imposed on it by fourths. The dissonance resolving to m loses the supplementary sign $\times$, owing to the fact that m becomes a fixed consonance (cf. $\S$ 209). If one of the indices is $Jv = 0$ a derivative fourth of this combination is not released from its limitations, otherwise an original fourth would have to be regarded as consonant, an impossibility inasmuch as the original is a two-voice combination.

$\S$ 224. Because of the absence of parallel fourths ($\S$ 219) and of $\overline{8}$ between the three upper voices (in conformity with the rules of simple counterpoint), these three voices can be transferred to different octaves on condition that none of them crosses the bass. In the absence of suspensions, no obstacle is encountered in such shifting of the three upper voices ($\S$ 220). But if suspensions are used these shifts are governed by the following rule: A voice forming $\overline{8}$ (or $-\underline{8}$) in relation to the bass cannot approach the latter any closer, since doing so would contract the ninth to a second—resolving to a unison—a progression forbidden in the strict style. Aside from this, all shifts of the three upper voices in double counterpoint at the octave are possible.

The conditions at which any of the three upper voices—suspensions being absent—could function as lower voices were explained in $\S$ 220. But if suspensions are applied another condition must be added to those already in force: A voice that contains a ninth resolving to an octave cannot appear as lowest voice.

$\S$ 225. A table will be compiled of the conditions for $\mathrm{I}^{d=\,-9} + \mathrm{II}^{d=\,-9}$. Here the original combination is for the alto and tenor, the soprano and bass take the duplications.

$$\text{Original}\begin{cases} \text{S.} & \quad \mathrm{II}^{v=\,-9} \\[4pt] \begin{bmatrix}\text{A.} \\[6pt] \text{T.}\end{bmatrix} & \begin{bmatrix}\ \mathrm{I} \\[6pt] \ \mathrm{II}\end{bmatrix} \\[4pt] \text{B.} & \quad \mathrm{I}^{v=\,-9} \end{cases}$$

Corresponding to this diagram are these duplications:

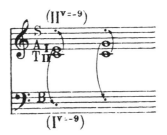

The original combination I + II (A.+ T.) yields the following derivatives:

$$\text{(a)} \quad (\text{I}^{v=-9} + \text{II}) \ Jv = -9 \ \text{B.} + \text{T.;}$$

$$\text{(b)} \cdot (\text{I} + \text{II}^{v=-9}) \ Jv = -9\text{: A.} + \text{S.;}$$

$$\text{(c)} \quad (\text{I}^{v=-9} + \text{II}^{v=-9}) \ Jv = -18\text{: B.} + \text{S.}$$

Since (a) and (b) have the same index, $Jv = -9$, that of the original is not triple but double: $Jv = -9 >, -18$, equivalent to $Jv = -9 >, -11$ (cf. table in § 190).

Next is to determine the changes that must be inserted into the table for this compound index. There are two combinations in which the bass does not participate: the original (A. + T.) and derivative (b): (A. + S.) $Jv = -9$. To prevent the appearance of a ninth resolving to an octave, the former required the supplementary condition $\overset{\leftharpoonup}{8}$; the latter $\underset{\leftrightharpoons}{1}$ (§ 222). As for consonant fourths, they cannot appear at all in the original, only in a derivative, and then only when the lowest voice is not involved (§ 223). But since combination (b), alone satisfying this condition, represents a shift at $Jv = -9$, wherein m, giving a fourth, is dissonant ($m = -3 + 9 = 6$, § 61), a derivative fourth can not appear as a consonance, and therefore must be inserted as a change in the table for this compound index. Writing in the supplementary conditions in the table for the double index $Jv = -9$, -11, the conditions are obtained for the above-mentioned duplications: $\text{I}^{d=-9} + \text{II}^{d=-9}$

$$^2 Jv = -9, -11: \qquad\qquad \overset{\leftharpoonup}{\underset{-}{3}} \quad \overset{\leftharpoonup}{\underset{-\times}{5}} \quad \overset{-\times}{\underset{\leftharpoonup}{6}} \quad \overset{-}{\underset{\leftharpoonup}{8}} \quad (v.\ \S\ 190, [2])$$

Supplementary conditions: $\qquad\qquad \underset{\leftrightharpoons}{1} \qquad\qquad\qquad \overset{\leftharpoonup}{8}$

Conditions for $\text{I}^{d=-9} + \text{II}^{d=-9}$: $\quad \overset{\leftharpoonup}{\underset{\leftrightharpoons}{1}} \quad \overset{\leftharpoonup}{\underset{-}{3}} \quad \overset{\leftharpoonup}{\underset{-\times}{5}} \quad \overset{-\times}{\underset{\leftharpoonup}{6}} \quad \overset{-}{\underset{\leftharpoonup}{8}}$

These conditions are met in the following combination:

Ex. 119

$\text{I}^{d=-9} + \text{II}^{d=-9}$

§ 226. Table for the duplications $I^{d=-9} + II^{d=-2}$.

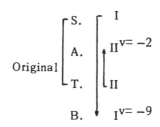

corresponding to:

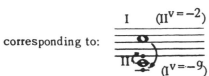

Original: I + II, S. + T.

Derivatives:

   (a) $(I^{v=-9} + II)$ $Jv = -9$, B. + T.;

   (b) $(I + II^{v=-2})$ $Jv = -2$, S. + A.;

   (c) $(I^{v=-9} + II^{v=-2})$ $Jv = -11$, B. + A.

Triple index for the original: $(I + II)$ $^2Jv = -2 <, -9>, -11$. Conditions not involving the bass, original: (S. + T.) and derivative (b): (S.+ A.).

Supplementary conditions: (1) the ninth, resolving to the octave (§ 222), excluded from the original (hence $\overset{(-)}{8}$) and from derivative (b) ($Jv = -2$, supplementary condition $\overset{(-)}{10}$). Because of the limiting interval $9 >$ the latter need not appear in the table.

(2) The fourth can not be used as a consonant interval. The only derivative in which it could be found is (b) (S. + A.) and here it is obtained from a dissonance ($m = 3 -2 = 1$). It is therefore not inserted as a change in the table.

$^2\mathbf{Jv} = -2 \prec, -9 \succ, -11$:	$\overset{(-)}{3}$	$\overset{(-)}{5}$	$\overset{-x}{6}$	$\overset{-}{8}$
	$\underset{-}{}$	$\underset{-x}{}$	$\underset{(-)}{}$	$\underset{(-)}{}$
Supplementary condition:				$\overset{(-)}{8}$
Conditions for $I^{d=-9} + II^{d=-2}$:	$\overset{(-)}{3}$	$\overset{(-)}{5}$	$\overset{-x}{6}$	$\overset{(\ )}{8}$
	$\underset{-}{}$	$\underset{-x}{}$	$\underset{(\cdots)}{}$	$\underset{(\ )}{}$

Ex. 120 $I^{d=\,-9} + II^{d=\,-2}$

Obs.—Comparing the preceding table with that in § 225 ($I^{d=\,-9} + II^{d=\,-9}$) it will be seen that they are identical except that the table last considered has the limiting interval 2<, absent in the table in § 225. The similarity is explained by the fact that both tables have the indices $Jv = -9$ and $Jv = -11$ and both the supplementary condition $\overset{\frown}{8}$. In the latter table the addition of $Jv = -2$ to these JJv inserted no changes except the limiting interval 2<. Ex. 120, in which the voices of the original do not approach closer than a third, also satisfies the conditions of $I^{d=\,-9} + II^{d=\,-9}$:

$I^{d=-9} + II^{d=-9}$

Ex. 121

§ 227. Table for the duplications $I^{d=2} + II^{d=-2}$.

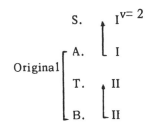

corresponding to:

Original: I + II, A. + B.;
Derivatives:

    (a) $(I^{v=2} + II)\ Jv = 2$, S. + B.;

    (b) $(I + II^{v=-2})\ Jv = -2$, A. + T.;

    (c) $(I^{v=2} + II^{v=-2})\ Jv = 0$, S. + T.

Double index: $^2Jv = 2, -2 <$.

Combinations in which the bass does not participate: derivatives (b) (A. + T.) and (c) (S. + T.).

Supplementary conditions: (1) in accordance with § 222 the ninth resolving to the octave ($\overline{8}$, $-\underline{8}$) is excluded from derivative (b) ($Jv = -2$, hence the supplementary condition $\overrightarrow{10}$) and from derivative (c) ($Jv = 0$, supplementary condition $\overleftrightarrow{8}$).

(2) In combination (b) the fourth can be consonant. It is obtained from an original sixth ($m = 3 + 2 = 5$), which appears as a fixed consonance at the other two indices ($Jv = -2$, $Jv = 0$), i.e. it enters into the structure of consonant harmony:

Therefore 5 is a fixed consonance in combination (b). As regards combination (c), the fourth in it is dissonant. This is a combination at $Jv = 0$, consequently a fourth in it would be derived from a fourth in the original, an impossibility, because in a two-voice original a fourth can not be consonant (§ 223).

The supplementary conditions $\overleftrightarrow{8}$, $\overrightarrow{10}$, and the use of the fixed consonance 5 are therefore obtained, all of which are inserted in the table for the double index: $Jv = 2, -2<$.

Consonance 5 is absent from the lower row, since it is fixed. Also, because the limiting interval is $2<$, interval 1, which is outside of this limit, is not included in the table.

Obs.—What was said in §§ 203-8 about uniting the conditions of duplications with the conditions of every index is valid also for the simultaneous duplication of two voices, and for all cases of duplication in general.

§ 228. With the simultaneous duplication of two voices in imperfect consonances is completed the study of two-voice vertical-shifting counterpoint. The remainder of Division A consists of additional matter referring to questions previously brought up.

The Six-Four Chord in the Strict Style

§ 229. In connection with the use of fourths there arises the question as to the application in the strict style of triads in the second inversion. Although this is within the province of simple counterpoint it is necessary to refer to it here because of the frequent appearance of opinions that are unintelligible in view of certain facts. Such, for instance, is the common assertion that six-four chords are forbidden in the strict style, whereas in reality they are often found. In order to define the conditions under which six-four chords are in keeping with the character of the strict style, they are brought under the following general rule, which refers to all dissonant chords:

Every union of sounds, dissonant intervals included, by whatever term it is known in the study of harmony, may be found in the strict style under circumstances in which the dissonance may be analysed according to the rules of two-voice counterpoint as a suspension, a passing-note, or an **auxiliary-note.** This is based on the proposition that every combination in the strict style is correct if each voice forms correct two-voice counterpoint with every other voice, taking into consideration the changes in the rules of two-voice counterpoint when this passes into multi-voice counterpoint. This involves, as previously observed, greater freedom as to hidden consecutives (§74,[1]) and the use of fourths as true consonances between the upper and middle voices or both middle voices (§ 83).

Take, for example, this "seventh-chord": Here there is a dissonant interval between the outer voices: $\overline{13}$; this dissonance must be both prepared and resolved correctly; besides which the free note may progress to another note at the moment of resolution:

 etc.

The remaining voices do not participate in the dissonance but form consonant intervals with each other, therefore they are free to move either stepwise or by leap, on condition that they do not form dissonances at the moment the dissonance in the outer voices is resolved. Hence is obtained a large number of "resolutions" of this chord:

---

*0 is beyond the limiting interval 2<. therefore at this place the alto and tenor cross.

§ 230. Six-four chords are also found in the preceding illustrations (at the places indicated*); they result from the movement of the voices, according to the general principle mentioned. One dissonance, 3, is a component of the six-four chord, and if this dissonance is prepared and resolved according to the rules of two-voice counterpoint of the strict style, then the six-four chord that results is correct. But here a reservation must be made: it has been seen that in two-voice counterpoint the resolution of fourths ($\overline{3}$ and $\underline{3}$) to fifths sounds very empty. This is because the inherent meagerness of the dissonant fourth is further accentuated by its association with an empty-sounding fifth. In multi-voice counterpoint this use of $\underline{3}$ is always aided by the sharper dissonance of

the second: [music] This does not include those instances where the fourth

is the only dissonance in the given harmony: [music] though such use of the

six-four chord is by no means unknown in the strict style.

Passing to specific cases, the six-four chord may be used in the following situations:

(1) On accented beats, as preparation and resolution of a dissonant fourth:

(2) As the resolution of a suspended seventh ($\overline{6}$), which as passing-note forms a fourth with the bass:

(3) Simultaneously with the resolution of a suspended seventh:

(4) As the result of passing-notes:

(5) Formed by an anticipation:

Many other examples might be cited.

§ 231. It is difficult to assume that these tonal combinations, known in modern harmony as six-four chords, were regarded as such by the masters of the strict style. There also appeared a number of other effects that are now analysed as secondary seventh-chords, ninth-chords, etc., but which in the period considered were not designated by any terms, nor understood as situations that could be classified according to the rules of any system or theory. In only one case can a ''six-four''chord—or more accurately, a dissonant fourth—be regarded as a departure from the normal usage of the strict style. This is when it is used as a preparing chord. Here the dual nature of the fourth is evident, as it functions as a consonance though really a dissonance. Entering as a syncopation, usually by conjunct movement, the fourth on an unaccented beat plays the part of a preparing consonance.* On the accented beat following it is understood as a dissonance, and accordingly resolves one degree downward. Such use of fourths, whereby a ''six-four'' chord is obtained at the moment of resolution, is a special effect intended by the composer, and is exceptional inasmuch as it ignores the conditions under which suspensions are ordinarily employed. Following are some examples of this use of the ''six-four'' chord:

*Cf. Bellermann, ''Der Kontrapunkt,'' 4-te Auf., s. 200.

Tonal Combination Resulting from the Duplication of Suspensions;
Their Importance for the Development of Harmonic Technique

§ 232. In two-voice counterpoint there is of course no difficulty about holding the free note during the resolution of a suspension. Such is the normal treatment of the free note; the more exceptional treatment is when it progresses to another note at the moment of resolution. But when duplicated in imperfect consonances situations are encountered where the note to which the dissonance resolves forms a dissonance with another voice. When this happens, either the free note progresses to a note consonant with the note of resolution, or else the latter continues in conjunct movement. These and other cases result in various harmonic combinations.

Taking, for example, the dissonance of the seventh at the duplication $I^{d=\,-9}\,+$

$II^{d=\,-9}$ (§ 225): 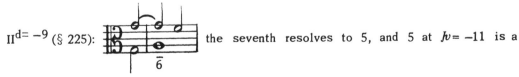 the seventh resolves to 5, and 5 at $J\!v=\,-11$ is a

variable consonance; therefore at the moment of resolution it yields dissonant harmony. Consequently either the free note must progress at the moment of resolution to a note consonant with the other voices:

or the free note is held and the other voices continue one degree downward from the note of resolution:

or the note of resolution progresses one degree upward, so that the progression of the free note forms the resolution of an auxiliary dissonance:

or finally, a new dissonance is formed by the free note at the moment of resolution and in turn resolves according to rule:

Hence a considerable variety of harmonic combinations is possible when dissonant chords are formed by the methods described. Chords interconnect—one progresses to another—and a valid, durable harmonic texture results thereby; it is the logical result of applying the rules of two-voice counterpoint that refer to suspensions.

The introduction of these dissonances—also variable consonances—in exercises with duplications provides, therefore, the means of developing not only contrapuntal skill, but to an important extent harmonic technique also, as it enriches harmony to an extent inaccessible by other methods.

There are other harmonic effects where dissonant chords are obtained not only at the place where the suspension sounds, but also at the resolution; they result from the parallel motion of the voices in imperfect consonances:

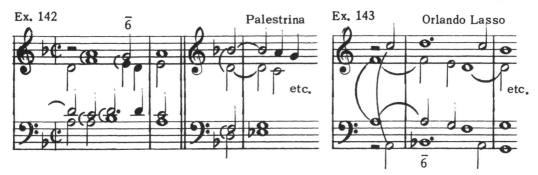

These are best mastered by the continued study of exercises in duplication, using variable consonances and suspensions.

§ 233. There is a very important problem as to the use of suspensions and imperfect consonances that hitherto has escaped the attention of theorists. It is customary in teaching counterpoint to pass in silence the possibility of applying these intervals in cases where they might be used and to limit the accented beats to certain fixed consonances. In the examples in duplication cited by Zarlino tied intervals—dissonances and variable consonances—are entirely absent. Zarlino throws no light on the subject, as he fails to isolate the problem, confusing it with the use of variable sixths and sevenths in double counterpoint at the twelfth.* In their treatment of duplications Fux, in his *Gradus ad Parnassum*, and Marpurg, in his *Abhandlung von der Fuge*, allow a fixed consonance on accented beats and exclude the sixth and all suspensions. Most later theorists were too concerned in supporting Marpurg—repeating what he said and quoting the same examples. Marpurg's authority was thereby confirmed, as though the absence of suspensions were a necessary condition when imperfect consonances are duplicated. The fallacy of this attitude must be shown, for his treatment of duplication is not only meaningless but he closes the way of approach to those combinations which in a high degree are useful for the development of harmonic technique.

§ 234. Exercises in two-voice florid counterpoint contribute greatly to the development of this technique in the direction stated. In them the pupil for the first time encounters the situations described, where suspensions are resolved to notes that are dissonant in relation to the implied harmony. In this connection it may be of interest to consult Bellermann, *Der Contrapunkt*, 4th edition, pp. 227-37 and 266-8.

§ 235. Mention has been made of the significance for the development of harmonic technique of the application in multi-voice counterpoint of those suspensions wherein a note, dissonant in relation to one voice, forms at the resolution a new dissonance with the other voice, forcing the latter to pass into consonant harmony, with the result that various resolutions of dissonant harmony are obtained. Theorists, in excluding dissonances and variable consonances from these two-voice combinations that admit of duplication, thereby eliminate the very combinations that are of most value in improving harmonic technique. Not only this, but some writers make the assertion that these forms of resolution are entirely forbidden in the strict style. Fétis, for instance, in his *Traite du contrepoint et de la Fugue* (2nd edition, part I, pp. 51-2) says that consonant chords only are the basis of the strict style; he therefore allows only those suspensions that resolve to a note consonant with the other voices, for example:

---

*Cf. footnote. § 151.

as if only such suspensions as these could at the moment of resolution be followed by another chord:

Those cases where the changing of the chord at the moment of resolution appears obligatory, owing to the fact that had the voices remained stationary the resolution would have formed dissonant harmony, he rejects as wrong. According to this the following harmonies: (a) the seventh with the third and fifth, (b) the fifth and sixth with the third, and (c) the second with the fourth and sixth:

are rejected as "inadmissable dans le contrepoint simple." He also states that such instances are not found in the literature of the period and quotes a solitary example from Palestrina, calling it a mistake. This is what he says:

"All these circumstances have probably been noticed by the composers who preceded the invention of modern tonality and the use of natural dissonances. for *one cannot find examples of these harmonies in their works.** The following, an excerpt from the *Hymn of the Martyrs* of Palestrina, is the *only one* (!) in which I have found the harmony of the third, fifth and sixth, but his *resolution has the defect that I shall indicate,** and one must regard this example only as *a mistake on the part of the great master.* The passage follows:"

These statements of the French theorist can with entire justice be flatly contradicted. The composers of the era preceding our tonal system did not hold such views, and the progression criticized by Fétis was not considered a mistake. The assertion that such progressions cannot be found in their compositions, and that the one cited from Palestrina is unique cannot possibly be substantiated—they are often found. In addition to several already quoted in other connections[**] that illustrate the progression forbidden by Fétis, a

---

*The italics here and in later quotations are mine. —S. T.

**Cf. the following from Palestrina: Exs. 39, 45, 46, 47, 131, 136; from de Pres: Ex. 43; from Orlando Lasso, Ex. 56.

series of several more are herewith quoted from Vol. 1 of Ambros' History of Music. These examples illustrate in particular the harmony of the third, fifth and sixth that Fétis calls a mistake of Palestrina.

It is freely admitted that considering the extensive literature of the period Fétis may not have come across the works from which these examples are taken. Turning now to a well-known composition, Palestrina's *Missa Papae Marcelli*, a statement in regard to it is available. In his *Biographie universelle des musiciens*, article on Palestrina, Fétis says:

"Few historic monuments of art present so much interest for study as this mass dedicated to Pope Marcellus, for it marks one of those rare epochs when genius, over-leaping the obstacles by which the spirit of his times was surrounded, suddenly opens up an undiscovered vista which it takes with giant strides . . . With regard to the technique—the purity of the harmony, the simple and natural voice-leading within the range of each, the melodic conduct of six parts with all the combinations known to scientific composition, in the narrow range of two and one—half octaves—*all this, I say, is above praise; it is the despair of whoever has seriously studied the mechanics and the difficulties of the art of writing.*"

And in this mass, the merit of which, according to Fétis himself, is "above praise," on the very first page, extending twelve measures from measure 7, are found the same progressions which in his opinion must be called mistakes of Palestrina—namely these "erreurs de se grand maitre:"

Ex. 156   Palestrina

Such, according to Fetis, are the "inadmissable" cases that are of frequent occurrence in the strict style, and which are found not only in those compositions of Palestrina cited by Fétis in Part I of his book as exemplary models,* but even in his own examples, for instance in measure 2 of the first example on page 54:

and in measure 11 of the five-voice example on page 84:

---

*P. 123 (last measure), p. 127 (m. 9), p. 132 (m. 6), p. 135 (last m.) p. 136 (m. 3), p. 139 (m. 18).

It is not hard to find a more or less plausible explanation of how the distinguished theorist came to fall into such contradiction. The study of strict counterpoint begins, of course, with two-voice writing in the first species (note against note), from which dissonant intervals are excluded altogether. Therefore Fétis concluded that the beginning of the strict style established a basic principle. This idea, expanded to include consonant chords, offered a simple explanation of the difference between the strict and free styles: the former, based on consonant harmony as opposed to contemporary harmony, which allows the independent use of dissonant chords. This generalization, concerning only the first species of strict counterpoint, was adopted as a guiding principle for the entire domain of the strict style. From this basic assumption Fétis drew the furthest inferences, not noticing that the laws he deduced were in opposition to the musical literature of the period he was dealing with. It is not surprising that the first attempt to verify these situations by reference to the classic composers ended unsuccessfully; Fétis found in Palestrina a harmony that contradicted his theoretical assumptions. But this failure did not raise any doubts as to the correctness of his theory, nor prevent him from continuing to verify it to his own satisfaction. He preferred to attribute this one instance to a lapse on the part of Palestrina, and presumably abandoned further investigation. Nothing else can explain how he came to regard this one example as unique when, as has been shown, such examples are to be found in abundance.

There is a further significance about the basic principles of the strict style as understood by Fétis. In a reference on page 81 he says, a propos the obscure matter of suspensions: "these considerations throw a bright light upon the origin and classification of secondary seventh-chords."*

An inconsistent judgment can do much harm when sanctioned by authority. Much space has therefore been given to a refutation of Fétis' statements, though in other regards his treatment of the subject is a valuable contribution to theoretical literature.

§ 236. In approaching vertical-shifting counterpoint from these various angles the first result is the possibility that double counterpoint at the twelfth may become more familiar. Counterpoint at this interval, so important in this period of both Palestrina and Bach, in now passing into disuse. This is due both to lack of cooperation on the part of teachers of composition and to the superficiality which ignores the technique of the preceding era. For example Marx, in the fourth edition of his *Kompositionlehre*, presents double counterpoint only at the octave. The previous editions were no better in this regard, and the author attempts to justify his lack of thoroughness by referring to counterpoint at other intervals as a weakness to which he is determined not to yield.* But such an opinion as to complex counterpoint by one of the most authoritative theorists of the nineteenth century cannot be regarded as binding on his successors; his lack of cooperation has only impoverished contemporary contrapuntal technique.

To raise their technique to the level of the preceding era means that composers of the present day should face the problems involved and act accordingly. Here the right course to follow is indicated by Beethoven, whose later works show a striking novelty and originality, due to a return to the older contrapuntal methods. The way in which he used

---

*E.g., cf.

*"He [the author] will not deny that the appearance of completeness has been carefully avoided. To retain worthless details against the reproach of incompleteness is only a weakness to which the author will not yield." (PP. 595-6)

these resources is illustrated in the first movement of his Sonata Op. 106, where he has a two-voice imitation in double counterpoint at the twelfth:

Later it occurs with both voices duplicated, first in tenths, then in thirds. Counterpoint at the same interval is used in the second section of the fugue from the Sonata Op. 110. The following examples are from the Finale to the C♯ minor Quartet Op. 131, showing double counterpoint at $Jv = -4, -14, -18$:

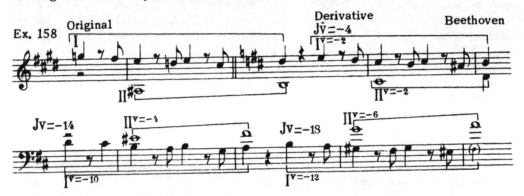

Later uses of these indices:

Modern music offers plenty of opportunity for the use of counterpoint at those indices which in the strict style are only found exceptionally, i.e., $Jv = \pm 1, \pm 6, -8, -13$. Counterpoint at these indices, troublesome in the strict style because they easily give augmented fourths in the melody and also because the abundance of variable consonances requires rigid observance of numerous conditions, loses its difficulty in contemporary music owing to the unrestricted use of chromatics and free dissonances. This opens up a vast expanse of unexplored territory, large enough to satisfy any modern composer in his striving for originality. Here again Beethoven points the way, with a use of vertical-shifting counterpoint that differs but little from the usual. In the following passage from the Missa

Solemnis, Op. 123 is found the application to free writing of counterpoint at the seventh: $Jv = 6$ (if one of the voices of the derivative is brought an octave lower, $Jv = 1$):

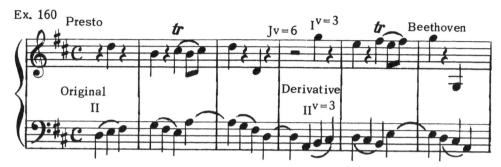

Ex. 160   Presto $Jv = 6$ $I^{v=3}$ Beethoven

Original
II

Derivative
$II^{v=3}$

(The original combination admits of the duplications $I^{d=-16} + II$, $I^{d=2} + II$, and $I^{d=2} + II^{d=-2}$).

It may be said that the same intervals which were most carefully avoided in the era of the strict style—the augmented fourth and diminished fifth—are the ones that in contemporary counterpoint are often the chief cause of strange and unusual harmonic combination. Reference can be made, for instance, to a shift of the lower voice at a diminished fifth, to be found in Glinka's *Kamarinskoi:*

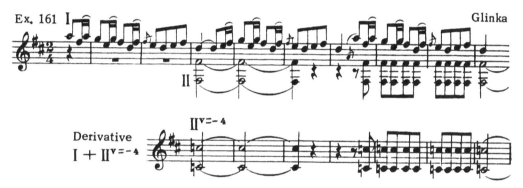

Ex. 161   I   Glinka

II

Derivative $II^{v=-4}$
$I + II^{v=-4}$

In Ex. 162 the augmented fourth (and its enharmonic equivalent the diminished fifth) is used as the motive for the two voices that shift, with the upper voice as soprano ostinato; a style of writing often found in the works of the Russian composers.

Rimsky-Korsakow

Ex. 162

An interesting example of a ground-motive shifting a second above while the upper voices are repeated without change is found in the Finale of Tschaikowsky's Second Symphony:

Ex. 163   Tschaikowsky

The last two examples are in three-voice vertical-shifting counterpoint, the detailed study of which, applied to the strict style, will be the subject of Division B.

DIVISION B

THREE-VOICE VERTICAL-SHIFTING COUNTERPOINT

THREE-VOICE VERTICAL-SHIFTING COUNTERPOINT

CHAPTER XI

THEORY OF THE TECHNIQUE
OF THREE-VOICE VERTICAL-SHIFTING COUNTERPOINT

Preliminaries

§ 237. The next problem is the study of those three-voice combinations that yield derivatives as a result of shifting the voices vertically. Such counterpoint will be termed three-voice vertical-shifting. A necessary condition is the presence in the derivative of all three melodies of the original. If, therefore, one melody appears that was not in the original, even though the other two shift, the whole texture will be termed two-voice vertical-shifting counterpoint, not three-voice. Various relations are possible, involving either the direct or the inverse shift, or both. The derivative may show the result of shifting one voice:

Ex. 164

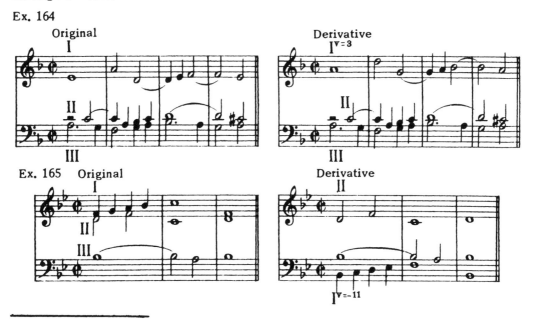

*Voice II is shifted an octave lower; this shift is indicated $II^{v=\pm7}$ (cf. § 241).

or of two at the same time:

Ex. 166 ·· Original

Derivative

Every combination that represents a shift of all three voices may be so transferred to other degrees that one voice does not appear to be shifted. Conversely, every derivative in which one or two voices have not shifted, as in the preceding examples, may be transferred to other degrees so that all three voices show a vertical shift. The various relationships in which a derivative may stand to its original, due to the possibility of transferring the derivative to other degrees, involves the uniting of indices, a matter requiring detailed treatment.

§ 238. An original combination may have one or several derivatives. An example of counterpoint giving several derivatives may illustrate the so-called triple counterpoint at the octave. Its derivatives show the result of shifting the voices to other octaves, and any voice may function as upper, middle, or lower part. Most textbooks, in applying to three-voice counterpoint the process called in this book the vertical shift, do so only to the extent of giving triple counterpoint at the octave, a knowledge of which, together with quadruple counterpoint at the octave, is generally regarded as necessary for a basic technique in counterpoint. The present work goes further, and applies the shift at $Jv = -11$, i.e. double counterpoint at the twelfth, as also necessary. In general, double counterpoint at the twelfth, as stated at the end of Division A, claims consideration on the ground that earlier usages, significant for the technique of composition, may thereby be restored. Several phases of its application will be dealt with separately. If to the shifts in double counterpoint at the octave and twelfth is added the shift at $Jv = -9$, making possible the duplication of voices, together with what has already been given in Chapter X, the resources of three-voice vertical-shifting counterpoint are almost exhausted. What remain are some combinations that have not been fully studied and others not investigated at all and still untried. Three-voice vertical-shifting counterpoint, within the limits indicated, is one of the most difficult phases of the whole subject of complex counterpoint. It has reference more to the virtuoso aspect of contrapuntal technique, and the skill necessary for its mastery means the meeting of almost innumerable requirements. The approach to learning it can only be by way of a firm grasp of two-voice vertical-shifting counterpoint.

§ 239. Also, the rules of simple counterpoint for more than two voices are only a further development of those governing two voices, in the same way that vertical-shifting counterpoint for two voices is the basis for the vertical shift in some parts. An original multi-voice combination must be dissected into two-voice combinations, implying that each voice must combine with any other. In finding the index for each of the resulting combinations the possibility of explaining the conditions that must satisfy the original multi-voice combination will be obtained. To increase the number of voices in simple counterpoint means that changes must be inserted into the rules covering two parts, and in the same way the rules for two-voice vertical-shifting counterpoint undergo analogous changes when these two-voice combinations are parts of a multi-voice texture. Therefore the problems to be investigated are: the ways in which three-voice combinations differ from those in two; the relations between the indices of these two-voice combinations, and the nature of the changes that have to be inserted in the rules for these indices, owing to the fact that a two-voice combination is part of a larger one. But first it is necessary to explain how the voices and their shifts are indicated.

Notation of Voices and Shifts

§ 240. A voice of a three-voice combination will be indicated according to its position as highest, inner, or lowest voice, figure I, II, III respectively. The sign + unites these figures, showing that the voices represented form a contrapuntal union. Therefore the formula for the original combination is: I + II + III.

§ 241. The shifting of the outer voices (highest I, lowest III) will be indicated as in two-voice counterpoint, i.e. the shift of the highest voice upward and of the lowest downward are regarded as positive operations and indicated by the plus sign; the shift of the same voices in the opposite direction are negative operations, indicated by the minus sign. As regards the middle voice (II) there is a double interpretation, according to its relation to the other voices. Therefore a shift of the middle voice will be indicated by the use of both the plus and minus signs, placed one under the other, the upward shift by the sign $\mp$, the downward shift by $\pm$. The upper part of the sign refers to the union of voice II with voice I, the lower to its union with voice III. For example, the expression $I^{v=-9} + II^{v=\pm3} + III^{v=-5}$ means that voice I shifts a tenth below, II a fourth below, and III a sixth above. $I^{v=0} + II^{v=\mp8} + III^{v=0}$ means that the middle voice shifts a ninth above, and I and III remain unshifted. If separate combinations of voice II with either I or III are taken (I + II or II + III), one sign for voice II is sufficient, referring to its union with whichever outer voice is given. For example, the shift of a fourth below for voice II would be indicated either $I + II^{v=3}$ or $II^{v=-3} + III$. The shifting of the voices may be represented by this diagram:

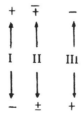

§ 242. In solving multi-voice problems in vertical-shifting counterpoint the combination must be analysed into its components, each of two voices, so that any voice may appear in relationship with each of the other voices (§ 239). In three-voice counterpoint there are three such pairs of combinations: I + II, II + III and I + III. For each of these combinations it is necessary to find the index which, according to § 27, equals the algebraic sum of the shifts of both voices. The shift of the middle voice will take a double designation (§ 241), of which the upper sign indicates the union of II with I, the lower sign the union of II with III.

The Indices Jv' Jv'' $Jv\Sigma$ and Their Relationships

§ 243. The index for the combination I + II will be indicated by Jv'; for II + III, Jv''. The third index, retering to the union of the outer voices, I + III, is always equal to the sum of the first two indices.* It will be indicated: $Jv\Sigma$, the Greek sigma standing for "sum". As an example of the relationship described, take the derivative: $I^{v=a} + II^{v=\pm b} + III^{v=c}$. In the first two indices ($Jv' + Jv''$) the quantity b enters into the equation with both positive and negative signs; these cancel each other and the result is $a + c$, the index for the combination I + III.

$$(I^{v=a} \quad + II^{v=b})\, Jv' = a + b$$
$$(II^{v=-b} + III^{v=c})\, Jv'' = \quad -b + c$$
$$(I^{v=a} \quad + III^{v=c})\, Jv\Sigma = a + c$$

Problem: To find the indices for the derivative $I^{v=-10} + II^{v=\pm 5} + III^{v=3}$:

$$(I^{v=-10} + II^{v=5})\, Jv' = -5$$
$$(II^{v=-5} + III^{v=3})\, Jv'' = -2$$
$$(I^{v=-10} + III^{v=3})\, Jv\Sigma = -7$$

§ 244. The correlation of indices is expressed by the equation:

$$Jv' + Jv'' = Jv\Sigma$$

Determining the value of each term of the equation:

$$Jv' = Jv\Sigma - Jv''$$
$$Jv'' = Jv\Sigma - Jv'$$
$$Jv\Sigma = Jv' + Jv''$$

Hence it follows that: (1) a derivative can take only two indices, the third is not obtained independently; (2) one of the indices may equal 0; (3) all three indices may equal 0; (4) two indices can not equal 0 except on condition that the third index also equals 0.

---

*It should be observed that this refers to the index of a single derivative, not to an index that unites the conditions of several derivatives. In the latter case it is not necessary to indicate the correlation between indices (cf. Obs. to § 281).

§ 245. In finding the three indices for a given combination it is possible, without changing their values, to substitute other numbers for the vv of the separate voices. The series of intervals for each derivative will remain the same, though a voice may be transferred to other degrees. For example, for $I^{v=-2} + II^{v=\pm9} + III^{v=-2}$ may be substituted $I^{v=0} + II^{v=\pm7} + III^{v=-4}$, since in both cases the values of the indices are identical; that is, the algebraic sum of each pair of voices remains unchanged: $Jv' = 7, Jv'' = -11, Jv\Sigma = -4.$

§ 246. Whatever indices there are, any voices of the derivative may remain unshifted, that is, can be taken at $v=0$. In the preceding section, for instance, the highest voice remains, and the vv of the other voices would be indicated: $I^{v=0} + II^{v=\pm7} + III^{v=-4}$.

If the middle voice remains unshifted the derivative combination will be: $I^{v=7} + II^{v=0} + III^{v=-11}$. Here as in other cases JJv remains without change, the derivative shifting to other degrees.

§ 247. If all three indices are numerically equal but cancel each other by opposite signs so that the result is 0, various shifts may be assumed; for instance $I^{v=-3} + II^{v=\pm3} + III^{v=3}$; $I^{v=5} + II^{v=\mp5} + III^{v=-5}$ etc. The result of such shifts is a series of combinations identical with the original. In this way every recurrence of an original combination or its transferrence to other degrees, the intervals between the voices remaining constant, may represent a shift at indices equal to zero. This, and simple counterpoint in general, is only a special case of the vertical shift.

§ 248. As in the two-voice examples, the crossing of voices will be avoided in both the original and derivative combinations, therefore each index can show either the direct or the inverse shift. This enables the voices of the derivative to be disposed in any one of six ways; these permutations may be represented as follows:

(1)   (2)   (3)   (4)   (5)   (6)
I ——— I   I   II   I ——— I   I   III   I   II   I   III
II ——— II   II   I   II   III   II   I   II   III   II   II
III ——— III III ——— III III   II   III   II   III   I   III   I

In each diagram the numbers on the left refer to the location of the voices in the original combination, those on the right the location of the same voices in the derivative. Each number on the right is connected by a line with the same number on the left. A line crossing another means that the corresponding voice has the inverse shift; if the lines do not cross the shift is direct. It must be observed that these diagrams illustrate only the process of shifting, not the final result of the shift itself. For example, in diagram (2) voices I and II take the inverse shift, and this is all the diagram is intended to represent. The same applies to the other diagrams, their purpose is only to show the different locations of the voices. The diagrams are abbreviated thus:

(1)   (2)   (3)   (4)   (5)   (6)

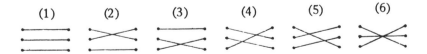

The dots to the left refer to the positions of the voices in the original, those on the right to the same voices in the derivative. For instance, the disposition of voices in Ex. 164 would be represented by diagram (1):   ; in Ex. 165 by diagram (5):   ; in Ex. 166 by diagram (3):

The following table shows how the signs for the shifts (§ 23) are applied to each index, for all six diagrams:

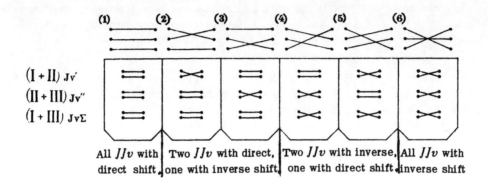

In working out exercises attention must first be given as to which one of the six diagrams the disposition of voices in the derivative shall conform. Stating the problem more definitely, the arrangement of voices in the derivative must be decided upon, and for the shifting of the voices, those intervals not chosen that would bring about the mixed shift, or cause a shifting voice to approach too closely to another that does not shift, or cause them to recede too far apart.

§ 249. Three-voice vertical-shifting counterpoint may be regarded as a union of three two-voice combinations: I + II, II + III and I + III, represented by the indices Jv', Jv'' and $Jv\Sigma$. Each pair of voices must conform to the rules of the corresponding index, i.e. it must satisfy the conditions of two-voice vertical-shifting counterpoint, but some changes must be inserted into these conditions, owing to the fact that two-voice counterpoint is here a constituent of three-voice.

§ 250. These changes consist, first, in allowing the use of certain hidden consecutives. The possibility of doing this relaxes the strict rules by which similar motion at indices of the second group (^2JJv) was forbidden. Between two voices combined according to a ^2Jv the hidden progressions (similar motion to fixed perfect consonances) which are forbidden in simple counterpoint may be freely used in the original combination.

§ 251. Secondly, into the conditions of two-voice counterpoint to which the pairs of voices in three-voice counterpoint must conform, there is incorporated a series of changes that are the result of the different uses of the ninth and fourth in multi-voice counterpoint. This difference, as has already been stated, consists in the fact that multi-voice counterpoint, as compared to two-voice, imposes on the ninth only the limitation that this interval ($\overline{8}$ or $-\underline{8}$) is not allowed except where the bass voice is concerned. Therefore in three-voice counterpoint the necessary condition for the union of upper and middle voices is $\overset{\frown}{8}$ and $-\underline{8}$. As for the other interval, the fourth, the opposite holds good. The fourth, when occurring between the same two voices, is released from the limitations of a tied dissonance and may be used correctly as an imperfect consonance (3 instead of $\overline{3}$). These are conditions of simple counterpoint; in complex counterpoint they must be observed both with reference to the original and derivative combinations. Hence for each of these two intervals there arises two rules which for convenience will be indicated by the first four letters of the alphabet: Rules A and B will secure correctness in the use of the original and derivative ninth, Rules C and D for the original and derivative fourth.

I. Rules for Ninths

§ 252. As regards the use of ninths in the original combination, there results from the rules of simple counterpoint, forbidding $\overline{8}$ in I + II, the following rule of complex counterpoint:

Rule A *(for original ninths)*.— $\overset{\leftarrow}{8}$ is a condition obligatory for every Jv'.

§ 253. Correct use of ninths in the derivative is secured by the next rule:

Rule B *(for derivative ninths)*.— For an index referring to those voices which in the derivative function as upper and middle the sign (−) is obligatory for that m which gives the derivative ninth (i.e. which gives $n= \overline{8}$ or $n= -\underline{8}$). If Jv has the direct shift the sign must be placed above: $\overset{\leftarrow}{m}$; if the inverse shift, below: $\underset{\leftarrow}{m}$.

Therefore in applying Rule B it is necessary to take into consideration the shift—direct or inverse—of that Jv to which the rule refers. The following table shows this index for each of the six diagrams, also those in which m, giving a derivative ninth, takes the sign (−) above, and which below:

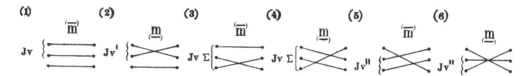

Hence it is seen that for diagrams (1) and (2) rule B refers to Jv'; for (5) and (6) to Jv''; for (3) and (4) to $Jv\Sigma$. A positive derivative ninth appears in the odd-numbered diagrams, in these the required condition is $\overset{\leftarrow}{m}$; the ninth in the even-numbered diagrams is negative, condition $\underset{\leftarrow}{m}$.

§ 254. In the following table is shown, for each index, the original interval that gives $n= \overline{8}$ or $n= -\underline{8}$.

Table of Supplementary Conditions Inserted into Rule B

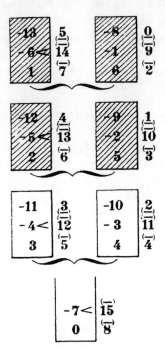

II. Rules for Fourths

§ 255. The rules for ninths were interdictory, since they imposed new limitations. In three-voice simple counterpoint consonant fourths are allowed between the upper and middle voices, though in general the treatment of fourths is similar to that of dissonances. If in three-voice vertical-shifting counterpoint only the rules are used that impose the limitations of two-voice, while the rules that release fourths from these limitations are not drawn upon, no errors will result, but to do this will deprive three-voice counterpoint of many advantages. This releasing of original and derivative fourths from their limitations adds many resources, especially with reference to some of the difficult indices, as will be seen presently.

§ 256. Rule C (*for original fourths*).—If an original fourth of an index that refers to a combination of the upper and middle voices (i.e. Jv') gives n equal to a consonance, this fourth is released from its limitations (3 and 10 instead of $\overline{3}$ and $\overline{10}$) and may be used correctly as a consonance. This fourth, indicated by the letter p. (i.e. giving n equal to a perfect consonance), is subject to the limitations of the latter. The conditions are expressed by the figures 3 and 10, to which the letter p. is added, deleting at the same time the tie-sign ($\overset{p.}{3}$ and $\overset{p.}{10}$ instead of $\overline{3}$ and $\overline{10}$).

§ 257. In the following table are given those indices at which the fourth yields a consonance (except a consonant fourth) in the derivative. The figures 3 and 10 to the right of each column, all without tie-signs, indicate that the corresponding intervals may be used as consonances; the sign p. means that the interval is subject to the limitations of a perfect consonance. These figures should be substituted for the same figure in the table for each index when this index applies to three-voice vertical-shifting counterpoint at the Jv' concerned.

Changes Inserted into Rule C

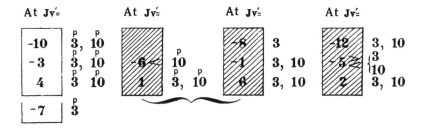

In this table the indices that have the direct shift apply in the Jv' concerned to diagrams (1), (3) and (5); those having the inverse shift to diagrams (2), (4) and (6).

The following examples illustrate cases of where original fourths are released from limitations, therefore of changes in Rule C.

Ex. 167

Ex. 168

Ex. 169

In each of these examples notice the fourths in the original, and the consonances obtained from them in the derivative. In Exs. 167, 168, 170 and 172 these consonances are perfect; in Ex. 169 and 171 imperfect, hence the possibility of parallel consonant fourths in the original of Ex. 171.

§ 258. To the indices listed in the preceding section must be added three more: $Jv' = 0$, $Jv' = -6 >$ and $Jv' = -13$. They all refer to one diagram, that of the indices at which a fourth in the original yields a fourth also in the derivative. Since fourths in any case can be consonant only when appearing between the upper and middle voices, the latter, the union of which each of these JJv refers to, must remain upper and middle. A positive derivative fourth is obtained from an original at $Jv = 0$, and corresponding to this, also at $Jv = 7$ and $Jv = -7 <$. Since these diagrams have the direct shift, they must, in order to satisfy the above condition, be used with diagram (1): Jv' {═══════}

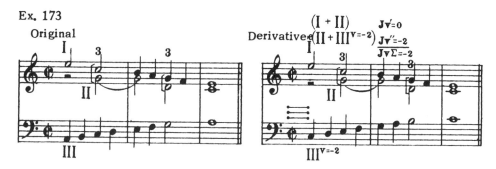

Ex. 173

A negative fourth can be obtained in the derivative according to diagram

(2): Jv' [⟩⟨] , where the voices concerned still remain upper and middle. In this case the required indices are $Jv' = -6 >$ and $Jv' = -13$.

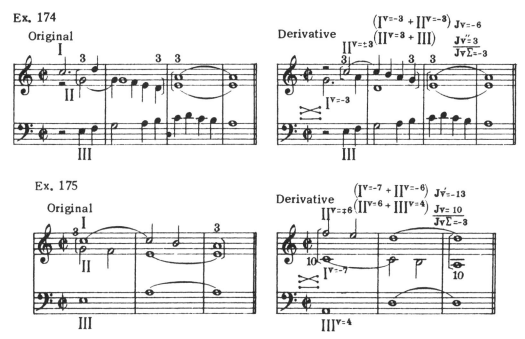

Ex. 174

Ex. 175

§ 259. Rule D, of which the object is the releasing of derivative fourths from the limitations of dissonances, refers, like Rule 3, to the two voices that in the derivative remain upper and middle (cf. table of diagrams, § 253).

Rule D *(for derivative fourths)*.—If at an index referring to the voices which in the derivative remain upper and middle (either ^1Jv or ^2Jv), from $m =$ consonance is obtained $n = \pm 3$ or $n = \pm 10$, then m is released from the sign required by the obligations of n. It becomes a fixed consonance, used in accordance with the rules of simple counterpoint. Therefore if m is an imperfect consonance, parallel progressions of this consonance are possible, and ipse facto, parallel motion at an index of the second group (^2Jv). A dissonance resolving to m loses the supplementary sign ×, since m becomes a fixed consonance.

In Ex. 167 the original third in the second measure: gives in the derivative a consonant fourth: at $Jv'= 1$. Therefore the rule requires that

a change be made in the table for this index: instead of $2\underset{\times}{\overset{\times}{3}}$ to substitute $2\overset{p\cdot}{3}$. In Ex. 171 the derivative fourth (10) between the upper and middle voices is obtained from a third (9) also at $Jv = 1$, in the table for which must be made the same substitution. Since the original consonance is imperfect its use in a parallel progression is possible, as in the first measure of Ex. 171, also the proximity of two of these consonances (mm. 2 and 3).

§ 260. A list is herewith given of those indices at which a derivative fourth is obtained from a consonance, hence its release from the tie-sign, i.e. it becomes fixed. Alongside of these consonances are the dissonances of which they are the resolutions. Since the consonance is now fixed, the dissonance that resolves to it loses the sign ×.

Changes Inserted into Rule D

$$Jv = \;\; \boxed{\;\; 3 \;\;}\;\; 0,\,7 \;\mid\; \overset{p}{\underline{8}}$$

$$\boxed{\begin{array}{l} -10 \\ -\;3 > \end{array}}\;\; \begin{array}{l} 0,\,7 \\ 0 \end{array} \;\mid\; \underset{-\times}{\overline{8}}$$

$$\boxed{\;-\;7\;}\;\; 4 \;\mid\; \overset{p}{\underline{3}}$$

$$\boxed{\;\;\;1\;\;\;}\;\; 2\quad 9 \;\mid\; \overset{(-)}{\underline{1}}\quad \overset{p}{\underline{3}}\quad \overset{p}{\underline{10}}$$

$$\boxed{\begin{array}{l} -\;8 \\ -\;1 \end{array}}\;\; \begin{array}{l} 5 \\ 4 \end{array} \;\mid\; \begin{array}{l} \underset{(-)}{\overline{6}} \\ \underset{-\times}{\underline{3}} \end{array}$$

$$\boxed{\begin{array}{l} -12 \\ -\;5 > \end{array}}\;\; \begin{array}{l} 2\quad 9 \\ 2 \end{array} \;\mid\; \begin{array}{ll} \overset{p}{\underset{(-)}{\underline{1}}} & \overset{p}{\underline{8}} \\ \overset{p}{\underset{(-)}{\underline{1}}} & \underset{-\times}{\overline{3}} \end{array}$$

$$\boxed{\begin{array}{l} -\;2 \\ \;\;\;5 \end{array}}\;\; \begin{array}{l} 5,\,12 \\ 5 \end{array} \;\mid\; \begin{array}{ll} \overset{p}{\underset{(-)}{\underline{6}}} & \overset{p}{\underset{(-)}{\underline{13}}} \\ \overset{p}{\underset{(-)}{\underline{6}}} \end{array}$$

Obs.–Numerous illustrations of changes in the tables of indices will be found in the twelve examples of Appendix B. To master thoroughly all the rules of three-voice vertical-shifting counterpoint one should make an exhaustive analysis of these examples and of the application to them of the tables.

§ 261. From a consideration of all these changes that two-voice counterpoint undergoes when it enters into the structure of multi-voice counterpoint, it is apparent that in the latter a union of the bass with any higher part differs but little from independent two-voice counterpoint. The only difference consists in the possibility of hidden consecutives, which in two-voice independent counterpoint are reduced to a minimum, if not entirely excluded. As for the other two-voice combinations that can be extracted from multi-voice counterpoint, that is, those from which the bass is absent, in addition to the use of hidden consecutives is added the possibility of the independent use of fourths as valid consonances.

Multi-Voice Counterpoint as Developed from Two-Voice; Verification of Multi-voice Combinations by Two-Voice

§ 262. To regard multi-voice counterpoint as the union of various combinations of two-voice counterpoint, and to accept this fact as a basic principle of the strict style, will mean a clearer understanding of the numerous complexities found in this province of composition.* From this principle may be deduced both the conditions of simple multi-voice counterpoint, beginning with the first species, and the conditions of complex counterpoint in all of its many phases. To say that the first species of multi-voice counterpoint yields concords in the form of triads and first inversions is to employ the terminology of harmony, and to assume that these harmonies are used, while their cause remains unexplained. But it is sufficient to return to the principle mentioned, and to observe that any two voices extracted from the whole must make correct two-voice counterpoint. Only such chords as consist of consonant intervals (including the fourth between the upper and middle voices) can form 'the two-voice combinations that enter into the structure of multi-voice counterpoint. In this way they provide for the conditions of multi-voice counterpoint in other species than the first. But every attempt to apply the terminology borrowed from harmonic theory only obscures the issue. In all intricate situations the principle stated is the sole one to be applied. Only its continued use makes freedom and facility in voice-leading possible, qualities of which the acquisition would be attempted in vain by means of the guidance provided by rules and terms taken from the study of harmony. To understand fully the significance of the strict style it is necessary to grasp the idea that the wide diversity of effect is the result of applying the principle here discussed, and to assimilate the facts by a study of them in clear and definite order.

§ 263. Therefore, two-voice counterpoint is the basis of the strict style. To know its rules is to possess the key to the whole domain of strict counterpoint. In analysing the conditions of this dependence of the strict style on two-voice counterpoint one may not observe immediately that these conditions are very simple. The strict style employs melodic progressions that are simple and above all easily sung. Everything is rejected that makes melody difficult to sing or to understand. The intervals formed by the combination of two melodies are also subject to simple and natural conditions. The free use of consonances, together with the precautions that surround the use of dissonances, is seen not as the result of rules arbitrarily imposed but have a deep-seated origin in the

*Cf. Bellermann, "Der Contrapunkt," 4-te Auf., s. 200.

auditory mechanism of mankind. One need not be a musician in order to appreciate the fact that the resolutions, for instance, of fourths to thirds, or sevenths to sixths, are entirely satisfactory to the musical instinct, and on the contrary, that the forbidden resolutions of seconds to unisons and of sevenths to octaves are unsatisfactory. This instinctive understanding of the functions of intervals in two-voice counterpoint is retained when the number of voices is increased, and the rich and intricate effects attained that are characteristic of the strict style. It is all evolved from the simple basis of two-voice counterpoint. Each voice in a multi-voice texture enters with notes that are easily sung. It moves with freedom yet without confusion with the other voices. Each of the latter contributes to the correct intonation of the first voice, supporting it and receiving support. With no other voice does it enter into irreconcilable contradiction. If with another voice it forms a more or less sharp dissonance this is soon resolved, simply and naturally. Silent, a voice is not abruptly cut off, but the melody quietly subsides, leaving the other voices free. The result of this simple and natural voice-movement is a rich harmonic texture and an imaginative interweaving of parts. The independent movement of the voices generates various dissonant harmonies—secondary sevenths chords. ninth chords, passing chords etc.—with a great variety of resolutions, but such chord combinations are not an impediment to the free movement of the voices. Due to the simplicity on which it is based, counterpoint of the strict style is an art unique with symmetry, naturalness and logic as its foundations. All its infinite variety is but an evolution from the basis, easily comprehensible, of two-voice counterpoint.

Cases of Multi-Voice Combinations
not Verifiable by Two-Voice

§ 264. In formulating the principle under discussion, according to which multi-voice counterpoint appears as developed from two-voice, Bellermann puts forward this method of verification: Three-voice counterpoint must be equivalent to three two-voice combinations (I + II, II + III, I + III). If each of these combinations forms correct two-voice counterpoint (in which may be found the exceptions mentioned, hidden motion and the independent use of fourths) the entire combination is correct.

If verification could proceed solely by the method recommended by Bellermann, if it were applicable to all cases without exception and no corrections were required, the problem with reference to three-voice vertical-shifting counterpoint would be definitely solved. It has already been shown how to find the indices for all three pairs of the combined set, and the nature of the changes to be inserted into the conditions of these indices because of the fact that they now refer not to independent two-voice combinations but to those entering into the structure of multi-voice counterpoint. In three-voice counterpoint written at these conditions both the original and derivative confirm this method of verification, and if separated into three two-voice combinations no errors emerge. But, as has just been seen, this does not in all cases guarantee the correctness of all multi-voice counterpoint. Errors may still creep into the derivative, since Bellermann's method of verification does not correct unconditionally, and must be taken with certain reservations.

§ 265. There are two situations where the method of verification just described does not hold good. It does not guard against errors caused by violating the rule that forbids doubling of the dissonance in a suspension, and it condemns as incorrect certain progressions in which no errors appear, but in which the free notes to suspensions are doubled.

§ 266. *Case 1.*—As already known, the dissonant note in a suspension should not be doubled. Therefore all progressions are incorrect in which the bass, used as a suspended fourth ($\underline{3}$ or $\underline{10}$) is doubled by another voice; for example:

If any of these incorrect combinations is dissected into three of two voices, each one shows correct two-voice counterpoint; therefore the method of verification just mentioned can not serve as a criterion of correct three-voice combinations. Since the fault does not extend to any of the three two-voice combinations, regarded individually, it is clear that the insertion of any supplementary conditions into the indices controlling them can not prevent the possibility of faults appearing in the derivative. However, this possibility can be avoided. In approaching the solution of a given problem it is first of all necessary to obtain the original for each of these instances of wrong doubling. Then from these originals must be discarded (1) those that contradict the conditions of simple counterpoint (because such cases are not found in originals), and (2) those in which the distribution of the voices departs from the normal: $\begin{smallmatrix}I\\II\\III\end{smallmatrix}$ (since voice-crossing is avoided). The remaining cases not excluded, i.e. originals that employ the conditions of simple counterpoint and in which no voice-crossings occur, must be kept in mind while working out problems; in them must be avoided whatever degrees cause errors. In the foregoing illustrations (a), (b) and (c) have fourths between the upper and middle voices. Obviously, if the original interval is a consonance that releases these fourths from their limitations for no other reason than that they become consonant, then notwithstanding the presence of the consonance in the original, an incorrect derivative results.

§ 267. Therefore, in order to prevent the doubling of dissonant notes at the interval of the fourth, it is necessary to find, for each of the given combinations, the indices of the originals that give the faulty derivatives. There are various ways of doing this, one of which is herewith indicated. In each of the illuatrations (a) to (f), § 266, the voices are provided with numbers in accordance with whatever diagram shows their allocation in the derivative. For instance, if they are arranged according to diaragm (1): ▬▬, the voices take the order $\begin{smallmatrix}I\\II\\III\end{smallmatrix}$; if according to diagram (2): ✕ , the order $\begin{smallmatrix}II\\I\\III\end{smallmatrix}$, etc.

In each illustration one voice is kept stationary; this is numbered II, and voices I and II are shifted, using for voice I v equal to Jv' taken with the opposite sign, and for voice II v equal to Jv'', also taken with the opposite sign. In this way the original is obtained of which the derivative shows the combination of voices that were shifted.

Problem No. 10 in Appendix B may be taken as an example. The voices of the derivative are arranged according to diagram (5): ✕ , therefore their order in the derivative is $\begin{smallmatrix}II\\III\\I\end{smallmatrix}$. The six illustrations in § 266 are in this order. Since $Jv'= -14$, and $Jv''= 1$, then for voice II to remain stationary the other two voices are shifted thus: $I^v= 14$, $I^v= -1$; and the corresponding originals are obtained:

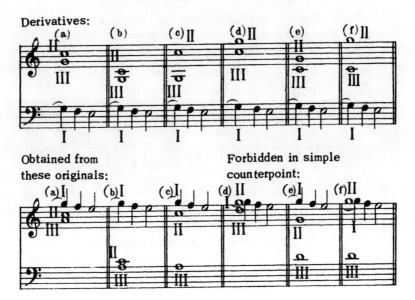

Derivatives:

Obtained from these originals:

Forbidden in simple counterpoint:

According to § 266, from the six originals found must be discarded (d), (e) and (f), because they violate the rules of simple counterpoint and double the dissonance (fourth from the bass). Moreover, (d) and (f) are useless because the voices are not arranged in normal order: $\frac{II}{I}$, crossing therefore results, which must be avoided. Three cases
III
remain: (a), (b) and (c), and these also are discarded. Correct usages are cited in No. 10, Appendix B.

§ 268. From the problems in Appendix B have been extracted all those original combinations that yield faulty derivatives; they are indicated by the same letters used in §§ 266-7, and refer to corresponding situations. The absence of these progressions in an original written according to the rules of the indices given will insure its correctness.

§ 269. *Case 2.*—Verification by dissecting three-voice counterpoint into three of two voices each also includes the following:

It is known that in suspensions in two voices a third voice may double the free note on the second half of beats, for example:

In the second and third measures the dissonance is formed on the accented beat between the voice suspended (the dissonance) and the whole-note (free note to the dissonance). The third voice, moving in quarter-notes, leaps to a note that doubles the free note (second quarter of the measure). If from this correct three-voice combination is taken one of two voices, consisting of the voice moving in quarters and that having the ties, such a combination, regarded as two-voice counterpoint, is incorrect, since the leap to the dissonance is not allowed, and can be justified only by the presence of the upper voice, which takes the note earlier in the measure, with the syncopated dissonance.

In the original combination such leaps are allowed in two instances. In the first a leap may be made to a note that forms a fixed consonance in relation to the free note and a variable dissonance in relation to the second note of the tie; in other words if the free note to which the voice progresses by leap is to appear in the derivative as a consonance to the two other voices; for example:

In the second, such a leap may be freely made where the voices represent only double counterpoint at the octave. Consequently, this leap is possible at all shifts in so-called triple counterpoint:

The cases examined in this section are of far less importance than the preceding ones. If in writing exercises what is here said about them is not used at all, no mistakes will arise in the derivative. But on the contrary, to neglect the first of the situations dealt with (§ 266) will involve the appearance in the derivative of progressions forbidden in the strict style.

CHAPTER XII

SPECIAL CASES OF THREE-VOICE
VERTICAL-SHIFTING COUNTERPOINT

§ 270. Up to this point only the general theory of three-voice vertical-shifting counterpoint has been dealt with. Before going on to the study of the original combinations
that yield several derivatives, of which among others is the so-called triple counterpoint
at the octave, it is advisable to dwell for awhile on a few special cases of originals with
one derivative, used in composition and having considerable importance for the development of contrapuntal technique. The situations referred to have much in common with
the shifts in double counterpoint where one of the two voices remains stationary.
The difference consists in the fact that here two voices remain stationary and one of
the outer voices shifts. If the lower voice shifts, the voices in the derivative are arranged according to diagram 4: $\bowtie$; if the upper shifts, according to diagram
3: $\bowtie$. But while in two-voice counterpoint it is a matter of indifference whether
the upper or the lower voice shifts at the given index, in three-voice counterpoint another combination of indices is necessary for shifting the lower voice than that required for shifting the upper, for as just seen, the diagrams referred to represent different
derivatives. Indicating by the letter a the interval at which one of the outer voices
shifts, while the other two do not, one of the following two formulas is obtained:

(1) $\mathrm{I} + \mathrm{II} + \mathrm{III}^{v=\,-a}$ Indices:
$$
\begin{aligned}
Jv' &= \;\;\,0 \\
Jv'' &= -a > \\
\hline
Jv\Sigma &= -a >
\end{aligned}
$$

(2) $\mathrm{I}^{v=\,-a} + \mathrm{II} + \mathrm{III}$ Indices:
$$
\begin{aligned}
Jv' &= -a > \\
Jv'' &= \;\;\,0 \\
\hline
Jv\Sigma &= -a >
\end{aligned}
$$

The difference between the two formulas is that in the first $Jv'= 0$ and in the
second $Jv''= 0$.

§ 271. First will be examined a shift at two of the most useful indices: $Jv= -11$ and
$Jv= -9$, then examples will be cited of some of the more difficult indices.

§ 272. The following example has $Jv''= -11$ and $Jv\Sigma= -11$, therefore it admits of
the shift $\mathrm{III}^{v=\,-11}$ (cf. the first formula in § 270).

174

Ex. 176

The original combination is taken from the Sanctus of Palestrina's mass *O admirable commercium,* and the derivative as far as the asterisk from the Benedictus of the same mass. This, a posthumous work of Palestrina's, was published in 1599. But also in Zarlino's book *Istitutioni armoniche* (first edition 1558) are found the following examples (in Chapter 62), both with the same shift as the preceding:

In combination I + II, measure 7 and 13, the voices cross. There are suspensions in measures 7 and 14. In Ex. 178 there are neither crossings nor suspensions. The absence of the latter makes the execution of the problem very easy. It all amounts to this: that for an outer voice to combine with each of the other two, the sixth can not be used in the capacity of a consonance. Then this outer voice admits of a shift at $Jv = -11$. It is understood that a shift cannot be made that is beyond the limiting interval of this index; such cases must be taken at $v = -18$, not at $v = 11$.

§ 273. This use of double counterpoint at the twelfth was passed on by tradition to the composers of the era of free counterpoint, as can be seen in the following, from *The Well-Tempered Clavichord* (Vol. I, Fugue 17):

Ex. 179

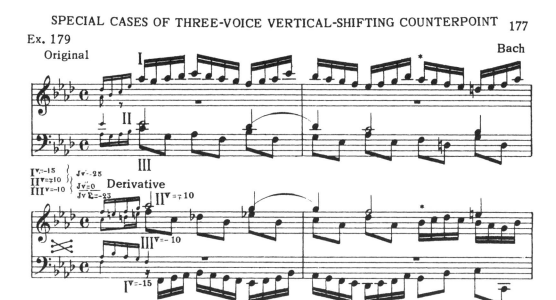

§ 274. If the application of this counterpoint to the free style is attended by some needless difficulties because of harmonic requirements, modulation in particular, on the other hand the possibility of the free use of sevenths (therefore sixths) opens up an extensive field for diversified harmonic combinations. Moerover, a detailed study of the application of complex counterpoint to the free style does not enter into the problem of actual composition. It may be observed that in analysing polyphonic works one is not limited to a study of the derivative combinations actually used; analysis can be carried further, and be made to include all possible derivatives, whether or not the composer employed them. This attitude contributed materially to the development of what may be called the spirit of contrapuntal combination. This may be illustrated by a few examples from *The Well-Tempered Clavichord* where double counterpoint at the twelfth is applicable. The derivatives given are only possibilities, they are not found in the works quoted.

Ex. 180

Possible Derivative

$III^{v=} -11$

Such shifts can be made also in four-voice counterpoint, as is seen in the two following examples, where the two lower voices are shifted a twelfth higher:

Ex. 181

Original   Bach

Possible Derivative

Ex. 182

Original   Bach   Possible Derivative

In conclusion is cited a four-voice example in which only one upper voice shifts in double counterpoint at the twelfth, relative to the other three voices ($I^{v=} -18$).

Ex. 183
Original

Bach

Possible Derivative

$I^{v=-18}$

§ 275. The skill to manage counterpoint at the tweltfh in all of its many aspects is what distinguishes the technique of earlier composers from that of present-day writers. Most recent theorists do not emphasize the importance of this counterpoint. From the fact that Bach assimilated the processes of composition—known to Zarlino—that existed at the time of strict style it would seem that the attention of theorists would have been directed to such passages as Ex. 179. But in the textbooks of van Bruck, Jadassohn and Riemann, dealing especially with the analysis of the preludes and fugues of this collection, is found only silence on this point. The attitude here taken toward counterpoint can have much significance for contemporary technique. Counterpoint at the twelfth, as compared with many other intervals, is very simple; its use is easy; multi-voice combinations where it is applied sound full because of the freedom with which thirds and fifths are employed. In this connection this counterpoint plays a predominant role in canonic imitation, about which details are given in *The Technique of Canon*. A general acquaintance with the various applications of counterpoint at the twelfth should be regarded as indispensible to the technique of today. The persistent and assiduous study of the exercises here indicated is recommended. To recover technical skill, now lost in contemporary music, would be in the highest degree desirable.

§ 276. In the following example counterpoint at the tenth is used. This example

gives the derivative: $I^{v=\,-16} + II + III.$

Indices:
$$Jv' = -16$$
$$Jv'' = \quad 0$$
$$Jv\Sigma = -16$$

Ex. 184

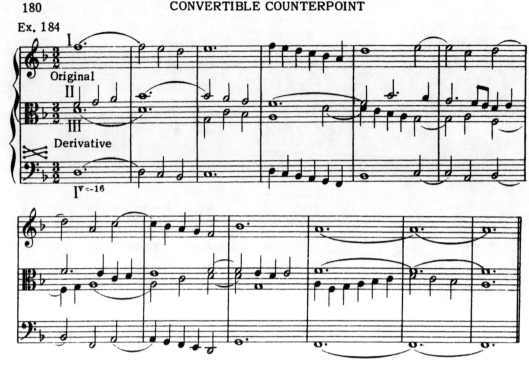

Regarded seperately, both the original and derivative combinations sound empty in places. On the contrary, the simultaneous execution of the original together with a shift at $I^{v=}-16$ gives complete four-voice harmony. Since $\bar{8}$ is absent in combination I + II and I + III there is no obstacle to this duplication.

§ 277. The most useful counterpoints are those at the twelfth and tenth. The next two examples illustrate the use of some difficult and infrequent indices. Ex. 185 gives

the derivative: ⋈ $I^{v=}-12$ + II + III.

Indices: $Jv' = -12$
             $Jv'' = 0$
             ────────────
             $Jv\Sigma = -12$

Ex. 185

This example, like the preceding, can be executed in four-voices. although the movement of the outer voices in parallel sixths sounds rather indolent and far less finished than would parallel motion in thirds.

In Ex. 186 an outer voice is shifted at the ninth ($I^{v=-15}$). Formula for derivative:

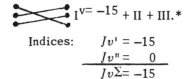 $I^{v=-15}$ + II + III.*

Indices: $Jv' = -15$
$$\underline{Jv'' = \quad 0}$$
$$Jv\Sigma = -15$$

Ex. 186

---

*Cf. also the shifts at the ninth in Nos. 7 and 8, Appendix B.

§ 278. It is doubtful if a single instance could be found in the literature of the Polyphonic Period of where shifts at $Jv= -8$ or -15 are used in three-voice vertical-shifting counterpoint. There are infrequent cases where along with $Jv= -3$ are also found $Jv= -13$ and $Jv= -21$, as in the following passage from Fugue 17, Vol. I of *The Well-Tempered Clavichord* (cf. Prout, *Double Counterpoint*, § 236), with derivative:

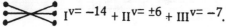 $I^{v=} -14 + II^{v=} \pm 6 + III^{v=} -7.$

Indices: $Jv' = -8$
$\underline{Jv'' = -13}$
$Jv\Sigma = -21$

Ex. 187

§ 279. It would be useless to look for illustrations in elementary counterpoint text-books as to how such shifts are obtained. The possibility of three-voice counterpoint admitting of a shift in double counterpoint at the ninth is a matter that exposes certain theorists to grave suspicions. For instance Sechter, in § 75 of *Von Doppelten Contrapunkt*, says: "The impossibility of three-voice counterpoint at the ninth is obvious if one remembers that at the doubling only the fifth is free. What then can the third voice do?" etc.

§ 280. In Appendix B are twelve examples of three-voice vertical-shifting counterpoint, each with one derivative, and arranged in the order of the diagrams. These examples can be used both for analysis and as guides for the writing of exercises.

CHAPTER XIII

COMBINATIONS GIVING MORE THAN ONE DERIVATIVE; TRIPLE COUNTERPOINT

§ 281. The methods of deducing the conditions of a compound Jv for two-voice combinations giving more than one derivative were stated in Chapter IX. The same methods will be applied to three-voice counterpoint, taking each of the three indices separately. For instance, if one of the required indices in a derivative combination is $Jv' = a$, and another $Jv' = b$, the compound index $Jv' = a, b$ is obtained. If two derivatives require the same index the latter remains without change. The conditions of the other indices Jv'' and $Jv\Sigma$ are defined in exactly the same way. To the conditions of two derivatives can be added those of a third, a fourth, etc.

Obs.—When uniting the conditions of indices that refer to several derivatives $Jv\Sigma$ is no longer equal to the sum of the two other indices. The general formula $Jv' + Jv'' = Jv\Sigma$ (§ 244) applies only to indices referring to one derivative, not to JJv that indicate the united conditions of several derivatives.

§ 282. All the problems of three-voice counterpoint giving more than one derivative can be solved by methods indicated in the preceding section. From the infinite number of possible combinations will first be examined some highly characteristic cases, first of all the so-called

Triple Counterpoint

§ 283. Theoretical works ordinarily deal with triple counterpoint at only one interval, the octave. By this term is to be understood three-voice counterpoint giving derivative combinations by shifting the voices at the octave, besides which each voice may be upper, middle, or lower. The result of these shifts is that arrangements of the voices are obtained according to all six diagrams (§ 248). In this way an original combination in which the arrangement of voices corresponds to diagram (1) gives five deriva-tives, with the voices arranged according to the remaining diagrams. An absolute condition of this counterpoint is that each voice must be written in double counterpoint at the octave with each of the other voices.

§ 284. Two questions arise in enumerating the features of triple counterpoint: (1) why does this counterpoint, though giving several derivatives, not require a compound index (as would follow from § 281), while each pair of voices takes only one: $Jv = -7$? (2) If the voices are written in double counterpoint at any interval other than the octave, can the same number of derivatives be obtained by shifting the voices? The answer to these questions gives the

General Formula for Triple Counterpoint

§ 285. To deduce this formula use is made of the definition of triple counterpoint at the octave (§ 283), substituting interval a instead of the octave for shifting the voices. Then the sum of the five derivatives is obtained to get the required index. The inverse shift will be assumed between the outer voices, so that each of them, shifting at $-a$, exchanges place with the others. Hence two diagrams are obtained: the shift of the lower voice at −a gives diagram (4): , and the shift of the upper at −a diagram

(5): . Diagrams (2): and (3): , with the direct shift be-
tween upper and lower voices do not show the result of shifting an outer voice, but only
the middle, which exchanges position with one of the outer voices. To obtain any of
these diagrams it is sufficient to shift only one voice. On the contrary the remaining

diagram: (6) requires the simultaneous shifting of both outer voices, the
middle voice retaining its position.

These are the shifts considered in the following table, where for each derivative is
given its indices according to the method indicated in § 281.

Derivatives:

$(I + II^{V = \mp a} + III)$ $Jv' = -a$, $Jv'' = a$, $Jv\Sigma = 0$.

$(I + II^{V = \pm a} + III)$ $Jv' = a$, $Jv'' = -a$, $Jv\Sigma = 0$.

$(I + II + III^{V = -a})$ $Jv' = 0$, $Jv'' = -a$, $Jv\Sigma = -a$.

$(I^{V = -a} + II + III)$ $Jv' = -a$, $Jv'' = 0$, $Jv\Sigma = -a$.

$(I^{V = -a} + II + III^{V = -a})$ $Jv' = -a$, $Jv'' = -a$, $Jv\Sigma = -2a$.

General formula for
triple counterpoint: $Jv' = -a, a$, $Jv'' = -a, a$, $Jv\Sigma = -a, -2a$.

The Difference Between Triple Counterpoint at the Octave
and Triple Counterpoint at Other Intervals

§ 286. A formula for triple counterpoint at the octave can be compiled, based on the
general formula. Substituting 7 for a is obtained:

$$Jv' = -7, 7; \ Jv'' = -7, 7; \ Jv\Sigma = -7, -14.$$

In the first two indices $Jv = 7$ must be discarded, since the derivative is only the
octave equivalent of the original (§ 47); therefore these indices are simple and not
compound: $Jv' = -7$ and $Jv'' = -7$. As regards $Jv\Sigma = -7, -14$, the latter value is superfluous, because of $Jv = -7$ (§ 50). And so the formula for triple counterpoint at the octave
assumes this form:

$$Jv' = -7, \ Jv'' = -7, \ Jv\Sigma = -7.$$

Therefore this counterpoint does not need a compound index. This answers the first
question brought up in § 284.

Obs.—The formula for triple counterpoint at the octave, in the way it is here presented, is inconvenient for practical application, since 7> is the limiting interval between the outer voices (for $Jv\Sigma = -7$) and restricts the freedom of their movements.
Another formula, more useful because it contains $Jv\Sigma = -14$>, is given in § 288.

§ 287. The absence of compound indices is characteristic of triple counterpoint at
the octave. Triple counterpoint at all other intervals absolutely requires all three double
indices, as the execution of such problems is in the highest degree difficult. If, for
example, a = 11 appears in the general formula, then is obtained:

$$Jv' = -11, 11; \ Jv'' = -11, 11; \ Jv\Sigma = -11, -22;$$

which in conformity with the statements in §§ 47 and 50 reduces to:

$$Jv' = -11, 4; \ Jv'' = -11, 4; \ Jv\Sigma = -11, -8.$$

Obs. 1.–The compound indices in this formula, especially the very difficult index $Jv = -8$, makes the execution of problems so hard that it would scarcely be possible to cite a single example in which all five derivatives are obtained by shifting the voices at the twelfth. To obtain the derivatives lacking it is customary to turn to the easier shifts at the octave, then, by combining with shifts at the twelfth or some other interval to get what Marpurg called "mixed triple counterpoint." But for such insoluble problems it is better to substitute easier ones.

Obs. 2.–Due only to the application of elementary mathematics, and associated with this, an exact terminology, it is possible to explain the difference that exists between triple counterpoint at the octave, on the one hand, and all other intervals, on the other. Theory up to this time, not taking advantage of mathematical resources and lacking an accurate terminology, was deprived of the means whereby could be analysed the complex relations that the shifting of voices exhibit in triple counterpoint, and was necessarily compelled to abandon these problems as admitting of no solution.

Triple Counterpoint at the Octave

§ 288. Therefore triple counterpoint at the octave is a case unique of its kind, for, requiring no index except $Jv = -7$ (or its more practical equivalent $Jv = -14$), it admits of shifts according to all six diagrams. Since each pair of voices is written in double counterpoint at the octave each voice can function as bass and can take part in two combinations, because the other two voices, shifting at the octave, can exchange places. There are six of these permutations. The formula is given in § 286 but its rigid application is inconvenient, due to the fact that in it $Jv\Sigma = -7$, whereby 7> is the limiting interval for the outer voices and prevents freedom of movement. In order for the limiting

interval to be 14> it is sufficient for derivatives  and (§ 285) to take $Jv\Sigma = -14$ instead of $Jv\Sigma = -7$ for shifting the outer voices. In this way $Jv = -7$ is removed altogether from the compound index $Jv\Sigma$, so that the formula as stated in § 286 is reduced to:

$$Jv' = -7, \quad Jv'' = -7, \quad Jv\Sigma = -14.$$

This formula, applied in the following examples, gives entirely natural voice-movements without any crossings. It is of far greater usefulness from a practical point of view than the formula in § 286.

Ex. 188

I+II+III

Original

$I^{v=-7} + II + III^{v=-7}$ $Jv' = -7$

$Jv'' = -7$

$Jv\Sigma = -14$

§ 289. Since in triple counterpoint at the octave each voice is written in double counterpoint at the octave with the other two, neither fourths nor fifths may be used as consonances, but must conform to the conditions of $Jv = -7$, i.e. $\overline{3}_{-x}$ and $\overline{4.}^{-x}$ There is a single exeception where a fourth is allowed with the bass (cf. § 231).

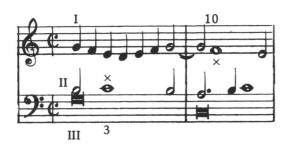

The shifts of this illustration in triple counterpoint at the octave show the use of consonant fourths and fifths:

Aside from such cases as these, neither fourths nor fifths may be used in the capacity of consonant intervals. If the condition $\overline{8}^{(-)}$ is added, obligatory at $Jv = -14$, it is also necessary, in avoiding crossings, to make Jv' and Jv'' conform to the limiting interval 7>, and $Jv\Sigma$ to 14>. By these conditions all the rules of triple counterpoint at the octave are exhausted. Therefore the impossibility of the free use of fifths in places where ties are absent results in incomplete harmony. This counterpoint attains harmonic completeness by the use of suspensions and complex forms of resolution, as was seen in the illustrations in § 289.

§ 290. Otherwise, harmonic completness can be attained only by reducing the number of derivatives, for in practice it is hardly ever necessary to use all six permutations. For instance the free fifth may be used in combination I + II, but then voice I can not appear as lower voice of the derivative. Therefore two derivatives are relinquished: 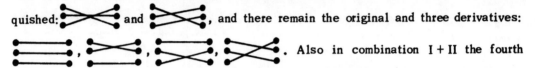 , and there remain the original and three derivatives: . Also in combination I + II the fourth

may be released from its limitations, using it as a perfect consonance, but not entirely releasing the fifth from its limitations ($\underline{4}$ instead of $\overset{-x}{\underline{4}}$, since the fourth becomes consonant). In this case voice II can not appear as lowest part in the derivative, therefore these two derivatives are eliminated:  , with these remaining: . If both situations apply to combination

I + II and both 4 and 3 are used (the latter as a perfect consonance), neither voice I nor II can function as lower part, and four of the derivatives are relinquished, leaving only 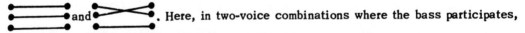 . Here, in two-voice combinations where the bass participates,

$\overline{8}$ may be admitted instead of $\overset{(-)}{8}$, but in this case the voices must not shift in such a way as to contract the ninth to a second. If combination I + II contains parallel fourths, any shift to these voices is possible, and the original combination remains, i.e. it is within the province of simple counterpoint.

This is so clear that no special illustrations are needed. The cases designated, not yielding all six permutations, might be called incomplete triple counterpoint, or else triple counterpoint with a specified number of derivatives; for instance, triple counterpoint with three derivatives, or with one derivative, etc.

Obs.—Those who have fully mastered triple counterpoint at the octave will have no difficulty with quadruple counterpoint at the same interval, where shifting the voices gives twenty-four permutations. Here also each voice is written in double counterpoint at the octave with each of the other voices. With such an abundance of derivatives several can be discarded, leaving plenty for obtaining the degree of harmonic completeness desired (§ 290).

§ 291. From a practical point of view triple counterpoint at the octave is of greater significance than any other aspect of three-voice vertical-shifting counterpoint. The ability to manipulate it is an indispensible requirement of good contrapuntal technique. Its use was more general in the era of free counterpoint, beginning with the first half of the seventeenth century, but it has not lost its importance for our time. In some textbooks are found many examples of this counterpoint, taken from the works of Bach, Handel, Mozart, Haydn and other composers. Some very valuable suggestions as to the use of triple and quadruple counterpoint at the octave, free style, are given by Prout in his *Double Counterpoint and Canon*, Chapter IX.

CHAPTER XIV

COMBINATIONS GIVING MORE THAN ONE DERIVATIVE
(Continued)

§ 292. The theory of three-voice vertical-shifting counterpoint was explained in the preceding chapter, together with a detailed study of one phase of it: triple counterpoint at the octave. Some other phases of it, where voices shift at other intervals, are given in the present chapter. It was seen how few conditions were required in certain cases in order for shifts in triple counterpoint at the octave to be practicable. For instance, to shift the middle voice an octave higher, so that it exchanges position with the upper voice, requires only one condition: the absence of parallel fourths; also to avoid crossing these voices the distances between them must be limited to 7>. Three-voice combinations in which I + II use both of these conditions are constantly found. In this way almost every combination in which the shifting of the voices in double counterpoint at the octave was not intended nevertheless admit of it. From this point of view further examples would refer to what Marpurg called "mixed triple counterpoint" *(Obs. 1, § 287)*. But this term is unnecessary, it refers to octave shifts and how they are obtained. To avoid needless complications it will not be introduced into the conditions of future problems. These can, when necessary, be treated as individual cases.

§ 293. Triple counterpoint at the octave, as has been seen, has two main features: (1) it gives all six diagrams when the voices are shifted at the octave; and (2) each voice is written in double counterpoint with each of the other two voices at the same interval. It is advisable to dwell for awhile on the second of these attributes, and inquire: How is a derivative obtained when each voice is written with every other in double counterpoint, not at the octave but at some other interval, which for the present will be designated by the letter a? This question is easily answered by the help of the general formula for triple counterpoint (§ 285); all that is necessary is to remove all indices from it except $Jv = a$, namely: $Jv' = a$, $Jv'' = a$ and $Jv\Sigma = -2a$. This excludes from the total number of

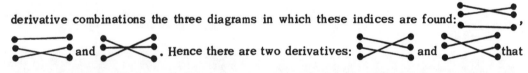

derivative combinations the three diagrams in which these indices are found: , and . Hence there are two derivatives: and that are obtained at the given conditions, i.e. the three indices $Jv' = -a$, $Jv'' = -a$, $Jv\Sigma = -2a$.

§ 294. Applying $a = 11$:

Ex. 189

$Jv' = -11$, $Jv'' = -11$, $Jv\Sigma = -11$
Original

(§§ 267-8)

190

§ 295. In this example only the two outer voices shifted at $-a$, forming two derivatives: ⟨diagram⟩ and ⟨diagram⟩. Now to these shifts is added an upward shift of the middle voice at the same interval: $II^{v=\overline{\mp}a}$. Hence the number of derivatives is increased to three, and to the two former diagrams is added one more: ⟨diagram⟩. Also Jv'' becomes a compound index: $Jv'' = -a, a$.

In Ex. 190 $a = -9$. Uniting the indices of each derivative (§ 281) and taking $Jv = 2$ instead of $Jv = 9$ (§ 47) gives: $Jv' = -9$, $Jv'' = -9$, $Jv\Sigma = -9$.

Ex. 190

In this example the three-voice combinations, original and derivative, are empty if regarded separately. Harmonic completeness can be attained by the inclusion of a fourth voice, when a shift of one of the voices is added to the original. This involves no difficulty, due to the fact that $\overline{8}$ is absent as between the upper and each of the inner voices, also between the inner voices themselves.

§ 296. Hitherto all voices have shifted at one and the same interval. Ex. 191 has three derivatives, the first resulting from the shift $I^{v=}\,2$, the second from $II^{v=}\,\pm11$, and the third from $I^{v=}\,-2$ and $II^{v=}\,\pm11$ together. The first derivative takes only the direct shift. Combining the indices for each derivative (§ 281) and taking $Jv=2$ instead of $Jv=9$ and $Jv=4$ instead of $Jv=11$ (§ 47) gives $Jv'=2$, $Jv''=-11$; $Jv\Sigma=2,-2$.

The first derivative has $Jv' = 2$, an index corresponding to an imperfect consonance. In three-voice vertical-shifting counterpoint, as in two-voice (§196,[1]), when the upper voice is shifted at an imperfect consonance this voice may be executed together with its own duplication, forming four-voice counterpoint:

The same applies to the second derivative, where duplicating the upper voice at $I^{v= -2}$ gives this:

Further details as to duplications will be discussed in the next chapter.

Extracting Derivatives from a Given Combination

§ 297. Up to this point the indices for a given three-voice derivative have been obtained by applying the formula for derivative combinations. The opposite problem is now to be considered: how derivatives may be extracted from a given combination.

To do this exact values of Jv', Jv'' and $Jv\Sigma$ must be determined. If any of these indices are compound, i.e. if they conform to the conditions of several indices, then their sums must be taken. In obtaining their values in this way the combinations must be united which would correspond to the formula $Jv' + Jv'' + Jv\Sigma$. The derivative combinations obtained from a given original are controlled by these values.

§ 298. The conditions of the indices that satisfy the requirements for Jv', Jv'' and $Jv\Sigma$ in the following example will be determined.

Ex. 192   Original

This example was written with the object of obtaining the largest possible number of derivatives. Similar motion is absent from all three pairs of voices, therefore the usable consonances are very limited in number. For instance between voices I and II only three consonances, used without preparation, are found: 0, 2 and 7. In the third and sixth measures are fifths between voices I + II, used according to a limitation of a variable consonance (4). Sixths are absent altogether. Examining in order the combinations I + II, II + III and I + III it will be observed that each of these combinations satisfies the conditions of the indices of the fifth column: $JJv = -9, -2, 5$. Besides this they all admit of a shift at $Jv = -11$. Finally, Jv' fully meets the requirements of $Jv = -7$, while Jv'' and $Jv\Sigma$ meet those requirements conditionally: because of the free use of fifths, the combinations to which these indices refer (II + III and I + III) can be shifted at $Jv = -7$ only according to diagrams in which the voices appear in the derivative as upper and middle. These diagrams are, for Jv'', [⤬] for $Jv\Sigma$ [⤬]

The JJv common to all three indices have been pointed out. To them must be added $Jv = 2$, but only to one Jv'. Therefore each of the three indices combines the conditions as follows:

$$Jv' = -11, -7, \ -9, \pm 2, 5;$$
$$Jv'' = -11, -7^*, -9, -2, 5;$$
$$Jv\Sigma = -11, -7^*, -9, -2, 5;$$

* conditional.

From these values must be put down a formula for each separate derivative. The indices may amount to a considerable number, in view of the fact that voices of the derivative may be shifted an octave and therefore take $Jv = -18$ instead of $Jv = -11$; $Jv = -16$ instead of $Jv = -9$; $Jv = -14$ instead of $Jv = -7$, etc. Similarly an index with the direct shift may be substituted for another index with the same shift, to the value of which is added 7, for example instead of $Jv = 2$ to use $Jv = 9$ etc. Also $Jv = 0$ or $Jv = 7$ may be freely taken for any combination.

§ 299. Now, with the resources given, formulas for derivative combinations can be compiled of which each presents the equation $Jv' + Jv'' = Jv\Sigma$. Any index is retained of which the value is a term in this equation for $Jv\Sigma$. For instance, taking $Jv\Sigma = -11$ (or its equivalent $Jv\Sigma = -18$), from the lists of combined indices are selected for Jv' and Jv'' those of which the sum would be equal to -11 or -18:

$$
\begin{array}{ccc}
Jv' = -11 & Jv' = -16 & Jv' = -9 \\
Jv'' = 0 & Jv'' = 5 & Jv'' = -9 \\
\hline
Jv\Sigma = -11 & Jv\Sigma = -11 & Jv\Sigma = -18 \quad \text{etc.}
\end{array}
$$

These correspond to derivatives 12, 13 and 14 at the end of this section.

The original combination has as many derivatives as there are formulas compiled by these methods. Following are fourteen derivatives, arranged in order of the diagrams, each with its formula.

1st Derivative

$I^{V=5} + II + III$
$Jv' = 5$
$Jv'' = 0$
$Jv\Sigma = 5$

2nd Derivative

$I^{V=5} + II^{V=\mp3} + III^{V=2}$
$Jv' = 2$
$Jv'' = 5$
$Jv\Sigma = 7$

3rd Derivative

$I^{V=-4} + II^{V=\mp3} + III^{V=4}$
$Jv' = -7$
$Jv'' = 7$
$Jv\Sigma = 0$

4th Derivative

$I^{V=-4} + II^{V=\mp5} + III^{V=2}$
$Jv' = -9$
$Jv'' = 7$
$Jv\Sigma = -2$

12th Derivative

$I^{v=-8} + II^{v=-3} + III^{v=-3}$ $Jv'=-11$
$Jv''= 0$
$Jv \Sigma =-11$

13th Derivative

$I^{v=-8} + II^{v=-8} + III^{v=-3}$ $Jv'=-16$
$Jv''= 5$
$Jv\Sigma=-11$

14th Derivative

$I^{v=-7} + II^{v=-2} + III^{v=-11}$ $Jv'=-9$
$Jv''=-9$
$Jv\Sigma=-18$

CHAPTER XV

DUPLICATIONS IN THREE-VOICE COUNTERPOINT

§ 300. Continuing the order of subjects as given in Division A, the next is the duplication of three-voice vertical-shifting counterpoint at imperfect consonances. Here the requirements are more limited, so that the original combination yields only one derivative in which the number of voices is increased as the result of duplication. The following cases will be dealt with in succession: (a) the duplication of one voice—four-voice counterpoint; (b) the duplication of two voices—five-voice counterpoint; (c) the duplication of all three voices—six-voice counterpoint.

(A) The Duplication of One Voice; Four-Voice Counterpoint

§ 301. In a former chapter were found cases of where one of the outer voices was duplicated, namely: $I^{d=-9}$. In accordance with § 222, $\overset{(-)}{8}$ (and $\underset{(-)}{-8}$) is an obligatory condition for every two-voice combination that does not include the bass. For example this progression:

although it gives a correct derivative at the shift $I^{v=-12} + II^{v=0} + III^{v=0}$,

will still not admit of the duplication $I^{d=-12}$. Fourths also must be considered. it is not necessary that a three-voice derivative, apart from the duplication, shall exhibit correct three-voice counterpoint as far as fourths are concerned; it is enough that the total, consisting of the original and the four-voice derivative, shall be correct. Therefore in the latter the free use of fourths is allowed, which are made possible by means of the duplication; for example:

198

Ex. 193

The writing of such combinations is facilitated considerably by the use of consonant fourths, although they render impractical the use of the particular three-voice derivative $I + II + III^{v= -9}$.

§ 302. In duplications at imperfect consonances the original combination must conform to the conditions of the Jv corresponding to the consonance giving the duplication. As already known, all JJv corresponding to imperfect consonances are those of the second group (^2JJv), i.e. indices not admitting of similar motion (except possible hidden progressions). But in certain cases duplicating at imperfect consonances does not preclude the use of similar motion, in particular, parallel motion. Progressions of thirds do not prevent duplication at sixths, nor do progressions of sixths prevent duplication at thirds (§ 212). The result is a series of first inversions.

The following example shows the bass duplicated in sixths: $I + II + III^{d= -12}$.

Ex. 194

Here it is necessary to conform to these indices:

$$Jv' = 0$$
$$^2Jv'' = -12$$
$$\overline{^2Jv\Sigma = -12}$$

Although Jv'' and $Jv\Sigma$ are both indices of the second group (^2JJv), duplicating the bass in sixths does not prevent parallel motion in thirds between the voices to which the indices refer, namely: $I + II$ and $I + III$.

As for $I + II$, parallel motion is possible between these voices both in thirds and sixths, because $Jv' = 0$. Therefore the thirds and tenths in Jv'' and $Jv\Sigma$ give derivative consonant fourths, functioning as fixed consonances.

Obs.—Such an example, where the voice duplicated is the bass, is easier to write than where the voice duplicated is highest in the original combination. In the latter case consonant fourths are prevented between soprano and alto and between soprano and tenor.

§ 303. In Ex. 194 the duplication in sixths allowed parallel motion in thirds at a ^2Jv. In the next example duplication in thirds allows parallel motion in sixths, also at a ^2Jv (in combination I + II).

Ex. 195

This example illustrates the duplication I + II$^{d= \mp 2}$ + III. Indices:

$$Jv' = -2$$
$$Jv'' = 2$$
$$\overline{Jv\Sigma = 0}$$

Into the conditions of Jv' is inserted a change: the sixth, giving a consonant fourth (5 −2= 3) becomes a fixed consonance. Parallel sixths are found in the second measure and in the last two measures.

§ 304. The duplication I$^{d= 5}$ also allows parallel sixths between the alto and tenor; this example sounds rather strange but can not be considered incorrect.

Ex. 196

Formula: I$^{d= 5}$ + II + III; indices:

$$Jv' = 5$$
$$Jv'' = 0$$
$$\overline{Jv\Sigma = 5}$$

There is a change in the conditions of $Jv'= 5$: the sixth, giving a consonant fourth (5 + 5 = 10) remains a fixed consonance. Parallel sixths in the original combination are found in the second measure.

§ 305. Often such a combination allows a shift that was not planned for when it was written. In finding these unintentional combinations it is usual to arrive at them quickly enough. Whenever similar motion between voices is absent a duplication that is more or less tentative can be thought of. If parallel motion in thirds is found the only possible duplication is that in sixths. Unless such thirds come underneath, the given combination will not admit of any duplication at all. It is the same with parallel sixths, the number of duplications is limited to a possible duplication at the third (less often at the lower sixth), as in Ex. 196. This example can give the following shifts:

(B) Simultaneous Duplication of Two Voices;

Five-Voice Counterpoint

§ 306. It was seen that four-voice counterpoint obtained by duplicating two voices in imperfect consonances includes three derivative combinations and that an index referring to the original two-voice combination is a compound Jv, the result of uniting three indices (§ 216). Exactly the same happens when two voices in a three-voice combination are duplicated, three derivatives result, and the index is compound, uniting the conditions of three indices.

Obs.—If all three indices are different the index is triple; if two of them are alike and the third does not equal zero it is double; if two are alike and the third equals zero it is simple.

§ 307. The duplication $I^{d=-16} + II^{d=\pm2} + III$ will be taken. Here are five voices: $I + I^{v=-16} + II + II^{v=\pm2} + III$. I and II are duplicated. The Jv' of each must show the result of combining three indices. Therefore combination I + II has three derivatives: $I + II^{v=2}$, $I^{v=-16} + II$ and $I^{v=-16} + II^{v=2}$ (here are all combinations of voice I with II except I + II, which is the original). The indices for each of these derivatives are:

$$
\begin{array}{ll}
(I + II^{v=2}) & Jv' = 2 \\
(I^{v=-16} + II) & Jv' = -16 \\
(I^{v=-16} + II^{v=2}) & Jv' = -14
\end{array}
$$

Hence Jv' appears as a compound index: $Jv' = 2, -16, -14$. The two remaining indices are:

$$
\begin{array}{ll}
(II^{v=-2} + III) & Jv'' = -2 \\
(I^{v=-16} + III) & Jv\Sigma = -16
\end{array}
$$

Compiling a table for Jv':

$$
\begin{array}{llll}
Jv = -2: & \overline{3}_{-x} & \overset{-x}{\underset{(-)}{4}} & \\[2mm]
Jv = -16 \ (= -9): & \overset{(-)}{\underline{3}} & & \overset{-}{\underset{(-)}{8}} \\[2mm]
Jv = -14: & \overset{\text{p.}}{\underset{-x}{3}} & \overset{-x}{\underset{(-)}{4}} & \overset{(-)}{8} \\[2mm]
\hline
{}^{2}Jv' = -2<,-16,-14>: & \overset{(\text{p.})}{\underset{-x}{3}} & \overset{-x}{\underset{(-)}{4}} & \overset{(-)}{\underset{(-)}{8}}
\end{array}
$$

$\overset{(\text{p.})}{\underset{-x}{3}}$ can not be released from signs, since at $Jv = -9$ it is a fixed dissonance.

At $Jv'' = -2$ the sixth, giving a consonant fourth, becomes a fixed dissonance. 5 and $\underset{(-)}{\overset{\text{p.}}{6}}$ appear as changed in the conditions of $Jv = -2$. $\overline{8}$ is excluded from the original combination, since II when duplicated becomes an inner voice. The following is written according to the preceding plan:

Ex. 197

$I^{d=16}+II^{d=\pm2}+III$

§ 308. The next example has the duplication $I^{d=-2}+II+III^{d=-2}$. The first two indices are: $Jv'=-2$, $Jv''=-2$. $Jv\Sigma$ refers to the two voices duplicated (I + III) and therefore takes a compound index:

$$(I + III^{v=-2}) \quad Jv\Sigma = -2$$
$$(I^{v=-2} + III) \quad Jv\Sigma = -2$$
$$(I^{v=-2} + III^{v=-2}) \quad Jv\Sigma = -4$$

Since $Jv\Sigma$ refers to the outer voices $Jv = -4<$ must apply. Hence $^2Jv\Sigma = -2, -4<$. Table:

Jv $= -2$:	$\dfrac{-}{5}_{-\times}$	$\dfrac{\overset{p}{6}}{\scriptstyle(-)}\times$		
Jv $= -4<$:	$\dfrac{\scriptstyle(-)}{5}_{-\times}$	$\dfrac{-\times}{6}_{\scriptstyle(-)}$	$\dfrac{-\times}{7}_{-\times}$	$\dfrac{-\times}{8}_{-}$
^{2}**Jv**$\Sigma = -2, -4<$:	$\dfrac{\scriptstyle(-)}{5}_{-\times}$	$\dfrac{\overset{p}{6}}{\scriptstyle(-)}\times$	$\dfrac{-\times}{7}_{-\langle}$	$\dfrac{-\times}{8}_{-}$

3 does not appear in the table since it is beyond the limiting interval $4<$.

Ex. 198

(C) Simultaneous Duplication of Three Voices;

Six-Voice Counterpoint

§ 309. When all three voices are duplicated, in each pair of combinations both voices are duplicated, consequently they give three derivative combinations. Therefore each index is compound, consisting of three indices (cf. *Obs.*, § 306).

§ 310. Indices for this problem $I^{d=-9}+II^{d=+9}+III^{d=-9}$.

Beginning with Jv':

$$(I + II^{v\,=\,-9})\quad Jv' = \;\;-9$$
$$(I^{v\,=\,-9} + II)\quad Jv' = \;\;-9$$
$$(I^{v\,=\,-9} + II^{v\,=\,-9})\quad Jv' = -18$$

Hence: $^2Jv' = -9, -18.$
Passing to Jv'':

$$(II + III^{v\,=\,-9})\quad Jv'' = -9$$
$$(II^{v\,=\,9} + III)\quad Jv'' = \;\;9$$
$$(II^{v\,=\,9} + III^{v\,=\,-9})\quad Jv'' = \;\;0$$

Hence: $^2Jv'' = -9, 9$ (or $Jv'' = -9,2$; § 47).
Last, $Jv\Sigma$:

$$(I + III^{v\,=\,-9})\quad Jv\Sigma = \;\;-9$$
$$(I^{v\,=\,-9} + III)\quad Jv\Sigma = \;\;-9$$
$$(I^{v\,=\,-9} + III^{v\,=\,-9})\quad Jv\Sigma = -18$$

Hence: $^2Jv\Sigma = -9, -18.$
Therefore the three indices are:

$$Jv' = -9, -18$$
$$Jv'' = -9, 2$$
$$Jv\Sigma = -9, -18$$

A table for the double indices of Jv' and $Jv\Sigma$ is given in § 190; (2). It remains to compile a table for $Jv'' = -9, 2$:

$\mathbf{Jv} =$	2:	$\overset{-}{3}$	$\overset{-\times}{4}$	
		$\underset{-\times}{}$	$\underset{(-)}{}$	
$\mathbf{Jv} = -9$:		$\overset{(-)}{3}$		$\overset{-}{8}$
		$\underset{-}{}$		$\underset{(-)}{}$
$^2\mathbf{Jv''} = -9 \succ$,	2:	$\overset{(-)}{3}$	$\overset{-\times}{4}$	$\overset{-}{8}$
		$\underset{-}{}$	$\underset{(-)}{}$	$\underset{(-)}{}$

The following six-voice example presents the solution of this problem:

Ex. 199

Notice that in neither the original combination (I + II + III) nor in the derivative is there any crossing of voices. But the middle voices of the original and derivative (II + III$^{v\,=\,-9}$) continually cross. Such crossing gives more room for the voices, without which they would be too cramped in their movements.

§ 311. The duplication of all three voices completes the study of three-voice vertical-shifting counterpoint, and with it the study of vertical-shifting counterpoint in general.

PART TWO

DIVISION C

TWO-VOICE HORIZONTAL- AND DOUBLE-SHIFTING COUNTERPOINT

PART TWO

DIVISION C

TWO-VOICE HORIZONTAL-SHIFTING AND DOUBLE-SHIFTING COUNTERPOINT

CHAPTER XVI

GENERAL PRINCIPLES

§ 312. The vertical shifting of voices was investigated in Part One. The present subject is that of combinations giving derivatives by means of the temporal shifting of voices, i.e. by changing the relationship between the time-intervals of their entries. This kind of shifting is called horizontal, and counterpoint admitting of it, horizontal-shifting counterpoint. Double-shifting counterpoint is the use of the vertical and horizontal shift at the same time. As this counterpoint is written by the same methods as horizontal-shifting counterpoint alone the two will be dealt with together. In classifying complex counterpoint in this way all possible cases of voice-shifting are exausted.

§ 313. To shift a melody by a whole measure, or by an intergral number of measures, does not change it in any essential respect. But to shift it by some fraction of a measure—at a half-measure, or a measure and a half—transfers the melody from one part of a measure to another. This is the only change that a melody undergoes in the horizontal shift. All other changes not resulting from either the vertical or the horizontal shift such as augmentation, diminution, contrary motion, etc. are outside the province of shifting counterpoint, though in the ensuing chapters they will be referred to when necessary for explaining their connections with shifting counterpoint.

§ 314. Comparing the following two combinations—

Ex. 200 (a)

it will be observed that each of them consists of the same two melodies (I + II) on the same degrees. But the melodies enter differently: in (a) voice I enters first, in (b) voice II. This concerns the horizontal shift. Regarding combination (b) as the derivative, it can be investigated as the result of shifting either I or II, the voice not shifted not being concerned in the process. In the first case the derivative results from shifting I two measures to the left.

The Basic Version

§ 315. The possibility of a two-voice horizontal shift such as shown in Ex. 200 is arrived at as follows:

An original is written in two-voice canonic imitation, and to it is added a third contrapuntal part. From this three-voice combination, called the basic version, is taken the counterpointing voice, first in union with the voice of initial entry, or voice to be imitated (proposta) and next with the imitating voice (risposta). This was how Ex. 200 was obtained. The voices of the basic version will be designated: proposta, P (plural PP); risposta, R (plural RR); counterpoint Cp. In the basic version, Ex. 200 (b) the distance of entry between P and R is two measures, the entrance interval O.

From this are taken the two combinations $Cp + P$ and $Cp + R$ of Ex. 200 (a).

§ 316. Therefore the combination of voices that serves as the basis for horizontal-shifting counterpoint, and of which the indispensable attribute is canonic imitation, is termed the basic version. By means of it are solved problems in horizontal-shifting counterpoint and, as explained later, in double-shifting counterpoint.

§ 317. For two-voice horizontal-shifting counterpoint with one derivative the basic version consists of a two-voice imitation at the unison $(P + R)$ and the counterpointing voice (Cp). Hence two two-voice combinations result: $Cp + P$ and $Cp + R$, of which the first is taken as the original, the second as the derivative.

Obs.—Two-voice canonic imitation is properly within the province of simple counterpoint. With the exception of the infinite canon this imitation does not require the application of complex counterpoint. Its scope consists of: first, the writing of P as far as the entry of R; this section of P is then transferred to the other voice, forming the beginning of R. The voice that first enters continues as counterpoint with the entry of R; this continuing melody is also transferred to the later entering voice, etc.*

§ 318. A special case of the basic version is where P is silent at the entry of R, so that instead of a three-voice combination only two voices are actually present:

---

*A more complete explanation is given in "The Technique of Canon, § 15. —Tr.

§ 319. In the basic version both the imitating voice (R) and the counterpointing voice (Cp) are written in simple counterpoint, as no application of complex counterpoint is needed.

§ 320. Counterpoint that admits of horizontal shifting can hardly be regarded as complete and independent in itself. Ordinarily it is a constituent part of a passage of greater dimensions and for a larger number of voices.* Therefore it is not considered a disadvantage when the voices that in the original combination end together with a cadence do not do so in the derivative, where in ending at different times one voice is silent, as in Ex. 200 (b). It is assumed that such vacant places may be filled up by other participating voices. If they do not, and the necessity arises to fill the vacancies anyway, the voice about to end continues as long as conditions demand.

§ 321. Another matter is that combinations admitting of the horizontal shift, and intended to enter into the structure of passages of larger dimensions, may in the basic version be found where the two voices concerned do not make correct two-voice counterpoint without a third supplementary voice. This fact impedes the free use of such combinations, and with their application in view it is first advisable to be clear as to what kind of basic version may be used independently, which requires a supplementary voice, and what is inadmissable. Hidden progressions and unprepared fourths need a lower supplementary voice; a ninth resolving to an octave ($\overline{8}$) is not allowed at all (§ 83).

Basic Version and Imaginary Risposta

§ 322. As seen in the preceding section, a basic version consisting of correct three-voice counterpoint may be composed to two-voice combinations that do not form correct two-voice counterpoint. But a basic version, complete in itself, may present a combination that is not contrapuntally correct. A cantus firmus may be taken, transferred to another voice, entered at any favorable time and at any interval that is *not* allowed between the voices. In order to distinguish the risposta of such a fictitious imitation from the more legitimate kind, it will be termed an imaginary risposta or imaginary voice, and will be indicated by the initial letter and four dots: R.... . To an imitation with imaginary risposta is added Cp that forms a correct two-voice combination separately with P and also with R.... , for example:

Ex. 202 (a)   Basic Version

Hence two combinations are obtained with horizontal-shifting voices: Cp + P and Cp + R...., of which the first is the original, the second the derivative:

---

*The infrequent cases where this counterpoint is independent (termed counterpoint with and without rests) will be discussed in Division D.

(b) Original   (Cp +P)

Derivative (Cp +R...)

Obs.—In view of the fact that the voices of a basic version may not form a canonic imitation that is contrapuntally valid, the term "basic version" is more suitable than "basic combination." The word "combination" implies a relationship that is contrapuntally correct, while "version" may include a fortuitous relation of voices, such as the preceding imitation with an imaginary R.

§ 323. The combination $Cp + R....$ will be termed the imaginary combination. In contradistinction to imaginary, $Cp + P$ will be termed the real combination, and each voice entering into it a real voice. Both imaginary and real combinations are contrapuntally correct. On the contrary, P and $R....$ of the basic version do not combine, though they may form correct counterpoint accidentally.

§ 324. The real combination corresponds to the original, the imaginary to the derivative.

§ 325. To indicate which voice of the basic version is $R....$ (= imaginary voice), the voice number will be followed by four dots. Therefore the formula of an imaginary combination shows two forms: $I.... + II$ or $I + II....$; the voice unaccompanied by dots is Cp. But such an expression as this is an incomplete formula. In writing a basic version giving a predetermined horizontal shift it is not enough to know which voice has the imaginary risposta. The number of measures or fractions thereof that the proposta must be shifted to the right, in order to yield the risposta, must be known. This, relating to the horizontal shifting of voices, will be discussed in the next chapter.

§ 326. Working out the Cp to a previously written P and $R....$ that does not form a correct combination is a process which though unusual contributes materially to the development of the polyphonic spirit. A problem in horizontal shifting where the cantus firmus is given can be solved otherwise only if the cantus gives a correct canonic imitation accidentally. Therefore, referring to problems on a cantus firmus (as in the following section), it will be assumed that the corresponding basic version retains the imaginary risposta and that P and $R....$ of this version are written so as to adjust to both. But there is another and easier method, giving better musical results; the basic version, retaining the imaginary R, is divided vertically into parts that are written one after another. This will be explained more fully in § 376.

Conditions of a Difficult Problem on a Cantus Firmus

§ 327. The degree of difficulty shown by a two-voice problem on a cantus firmus with horizontal shift or with this and a vertical shift at the same time depends on the nature of the intervals that happen to occur between P and $R....$ of the basic version. The further apart the voices are—unison to octave—the easier the problem. Under these conditions, to write counterpoint against the two voices is almost equivalent to writing it against one. The Cp offers no difficulty when there are consonances between P and $R.....$ Difficulties arise if among the consonances are found dissonances. As their number increases embarrassments increase, especially if two or more dissonances come in succession. Finally, parallel dissonances can make a problem entirely unworkable. For instance, with a row of seconds or sevenths it is quite impossible to write a voice that will make correct counterpoint with each voice of the dissonance. In working out exercises favorable cases should be chosen—consonances prevailing over dissonances—and problems not attempted in which progressions such as these are found:

Obs.—It is necessary to remember that these statements of difficult conditions refer only to those versions where the proposta functions as the given voice, and P and R.... are written beforehand, together with Cp. These conditions have no meaning for those basic versions where, in the absence of a given voice, P and R.... are written in sections, as well as Cp. More will be said about this later (§ 376). Basic versions written according to these methods uniformly use intervals that are admissable between P and R.....

Basic Version for Double-shifting Counterpoint

§ 328. From a basic version with canonic imitation at the unison (with either real or imaginary risposta) is obtained two-voice counterpoint giving a derivative by means of only a horizontal shift. If an imitation at some other interval is taken for the basic version and its associated Cp, then from such basic version is obtained the original combination $Cp + P$ with a derivative $Cp + R$ (or $Cp + R$....), representing a simultaneous horizontal and vertical shift of the voices. Such counterpoint is termed double-shifting (§ 312).

§ 329. In a basic version for double-shifting counterpoint Cp may appear as either outer or inner voice. If Cp is an outer voice the derivative combination will show the

direct shift (); if Cp is an inner voice, the inverse shift ( ).

§ 330. A basic version for double-shifting counterpoint requires no changes in the rules of vertical-shifting counterpoint; Cp is written with P and R (or R....) in simple counterpoint.

§ 331. Exs. 203 and 204, each in double-shifting counterpoint illustrating a basic version with real R, are taken from the works of Palestrina. In both of them Cp is an outer voice, therefore the vertical shift is direct (§ 329).

R imitates P at the third above and enters two measures later. $P + R$, constituting part of a correct three-voice texture, do not form correct two-voice counterpoint by themselves, because of the two unprepared fourths. They require a lower supplementary voice (§ 321). From this basic version is obtained:

The derivative is obtained by shifting I two measures to the right and a third higher, or what amounts to the same thing, shifting II two measures to the left (§ 413) and I a third higher.

In the second measure of Ex. 204 is found a hidden fifth and the free entry of a fourth between P and R, therefore the combination $P + R$ requires a supplementary voice. The derivative was obtained by shifting I a half-measure to the right and a fourth lower (or a half-measure to the left and I a fourth lower).

The combination $Cp + R$, from the basic version, is found three times in Palestrina, each time transferred to other degrees and with long note values in the upper voice:

In two of these instances both voices shift at the half-measure (§ 335):

§ 332. In the two preceding examples Cp appears as the lower voice, therefore the shift in the derivative is direct. In the next example Cp is an inner voice, hence the shift is inverse (§ 329). R.... enters one measure later than P, at the seventh above:

Ex. 205

Basic Version

In the derivative the c.f. is shifted one measure to the right and a seventh higher.

§ 333. In the preceding example the c.f. in the derivative appeared as shifted to another degree. In order to retain it on the same degrees as in the original the Cp would have to be shifted a seventh lower. Such a shift, not intended when the basic version was written, might easily result in an augmented fourth or a diminished fifth, f-b, in the third and fourth measure:

etc.

Such situations can be avoided as follows: in the basic version take for the imaginary voice a key-signature that gives the first note the same relative position in the scale as the first note of the c.f., using a separate staff for the purpose. For instance the c.f. of the basic version of Ex. 205 begins on g, the fifth degree of C major, and in the imaginary voice it begins on f. To make this f the fifth degree of a major scale a signature of two flats must be taken for the imaginary voice, as in Ex. 206. Here, in writing Cp simultaneously with P and $R....$, its relation to P must be according to C major and to $R....$ according to B-flat:

Ex. 206 (a)

Basic Version

The derivative $Cp + R....$ must be transposed so that its key-signature is the same as that of the original; the c.f. then appears on the same degree:

This process is used in some of the problems in Appendix C.

Shifting Voices from One Part of the Measure to Another

§ 334. In Ex. 203 was an instance of where a voice was shifted from one part of the measure to another; this happens when a shift is made at some fractional part of a measure, such as a half-measure, one and one-half measures, a third-measure, etc. A voice of the basic version must be so written that when it is shifted to another part of the measure no rhythmical errors will result. For instance, when a shift is made at the half-measure it is bad to tie over a note that occupies a whole measure: , because these give incorrect ties between two notes of which the first is shorter than the second: .

In triple time it is also bad to shift a long tied note one-third of a measure to the right: ; since ties give: .

The same thing happens when a shift is made to the third beat: , since these ties give and .

The following rule is recommended for avoiding the rhythmical figure : in shifting at the half-measure do not use the rhythmical sucession .

Obs.—Exceptions to this rule are sometimes found in the strict style:

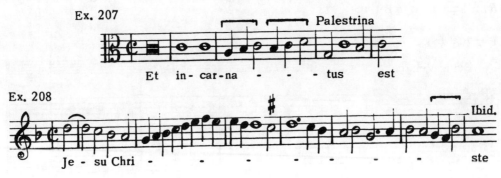

§ 335. When two voices at $Jv= 0$ are shifted from one part of a measure to another, forming a contrapuntal combination which except for rhythmical conditions refers to each voice separately, some conditions must be considered that refer to their united effect. These conditions have reference to the place that suspensions and their resolutions occupy in the measure.

The resolution of a prepared dissonance must not appear at any part of a measure which would cause the resolution when shifted to come on an accented beat. For instance in shifting at a half-measure it would be bad to write:  , since the dissonance would appear on the weak half of the measure and the resolution on the accent: . On the contrary a resolution of the same dissonance on the second quarter: is entirely practicable, for shifting at the half-measure gives: .

Also in triple time with a shift at one-third of a measure to the right it would be bad to write: , which would give: ; shifting it at two-thirds of a measure: would give: .

When a shift is made at the half-measure a passing-note cannot be used on the third quarter: because when shifted it would come on the accented beat:

Guided by such considerations it is easy to understand that similar situations must be avoided in the basic version when shifts are made at one-quarter of a measure, or three-quarters, etc.

Functions of the Basic Version

§ 336. By means of a basic version are obtained the derivative combinations for horizontal- and double-shifting counterpoint (§ 328). But the functions of a basic version are not limited to these. Its application to other categories of complex counterpoint will herewith be examined.

§ 337. Of the two imitating voices in a basic version P may be considered as a voice not shifting, and R as a voice shifting horizontally. At each shift of this voice a new problem arises that requires a new basic version. But at all shifts the fundamental problem is one and the same: To two voices that imitate must be added Cp that forms correct two-voice counterpoint with each of them. Shifting R in the direction of P can bring it in such a position that their entries coincide, for the term imitation, in its generally accepted meaning, applies to these two voices. A further shift of R in the same direction makes it the earlier entering voice, i.e. R becomes P and the previous P is changed to R.

Returning to the case where the entries of P and R coincide, if at such a shift R is found on the same degrees as P, simple counterpoint results, for because of the complete coincidence of the two voices Cp is written not to two voices but only to one. If the voice that shifts horizontally also shifts vertically at the same time to other degrees, then at the coinciding entries is obtained vertical-shifting counterpoint; of the two combinations $Cp + P$ and $Cp + R$ one is taken as the original, the other as the derivative. Therefore, to the two functions of the basic version already known may be added a third: it may serve also as a basis for vertical-shifting counterpoint. But in practice this is of little utility; it is mentioned only as one of the functions of the basic version, not with any idea of recommending its use.

Obs.—The coincidence mentioned—the entries of P and R in the basic version—depends on the possibility of a consonant and uniform relation between the intervals of the original and derivative, thereby allowing the application of the general rules governing intervals, the shifting of voices, etc. Hence arises the study of vertical-shifting counterpoint. By mastering this study a command over tonal combinations and a facility in writing derivatives will be acquired that can be obtained by no other means. Counterpoint textbooks often recommend the direct solving of problems by the help of supplementary voices, without previous study of double counterpoint. This method is almost worthless, as the basic version in which the entries of P and R coincide include also Cp as middle voice, agreeing with the other two, and forming correct counterpoint with each of them individually. Superficially this method of applying vertical-shifting counterpoint would appear to be the simplest, leading at once to the desired result and requiring no preliminary training except a knowledge of simple counterpoint. This delusion could be kept up as long as easy problems only were attempted. But passing to problems with difficult indices, or to those combining the conditions of several indices, or to the simultaneous shift of three voices, etc., the fallacy of the method would at once become apparent. Having no other resources than supplementary voices, the situation would be hopeless, and all attempts to solve such problems would in most cases end in failure.

§ 338. In a two-voice imitation R can reproduce P in a variety of ways; in augmentation or diminution, in contrary motion, etc. Such imitations are written in simple counterpoint, according to the method described in § 317, *Obs.* Applying these execptional forms of imitation to the basic version, derivatives are obtained where one appears in augmentation, diminution, contrary motion, etc.

§ 339. In the derivative of the following example I gives notes of twice the value of those in the original:

Ex. 209 (a)

Original

This counterpoint is taken from a basic version where *R*.... imitates *P* in augmentation:

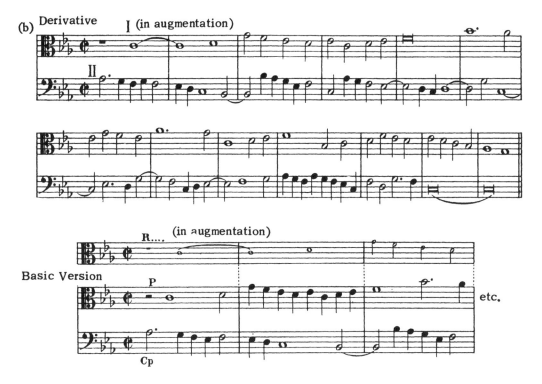

An example in diminution would be obtained by taking the derivative as the original.

In the next example I in the derivative is· a shift of the same voice in the original, one measure to the right, and in contrary motion.

Ex. 210

Basic Version

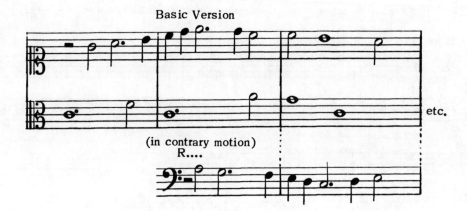

(in contrary motion)
R....

This combination is taken from the following basic version, which, like the preceding, was written according to the method indicated in § 376.

The exceptional forms of imitation may be united in one voice; for example R may imitate in augmentation and contrary motion at the same time, giving a corresponding imitation of this voice in the derivative.

Obs.—If it is necessary that both voices of the derivative shall be taken in contrary motion the problem can not be solved by means of a basic version. It refers to the province of metamorphosed counterpoint, having special conditions. The use of exceptional forms of imitation in the basic version establishes the boundaries that shifting counterpoint can explore. The matter is referred to here only for the purpose of explaining the functions of the basic version in complex counterpoint in general.

§ 340. The student who has assimilated the comprehensive materal in this chapter will have acquired the technique necessary for the successful handling of a wide variety of derivatives that can be applied in multi-voice work—inventions, fugues, compositions with text, etc.* For such practical purposes the knowledge acquired is sufficient.

But for the solving of problems with a predetermined shift of voices, for finding their corresponding basic versions, and to prepare for the study of three-voice horizontal-shifting counterpoint, it is first necessary to master the contents of the next chapter.

---

*Examples of the horizontal shift in contrary motion will be found at the end of this Division. Cf. also Habert, "Die Lehre von der Nachamung," § 13.

CHAPTER XVII

NOTATION OF HORIZONTAL-SHIFTING VOICES; POSITIVE AND NEGATIVE MEASURES; THE SHIFTS; INDEX FOR HORIZONTAL-SHIFTING COUNTERPOINT; FORMULAS; METHODS OF WORKING OUT EXERCISES

§ 341. The concepts introduced into the study of vertical-shifting counterpoint—addition, subtraction, positive and negative shifts, contrapuntal indices etc.—are found also in the study of horizontal-shifting counterpoint.

§ 342. In the vertical shift the unit of distance is the second; in the horizontal shift (right and left, referring to the notation) the measure is the unit of distance. When a voice is shifted from one part of a measure to another the necessity was seen for using fractions. This concerned the metre in which a given combination was written; shifting at a half-measure, or at one and one-half measures etc. referred to duple time; at a third or at two-thirds of a measure, to triple time.

§ 343. The voices of an original combination are indicated according to the order of their entries; I is the earlier entering voice, II the later. In adding any number of measures to the distance between their entries I may be advanced to the left or II to the right. Subtraction causes each to shift in the opposite direction. In other words, I is the voice for which positive shift is to the left, II the voice for which the positive shift is to the right. Expressed in a diagram: $+\leftarrow I \rightarrow - \leftarrow II \rightarrow +$

§ 344. Shifting horizontally, a voice may either recede from the other or approach it, or even take up such a position that II will precede I. The distance (temporal) between voices that enter in the order II-I is termed negative. In this way measures will be positive or negative, analogous to the positive and negative intervals of vertical-shifting counterpoint.

§ 345. The treatment of measures as positive and negative allows the distinction of direct and inverse shifts also in horizontal-shifting counterpoint. At the direct shift the quantities that define the distance between the entries of voices in original and derivative combinations, in terms of measures or parts of measures, have the same signs; at the inverse shift the opposite signs (cf. § 25).

Obs.—The signs ![symbol] and ![symbol] refer only to the vertical shifts of the voices.

§ 346. If the voices of the original combination enter either in the order I-II or II-I, in both cases the upper voice (I) is considered as the voice of earliest entry, in the sense that shifting it to the left is a positive operation; and the lower voice (II) as that of later entry, with its positive shift to the right. The only difference is that in the first case the distance between the entries is a positive number of measures, in the second, a negative number.

Obs.—This method removes the difficulties that arise when the lower voice enters before the upper. As voice of first entry it would have to be indicated by the figure I, as lower voice by II, besides which it would require a special sign, as these refer to both the vertical and the horizontal shift.

§ 347. The following diagram shows the positive and negative shifts of upper (I) and lower (II) voices in both vertical and horizontal directions:

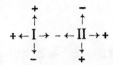

Each voice retains its sign in the derivative. The voices of the original combination, I + II, will be regarded as before, in vertical order, so that positive intervals are obtained between them, i.e. I is in fact the upper voice, II the lower. As for their relative positions in horizontal order, the distance between their entries in the original combination can only be positive (when the voices enter in the order I-II), or negative (if the order of entry is II-I), or equal to zero (if both voices enter simultaneously).

Notation of the Horizontal Shift: h, hh;
Formulas for the Derivative Combination

§ 348. The horizontal shift of a single voice will be indicated by the letter h (plural hh). The quantity indicating the direction and number of measures in the shift is united to h by the sign of equality and placed after the roman numeral instead of v. For example the expression $\mathrm{I}^{h=1} + \mathrm{II}^{h=\frac{1}{2}}$ means that both voices shift to the left, the upper one measure, the lower a half-measure; $\mathrm{I}^{h=1\frac{1}{2}} + \mathrm{II}^{h=2}$ means that the upper voice shifts one and one-half measures to the left, the lower two measures to the right, etc. The sign + means that the voices shifted form correct counterpoint. The preceding expressions are formulas of derivative combinations for horizontal-shifting counterpoint (cf. § 21).

Obs.—In horizontal-shifting counterpoint vertical shifts are excluded only at $Jv=0$.

§ 349. A voice that does not shift horizontally is represented by its figure with either h omitted or with $h=0$.

§ 350. In the formula for the derivative combination for double-shifting counterpoint the letter v is placed underneath h. For example the formula of the derivative combination $\mathrm{I}^{\substack{h=\ 0\\ v=-8}} + \mathrm{II}^{\substack{h=1\\ v=5}}$ means that the upper voice (I) does not shift horizontally, but shifts vertically a ninth below; the lower voice (II) shifts one measure to the right and at the same time a sixth below. The formula $\mathrm{I}^{\substack{h=-1\\ v=\ \ 0}} + \mathrm{II}^{\substack{h=0\\ v=3}}$ means a shift of the upper voice (I) one measure to the right and the lower (II) a fourth below, etc.

Index for Horizontal-Shifting Counterpoint: Jh

§ 351. To define the distance between the entries of the voices of the derivative the algebraic sum of their hh is added to the number of measures in the original distance (cf. § 26).

§ 352. The algebraic sum hh of two voices is called the index of horizontal-shifting counterpoint; similar to vertical-shifting; it is indicated $Jh; Jhh$ (cf. § 27).

§ 353. Jh may be added to the original distance between any two notes (cf. § 26). As a result the derivative distance is obtained between the corresponding notes.

§ 354. To indicate what shift of voices is made at a given Jh the formula of the derivative combination is enclosed in parentheses and after it is placed Jh, e.g.: $(\mathrm{I}^{h=2} + \mathrm{II}^{h=-\frac{1}{2}})\ Jh=1\frac{1}{2}$. If the formula also includes a vertical shift, after the parentheses first comes Jh, then Jv: $(\mathrm{I}^{\substack{h=\ 0\\ v=-8}} + \mathrm{II}^{\substack{h=1\\ v=5}})\ Jh=1, Jv=-3$.

§ 355. If to a horizontal shift is added a vertical shift at $Jv = 0$ the result has to do with horizontal shifting only, not with double shifting (*Obs.*, § 348).

§ 356. If one and the same combination admits of shifts at two or more JJh the corresponding figures, separated by commas, follow the sign of equality. Such a Jh, referring to one original and more than one derivative, is called a compound index. It may be double, triple etc., according to how many simple indices are present (cf. § 28). For instance, $Jh = 1$, ½; $Jh = 2$, −2 are double indices; $Jh = 1$, ½, −1 is a triple index, etc.

§ 357. A shift of voices I + II at a given Jh may be substituted for another and give as a result the same distance between entries, if the algebraic sum of the shifts remains without change (cf. § 29). A voice may appear as shifted to other parts of measures, depending upon the value of h of the corresponding fraction; this change is the only one inserted into the horizontal shifting of a melody.

§ 358. If for one of the voices $h = 0$, then for the other $Jh = h$. In other words, when only one voice is shifted $Jh = h$ of that voice. This follows from the fact that Jh equals the algebraic sum hh of both voices (§ 352).

§ 359. If a shift of one voice is substituted for a shift of the other with the same value (positive or negative) the distance between entries is in both cases identical. Therefore the expression $I^{h=1}$ + II and I + $II^{h=1}$ are equivalent. It is the same if h is equal to a fraction; whichever voice it represents is merely moved from one part of a measure to another.

The Formula a + Jh= b

§ 360. Adding Jh to the number of measures equal to the original distance yields the derivative distance (§ 351). Indicating the original distance by a and the corresponding derivative distance by b, the formula (cf. § 31) is expressed by the equation $a + Jh = b$. Hence the value of Jh is determined by the equation $Jh = b - a$, i.e. Jh is equal to the derivative distance, to which the original is added, taken with the opposite sign.

Conditions of the Shifts

§ 361. Jh may be either a positive or a negative quantity or may equal zero (cf. § 24). At $Jh = 0$, after shifting both voices of the original combination the distance between their entries in the derivative remains unchanged, even though the voices may shift from one part of the measure to another.

§ 362. The conditions of the shifts follow from the equation $a + Jh = b$ (§ 360) and from the statements in § 343 (cf. § 34):

(1) If a and Jh are both positive or both negative the shift is direct.

(2) If of the two values of a and Jh one is positive and the other negative, then—

(a) If the absolute value of a is greater than that of Jh the shift is direct;

(b) If the absolute value of a is less than that of Jh the shift is inverse;

(c) If the absolute value of a equals that of Jh the result is 0, i.e. the coincidental entries of the voices.

§ 363. From the equation $a + Jh = b$ it follows: it $a = 0$, $b = Jh$.

§ 364. Any combination in simple counterpoint may be regarded as the result of a horizontal shift of the voices at $Jh = 0$ (cf. § 44). In general, Jh in horizontal-shifting counterpoint has the same functions that Jv does in vertical-shifting.

Application of h and v to the Basic Version;
Formula of the Imaginary Combination

§ 365. By means of the sign h can be exactly designated by how many measures in the basic version R (or $R.....$, § 322) stands from P.

§ 366. R is only a shift of P to the right. Therefore h is a positive quantity if P (therefore also R) is voice II (P II, R II); and vice versa, at P I (and R I) h is a negative quantity (§ 343). Indicating by a the number of measures that R shifts relative to P, the combination $Cp + R$, taken as the derivative, shows two phases:

$$Cp \text{ I} + R \text{ II}^{h=\,a} \text{ or } R \text{ I}^{h=\,-a} + Cp \text{ II}.$$

Obs.—The Roman numerals I and II designate the upper and lower voices (§ 347). Therefore P I indicates P, forming the upper voice of the original combination. Cp II indicates Cp, consisting of the lower voice of this combination, etc. Adding the Roman numerals to P, R, and Cp enables the shifts applied to these voices to be indicated.

§ 367. If R is imaginary ($R....$) the preceding formula takes these forms:

$$\text{I}^{h=\,-a}_{....} + \text{II} \text{ or } \text{I} + \text{II}^{h=\,a}_{....};$$

they are called formulas of imaginary combinations (§ 323).

Obs.—The formula of an imaginary combination in two-voice counterpoint is at the same time the formula of the basic version according to its construction. But in three-voice counterpoint, as will be explained in Division D, three formulas are necessary for the purpose of the imaginary combination; united, they constitute the formula of the basic version.

§ 368. To simplify and generalize to the furthest extent, use will be made of the formula for the imaginary combination for every basic version, irrespective as to whether its R is imaginary or not. This is entirely admissable, because the actual R may be regarded, like the imaginary, as fortuitously forming correct counterpoint with P (§ 323).

Stated in this way, the formula for the imaginary combination, representing every factor in the basic version, does not determine beforehand whether the latter is written with the real or the imaginary R.

§ 369. For double-shifting counterpoint the formula of the imaginary combination must indicate at what interval $R....$ shifts—above or below—according to its relationship to P. Indicating this interval by b, the two views of the formula are:

$$\text{I} + \text{II}^{h=\,a}_{v=\,\pm b} \text{ and } \text{I}^{h=\,-a}_{v=\,\pm b} + \text{II}.$$

In this way, for the basic version, Ex. 203 (a)—

etc.

the formula of the imaginary combination is $I_{v=}^{h=-2} \, ^2 + II.$

For Ex. 204 (a)—

the formula of the imaginary combination is $I_{v=-3}^{h=-\frac{1}{2}} + II.$

For Ex. 205 (a)—

it is $I + II_{v=-6}^{h=1}$, etc.

§ 370. The imaginary combination corresponds to the derivative (§ 324). This correspondence obtains in the fact that the distance apart at which the voices enter, also the order of intervals formed by their union, are identical in both combinations. In other words, both imaginary and derivative combinations show a shift of the original at Jh and Jv alike. Both imaginary and derivative combinations may, therefore, be regarded as a shift of the other at $Jh = 0$ or at $Jv = 0$.

General Formula of Horizontal-Shifting Counterpoint

§ 371. The formula of the derivative combination states the requirements of a given problem; the formula of the imaginary combination indicates the kind of basic version that solves the problem but does not determine in advance how it shall be written (§ 368). Therefore in solving problems the formula of the derivative combination must be converted into the formula of the imaginary. Since Jh is identical in both combinations (§ 370) and in the combination $Cp + R....$ only one voice shifts: $R....$, and $h = 0$ for the other voice; thus $R....$ has $h = Jh$ (§ 358). Therefore—

$$Cp + R_{....}^{h=Jh}$$

is the general formula for horizontal-shifting counterpoint, solving all problems in this category.

§ 372. Corollary to this, whether h (therefore also Jh) is a positive or a negative value, the formula may be double (§ 367):

$$\text{I} + \text{II}\overset{h=}{\underset{\dots}{}}Jh= a \text{ or } \text{I}\overset{h=}{\underset{\dots}{}}Jh= -a + \text{II}.$$

Obs.—Since the interval of imitation in the basic version for horizontal-shifting counterpoint is the unison (0), in the formula for the imaginary combination of this counterpoint $v= 0$ is always understood.

General Formula of Double-Shifting Counterpoint

§ 373. To convert the formula of the derivative into that of the imaginary combination $v= Jv$ is added to the imaginary R, in the same way that $h= Jh$ was (§ 371). Hence the general formula for double-shifting counterpoint is:

$$h= Jh$$
$$Cp + R\overset{v=}{\underset{\dots}{}}Jv.$$

§ 374. This also has two forms (§ 372):

$$h= Jh =a \qquad h= Jh=-a$$
$$\text{I} + \text{II}\overset{v=}{\underset{\dots}{}}Jv \quad \text{or } \text{I}\overset{v=}{} Jv \qquad + \text{II}.$$

§ 375. Therefore, for the solution of problems in horizontal-shifting or in double-shifting counterpoint it is necessary that the problem be stated as a formula for the derivative (§ 348), completed by Jh and Jv; hence a positive or a negative Jh can be taken for the corresponding formula of the imaginary combination (§ 367), writing in $h= Jh$ and $v= Jv$ for the imaginary voice (§§ 371, 373). Examples of formulas are given at the beginning of each problem in Appendix C.

Obs.—The original combinations (hence also derivatives) studied have consisted of two different melodies. But it also happens that the original may consists of only one melody, imitated canonically. Such an original, as a special case of the combination I + II, will be examined, indicating each voice by its figure, and the shift in the derivative. The following is from Palestrina:

Ex. 211

$$(\text{I}\overset{h=\ 0}{\underset{v=\ 7}{}} + \text{II}\overset{h=\ 1}{\underset{v=\ -7}{}}) \; Jh= 1, \; Jv= 0;$$ formula of the imaginary combination: $\text{I} + \text{II}\overset{h=\ 1}{\underset{\dots}{}}$. Corresponding to this formula is a basic version representing a three-voice canon:

Basic Version

The combination I + II is the original (a), and I + II$^{h=1}$, shifted an octave higher, the derivative (b). The basic version, though contrapuntally correct, is not found in Palestrina, only the two-voice combinations (a) and (b). In view of the fact that three-voice canonic imitation can not be explained here, future examples will be limited to where voices I + II represent two different melodies.

Methods of Working Out Problems

§ 376. Two methods have been indicated of writing basic versions—with real and with imaginary R. In both cases Cp correlates to the two voices, previously written, of the basic version. A third method is possible, not utilizing previously written voices and therefore applicable only to problems without a given voice. This method consists in writing all three voices—P, R.....and Cp—by sections in definite order (v. diagram below). The whole problem is broken up into columns, each of which represents the distance from the beginning of the exercise to the entry of the imaginary voice. Melody P is represented by the bold-face figures **A, B, C**, etc. Underneath these Cp is indicated by the corresponding small letters. The divisions of R.....are indicated by the same capital letters as those for P, each letter followed by dots: $A....$, $B.....$, $C.....$, etc. A problem is worked out as follows:

First column 1 is written $(Cp+P)$. Next the section written for P is transferred to the second column, where it forms the beginning of the imaginary voice. With the entry of R.....each succeeding column is written in the same order, beginning with the imaginary combination (i.e. Cp is written to R....), which thereafter is real; to Cp is written P, which is then transferred to the third column, etc. The diagonal arrows from each column to the next show the transferrence of P to the imaginary voice. The curved arrows inside the columns show the order in which the melodies are counterpointed to one another; the voice to which an arrow points is written as counterpoint to that from which the arrow starts:

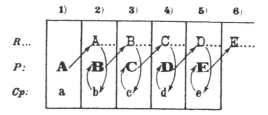

In going from one section to another care must be taken that the melody of a given section must each time form a natural continuation of the melody in the preceding section.

§ 377. In the following illustration (the beginning of Example No. 2 in Appendix C, formula of the imaginary combination $I^{h=-2}+II$) the divisions into sections are lettered in accordance with the preceding diagram. The composition of the basic version can here be traced step by step.

Obs.—In this illustration, also in the examples in Appendix C, the indications *P*, *R*..... and *Cp* are omitted. The voice forming *Cp* is indicated by a star to the left of the figure (*II). After the figure for the imaginary voice is placed in parentheses the figure of the voice counterpointing with it: $I^{h=-2}_{....}$ (+ II).

§ 378. Therefore there are three methods of working out problems in horizontal-shifting and double-shifting counterpoint.

(1) In the first method, to a basic version that imitates canonically is written a contrapuntal part that is first of all useful in combination with it; this has the advantage over the other methods in that when applied the basic version not only gives two-voice combinations of horizontal-shifting melodies but also presents them enriched by new contrapuntal material. The disadvantage of this method is that a two-voice combination extracted from three-voice counterpoint may not sound full enough without the assistance of a supplementary voice.

(2) In the second method a basic version with *R*.... is previously written with *P*, to which *Cp* is adjusted. This is a difficult and mechanical method, though useful from a purely technical point of view, and indispensible in solving a problem with a voice given beforehand. Otherwise, if such a problem does not show just what kind of horizontal shift is required, this method can be avoided and a search made for such entry of the imitating voice as will yield a real and not an imaginary *R*. In this event the problem is solved by the first method.

(3) As for the third method, explained in § 376, giving both combinations—a two-voice original and its derivative—it is hardly ever applied in composition.* Its principal use is for the working of exercises, for which purpose it excels both other methods in the extreme ease with which it employs all possible shifts of three voices, giving two-voice combinations that sound full and do not require supplementary parts. The examples in Appendix C were written by this method. The same process, but more complicated and using a larger number of voices, will be applied in three-voice horizontal-shifting counterpoint.

Obs.—Exs. 209 and 210 were written by this method. In applying it to imitation in augmentation each successive section is as many times the length of the preceding as the increased values of the imitating voice.

---

*Because it is unknown? Method (3) has unrealized possibilities. —Tr.

CHAPTER XVIII

INTERCHANGE OF ORIGINAL AND DERIVATIVE; PROBLEMS ON A CANTUS FIRMUS

Interchange of Original and Derivative Combinations in Horizontal-Shifting Counterpoint

§ 379. When the original and derivative combinations are interchanged (cf. § 68) the formula of the derivative, and corresponding to it, the formula of the imaginary combination, is altered as follows:

(1) In the formula of the derivative combination h of each voice, therefore also Jh, change their signs (+ or −) to the opposite.

(2) In the formula of the imaginary combination, because of the conversion of Jh to positive or negative or vice versa, h of the imaginary voice, equal to Jh, also requires the opposite sign and therefore is transferred to the other voice (§ 372), which becomes the imaginary voice of the new formula. Since R (therefore also P) may be either of the two voices (depending on which combination is taken as the original), for horizontal-shifting counterpoint with one derivative there are two basic versions available for the solving of problems.

Obs.—This does not refer to those combinations where one of the voices is a c.f.; in this case a problem is solved by the use of only one basic version, namely that in which P serves as c.f. (§ 326).

Problem No. 1 in Appendix C has the formula $(\mathrm{I}^{h=1} + \mathrm{II})\ Jh = 1$ for the derivative combination; hence the formula of the imaginary combination is: $\mathrm{I} + \mathrm{II}^{h=1}_{\cdots}$.

The beginning of the basic version (cf. *Obs.*, § 377) is as follows: (I + II is the original, $\mathrm{I} + \mathrm{II}^{h=1}_{\cdots}$ the derivative):

·Taking the derivative for the original, the signs for the derivative formula are changed: $(\mathrm{I}^{h=-1} + \mathrm{II})\ Jh = -1$ and a new formula obtained for the imaginary combination: $\mathrm{I}^{h=-1}_{\cdots} + \mathrm{II}$. This formula corresponds to the following second basic version (original I + II, derivative $\mathrm{I}^{h=-1}_{\cdots} + \mathrm{II}$):

Interchange of Original and Derivative
in Double-Shifting Counterpoint

§ 380. Here two cases are to be distinguished, according to whether Jv has the direct or the inverse shift.

§ 381. *Case 1.*—Jv has the direct shift: ══════ (*Cp* is an outer voice of the basic version, § 329). The rules concerning h and Jh (§379,[1]) are extended to include also v and Jv, viz.:

(1) In the formula of the derivative combination the signs for h and v of each voice, therefore Jh and Jv, are changed to the opposite.

(2) In the formula of the imaginary combination h and v of the imaginary voice change their signs, these being transferred to the other voice, which now stands as the imaginary voice of the new formula.

Problem No. 6 in Appendix C has the following formula:

$$(\mathrm{I}^{\substack{h=1\\v=0}} + \mathrm{II}^{\substack{h=0\\v=1}})\, Jh=1,\ Jv=1;\ \mathrm{I} + \mathrm{II}^{\substack{h=1\\v=1}}.$$

The formula of the derivative combination at the exchange of derivative and original is converted to:

$$(\mathrm{I}^{\substack{h=-1\\v=0}} + \mathrm{II}^{\substack{h=0\\v=-1}})\, Jh=-1,\ Jv=-1:$$

hence the new formula of the imaginary combination is: $\mathrm{I}^{\substack{h=-1\\v=-1}} + \mathrm{II}$.

Corresponding to this formula is the beginning of the second basic version:

As to the key-signature of the imaginary voice cf. § 333.

§ 382. *Case 2*—Jv has the inverse shift: ⤬ (*Cp* is the inner voice of the basic version, § 379). Exchanging original and derivative combinations:

(1) In the formula of the derivative h and v of voice I are transferred with their signs to voice II, and h and v of voice II to I; Jh and Jv therefore remain without change, hence:

(2) The formula of the imaginary combination remains without change.

Exchanging original and derivative in example No. 7, Appendix C, the former I now appears as II and vice versa:

The previous formula of the derivative was:

$$(\mathrm{I}^{\substack{h=\ 0 \\ v=\ -6}} + \mathrm{II}^{\substack{h=\ -1 \\ v=\ -2}})\ Jh= -1,\ Jv= -8;$$

converted to:

$$(\mathrm{I}^{\substack{h=\ -1 \\ v=\ -2}} + \mathrm{II}^{\substack{h=\ 0 \\ v=\ -6}})\ Jh= -1,\ Jv= -8;$$

Jh and Jv remaining as before. The formula of the imaginary combination is the same for both: $\mathrm{I}^{\substack{h=-1 \\ v=-8}} + \mathrm{II}$. It must not be forgotten that I refers now to the former II and II to the former I. Corresponding to the new formula is the second basic version:

§ 383. Therefore to obtain the second basic version the previous derivative is taken as the original combination. If the vertical shift is direct ( ) the formula of the imaginary combination changes thus: h and v with change of signs (+ and −) are transferred to the other voice, which now functions as the imaginary voice of the new formula. At the inverse shift ( ) the formula of the imaginary combination remains without change.

Problems on a Cantus Firmus

§ 384. In problems on a c.f. the method described in § 376 of composing the basic version cannot be used, since it does not admit of the writing of a voice in advance. These problems are written with the aid of a basic version in which the c.f. forms the proposta, and when shifted, the imaginary risposta. To these voices, previously written, is then added Cp. Therefore only one basic version is possible for a problem on a cantus firmus.

Obs.—Strictly speaking, a second basic version is possible for a problem on a c.f., but for this canonic imitation must be used—a very difficult matter and one not related to the subject under discussion.*

§ 385. Of the two voices of the original combination, if the c.f. is the upper (c.f. I) and in the formula of the derivative Jh is negative; or if the c.f. is the lower voice (c.f. II) and Jh is positive, the problem is no different from the preceding; the c.f. shifts to the right at $h= Jh$, forming $R....$, the usual method of composing the formula of the imaginary combination according to the basic version.

§ 386. If the c.f. and Jh are found in the reverse relationship, that is, c.f. I at a positive Jh or c.f. II at a negative, the c.f. must shift to the left and therefore cannot form $R.....$. In this case the derivative combination must temporarily be taken for the original, consequently its c.f. and Jh stand in the same relationship as that described in § 385, and the problem is solved in the usual way. Taking the derivative for the original and writing the basic version according to the formula of the imaginary combination, the original must be considered not as $Cp + P$ but as $Cp + R.....$ If the c.f. appears on other degrees or on other parts of the measure than those given, all com-

---

*It is dealt with in the author's sequel to the present work, "The Technique of Canon," —Tr.

binations shift in vertical and horizontal directions (at $Jh= 0$ and at $Jv= 0$), in such a way that the c.f. appears as at first. The derivative combination is arrived at by applying the requirements of the problem to the original by this method.

(1) Direct Shift.—

$$\text{(C.f. } I^{v=\overset{h=1}{0}} + II^{v=\overset{h=0}{-1}}) \; Jh= 1, \; Jv= -1.$$

In view of the fact that the c.f. is I and Jh is a positive quantity (§ 386), the original is replaced by the derivative. $Jh= 1$ and $Jv= -1$ are changed to $Jh= -1$ and $Jv= 1$ (§ 381). Hence the formula of the imaginary combination is:

$$\text{C.f. } I^{v=\overset{h=-1}{1}} + II.$$

The basic version corresponding to this formula is:

Ex. 212 (a)   Basic Version

Taking the imaginary combination $(Cp + R....)$ in the capacity of original, it is shifted so that the c.f. appears on the appropriate degrees, and the desired original is obtained:

(b)

Shifting the voices of the original according to the requirements of the problem:

$$\text{C.f. } I^{v=\overset{h=1}{0}} + II^{v=\overset{h=0}{-1}}, \text{ yields—}$$

(c)

Derivative

Obs.—In the preceding basic version the c.f. (= P) was taken in the register specified in the problem. But this is not essential; it may be transferred to other octaves, taken with other key-signatures, etc., whatever is desired. For instances, in the basic version of the following problem the c.f. is taken an eleventh higher, otherwise the imaginary voice would appear too low.

(2) Inverse Shift.—   Cf.

$$(I^{v=-2}_{h=-1\frac{1}{2}} + c.f. \ II^{v=-11}_{h=1}) \ Jh=-\frac{1}{2}, \ Jv=-13; \ I^{v=-13}_{h=-\frac{1}{2}} + II.$$

In view of the fact that the c.f. is II and that Jh is negative (§ 386), replacing the original by the derivative does not change the formula of the imaginary combination (§ 382).

Ex. 213 (a)

The key-signature of the imaginary voice is so calculated that the combination $Cp + R$......represents a transposition of the original (§ 333). With reference to shifting the c.f. at the half-measure, v. §§ 334-5.

From the basic version the imaginary is retained as original, but shifted so that the c.f. is in the register and at the part of the measure required by the conditions of the problem.

(b) Original

Shifting the voices according to the requirements specified:

$$I^{v=-2}_{h=-1\frac{1}{2}} + c.f. \ II^{v=-11}_{h=1}$$

is obtained:

(c) Derivative

CHAPTER XIX

ANALYSIS

Composition of the Basic Version
According to Original and Derivative

§ 387. In analysing horizontal-shifting and double-shifting counterpoint it is not enough merely to indicate by how many measures and at what intervals the voices of the derivative shift. Analysis must give in the resulting basic versions the factors of both combinations—original and derivative. There are two basic versions for a combination with one derivative, because each of the two combinations may be taken as an original. Taking one of the two-voice combinations as the original it is necessary to indicate how the voices in the derivative shift horizontally and vertically, to find Jh and Jv, to compile a formula for the imaginary combination (§ 375) and to write accordingly R to the original combination. Using a previous derivative for the original, the formula of the imaginary combination must be changed to agree if the vertical shift is direct, or retained if the shift is inverse (§ 383), and the second basic version written in conformity with it.

Obs.—The basic version may be found by other means than using the formula of the imaginary combination. Taking one of the voices as Cp, one of the combinations can be mentally adjusted to the other so that this voice coincides in both, the entry of R is then defined. The coincidence must be complete, and to assure this the Cp in the derivative must be on the same degrees and on the same parts of the measure as in the original. If this condition is not satisfied in the derivative the adjustment must be made by applying the method already given.

§ 388. Either of the basic versions will solve the given problem. But it is of primary importance that the basic version shall represent correct counterpoint; in analysing they must be abstracted from the general background and their occurrence in the composition noted. Consisting of the same two melodies but in highly complex relationships (since one of the melodies imitates canonically), such a basic version enriches the contrapuntal resources of composition to an important extent. Often the result of previously written two-voice combinations, it not only retains its own melodies but also separates them from and unites them with other melodies, thus becoming a crucial factor in all thematic invention.

§ 389. The two basic versions referred to in § 387 differ in this regard, that the voices of one of them consists of $Cp + P$, in the other of $Cp + R$ (or $Cp + R....$) and vice versa.

§ 390. These basic versions may appear as one of three cases: (1) RR of both versions are imaginary; (2) one basic version contains the imaginary R, the other is contrapuntally valid; and (3) both basic versions are contrapuntally valid.

§ 391. *Case 1: RR of Both Versions Imaginary.*—This situation represents the methods of composition explained in § 378, (2), (3); though useful for scholastic exercises they are not applicable in composition. It can hardly be assumed that a composer, having in view a combination with horizontal-shifting voices, would begin by writing a basic version with the aid of an imaginary R, or by adjusting Cp to voices not contrapuntally associated, or composing the whole according to its parts—preferring these mechanical expedients to the far more natural and simple process of writing a contrapuntally correct basic version and taking from it the required combination. It would be difficult to cite an instance of horizontal-shifting counterpoint where analysis would show two basic versions each having an imaginary R. The following is from Palestrina:

Ex. 214 (a) Original   Palestrina

It admits of this derivative (not found in Palestrina):

Derivative

(b)

The formula of the derivative is: $(I + II^{h=1}) Jv = 1$; that of the imaginary $I + II^{h=1}_{....}$. According to the formula of the imaginary a first basic version may be written with imaginary R:

(c)   1st Basic Version

Then the former derivative is taken as the original and the former original for the derivative, the corresponding changes being made in the formula of the imaginary combination (§ 383): $I^{h=-1}_{....} + II$. According to the latter a second basic version is possible, also having an imaginary R:

2nd Basic Version

(d)

If horizontal-shifting counterpoint of which both basic versions has an imaginary R were found in a composition it would be reasonable to consider it as entirely fortuitous, as in the preceding example.

§ 392. *Case 2: One Basic Version Contrapuntally Correct.*—In Ex. 215 the voices of the derivative also shift vertically, but at $Jv = 0$, therefore the shift is practically only horizontal.

Ex. 215 (a) Original   Palestrina   Derivative

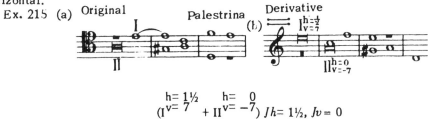

$$\left(I^{h=1\frac{1}{2}}_{v=7} + II^{h=0}_{v=-7}\right) Jh = 1\frac{1}{2}, Jv = 0$$

Formula of the imaginary combination: $I + II^{h=1\frac{1}{2}}_{....}$. Corresponding basic version:

(c)   1st Basic Version

$R\ \mathrm{II}^{h\,=\,1\frac{1}{2}}$

The second basic version, as it contains the imaginary R, is not given here; it will be referred to later in connection with double-shifting counterpoint.

Ex. 216 is from the five-voice *Gloria in excelsis (Qui tollis)* of Palestrina's mass *Ad coenam Agni providi*. These three two-voice combinations are found:

Ex. 216 (a)   (b)   (c)
Original   Palestrina   1st Derivative   2nd Derivative

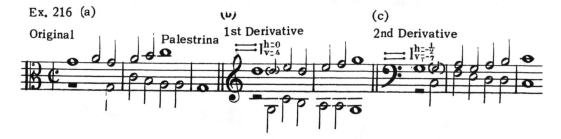

Here the two derivatives differ only in their vertical shifts (the first derivative is the separation at the octave of the second) and Jh is identical for both, as is seen by their formulas. That for the first derivative is:

$$(\mathrm{I}^{\,v=\,4}_{\ \ \ h=\,0} + \mathrm{II}^{\,v=\,0}_{\ \ \ h=-\frac{1}{2}})\, Jh = -\tfrac{1}{2},\ Jv = 4;\ \mathrm{I}^{\,v=\,4}_{\ \ \ h=-\frac{1}{2}} + \mathrm{II}.$$

For the second derivative:

$$(\mathrm{I}^{\,v=-7}_{\ \ \ h=-\frac{1}{2}} + \mathrm{II}^{\,v=\,4}_{\ \ \ h=\,0})\, Jh = -\tfrac{1}{2},\ Jv = -3;\ \mathrm{I}^{\,v=-3}_{\ \ \ h=-\frac{1}{2}} + \mathrm{II}.$$

Since the horizontal shift is the same for both derivatives, one of them must be selected for the basic version. Combination (c) is chosen, because its basic version is contrapuntally correct:

(d)   Basic Version

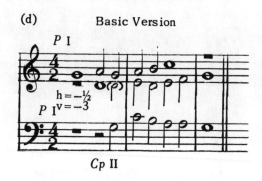

$Cp\ \mathrm{II}$

Hence the original is $Cp + P$; applied to the requirements of the problem as expressed by the formula for the second basic version, this derivative is obtained, and by separating the voices an octave, the first derivative. This basic version is found twice in Palestrina, the first time with a change of the initial note of R, c instead of d; the second time shifted a fifth below, with the initial note of R shortened.

Ex. 217

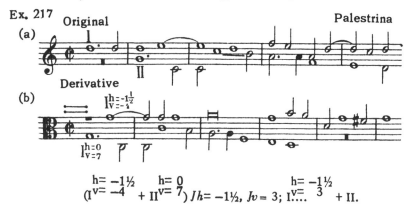

The following basic version corresponding to the formula of the imaginary combination, contains the original. $Cp + P$ is taken an octave lower:

If the last measure of Cp is discarded the second basic version shows correct counterpoint (cf. § 393). Formula of the imaginary combination: $I + II_{\cdots}^{\substack{h= \ 1\frac{1}{2} \\ v= -3}}$

Such instances, where an unimportant change in one of the voices gives a new basic version that is contrapuntally correct, should be observed in analysing, as they are applicable in composition.

§ 393. *Case 3: Both Basic Versions Contrapuntally Correct.—*

Ex. 218

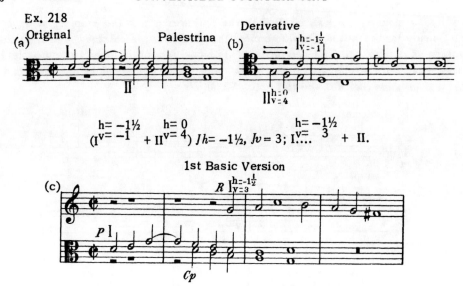

$$h= -1\tfrac{1}{2} \qquad h= 0 \qquad\qquad h= -1\tfrac{1}{2}$$
$$(I^{v=-1} + II^{v=4})\ Jh= -1\tfrac{1}{2},\ Jv= 3;\ I^{v=}_{\ldots}\ \overset{3}{} + II.$$

1st Basic Version

Taking the derivative as original and changing the indices (§ 383) to: $Jh= 1\tfrac{1}{2}$, $Jv= -3$
gives: $I + II^{v=-3}_{\ldots}$ $\overset{h=1\tfrac{1}{2}}{}$. Hence:

2nd Basic Version

Note the possibility of a second basic version with only a horizontal shifting of the voices—not found in Palestrina:

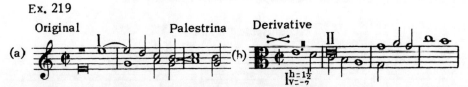

Ex. 219

In the basic version the original is found an octave lower:

1st Basic Version

Taking the derivative for the original and retaining the previous formula of the imaginary combination because of the inverse shift (§ 383) gives:

Ex. 220 Original   Palestrina

In order for this basic version to be contrapuntally correct up to the end it was necessary to interrupt Cp on the penultimate note, indicated*, after which the voice progression is free. The unprepared fourth in the third measure requires a supplementary voice. Taking the derivative as original and retaining the formula of the imaginary combination (because of the inverse shift) gives the second basic version, in which all melodies appear complete:

2nd Basic Version

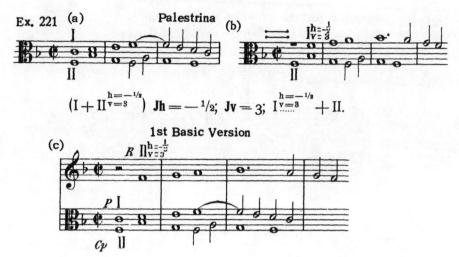

$$\left(I + II_{v=3}^{h=-1/2}\right)\ Jh = -1/2;\ Jv = 3;\ I_{v=3}^{h=-1/2} + II.$$

1st Basic Version

Exchanging as before and altering the formula of the imaginary combination to $I + II_{v=-3}^{h=1/2}$ gives:

2nd Basic Version

The slight alterations at the end of P make this basic version contrapuntally correct.

Obs.—The examples quoted from the works of Palestrina prove that horizontal-shifting counterpoint played no unimportant role in the era of the strict style. These examples may serve as material for the student's exercises (cf. § 423).

Analysis of Combinations on a Cantus Firmus

§ 394. It remains to discuss briefly how to find the basic version when one of the voices is a cantus firmus. In the basic version the c.f. must be P (§ 384). Therefore it is immaterial which of the two-voice combinations is taken as the original. If the c.f. is I, Jh must be negative; if it is II, Jh must be positive (§ 385). Of the two two-voice combinations the original will be whichever fulfils one of these conditions (§ 386).

Ex. 222 Original

$$\left(I_{v=-2}^{h=0} + C.f.\ II_{v=2}^{h=-2}\right)\ Jh = -2,\ Jv = 0.$$

Because the c.f. is II and Jh negative, the derivative is taken as the original. Instead of the former Jh, $Jh = 2$ is obtained (§ 383). Formula of the imaginary combination: $I + II_{\cdots}^{h=2}$. Writing R to the derivative gives:

Basic Version

$Cp + R$, taken a third higher, corresponds to the original, and $Cp + P$ to the derivative.

Ex. 223

$$\left(\text{C.f. } I_{v=-1}^{h=1} + II_{v=-7}^{h=1/2}\right) \quad Jh = 1^1/_2, \quad Jv = -8.$$

Since Jh is positive and the c.f. is I, the derivative is taken as the original. Because of the inverse shift, instead of c.f. I is obtained c.f. II; the indices remain without change (§ 382) and the formula of the imaginary combination is:

Hence:
$$I + \text{c.f. } II_{\cdots}^{h=1/2}{}_{v=-8}.$$

Basic Version

Combination $Cp + R \ldots$, shifting at the half-measure and an octave lower, corresponds to the original, and $Cp + P$ to the derivative.

Obs.—In analysing it is no disadvantage that a second basic version may not be contrapuntally correct, in which case the correct combination must be extracted. This basic version involves canonic imitation of a c.f. (*Obs.*, § 384), and refers to the study of canon. Instances are comparatively infrequent and present considerable difficulty in their working-out.

CHAPTER XX

COMBINATIONS GIVING SEVERAL DERIVATIVES

§ 395. A three-voice basic version (with one R) consists of the original combination and one derivative with horizontal-shifting voices. If R imitates P at the unison the derivative shows only the horizontal shift. If the imitation is at any other interval the derivative shows a double shift. Such a basic version, consisting of an original with one derivative, is written in simple counterpoint and does not require application of the conditions of any vertical index (§ 330). But if more derivatives are needed, without the addition of a new R in the basic version—i.e. retaining the three-voice texture—they can be obtained by writing the voices of the basic version according to the rules of any Jv. In meeting these requirements the voices will give a shift or a duplication at the given Jv, but this new derivative will consist of only one vertical shift of the voices: either a shift of the two-voice original, or of its derivative, or of the basic version, assuming that it is contrapuntally correct. The possibility of these shifts is dependent only on the conditions that the corresponding voices must satisfy the requirements of the given Jv, not that they shall enter into the structure of the basic version. Therefore at the vertical shift of the combination $Cp + R$ its Jh always remains unchanged; in other words, in obtaining new combinations by this method the derivatives are the result of a simple and not a compound Jh (§ 356).

§ 396. If, on the contrary, to increase the number of RR in the basic version and to write Cp not to a two-voice imitation but to one of three or four voices, means that each additional R gives a new two-voice derivative with a new Jh. In contrast to the preceding case, this gives derivatives at a compound Jh. It is understood that here the separate combinations or the entire basic version must conform to the rules of the Jv concerned, and that the new derivatives obtained in this way give only one vertical shift of voices.

§ 397. Both cases will be investigated in this chapter, first the combinations with several derivatives at a simple Jh, later those at a compound Jh.

Obs.—If vertical-shifting counterpoint is regarded as a function of the basic version (§ 336) and problems shifting in this counterpoint are solved by means of supplementary voices, that is, with coinciding entries of P and R in the basic version, then every two-voice derivative requires a separate R, shifting at some Jh or Jv or both at once. In such cases the number of RR in the basic version is equal to the number of two-voice combinations. Such a basic version is theoretically possible, but entirely useless for the practical solution of problems.

Combinations with Several Derivatives at a Simple Jh

§ 398. The application of Jv for obtaining derivative combinations at a simple Jh may be an elaborate process. These cases will present nothing new to those familiar with part I of the present work. In analysing combinations at one and the same Jh but at different JJv it is necessary to find the contrapuntally correct three-voice basic version, and to indicate what kind of vertical shift, as well as the duplications included in its two-voice combinations ($Cp + P$ and $Cp + R$) apply in the given situation, and what is possible in general; then to see if the same basic version admits of any derivative combinations. If the second basic version is also contrapuntally correct the relation to the two-voice combination already analysed should be written out and studied. Often the basic version sought for will be found in the course of analysing compositions; in other cases it must be deduced from the existing two-voice combinations, as explained in the preceding chapter. The following analysis of two examples from Palestrina will supplement what has just been discussed.

§ 399. In the first motet of Palestrina, *O admirabile commercium* (published in 1569), in the part for the lowest voice is found the following two phrases, separated by rests:

Ex. 224

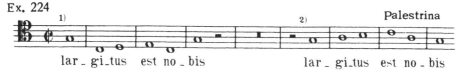

In a mass of the same title, published thirty years later (posthumous), in the *Sanctus* these two melodies are combined in the following way.*

Ex. 225

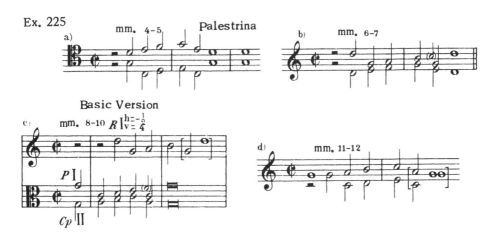

The two-voice combinations (b) and (d) represent vertical shifts of (a); combination (b) at $Jv = -11$, (d) at $Jv = -4$ (with the first note of twice the original value). But the three-voice combination (c) shows a more complex relationship of these two melodies, for it is the basic version, in the construction of which (a) and (b) enter. Consequently in combination (c) is found one of the melodies imitating canonically, at the same time the other (lower voice) acts as counterpoint to the imitation. The relation of the two-voice combination (a), (b) and (d) to the basic version is:

Combination (a) = $(Cp + P)$ shifting at $Jv = -11$;
" (b) = $(Cp + P)$;
" (d) = $(Cp + P)$ shifting at $Jv = -7$.

So, these derivatives show vertical shifts of one and the same combination: $Cp + P$. From the basic version can be written both combinations: $Cp + P$ and $Cp + R$, though the second of these Palestrina did not use:

_____

*In these quotations the small notes in parentheses are variants of the melody as found in Palestrina. The large notes in brackets are continuations of the melody, absent in the original.

Formula of the derivative combination:

$$(I^{v=\,\,4}_{}\,\,{}^{h=\,-\frac{1}{2}} + II)\,Jh= -\frac{1}{2},\,Jv= 4.$$

Formula of the imaginary:

$$I^{v=\,\,4}_{\cdots}\,\,{}^{h=\,-\frac{1}{2}} + II.$$

This formula corresponds to the first basic version (c).

The two-voice combinations (e) and (f) also admit of vertical shifts. The absence of consecutive sixths enables a shift to be made at $Jv= -11$. Moreover, combination (e), where fifths are absent, satisfies the conditions of $Jv= -7$. The absence of similar motion in (f) admits of a shift and duplication at $Jv= -9$. The indices of these combinations are:

$$(Cp + P)\,Jv= -7,\,-11;\,(Cp + R)\,Jv= -2,\,-9,\,-11.$$

$Cp + P$ also admits of duplications (§ 113):

$$I^{d= -9} + II;\,I + II^{d= -9}\,\text{and}\,I^{d= -9} + II^{d= -9}.$$

Numerous manipulations of combination (f) are possible; Palestrina did not use them, nor is the combination itself found, apart from the basic version. Here again may be emphasized the usefulness of analysing derivative combinations, irrespective of whether or not the composer employed them.

§ 400. Combination (c) of Ex. 225 is the first basic version. To obtain the second basic version the former derivative (f) is taken as the original (§ 381), with a corresponding change in the formula of the imaginary combination; instead of $I^{v=\,\,4}_{\cdots}\,\,{}^{h=\,-\frac{1}{2}} + II$ taking $I + II^{v= -4}\,{}^{h=\,\frac{1}{2}}$, which yields a second basic version that is contrapuntally correct.

2nd Basic Version

The former original appears here as derivative, therefore to express the relations of the two-voice combinations of § 399 to the second basic version $Cp + R$ must be substituted for $Cp + P$:

Combination   (a) = $(Cp + R)$ shifting at $Jv= -11$;
     "   (b) = $(Cp + R)$;
     "   (c) = $(Cp + R)$ shifting at $Jv= -7$.

In this basic version Cp is found in double counterpoint at the twelfth in relation to each of the other two voices: $(Cp + P)\ Jv = -11$, $(Cp + R)\ Jv = -11$, and can, therefore, be shifted a twelfth below, which gives a shift of the basic version according to diagram (5):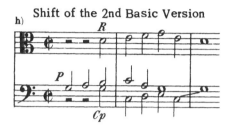

Shift of the 2nd Basic Version

This combination, similar to the two preceding, can also function as a basic version in relation to the two-voice combinations in § 399. It is found in another part of the same mass, the *Agnus Dei*, modified thus:

Ex. 226   Palestrina

§ 401. Ex. 227 is from Palestrina's mass *Regina coeli*, where the following combinations are found:

Ex. 227   Palestrina

Basic Version

Of these (b) is a shift of (a) $Jv=-11$. Here it is given with literal exactness; in the original it appears with unessential changes of note-values for the first note of each

voice:  etc. Combination (c) shows the basic version; $Cp + P$ in it corres-

ponds to combination (a), shifted a fourth higher. This basic version contains moreover the combination $Cp + R$, it is not found in Palestrina, and it requires a supplementary voice below because of the unprepared fourths. This combination, (d), is derived from (a) at $Jh=1$ and $Jv=-4$.

(d)

$$\left(I_{v=3}^{h=0} + II_{v=-7}^{h=1}\right)\ Jh = 1,\ Jv = -4.$$

So, in these combinations there is only one index of horizontal-shifting counterpoint: $Jh=1$. The vertical shifts and duplications of the four preceding combinations will now be listed, also which of them is to be regarded as the original:

Combination (a): $Jv=-9,\ -11$; $I^{d=-9}+II$; $I+II^{d=-9}$; $I^{d=-9}+II^{d=-9}$. At these duplications $d=-2$ must be substituted throughout for $d=-9$.

Combination (b) has the same indices and takes the same duplications.

Combination (d): $Jv=-12,\ 2$; $I+II^{d=2}$ or $I+II^{d=9}$.

The remaining combination (c) is the basic version, of which the voices are numbered in the order of altitude: I, II, III.

(e)

It admits of the following vertical shifts: $II^{v=\pm2}$; $II^{v=\pm9}$; $II^{v=\mp5}$; $I^{v=-2}+II^{v=\pm2}+$ III; $I^{v=2}+II+III^{v=-2}$; $I+II^{v=\pm9}+III^{v=-2}$; and these duplications: $II^{d=\pm9}$; $III^{d=-9}$;

$I+II^{d=\pm9}+III^{d=-9}$. These duplications also must take 2 instead of 9. This gives the following five-voice derivative:

(f) [musical example]

etc.

To those familiar with Part 1 of this work these multi-voice derivatives present nothing new. They are shifts at various JJv, and do not depend on whether or not a given combination admits of a horizontal shifting of voices.

Combinations with Several Derivatives at a Compound Jh

§ 402. If a three-voice imitation instead of a two-voice is taken for the basic version, i.e. if another R is added (RR according to the order of entries are indicated R_1, R_2, etc.), the basic version consists of an original ($Cp + P$) and a derivative ($Cp + R$) with the addition of a second derivative: $Cp + R_2$, having its own Jh. Adding R_3 (i.e. making a four-voice imitation) yields three derivatives: $Cp + R_1$, $Cp + R_2$, $Cp + R_3$, each with a special Jh, etc.

§ 403. The number of derivatives each having a separate Jh is equal to the number of RR in the basic version (§ 396). Therefore Jh will be double (§ 356) at two RR, triple at three, etc.

§ 404. The number of voices in the basic version equals the number of $RR + 2$, adding here the two voices forming the original combination.

§ 405. If R, entering into the composition of a given basic version, imitates P at the unison, the voices of this combination show a shift that is only horizontal (as the vertical shift is only at $Jv = 0$); at other intervals of imitation the voices will be double-shifting (§ 328).

§ 406. If Cp in relation to P and the given R is an outer voice its combination with this R gives the direct shift; if Cp is between these two voices its combination with R gives the inverse shift (§ 329).

§ 407. Here the conditions will be limited to two derivatives at a double Jh. The basic version, therefore, must be four-voice (§ 404) and will contain two RR (§ 390).

§ 408. The JJh that enter into the composition of a double Jh may have the same signs (both positive or both negative) or have opposite signs. These two cases correspond to basic versions of various forms.

§ 409. First, when the signs of both JJh are alike, the basic version consists of a three-voice imitation with Cp:

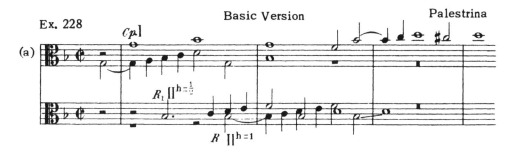

Hence an original ($Cp + P$) and two derivatives ($Cp + R_1$ and $Cp + R_2$). Since the imitation is at the unison both derivatives contain only horizontal-shifting voices.

Formula of first derivative:

$$(I + II^{h=1/2})\ Jh = 1/2; \text{ its imaginary: } I + II^{h=1/2}_{....}.$$

Formula of second derivative:

$$(I + II^{h=1})\ Jh = 1; \text{ its imaginary: } I + II^{h=1}_{....}.$$

Because of the fact that Jh in both derivatives is positive the imaginary voice is the same in both formulas: $II....$. Shifted at the half-measure ($II^{h=1/2}_{...}$), it forms R_1 and takes part in a combination corresponding to the first derivative; shifted at the whole-measure ($II^{h=1}_{...}$) it forms R_2 and enters into a combination corresponding to the second derivative. In these situations, where JJh are both positive or both negative, the Jh of the lesser absolute value refers to the first derivative, that of the greater to the second derivative. In analysing such cases the order of arranging the two derivatives should be the same, i.e. the derivative of the lesser absolute value should come first.

Obs.—Multi-voice canonic imitation may appear in many different forms. It refers to the study of canon, a subject exhaustively treated in the sequel to this book. For those who have not studied canonic form multi-voice imitation at the unison, as found in Ex. 228 (a), is entirely accessible and does not require the application of complex counterpoint. The process of writing it is similar to that of writing two-voice canonic imitation (*Obs.*, § 317). The only difference is that in writing a part P is transferred not to one voice only but to two or three, according to the number of RR.

§ 410. Second, when the sign of one Jh is positive and the other negative the basic version corresponds to other forms. For a negative Jh R must be R I, for a positive, R II (§ 366), consequently P I and P II are found in one and the same basic version. In other words both voices of the original combination I + II are PP, and each has one R. The result is two simultaneous two-voice canons, the so-called double canon. The voices of the original combination I + II are indicated by two P's, the first according to the time of entry P^a, the second P^b. If both PP enter simultaneously it does not matter which is used. Each P has its own R, indicated by the same small letter: P^a and R^a is one of the canons, P^b and R^b the other.

§ 411. The following double canon is from the *Kyrie* of Palestrina's *Missa Papae Marcelli:*

Ex. 229   (a)   Palestrina

Taking this double canon as the basic version, in which $P^a + P^b$ forms the original combination, the pairs of combinations $R^a + R^b$ must be discarded, as this is only a shift of $P^a + P^b$ at $Jh = 0$; $P^a + R^a$ and $P^b + R^b$ are left, but each of them contain only

one imitating melody, while the derivative combination must consist of both voices of the original. Excluding these there remain, besides the original $P^a + P^b$, two derivatives: $P^a + R^b$ and $P^b + R^a$:

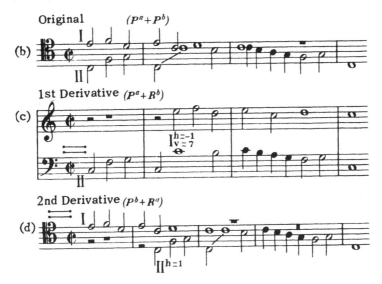

Formula of first derivative:

$$(\mathrm{I}^{\substack{h=\ -1\\ v=\ 7}} + \mathrm{II})\ Jh = -1,\ Jv = -7;\ \text{its imaginary: } \mathrm{I}^{\substack{h=\ -1\\ v=\ 7}}_{....} + \mathrm{II}.$$

Formula of second derivative:

$$(\mathrm{I} + \mathrm{II}^{h=\ 1})\ Jh = 1;\ \text{its imaginary: } \mathrm{I} + \mathrm{II}^{h=\ 1}_{....}.$$

Compound index of horizontal-shifting counterpoint: $Jh = -1, 1$. Since one of these values is positive and the other negative the imaginary voice in one case is I...., in the other II...., and the basic version is therefore a double canon (§ 410).

Obs.—A simple method of composing a double canon consists in writing part of the combination $P^a + P^b$ and transferring it to the same or to other degrees at $Jh = 0$ and $Jv = 0$, forming the beginning of $R^a + R^b$, which the first two voices accompany in simple counterpoint. This counterpointing section of $P^a + P^b$ is also transferred to the other two voices, forming the continuation of $R^a + R^b$, etc. The composition of such a double canon is analogous to that of the ordinary two-voice canon, each pair of voices corresponding to a single voice in the two-voice canon. Other phases of the double canon, where $R^a + R^b$ consists of a shift of $P^a + P^b$ not at $Jh = 0$ and $Jv = 0$ but at other intervals* can be applied only to a kind of basic version now unfamiliar—dealt with in a course in canonic form. An exception may be made for the shift at $Jv = -7$ (cf. Ex. 230).

§ 412. In those cases where both JJh have the same signs the derivatives are arranged in order according to the absolute values of Jh, writing the first derivative at the Jh of smallest value, the second Jh at the largest (§ 409). The original and the second derivative are termed outer combinations, the first derivative the inner combination.

§ 413. Taking one of the outer combinations as the original, a basic version in the form of a three-voice imitation + Cp is obtained by the method indicated in § 409. Getting now the two basic versions by the same method, it is seen that their only difference is that P of one forms Cp in the other. Here the reciprocal relation of the outer combinations

---

*If in this case $Jh \neq 0\ R^a + R^b$ contains a third derivative with a separate Jh.

is such that if either is regarded as the original the other is the derivative. Hence there is the same relation between the formulas of the derivative combination (and the imaginary) as there is when the original and derivative are exchanged (§§ 380-2).

§ 414. Taking the first derivative (inner combination) as the original, a basic version is obtained in the form of a double canon. Therefore in a double canon adopted as a basic version the inner ($P^a + P^b$) is the original combination and the outer ($P^a + R^b$ and $P^b + R^a$) the two derivatives. In the following is applied all that was said in § 413 about outer combinations.

§ 415. The double canon from Palestrina's mass *Inviolata* illustrates this use of the basic version. In this canon $R^a + R^b$ consists of a shift of $P^a + P^b$ at $Jv = -7$:

Formula of first derivative ($P^a + R^b$):
$$(I + II^{v=-7}) \, Jh = 1, \, Jv = -7; \, I + II^{v=-7}.$$
Formula of second derivative ($P^b + R^a$):
$$(I^{h=-1} + II) \, Jh = -1; \, I^{h=-1} + II.$$

Taking each of the derivative combinations (outer, § 412) in turn as the original, two basic versions are obtained, each in the form of a three-voice imitation + Cp. First taking $P^a + R^b$ for the original:

Formula of first derivative:
$$(I^{v=-7} + II) \, Jh = 1, \, Jv = -7; \, I + II^{v=-7}.$$
Formula of second derivative:
$$(I^{v=-7} + II) \, Jh = 2, \, Jv = -7; \, I + II^{v=-7}.$$

The second basic version (three-voice imitation + *Cp*) is constructed according to the formula of the imaginary combination:

Finally, taking the combination $P^b + R^a$ as the original:

Formula of first derivative:

$$(I + II^{h=1})\, Jh = 1;\ I + II^{h=1}_{\ldots}.$$

Formula of second derivative:

$$(I + II^{h=2}_{v=-7})\, Jh = 2,\ Jv = -7;\ I + II^{h=2}_{v=-7}.$$

The third basic version is constructed from the same formula of the imaginary as before. *P* of this version is the same voice as *Cp* of the preceding (§ 413).

The formula of the imaginary combination for the second derivative in both basic versions is the same, because of the inverse shift (§ 382).

§ 416. Of the three basic versions given in § 415 Palestrina used only the first, the double canon. The other two were obtained by the process indicated, and could have served as material for the composition, on an equal footing with the first. These three basic versions are unusual in that all of them are contrapuntally correct. For instance if the double canon in Ex. 229 were taken as a basic version only one of the two remaining basic versions would give a correct union of voices; this version is obtained if the second derivative ($P^b + R^a$) is taken as the original. According to the formula of the imaginary combination, which the reader can easily find himself, the following basic version of the first form is obtained:

2nd Basic Version

§ 417. It is impossible to indicate the characteristics that would enable one to determine in advance which of the possible basic versions exhibited correct counterpoint and which contains *R....* , and therefore useless as material for composition. This can be done only by writing out all the versions. Very often only the basic version as originally written contains correct counterpoint. For example the four-voice combination in measure 4 to 8 of the following passage from the *Gloria* of Palestrina's mass *Aeterna Christe munera* satisfies all the requirements of a basic version:

Palestrina

Ex. 231

§ 418. In continuing with the study of canonic form using multi-voice imitation no difficulty will be experienced in applying canonic imitation in four or five voices to the basic version. But from a practical point of view this is hardly necessary. The number of derivative combinations available increases according to the degree of advancement made in the study of shifting counterpoint. It must not be forgotten that in combinations such as have been studied, for example, the conditions of various *JJv* may be applied and new derivatives obtained with only one horizontal shift. Instead of being too concerned about methods of obtaining new derivatives a far more important matter is now to learn how to arrange them to the greatest advantage from the esthetic point of view.

Arrangement of Contrapuntal Combinations in the Reverse Order of their Composition

§ 419. With the increase number of derivative combinations intended to serve as material for composition, the important question arises as to the order of their presentation. The most expedient way of assigning different combinations of the same melodies is according to the degree of their complexity; at first melodies comparatively simple in structure, and for elementary thematic work more complicated ones. The progressive increase of interest throughout the composition and the ease or otherwise with which parts are heard is what governs this apportionment of contrapuntal material.

Proceeding on this plan, it is not infrequent to change the order in which these combinations arise, presenting first the ones that are written later and vice versa. For example it is advantageous to place a contrapuntally correct basic version later than the two-voice combinations extracted from it; in general, a multi-voice imitation, previously written, after a two-voice imitation on the same themes. In fugues with more than one subject—double, triple etc.—the combination of subjects is written first of all and is generally reserved for the concluding section, from which working-out of the subjects in the preceding sections is taken. In the same way subjects of a stretto fugue can be extracted from a previously written canon.

§ 420. The following basic version is from the *Benedictus* of Palestrina's mass *Jam Christus astra ascenderat:*

In combination *Cp + P* is found the free use of fourths, requiring a lower supplementary voice. On the contrary, *Cp + R* presents an independent two-voice combination, at the beginning of the *Benedictus* (Ex. 233) with the voices brought an octave closer together. In order of entry *P* is the first subject, *Cp* the second. After the two-voice union of these subjects, on the latter half of the fourth measure, the lowest voice enters, with an imitation of the second subject. On its final note in the seventh measure the basic version begins, presenting a more interesting union of the same two subjects. Here the first subject enters again, forming a canonic imitation in the outer voices at the distance of one measure. Beginning with the ninth measure the second subject joins the canon, it

is unchanged up to its final note. To these three voices a fourth supplementary voice is
added, an active, pliant melody that forms an excellent counterpoint to the notes of the
basic subjects.

Ex. 233   Palestrina

In reading these scores the question will inevitably arise as to how this gradual
increase of interest shown by the various unions of subjects is brought about. The
answer is simple: the combination of greatest complexity—the basic version—is written
first: from it are taken the simpler combinations, placing them first, then the basic version, appearing as the culmination of the entire thematic material.

§ 421. At the beginning of Ex. 234, from the second part of Palestrina's motet *Manifesto vobis veritatem*, the following combinations are found:

The initial note of II in combination (a) is here shortened in order that the melody shall conform to future appearances. Formulas:

$$(I + II^{\substack{h=-1\\v=-7}})\; Jh = -1,\; Jv = -7;\; I^{\substack{h=-1\\v=-7}}_{\dots} + II.$$

The first basic version follows the formula of the imaginary combination.

1st Basic Version

It is found in measures 8-10 of Ex. 234, shifted an octave higher.

The derivative is taken as original for the second basic version, and in accordance with § 382 retains the formula of the imaginary combination:

2nd Basic Version

Retaining the imaginary R, this combination cannot be applied in the work. If R.... is shifted a twelfth higher (cf. combination (e)) or a tenth (f), a correct contrapuntal union is obtained in certain places. The first of these (with a shift of R.... at the twelfth) is found in measures 4-5, all voices shifted one-half measure:

The second combination (with a shift of R.... at the tenth) is found in measures 6-8:

But in both instances the melodies that enter first must soon be discontinued, since they cease to form a correct union. Hence it is clear that combination (a) must be regarded as the principal basic·version, for in it the subjects form a correct contrapuntal union from beginning to end. This version, as the more complete, follows the above-mentioned variants of the second basic version (mm. 8-10). After this combination (a) and (b) again appear in the former order: Cp + P (mm. 10-13) and Cp + R twice (mm. 12-17), but with this difference: that whereas these combinations first appear on the same degrees as in the basic version, here they are on other degrees; the result is an increase of harmonic interest. In measures 17-19 only one theme (P) appears, but in a more complicated setting: instead of the former two-voice imitation it is here three-voice, and instead of a distance of one measure between entries, a distance of one-half measure (stretto announcement):

Ex. 234   Palestrina

§ 422. No difficulty will be found in analysing the following examples from the Benedictus of Palestrina's mass *Tu est pastor ovium*. Observe the absence of similar motion in combination $P + R_1$, making possible a duplication at the tenth; this is found at the beginning of the extract (mm. 1-3) and again immediately after the basic version (mm. 11-12).

Ex. 235   Palestrina

§ 423. The composition of such examples, where from a previously written basic version is taken thematic combinations of different degrees of intricacy, presented in an order of progressive interest, is of the utmost profit to the student. At first the basic versions given in Chapter XIX may be used. These exercises should preferably be set to a text.

Obs.—Imitative forms have more significance when the same melody is set to the same text. As a subject is interwoven with other voices, each with its own words, both music and words appear as the expression of a single purpose, a fact that facilitates the understanding of contrapuntal forms and the meaning of texts. The words assist in disengaging the principal subject from amid the surrounding melodies and acquaintance with the melodies inevitably forces the listener to remember their close association with the words.*

§ 424. The ways described, by which the parts of a composition are allocated in the reverse order of their origin, lead to widely different results. For instance, a two-voice canonic imitation is often found, followed by a multi-voice imitation—obviously written first—on the same themes. In the following example the two-voice imitation in the first two measures was undoubtedly extracted from the three-voice imitation in measures 3-5:

Ex. 236   Meyer

§ 425. A fine example showing the application of this method is the Finale of Mozart's C major Symphony (K.V. 551, "Jupiter"). Here a five-voice combination, including the cantus firmus, was first composed in quintuple counterpoint:

Ex. 237   Mozart

From this the themes of the Finale are taken, and the original combination itself, with shifts in quintuple counterpoint, is found in the coda as the climax of the movement (cf. m. 36 from end).

---

*With reference to the setting of texts, c.f. J. Quadflieg, "Ueber Textunterlage und Text-behandlung in Kirchlichen Tonwerken," in Haberl, "Kirchen musicalisches Jahrbuch, 1893, pp. 109-128, and 1906 (XX Jahrgang), pp. 197-233. Also cf. in Bellermann's work already re-ferred to, the chapter ("Vom Unterlagen der Textworts," [Cf., for more accessible references, the following: "The style of Palestrina and the Dissonance," by Knud Jeppesen, translated by Margaret W. Hamerik (Oxford University Press), pp. 34-42; "Counterpoint," by Jeppesen, trans-lated by Glen Haydon (New York: Prentice-Hall, Inc.), pp. 158-60 and 255-61; "Contrapuntal Technique in the Sixteenth Century," by R.O. Morris (Oxford), Chapter VII. —Tr.]

Obs.—It is of interest to observe that in the *Christe eleison* from Palestrina's mass *Jesu nostra redemptio* not only the same c.f. is found, but also contrapuntal parts that recall the themes from Mozart's C major Symphony:

The entry of the first two voices has a certain affinity with the beginning of the fugato in the Finale (m. 36); the first notes of motive (a) in the upper voice are reproduced literally in the symphony (voice IV of the five-voice combination), and motive (b) in the tenor recalls Mozart's subject I in contrary motion.

§ 426. Another example of thematic material presented in the reverse order of composition can be cited from the last movement of Beethoven's Ninth Symphony. The theme to which the words "Seid umschlungen Millionen" are set, first appearing in the Andante maestoso, in the counterpoint, previously written at $Jv = -7$, to the principal theme of the movement, "Freude schöner Gotterfunken"—

and then taken as a separate theme which appears earlier.

§ 427. The same thing occurs in Borodine's *In Central Asia*, where there is a combination of two themes: a Russian song and with it a contrapuntal part of distinctly oriental character. It appears after the separate statement of the two themes:

§ 428. Horizontal-shifting counterpoint can be used to advantage in all situations where two themes are developed together. It is applicable in double fugues, in the development section of sonata movements etc. Horizontal shifting brings the greatest variety into the combination of themes, both in their contrapuntal and harmonic relationships, especially if the vertical shift is used in connection with the horizontal, and with the application of some Jv applied at the same time in the separate combinations. It may be observed that except in those cases where the derivatives succeed the original the experienced eye of the contrapuntist will often detect the purpose of a series of combinations. The sharpening of this faculty of contrapuntal thinking should be one of the chief objects in studying the present work.

§ 429. As an example of horizontal shifting applied to the subjects of a double fugue the following may be cited, from a fugue by Battiferro, a seventeenth-century composer; an excerpt is quoted by Marpurg in his *Abhandlung von der Fuge*. The two subjects, combined first in this way:

later appear with these horizontal shifts:

According to the formula of the imaginary combination $I + II_{v.=-11}^{h=1}$ the following basic version is obtained:

The two-voice combination contained in this basic version admits of the following shifts: $(Cp + P)$ $Jv = -11$, -14; $(Cp + R)$ $Jv = -9$, -11. The latter combination admits also of various duplications in imperfect consonances. Another double fugue by the same composer, also using horizontal-shifting subjects, is quoted in Dehn's *Lehre vom Kontrapunkt*.

§ 430. In Vol. II of Ambros' *Geschichte der Musik*, chapter on "Die Kunst der Niederlander" he says that the compositions of J. S. Bach recall the contrapuntal methods of the old Netherlanders. One would therefore expect to find horizontal shifting among the resources used by Bach. Riemann observed this in his *Cathechismus der Fugenlehre* (Teil II, pp. 149, 205) in connection with fugues 17 and 23, Vol. II of The *Well-Tempered Clavichord*. Reference may here be made to the following combination from Fugue 18, Vol. 1 of the same work:

Another reference is to the triple fugue in E♭ for organ*, where there is a combination in horizontal-shifting counterpoint of the first subject:

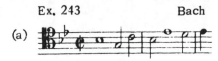

with the third (cf. beginning at m. 30):

An analysis of this fugue will be found in Prout's *Fugal Analysis*, pp. 171-89.

Horizontal shifting can also be found in Handel—in the double fugues for piano in g minor and f♯ minor, in the concluding chorus of the oratorio *Alexanderfest*, and elsewhere.

§ 431. As an unusual example of the application of two-voice horizontal-shifting counterpoint by a later composer the following passage can be cited from the Seventh Symphony, Op. 77, of Glazounow:

---

*Organ compositions, Peters Ed., Vol. No. 1. [Cf. also: Bach, Two-Voice Invention No. 11, mm. 1-2 and 3-5 (horizontal shift and contrary motion); "The Well-Tempered Clavichord," Vol. 1, Fugue 1, mm. 2-3 and 4-5; Vol. 88, Fugue 4, mm. 55-6 and 67-8; "The Art of Fugue," Contrapunctus VIII, mm. 39 and 125; Contrapunctus XIV (the last, unfinished, fugue), mm. 147-53 and 167-74 (see note at end of chapter). —Tr.]

§ 432. The last three examples quoted belong to the free style, in which the principles of horizontal-shifting counterpoint may be similarly applied. Here the study of horizontal-shifting counterpoint is to be distinguished from that of vertical-shifting. The rules of the latter are different, according to whether the style of the composition is strict or free, but for horizontal-shifting and double-shifting counterpoint this is of no importance. These rules are of a more general nature and do not lend themselves to a rigid classification according to strict and free styles. Such matters as the proper use of ties, the entrance-intervals of voices in the basic version, the extraction from it of the possible two-voice combination etc. do not affect the question as to whether the contrapuntal parts of the basic version are strict or free. It is only when the conditions of JJv are applied that a positive demarcation emerges between the strict and free styles. Aside from this the study of horizontal-shifting counterpoint can be extensively applied to problems in contemporary musical art. The introduction of horizontal-shifting into the technique of present-day composition will open up numerous untried resources and will enrich it by effects characteristic of this field of complex counterpoint, effects that are inaccessible by other methods.

[Translator's Note]

An interesting case—perhaps a unique one—of where the basic version was not discovered until long after the composer's death, is illustrated by the last fugue in Bach's "The Art of Fugue." Bach did not live to complete it; it breaks off at measure 239, after he had assigned a separate exposition to three subjects and had combined the first and second, and all three.

Of all the fugues in the collection this unfinished work is the only one that does not contain the "motto-theme" on which the entire work is based, a fact that has caused misunderstandings. The first was due to a theory advanced by Wilhelm Rust, who claimed that because this subject was absent the fugue did not belong to the collection at all, and was an independent work. Also, several theorists have misinterpreted this fugue for a similar reason; at least three—Prout, Goetschius and Gedalge—classify it as a triple fugue, which is unjustifiable, considering its unfinished state. This is still less excusable when it is remembered that long before these theorists wrote, Martin Nottebohm discovered a way in which the motto-theme in quadruple counterpoint with the three subjects developed by Bach up to measure 239, the obvious conclusion being that Bach was writing a quadruple fugue. Several attempts have been made to complete the fugue, on the basis of Nottebohm's discovery, but none were successful until Donald Francis Tovey wrote a thoroughly convincing completion in which the four subjects are combined in both direct and contrary motion. The basic version will be found in measures 271-6, Contrapunctus XIV, of Tovey's edition of "The Art of Fugue," Reference should also be made to his "Companion to the Art of Fugue"; both are published by the Oxford University Press.

DIVISION D

THREE-VOICE HORIZONTAL-SHIFTING AND DOUBLE-SHIFTING COUNTERPOINT

THREE-VOICE HORIZONTAL-SHIFTING AND DOUBLE-SHIFTING COUNTERPOINT

CHAPTER XXI

THEORY OF THE TECHNIQUE OF THREE-VOICE
HORIZONTAL-SHIFTING COUNTERPOINT

Preliminaries

§ 433. In three-voice horizontal-shifting and double-shifting counterpoint a derivative combination is obtained as the result of a horizontal shift (or also with vertical) of one or two melodies of the original combination. Instances of where all three melodies shift can be accounted for as the result of shifting only two, or if desired one melody may be regarded as not shifting.

§ 434. It is necessary that all three melodies of the original combination shall be present in the derivative. Therefore if one of them is replaced in the derivative by a new melody, even though the remaining two show a horizontal shift, the result is not three-voice horizontal-shifting counterpoint but only two-voice.

The Basic Version

§ 435. Three-voice horizontal-shifting and double-shifting counterpoint is written with the aid of a basic version that includes not less than four voices.

§ 436. If to a two-voice canonic imitation $(P + R)$ is written two contrapuntal parts: Cp_1 and Cp_2, a basic version is obtained from which two three-voice combinations can be taken: $Cp_1 + Cp_2 + P$ and $Cp_1 + Cp_2 + R$. These two combinations, of which the first is used as the original and the second the derivative, differ in that the voices concerned in the imitation appear in the derivative as a horizontal shift.

§ 437. If the imitation is at the unison the voices show only a horizontal shift; if at other intervals, a double shift (cf. § 328).

(1) Imitation at the unison; horizontal-shifting counterpoint:

Ex. 245 (a) Basic Version

The derivative is obtained by shifting the upper voice one measure to the right.

    (2) Imitation at the seventh below; double-shifting counterpoint:

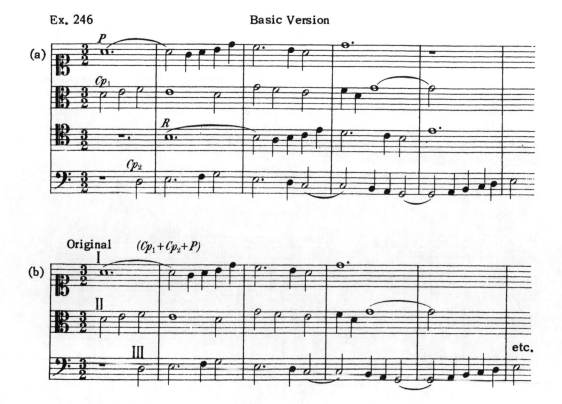

The derivative is obtained by shifting the upper voice one measure to the right and a seventh below, according to diagram (2) (cf. *Obs.*, § 442).

§ 438. The composition of such a four-voice basic version presents no difficulties. If not written in this way three-voice combinations will be obtained that are apt to sound empty, and impractical without a supplementary voice. The advantage of following the method is that a basic version will be obtained that represents correct four-voice counterpoint, and can be employed in the capacity of thematic material on an equal footing with the three-voice combinations taken from it.

§ 439. In a previously written basic version an imitation can appear as imaginary R. If this is done Cp_1 and Cp_2 must be so written that they form correct three-voice counterpoint with both P and $R....$ separately. This corresponds to the second method of solving problems discussed in § 378 and is the least useful for three-voice counterpoint. The difficulties involved in writing only one voice in such a basic version have already been noted, but with two voices, indispensible for three-voice horizontal-shifting counterpoint, these difficulties increase to an excessive degree. This method can be applied only in those situations where the simultaneous movement of P and $R....$ does not form dissonant harmony (§ 327), and where P continues only for a short time after the entry of $R.....$ for example:

Ex. 247   Basic Version with imaginary Risposta

Hence the original is $(Cp_1 + Cp_2 + P)$ and the derivative $(Cp_1 + Cp_2 + R)$, where the middle voice shifts two measures to the right.

§ 440. Writing horizontal-shifting counterpoint with the aid of a four-voice basic version gives a derivative combination in which the entries of two of the voices keep the same relationship that they had in the original. These two voices, therefore, may be regarded as non-shifting, and the derivative combination as having been obtained from the horizontal shifts of only one voice. To work out solutions of all possible shifts of voices in both horizontal- and double-shifting counterpoint another method will be given, consisting of an adaptation to three-voice counterpoint of the third method of solving problems explained in § 376. A basic version can be written by this method only if among the JJh no Jh is equal to zero. Six voices are concerned, three real and three imaginary, and the writing is done by sections, one after another. A detailed description is given in the next chapter.

Notation of Voices and Shifts

§ 441. From a three-voice original combination I + II + III will first be examined the shifts of the outer voices I and III. These voices are indicated in the same way that I and II were in two-voice counterpoint. In the original combination I is always the highest voice, III always the lowest. In relation to the horizontal shift I is the voice of earliest entry, though in fact it may enter later than III; III is always considered as the voice of latest entry. The vertical and horizontal shifts of these voices can be represented by the following diagram (cf. § 347):

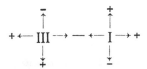

That is, for I the positive shifts are upward and to the left; for III downward and to the right. Thus the expression $I^{h=1}_{v=3} + III^{h=-2}_{v=1}$ means that the upper voice (I) shifts one measure to the left (h= 1) and at the same time a fourth higher (v= 3); the lowest voice (III) shifts two measures to the left (h= −2) and a second below (v= 1) etc.

§ 442. How to indicate the middle voice remains to be explained. The horizontal shift of this voice is expressed in the same way as was the vertical (§ 241). II in relation to I is regarded as the voice of later entry, for which the positive shift is to the right. In relation to III it is the voice of earlier entry, in which case a shift to the right is negative. Based on this, a horizontal shift of the middle voice (II), similar to the vertical shift, is indicated by the use of two signs together, placed one under the other; the upper referring to the combination of II to I, the lower to its combination with III. Therefore ± means a shift of II to the right, ∓ its shift to the left. Indicating the number of measures that II shifts by a, its shifts are shown in this diagram:

$$II^{h=\pm a} \quad \text{and} \quad II^{h=\mp a}$$
$$\longrightarrow \qquad\qquad \longleftarrow$$

For example, the expression $II^{h=\mp 1}$ means that II shifts one measure to the left, and $II^{h=\pm 2}$ two measures to the right. In indicating a shift of II where it is combined with one of the outer voices (I + II or II + III) one sign is enough, referring to its combination with the voice concerned. E.g., the expressions $I + II^{h=2}$ and $II^{h=-2} + III$ both indicate a shift of II two measures to the right.

Obs.—The six diagrams that show the permutations of voices in the derivative (§ 248) refer only to their vertical shifts, therefore they apply here only to double-shifting counterpoint.

§ 443. The use of these signs in the formulas of derivative combinations indicates the shifts that meet the conditions of a given problem. For example, in the three-voice combination of Ex. 245 the formula of the derivative is:

$$I^{h=-1} + II^{h=0} + III^{h=0}.$$

Voices II and III are here regarded as the two that remain stationary, but I could have been considered as the non-shifting voice, in which case the formula for the same derivative would have been:

$$I^{h=0} + II^{h=\mp 1} + III^{h=-1}.$$

In this way different formulas may refer to one and the same derivative. The essential similarity of such formulas is proved by the fact that their JJh are identical (cf. § 448).

<h3 style="text-align:center">The Indices Jh', Jh", JhΣ
and their Reciprocal Relationships</h3>

§ 444. In relation to the horizontal shift, three-voice counterpoint will be examined, as before, as the union of three two-voice combinations: I + II, II + III and I + III.

Given a formula for the derivative combination, indicating a horizontal shift, the corresponding Jh must be found for each of the three pairs of combinations. This done, three formulas for the imaginary combinations are then compiled, which when united constitute the formula of the basic version.

Obs.—In two-voice horizontal-shifting counterpoint the basic version is composed according to the formula of the imaginary combination, which at the same time shows the formula of the basic version. But in three-voice counterpoint these two formulas do not coincide; the formula of the basic version is compiled from three formulas of the imaginary combination, as there are three pairs of voices involved. If one of the JJh is equal to zero the formula of the basic version will consist of only two formulas of the imaginary combination (cf. § 461).

§ 445. Analogous with the indices Jv, Jv'' and $Jv\Sigma$ (§ 243), those of horizontal-shifting counterpoint are indicated: Jh', Jh'' and $Jh\Sigma$. Jh' refers to the combination I + II, Jh'' to II + III and $Jh\Sigma$ to I + III. The latter combination is equal to the sum of the first two, which can be demonstrated in the same way by which $Jv\Sigma = Jv' + Jv''$ was (§ 234).

§ 446. Expressing the relations of JJh by the equation $Jh' + Jh'' = Jh\Sigma$, the value of each term can be defined (cf. § 244):

$$Jh' = Jh\Sigma - Jh'';$$
$$Jh'' = Jh\Sigma - Jh'$$
$$Jh\Sigma = Jh' + Jh''$$

Hence it follows that: (1) only two JJh may arbitrarily be taken, the third necessarily follows; (2) one of the JJh may equal zero; (3) all three JJh may equal zero; (4) two JJh can not equal zero unless the third also does. When all three JJh equal zero the result is counterpoint in which the relations between the entries of all three voices remain unchanged, in other words, simple counterpoint, which may thus be regarded as a special case of the horizontal shift.

§ 447. Without altering the values of the three JJh substitutions of other hh values may be made for the individual voices; the relation between the entries in the derivative remains without change (cf. § 245). For example, $I^{h=1} + II^{h=\pm 2} + III^{h=0}$ may be substituted for $I^{h=2} + II^{h=\pm 1} + III^{h=-1}$, because the values of JJh are identical, namely: $Jh'=3$, $Jh''=-2$, $Jh\Sigma=1$. All this was explained in Division B with reference to the indices of vertical-shifting counterpoint. In general there is a uniform analogy between JJh and JJv.

§ 448. The formulas given in § 443 represented different expressions of one and the same arrangement of voices in the derivative. The identity of the formulas is seen when the JJh are found, these being the same in both cases. For the first formula ($I^{h=-1}$ + $II^{h=0}$ + $III^{h=0}$) the indices are:

$$(I^{h=-1} + II^{h=0})\ Jh' = -1$$
$$(II^{h=\ \ 0} + III^{h=0})\ Jh'' = \ \ 0$$
$$\overline{\phantom{(II^{h=0} + III^{h=0})}\ Jh\Sigma = -1}$$

For the second formula ($I^{h=0}$ + $II^{h=\mp 1}$ + $III^{h=-1}$) the indices are:

$$(I^{h=0} + II^{h=-1})\ Jh' = -1$$
$$(II^{h=1} + III^{h=-1})\ Jh'' = \ \ 0$$
$$\overline{\phantom{(II^{h=1} + III^{h=-1})}\ Jh\ = -1}$$

Formula of the Basic Version

§ 449. Three-voice horizontal-shifting counterpoint, like two-voice, is written with the aid of a basic version. According to the three indices Jh', Jh'' and $Jh\Sigma$ (if in none $Jh=0$) three formulas for the imaginary combination are compiled, each of them in the same order as was done in two-voice counterpoint: at a positive Jh the imaginary voice is indicated by the highest numeral, at a negative Jh by the lowest. In the imaginary voice is written $h=Jh$. Hence each of the three formulas of the imaginary combination can appear in either of two forms:

$$(1)\ I + II^{h=Jh'=a} \quad \text{or}\quad I^{h=Jh'=-a} + II;$$
$$(2)\ II + III^{h=Jh''=a} \quad \text{or}\quad II^{h=Jh''=-a} + III;$$
$$(3)\ I + III^{h=Jh\Sigma=a} \quad \text{or}\quad I^{h=Jh\Sigma=-a} + III.$$

The three formulas of the imaginary combination together constitute the formula of the basic version (§ 444).

§ 450. In the problems in horizontal-shifting counterpoint presently to be taken up, as also in the later problems in double-shifting counterpoint, two forms of the basic version will be distinguished. The first will refer to those cases in which no $Jh=0$, the second to those in which one $Jh=0$.

CHAPTER XXII

THREE-VOICE COUNTERPOINT WITH HORIZONTAL SHIFTS

(A) First Form of the Basic Version for
Horizontal-Shifting Counterpoint: Jh= 0 Absent

§ 451. Problems in which three JJh are found contain a formula for the imaginary combination for each pair of voices (§ 444); with $Jh = 0$ absent, the number of these formulas is therefore three.

The three formulas for the imaginary combination, which when united constitute the formula of the basic version, define the entries of its $RR....$ (imaginary voices).

§ 452. Assuming that the problem is: $I^{h=\,0} + II^{h=\,\pm2} + III^{h=\,1}$, the JJh for the three pairs of combinations are written out:

$$(I^{h=\,\,\,\,0} + II^{h=\,2})\, Jh' = \,\,\,\,2$$
$$(II^{h=\,-2} + III^{h=\,1})\, \underline{Jh'' = -1}$$
$$Jh\Sigma = \,\,\,\,1$$

From these three indices are compiled the formulas for the imaginary combinations, constituting the formula of the basic version:

$$I + II^{h=\,2}_{.....}, \; II^{h=\,-1}_{.....} + III, \; I + III^{h=\,1}_{.....}.$$

Of the three imaginary voices contained in the basic version two are indicated by the same numeral (II....). These two $RR....$ of one and the same P, i.e. of a real voice, are indicated by the same figure. The third imaginary voice is designated by the other figure (III....), and therefore functions as R relative to the second P. In this way the basic version includes a double imitation with imaginary $RR.....$ Of the three real voices one of them (in this case I) enters into two of the imaginary combinations, being united with the other two numerals II.... and III.... (combinations $I + II^{h=\,2}_{.....}$ and $I + III^{h=\,1}_{.....}$). These three voices—one real and two imaginary—must, as will be seen, always form correct counterpoint: this is the derivative. The vertical shift absent, as in the present instance, they reproduce the progression on the same degrees, and since h is not equal to a fraction (§ 359), also on the same parts of the measures. Thereupon it is seen that the other real voice (here III) enters into one imaginary combination ($II^{h=\,-1}_{.....} + III$). Finally, the last of the real voices (here II) does not participate in any of the imaginary combinations.

§ 453. According to the preceding it should be observed that with three imaginary voices one of the real voices enters into combination with two of them; another real voice combines with one imaginary, but the third real voice remains free and does not combine with any of the imaginary voices. This is a general characteristic of all basic versions that do not have $Jh= 0$ and where, therefore, there are three imaginary combinations.

To demonstrate this let it be assumed that of the three real voices in the basic version each one combines with one of the three imaginaries. In this case the formula of the basic version would be represented by one of these two combinations:

(a) I + II.... , II + III.... , I.... + III or
(b) I.... + II, II.... + III, I + III.... .

But neither of these is possible. From the way in which the imaginary voices are disposed in formula (a) it is clear that the first and second imaginary combinations have h as positive but the third is negative. And since for an imaginary voice $h=$ Jh of the corresponding combination, Jh' and Jh'' would be positive but $Jh\Sigma$ negative, an impossibility, for $Jh\Sigma$, as equal to the sum of the other two JJh (§ 445), would also have to be positive. The same reasoning proves the impossibility of formula (b), where $Jh\Sigma$ would have to be negative, but the sum of two positive quantities. Therefore all of the real voices cannot participate in the imaginary combinations. Neither can any one of the real voices participate in all three imaginary combinations, since one of the voices is absent from each of the three pairs of combinations: I + II, II + III and I + III. Therefore only two of the real voices can enter into the structure of a two-voice imaginary combination. But since there are three of the latter, one of the real voices must enter into two of them, and the third into one.

§ 454. The following is a solution of the formula in § 452:

$$I^{h=0}+II^{h=\pm2}+III^{h=1} \qquad \begin{array}{l}(I^{h=0}+II^{h=2}) \quad Jh'=2\\(II^{h=-2}+III^{h=1}) \quad Jh''=-1\\ \hline \qquad\qquad\qquad Jh\,\Sigma=1\end{array} \qquad I+II^{h=2}_{\ldots}, \; II^{h=-1}_{\ldots}+III, \; I+III^{h=1}_{\ldots}$$

Ex. 248 (a)   Basic Version

Derivative

The real voice that counterpoints two imaginary voices is indicated by two stars (**I); the one counterpointing one imaginary by a single star (*III). The two imaginary voices that counterpoint one and the same real voice, II.... (+ I) and III.... (+ I), are written on two adjoining staves, connected by bar-lines. The remaining imaginary voice, which counterpoints one real, may occupy a staff either above or below the two former. Observe that the derivative, given separately, is an exact reproduction of this combination formed by the real voice entering into the two imaginary combinations (**I), and the two imaginary voices which it counterpoints.

§ 455. As before, in approaching the solution of problems, it is first of all best to look over the general features and to place on the supplementary staves a clef for each imaginary voice, putting it to the right of the clef for the real voice, at a distance equal to the number of measures indicated by the figure for h of the imaginary voice. Next write the real combination up to the measure where an imaginary voice first enters (in Ex. 248, therefore, the first measure). This constitutes the first section of the problem. From this section the real voices are then transferred to the supplementary staves, as imaginary voices. This done, the next section is taken up (m. 2, Ex. 248), in which is the first entry of one of the imaginary voices. At its first entry this rule should invariably be followed: In each section the imaginary combinations (i.e. the union of the real voice with the imaginary) are written in advance of the real combination. At this point (beginning where all the imaginary voices have entered) the order in which the real voices are composed for each section is as follows:

(1) First write the real voice that counterpoints the two imaginaries (in Ex. 248, **1). It is composed in this way in order to form correct three-voice counterpoint with them.

(2) Write the real voice that counterpoints one of the imaginary voices (in Ex. 248, *III). The reason for this is that it must form two-voice counterpoint separately with its own imaginary and with the real voice of which part is already written.

(3) Finally write the real voice that does not participate in any of the imaginary combinations (in Ex. 248, II). It is written as counterpoint to the two real voices already existing, forming with them a correct three-voice combination. When a section is completed in this way the real voices, now established, are transferred to the supplementary staves as imaginary voices for the ensuing sections. These are composed in the same order, the real voices again being transferred to the supplementary staves, and so on.

§ 456. It is seen from the preceding that each real voice forms a contrapuntal combination with either of the other two voices. When these two voices are both real or both imaginary it is written so as to form correct three-voice counterpoint with them. If one of these two voices is real and the other imaginary, three-voice counterpoint is not obtained, but the real voice first mentioned forms correct counterpoint with each of them.

§ 457. In regard to the real voice that unites with one imaginary (in Ex. 248, *III), the following fact should be observed: the union of this voice with the imaginary is exactly the same as the combination of the two remaining imaginary voice (in Ex. 249 cf. combination II.... + III beginning with the second measure, with the combination of the remaining two imaginary voices, beginning with the third measure of the original). The importance of this real voice, uniting with one imaginary, is that this combination guarantees the correctness of the union of the imaginary voices at their recurrence. Therefore it must not be regraded as an independent two-voice combination, but always as entering into the structure of a three-voice, being reproduced exactly in the derivative. It follows that when this combination does not include the lowest voice of the derivative, unprepared fourths may be used in it, but not, on the contrary, $\overline{8}$. In Ex. 248 this combination (II.... + III) can function as independent two-voice counterpoint only because one of its voices is the lowest voice of the derivative.

§ 458. Since the combination of real and imaginary voices just discussed is only of secondary importance, being essential only because of the other two imaginary voices which counterpoint one and the same real (I + II.... and I + III.... , Ex. 248), this counterpointing of one real voice by one imaginary need not continue to the very end of the of the problem. To continue the imaginary voice as far as the next to the last section is enough, and if the derivative has a free ending this voice may be interrupted.

§ 459. In the preceding basic version the correct three-voice union of all three imaginary voices in the first measures was entirely fortuitous. Generally even two imaginary voices, counterpointing one and the same real, do not combine with the third imaginary as in the sixth measure of Ex. 248.

(B) Second Form of the Basic Version for
Horizontal-Shifting Counterpoint: Jh= 0 Present

§ 460. Having examined three-voice horizontal-shifting counterpoint in which none of the JJh were equal to zero, the next to be studied are those cases in which one of the JJh equals zero. Of three JJh, two of them can not be equal to zero—this was discussed in § 446—as the result of the equation $Jh' + Jh'' = Jh_{\Sigma}$. Therefore if only one voice is shifted its position is changed relative to the other two, and still neither of the two JJh that refer to the combination of the shifting voices with each other can equal zero.

§ 461. The presence of $Jh= 0$ means that the corresponding combination represents only a case of simple counterpoint; that it can not form an imaginary combination and must be excluded. The result of this is that the formulas to be examined contain not three but only two formulas for the imaginary combination. These two formulas may represent one of two cases: the voice common to both formulas can be either (a) real (e.g. I.... + II and II + III.... ; I + II.... and I + III....), or (b) imaginary (e.g. I + II.... and II.... + III; I.... + II and I.... + III).

§ 462. Hence there are two aspects of basic version with two imaginary voices, hereafter referred to as b.v. form 2 a and b.v. form 2 b, respectively. B.v. form 2 a contains two imaginary voices, these counterpoint one real voice, and constituting with it the required derivative. B.v. form 2 b contains one imaginary voice, which counterpoints two real voices, all three constituting the derivative. To indicate this imaginary voice in the basic version the numerals of both real voices with which it is associated will be placed in parentheses: II.... (+ I + III); I.... (+ II + III). Each of the foregoing sub-forms is herewith illustrated.

§ 463. *Case 1, B.V. Form 2* a.—The basic version contains two imaginary voices:

§ 464. *Case 2, B.V. Form 2* **b.**—The basic version contains one imaginary voice:

$$I^{h=-\frac{1}{2}} + II^{h=0} + III^{h=0} \qquad \begin{matrix}(I^{h=-\frac{1}{2}} + II) \\ (II^{h=0} + III^{h=0})\end{matrix} \quad \begin{matrix}Jh=-\frac{1}{2} \\ \frac{Jh''=0}{Jh\Sigma=-\frac{1}{2}}\end{matrix} \qquad I^{h=-\frac{1}{2}}_{...} + II, \; I^{h=-\frac{1}{2}}_{...} + III$$

Basic Version Second Form

Ex. 250 $I^{h=-\frac{1}{2}}_{...}$ (+II+III)

(a) Original

(b) Derivative

§ 465. Examination of a special application of horizontal-shifting counterpoint, called counterpoint "with and without rests" will be the subject of Chapter XXIV.

CHAPTER XXIII

THREE-VOICE COUNTERPOINT WITH SIMULTANEOUS
HORIZONTAL AND VERTICAL SHIFTS (DOUBLE-SHIFTING)

§ 466. At certain horizontal shifts in three-voice counterpoint each voice in the derivative retains the same position relative to the voices, as regards altitude, as it had in the original. In other words, all three voices are disposed according to diagram

(1): If the voices shift not only horizontally but at the same time vertically their arrangement in the derivative may correspond to any of the six possible diagrams (*Obs.*, § 442). In solving problems the particular diagram according to which the voices of the derivative are arranged must be taken into consideration; and in selecting intervals for the vertical shift care must be exercised to assure enough room for the shifting voices to move around in without confusion. Here one must be guided by the same considerations as in the problems in vertical-shifting counterpoint.

§ 467. As before, two forms of the basic version are distinguished. First will be examined those cases in which among the *JJh* none is equal to zero, then those in which one *Jh* equals zero.

(A) First Form of the Basic Version for
Double-Shifting Counterpoint; Jh= 0 Absent

§ 468. In the formula for the derivative combination the vertical shift of the voices must be indicated as well as that of the horizontal, besides which v for II must take a double designation ($\pm$ or $\mp$, § 241):

$$\text{I}^{\substack{h=\ 0\\v=\ -3}} + \text{II}^{\substack{h=\ \pm3\\v=\ \pm4}} + \text{III}^{\substack{h=\ 1\\v=\ -10}}$$

Preceding the formula is the diagram governing the disposition of voices in the derivative. According to this formula the values of Jh', Jh'', $Jh\Sigma$ and those of Jv', Jv'', $Jv\Sigma$ are then determined:

$$(\text{I}^{\substack{h=\ 0\\v=\ -3}} + \text{II}^{\substack{h=\ 3\\v=\ 4}} \ ) \, Jh' = \ \ 3, \, Jv' = \ \ 1$$
$$\underline{(\text{II}^{\substack{h=\ -3\\v=\ -4}} + \text{III}^{\substack{h=\ 1\\v=\ -10}}) \, Jh'' = -2, \, Jv'' = -14}$$
$$Jh\Sigma = \ \ 1, \, Jv\Sigma = -13$$

Then, using the *JJh* and *JJv* found, formulas for the three imaginary combinations are compiled, which together constitute the formula of the basic version (§ 444). In it each imaginary voice takes $h= Jh$ of the given combination and $v= Jv$ of the same combination (§ 373). In this way the formula of the basic version for the same preceding problem assumes this form:

$$\text{I} + \text{II} \overset{h=\ 3}{\underset{v=\ 1}{\ldots}}, \, \text{II} \overset{h=\ -2}{\underset{v=\ -14}{\ldots}} + \text{III}, \, \text{I} + \text{III} \overset{h=\ 1}{\underset{v=\ -13}{\ldots}}$$

According to this the clef for each imaginary voice is placed to the right of the clef for the real voice at the distance indicated by h of the imaginary voice. The voice that shifts vertically is transferred to a supplementary staff according to the indication for its v. For example, in the combination $I + II_{v=1}^{h=3}$ the imaginary voice must be transferred to a supplementary staff three measures later and a second below the real voice indicated by the same numeral; in the combination $II_{v=-14}^{h=-2} + III$ the imaginary voice enters two measures later and two octaves below the real voice etc. See Appendix D, No. 4, for a basic version written according to this formula.

§ 469. The two imaginary voices that counterpoint one and the same real must be arranged on the supplementary staves in accordance with the diagram of the given problem and in the positions which they take in the derivative, as indicated by the same numerals. Therefore in the basic version referred to (App. D, No. 4), conforming to diagram (4) ( ), voice III.... (+ I) is placed on the staff above voice II.... (+ I). The third imaginary voice, not being in contrapuntal relationship with the other two, occupies a staff either above or below the latter, depending on which it is nearest to, according to pitch. Therefore in this basic version the separate imaginary voice II.... (+ III) is placed underneath the other two.

§ 470. The introduction of the vertical shift does not involve any essential change in the methods of working out problems, which as before are written in sections, one after another. The parts for the real voices, written as far as the first entry of an imaginary voice, are transferred to the supplementary staves, forming the first section, which determines the size of all the later sections. A real voice, whether it counterpoints two imaginary or two real voices must, according to the preceding, form simple three-voice counterpoint with each pair. Counterpointing two different voices, one imaginary and one real, this voice forms simple two-voice counterpoint with each separately (§ 323). What was stated in § 457 about the combination of this voice with an imaginary applies also here.

§ 471. If the combined use of the horizontal and vertical shifts involves any new difficulties in the solutions of problems these difficulties are only of a kind that are characteristic in general of vertical-shifting voices. The necessity of avoiding augmented fourths and diminished fifths in the derivative, both as melodic progressions and as intervals between any two voices (except as passing notes) adds considerably to the limitations of these problems. Whereas in two-voice combinations such obstacles can often be overcome by chromatic alteration, in three-voice combinations this is seldom available because it can result in a cross-relation. Since one such mistake vitiates the whole problem, in writing the basic version it is necessary to take into consideration the possible appearance in the derivative of the forbidden intervals—the augmented fourth and diminished fifth. This is most easily done when the combination of two real voices that is reproduced as an imaginary combination, contrapuntally associated (in the examples the supplemantary staves with connecting bar-lines), has $Jv = 0, \pm 7,$ or ± 14. In this case a key-signature for the imaginary voices (always the same for both) must be chosen which causes the voices to appear on the same degrees of the scale as in the original, and consequently also in the derivative (because of the JJv indicated). By doing this neither augmented fourths nor diminished fifths will be encountered in the derivative, for they are absent in the original (cf. Nos. 3, 4, 6 in Appendix D). In order not to multiply difficulties a remaining precaution is that the real voice which counterpoints the two imaginaries has a melody that is valid with both key-signatures (§ 333). At other IIv, where both imaginary voices can not be on the same degrees as in the original, care must be taken that a voice functioning as imaginary does not start on the same degree of the scale as when it functions as real, and that in each section it does not form an augmented fourth in either case. The signature for the two contrapuntally associated voices having been decided, a signature for the derivative is next chosen that will give the corresponding voices on the same degrees of the scale. The third imaginary voice must then take a signature which will put it in the same relative scale-position as this voice has in the derivative.

§ 472. Sometimes during the writing of problems it appears more convenient to change the signature from that adopted at the beginning of the two imaginary voices. Such instances can not be brought under any rule. The overcoming of this or some other difficulty in each individual case helps to build up the experience in contrapuntal writing which these exercises will develop in the course of time.

§ 473. Before proceeding with exercises it will be of advantage to study minutely the six examples in Appendix D that have often been referred to.

(B) Second Form of the Basic Version for
Double-Shifting Counterpoint $Jh= 0$ Present

§ 474. In three-voice horizontal-shifting counterpoint a combination having $Jh= 0$ is excluded from the formula of the basic version, as was the case with simple counterpoint (§ 461). If with the horizontal shift is incorporated also the vertical, this rule remains in force only for those situations where, except in $Jh= 0$, the given combination also has $Jv= 0$. If, at $Jh= 0$, $Jv \neq 0$, this combination is an instance of vertical-shifting counterpoint and enters into the formula of the basic version, not in the capacity of imaginary but as a real combination, having its own Jv. The formula of the basic version in this case will consist of three formulas; two of these are formulas of the imaginary combination, one the formula of the real combination with determinate Jv. Here for the first time is found the requirement that in counterpoint with one derivative two real voices shall satisfy the conditions of vertical-shifting counterpoint. For instance, in the formula for the basic version in Ex. 251 there is, besides the two formulas for the imaginary combination, also a formula for the real combination, with the requirement that the real voices II + III shall be written in double counterpoint at the tenth, namely: (II + III) $Jv= -16$. Exactly the same formula for the basic version is found in Ex. 252; included in its formula is: (I + II) $Jv= 2$.

§ 475. The second form of the basic version now to be examined, appears in two aspeacts (§§ 461-2), which as before are referred to as b.v. form 2 a and b.v. form 2 b. The characteristics follow by which these two sub-forms are distinguished. A voice found in both formulas for the imaginary combinations may be either real (b.v. form 2 a), or imaginary (b.v. form 2 b).

§ 476. *Case 1, B.V. Form 2 a.*—If the voice that recurs in both formulas of the imaginary combination is real (e.g. I in the formula I + II...., I + III...., or II in I.... + II, II + III....), there enters into the construction of the basic version two imaginary voices, designated by different numerals, both of which counterpoint one real. These imaginary voices are shifted at the given Jv of the real combination, wherein $Jh= 0$. In counterpointing the real voice they form a three-voice combination, which is the derivative.

In Ex. 251 the real voices, II and III, are written in double counterpoint at the tenth ($Jv = -16$). The two imaginary voices represent a shift at this Jv. The problem is written section by section. The first two measures (as far as the entry of the imaginary voices)

are written not in simple counterpoint as before, but so that II and III form double counterpoint at the tenth. Then the voice parts are transferred to the supplementary staves
in accordance with vv of the imaginary voices, in addition to which they show a shift
at $Jv = -16$. Next the second section is written (third and fourth measures). Since the
imaginary combination must be written in advance of the real (§ 455) I is done first of
all in a given section, so that it will form three-voice counterpoint with the two imaginary
voices. Then II and III are counterpointed to I, but so that the two former voices will
be in double counterpoint at the tenth. The voice parts in measures 3 and 4 are now
transferred to the supplementary staves and the same process applied to the third section
(mm. 5-6) and so on to the end of the problem.

Ex. 251   (a)   Basic Version First Form

§ 477. *Case 2, B.V. .Form 2* b—The characteristic of this sub-form is that in both formulas of the imaginary combination the imaginary voice is represented by one and the same numeral (e.g. II + III.... and I + III.... ; I + II.... and II.... + III etc.). Since this voice enters at the same time in both combinations, then in the absence of the vertical shift it also enters at the same altitude in both. The result is that it could be written only once, as in Ex. 250, where the basic version has only one supplementary staff. When the vertical shift is incorporated with the horizontal this imaginary voice must be taken at a different altitude for each combination, and therefore must have a double presentation, although the time entries for both combinations are identical, as in the basic version of Ex. 252. This sub-form of the basic version exhibits still another peculiarity: the absence of that combination of real and imaginary voices which appears as the derivative; also the imaginary voices do not represent a shift of the real voices at the given *Jv*, as in the basic version of the first sub-form. The derivative, since it is broken up into its units, can not be written until the basic version is completed; the shift is then made according to the requirements of the problem.

(b) Derivative

In view of the fact that the lower voice does not participate in the real combination, having $Jv = 2$, the free use of fourths is possible, which at this Jv are variable dissonances. Since an original fourth at $Jv = 2$ gives a derivative imperfect consonance $(3 + 2 = 5)$, it may be regarded as having the characteristics of the latter, hence the fourths on the unaccented beats in the third measure, the two parallel fourths in the seventh measure, etc. Releasing fourths from their limitations facilitates considerably the solution of problems. Furthermore, the voices of the derivative are arranged according to diagram (1), consequently I and II, with a shift at $Jv = 2$, remain as upper and middle voices in the derivative. Hence it is necessary to exclude from the original the interval that gives a derivative $\overline{8}$, namely, $\overline{10}$.

§ 478. If in double-shifting counterpoint all $JJv = 0$, horizontal-shifting counterpoint is obtained; if all JJh, vertical-shifting; if all JJv and JJh are equal to zero, simple counterpoint. Therefore simple, vertical-shifting and horizontal-shifting counterpoint may all be regarded as special cases of double-shifting counterpoint.

§ 479. Combinations giving several derivatives will not be dwelt upon. To obtain them with the aid of a basic version, increasing the number of its imaginary RR, would be too difficult. Each additional $R\ldots$, imposing new restrictions on the real voices that counterpoint the imaginaries, only multiplies difficulties, and the problems are hard enough without them. The solution of such problems is possible with the aid of a basic version that is contrapuntally correct. But increasing their RR also increases the defects that are characteristic in general of such versions: the unavoidable emptiness of the three-voice combinations extracted from them. These versions may be obtained rather by writing two contrapuntal voices (Cp_1 and Cp_2) to a three-voice imitation, which gives an original and two derivatives ($Cp_1 + Cp_2 + P$; $Cp_1 + Cp_2 + R_1$, $Cp_1 + Cp_2 + R_2$), or by writing a fifth voice (Cp) to a double canon, which gives an original and three derivatives: ($Cp + P^a + P^b$, $Cp + R^a + R^b$, $Cp + P^a + R^b$, $Cp + P^b + R^a$), etc. Theoretically such cases present nothing new, and examples will not be quoted because of lack of space.

§ 480. With the study of three-voice double-shifting counterpoint the problems are ended. The shifting of voices in two directions, vertical and horizontal, has been investigated, and the methods whereby can be solved   any problem of shifts in either direction, as well as all possible combinations of shifts in both directions. The two chapters following may be regarded as supplementary.

CHAPTER XXIV

COUNTERPOINT WITH AND WITHOUT RESTS

§ 481. In explaining the technique of horizontal-shifting counterpoint numerous examples from different eras were quoted where both the original and derivative combinations—sometimes the basic version—entered into the structure of a composition, serving as thematic material. As supplementary to this study some very infrequent applications of this counterpoint will be examined, in which the entire composition presents an original combination that can be executed in another way, as derivative. This process was known in the Flemish Schools as counterpoint "with and without rests." In music histories mention is often made of a pupil of Josquin de Pres, Pierre Moulu, who wrote a mass that can be performed in two ways: as written, and also by omitting all rests.*From this mass, containing movements in from two to five voices, two examples—two-voice and three-voice—will be quoted, in order to explain the essential features of this process and to show that such a problem can be solved by means of what has already been learned.

§ 482. Rests found in the original are omitted in the derivative. However, not all of them are omitted, only those larger than a half-rest. This, and all rests of smaller values, are retained in the derivative. The half-rest, as will be seen in the examples, often precedes the first note that enters after a voice has been interrupted, and together with this note is transferred to the derivative. The note with which a new phrase begins may be of any desired length, but the note on which it ends occupies ordinarily not less than half a measure, because of the necessity of ending a melody quietly and not cutting it off abruptly on a short note. If some intermediate notes of a phrase occupy three-fourths of the measure, followed by a half-rest, and in the next mesaure a rest of the same value precedes the note of entry:

both rests, equal in value to a whole-rest, must be omitted in the derivative:

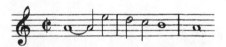

Such cases are not found in the derivatives of the following examples.

Obs.—The silencing of voices on a long note, whereby the melody ends naturally with a cadence in one part while the other voices continue their independent movement—the entry of a voice after a rest where the harmony needs completion, so that both harmonic and contrapuntal requirements are satisfied (as when the entering voice imitates)—all

---

*The manuscript of this mass, entitled "A deux visaiges et plus," or "Missa sans pause," is in the Public Library of Cambria. While the first edition of this book was in course of preparation the author was enabled to obtain a photographic copy through the efforts of V. A. Bulichev, who went from Paris to Cambria for this purpose, and to whom the author herewith expresses his thanks. [Cf. Grove, "Dictionary of Music and Musicians," article Moulu. —Tr.]

these are essentials of good contrapuntal style. In analysing it is necessary to pay special attention to the technical details that enter into the structure of a beautiful melodic line. It is impossible not to observe the beauty of the entrances in Mozart. In this connection his later string quartets, especially the one in C major (K. V. 465), should be the subject of constant and careful study. A finished work of voice-leading can only be the result of a course of study that starts with simple counterpoint, followed by imitation, especially imitation as applied in choral-figuration. Reference may again be made to Bellermann's work on counterpoint, the chapter *Von der Nachahmung* (pp. 293-5), also to Bussler's *Der Strenge Satz*, §§ 29-30.*

§ 483. The omission of rests in the derivative has the effect of shifting a melody to the left. Such a shift for the upper voice will be indicated by the sign +, for the lower by —, for the middle by ∓ (§§ 441-2). The omission of rests will be called rest-removal. This term refers, exclusively, to all rests larger than a half-rest.

§ 484. Since the omission of rests shifts the voices only horizontally, their pitch remaining as before, counterpoint with and without rests is a special case of horizontal-shifting counterpoint, not of vertical-shifting; otherwise there is nothing to prevent its use with vertically-shifting voices also (cf. Ex. 258).

§ 485. If rest-removal were found in one of the voices only at the beginning, this would be an ordinary case of horizontal-shifting counterpoint. But in the examples to be studied, rest-removal is found sometimes in one voice, sometimes in another, giving melodies that are divided into phrases. Therefore an instance of this kind must be regarded as the association of several examples in horizontal-shifting counterpoint.

§ 486. Each time that a voice shows that rests have been removed there will be placed above the staff, immediately after the last rest, a figure equal to their total sum, taking as usual the measure as the unit of value. If the highest voice, no sign will be placed before the figure, + being understood; if the lowest voice the figure will be preceded by the sign —; if the middle voice, by ∓ After this figure is a comma, followed by h, indicating the shift of this voice in the derivative. The quantity h is equal to the sum of the first rests:

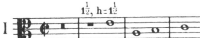

But following this, rests that again shift the voice in the same direction are indicated by a new h, equal to the sum of the new rests, added to the preceding h:

The same voice as derivative:

*Cf. also: Goetschius: "Applied Counterpoint," Chapters X and XI; Dunhill: "Chamber Music." —Tr.

The concluding note where each phrase is silent is indicated by a star: *. By numbering the measures each shift to the left is easily verified. For example, the second phrase in the original enters on the second half of measure 5, and has $h = 2\frac{1}{2}$; therefore in the derivative its entry occurs at the beginning of measure 3. The third phrase in the original $(h = 3)$ begins on the second half of measure 8, shifted to the second half of measures 5 in the derivative. Next comes $h = 5$, therefore measures 14 in the original and 9 in the derivative correspond, etc.

§ 487. Such problems are solved by the methods previously described: with the aid of a basic version written according to the formulas of imaginary combinations. Here the only difference is that instead of one formula for the imaginary combination (= basic version) each problem must have several of these formulas, because of the changing values of Jh.

(A) Two-Voice Counterpoint With and Without Rests

§ 488. The first formula of the derivative with corresponding Jh, and according to it the formula of the imaginary combination, are compiled in their entirety, as in all other cases of horizontal-shifting counterpoint. As long as rest-removal is not in effect in either voice the imaginary voice is written without interruption. If rest-removal is in effect in a real voice that is identical with the imaginary, and only in this one voice, the imaginary voice is written as far as the end of the given phrase, stopping on the note indicated by the star in the real voice (cf. imaginary voice in Ex. 254, mm. 11 and 22, and similar places in Ex. 255). After such interruption of the imaginary voice a new formula for the imaginary combination is substituted for the previous formula; the writing of the imaginary voice then continues according to the new formula. If in this the imaginary voice remains the same voice as it was in the previous formula, it enters somewhat later than the first entry of the real voice after the latter is silent, as in Ex. 254, where the imaginary voice continues the same (I....), and I enters after the rest in measure 11. The new formula ($I_{....}^{h=-1}$) is now applied, beginning with measure 12; the same I enters after the rest in measure 21, and a new formula goes into effect in measure 22, etc.

If rest-removal is effective in a voice that is not identical with the voice it counterpoints, the imaginary voice is interrupted at the place where the voice counterpointing it is silent, i.e. at the sign * (Ex. 254; m. 17). At this interruption the previous formula of the imaginary combination is cancelled, and a new formula takes effect at the next entry after the silencing of the real voice; if this entry precedes the rest-removal (§ 482) then a quarter of a measure earlier.

§ 489. Whatever rest-removal is in effect—consequently a new h—a new formula for the derivative is compiled, the voice concerned takes its new h (immediately after a rest), and the other voice the h that it had before. Jh is equal to their algebraic sum and defines the value of h of the imaginary voice in the new formula (cf. the formula for the next examples).

If the new imaginary formula is identical with the preceding formula its repetition is not necessary, and the imaginary voice is continued without further interruption. If in the new formula $h = 0$ the imaginary voice is discontinued until the next formula takes effect.

§ 490. The following example from Moulu's mass, with the accompanying formulas of derivative and imaginary combinations, illustrate fully these explanations.

Pierre Moulu. Pleni sunt coeli.
Ex. 254 (a)
Original (with rests)

*In the examples taken from this mass the liberties in the use of dissonances, characteristic in general of the old Flemish composers, are not indicated. The reader familiar with the rules of the srtict style can easily locate these places himself.

Formulas for the preceding example:

Meas. 3: $(I + II^{h=-2})$ $Jh = -2$; $I^{h=-2}_{....} + II$

"   11: $(I^{h=1} + II^{h=-2})$ $Jh = -1$; $I^{h=-1}_{....} + II$ (m. 12)

"   18: $(I^{h=1} + II^{h=-3})$ $Jh = -2$; $I^{h=-2}_{....} + II$

"   21: $(I^{h=2} + II^{h=-3})$ $Jh = -1$; $I^{h=-1}_{....} + II$ (m. 22)

(b)   Derivative (without rests)

§ 491. In the preceding example from Moulu (and also in two other two-voice sections from the same mass, the *Crucifixus* and *Et ascendit*), *Jh* in all derivative formulas has the same sign (negative), therefore the imaginary voice also remains constant: I$_{....}$. In the next example *Jh* is alternately negative and positive, giving for imaginary voices I$_{....}$ and II$_{....}$ respectively.

Ex. 255
(a)

Original (with rests)

Formulas for the preceding example:

Meas. 2: $(I^{h=1} + II)$ $Jh = $ 1; $I + II_{....}^{h=1}$

"   6: $(I^{h=1} + II^{h=-1\frac{1}{2}})$ $Jh = -\frac{1}{2}$; $I_{....}^{h=} -1\frac{1}{2} + II$

"   9: $(I^{h=2} + II^{h=-1\frac{1}{2}})$ $Jh = $ $\frac{1}{2}$; $I + II_{....}^{h=\frac{1}{2}}$

"   12: $(I^{h=2} + II^{h=-2\frac{1}{2}})$ $Jh = -\frac{1}{2}$; $I_{....}^{h=} -\frac{1}{2} + II$

Derivative (without rests)
(b)

(B) Three-Voice Counterpoint With and Without Rests

§ 492. When rest-removal is in effect in any voice of a three-voice texture two formulas for the derivative must be compiled, taking the voice concerned alternately in combination with each of the other two. The procedure according to each formula is the same as indicated in §§ 488-91. All that was said regarding imaginary voices applies also here.

Pierre Moulu

Ex. 256   (a)

Original (with rests)

Formulas for the preceding example:

Meas. 4: $(\mathrm{II} + \mathrm{III}^{h=-3})$ $Jh'' = -3$; $\mathrm{II}^{h=-3}_{\ldots} + \mathrm{III}$

       $(\mathrm{I} + \mathrm{III}^{h=-3})$ $Jh\Sigma = -3$; $\mathrm{I}^{h=-3}_{\ldots} + \mathrm{III}$

"   7: $(\mathrm{I} + \mathrm{II}^{h=-3})$ $Jh' = -3$; $\mathrm{I}^{h=-3}_{\ldots} + \mathrm{II}$

       $(\mathrm{II}^{h=3} + \mathrm{III}^{h=-3})$ $Jh'' = 0$

" 12: $(\mathrm{I}^{h=3} + \mathrm{II}^{h=-3})$ $Jh' = 0$

       $(\mathrm{I}^{h=3} + \mathrm{III}^{h=-3})$ $Jh\Sigma = 0$

" 15: $(\mathrm{II}^{h=3} + \mathrm{III}^{h=-4})$ $Jh'' = -1$; $\mathrm{II}^{h=-1}_{\ldots} + \mathrm{III}$

       $(\mathrm{I}^{h=3} + \mathrm{III}^{h=-4})$ $Jh\Sigma = -1$; $\mathrm{I}^{h=-1}_{\ldots} + \mathrm{III}$

" 18: $(\mathrm{I}^{h=3} + \mathrm{II}^{h=-4})$ $Jh' = -1$; $\mathrm{I}^{h=-1}_{\ldots} + \mathrm{II}$

       $(\mathrm{II}^{h=4} + \mathrm{III}^{h=-4})$ $Jh'' = 0$

" 25: $(\mathrm{I}^{h=5} + \mathrm{II}^{h=-4})$ $Jh' = 1$; $\mathrm{I} + \mathrm{II}^{h=1}_{\ldots}$

       $(\mathrm{I}^{h=5} + \mathrm{III}^{h=-4})$ $Jh\Sigma = 1$; $\mathrm{I} = \mathrm{III}^{h=1}_{\ldots}$

(b) Derivative (without rests)

§ 493. In conclusion is quoted a three-voice example from Berardi's book,* illustrating counterpoint with and without rests, the only specimen of the kind that the present author has found in theoretical literature.

Angelo Berardi

Ex. 257 (a)

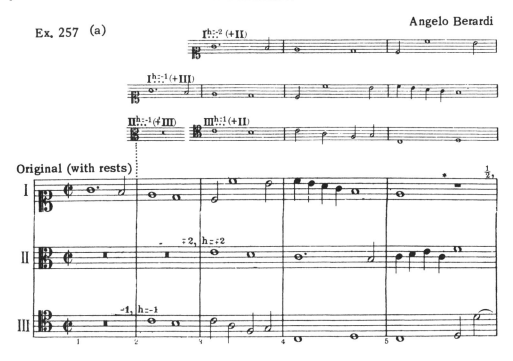

*Angelo Berardi: "Documenti armonici." Libro Primo, doc. 30. "Cantilena con le pause a senza."

Formulas for the preceding example:

Meas. 2: $(I + III^{h=1})$ $Jh\Sigma = -1;$ $I^{h=-1}_{\dots\dots} (+ III)$

    $(II + III^{h=-1})$ $Jh'' = -1;$ $II^{h=-1}_{\dots\dots} (+ III)$

" 3: $(I + II^{h=-2})$ $Jh' = -2;$ $I^{h=-2}_{\dots\dots} + II$

    $(II^{h=2} + III^{h=-1})$ $Jh'' = 1;$ $II + III^{h=1}_{\dots\dots}$

" 6: $(I^{h=\frac{1}{2}} + II^{h=-2})$ $Jh' = -1\frac{1}{2};$ $I^{h=-1\frac{1}{2}}_{\dots\dots} + II$ (m. 7)

    $(I^{h=\frac{1}{2}} + III^{h=-1})$ $Jh\Sigma = -\frac{1}{2};$ $I^{h=-1\frac{1}{2}}_{\dots\dots} + III$

" 7: $(II^{h=2} + III^{h=-1\frac{1}{2}})$ $Jh'' = \frac{1}{2};$ $II + III^{h=\frac{1}{2}}_{\dots\dots}$ (m. 8)

    $(I^{h=\frac{1}{2}} + III^{h=-1\frac{1}{2}})$ $Jh\Sigma = -1;$ $I^{h=-1}_{\dots\dots} + III$

" 8: $(I^{h=\frac{1}{2}} + II^{h=-2\frac{1}{2}})$ $Jh' = -2;$ $I^{h=-2}_{\dots\dots} + II$

    $(II^{h=2\frac{1}{2}} + III^{h=-1\frac{1}{2}})$ $Jh'' = 1;$ $II + III^{h=1}_{\dots\dots}$

" 11: $(I^{h=1\frac{1}{2}} + II^{h=-2\frac{1}{2}})$ $Jh' = -1;$ $I^{h=-1}_{\dots\dots} + II$ (m. 12)

    $(I^{h=1\frac{1}{2}} + III^{h=-1\frac{1}{2}})$ $Jh\Sigma = 0$

" 12: $(II^{h=2\frac{1}{2}} + III^{h=-2\frac{1}{2}})$ $Jh'' = 0$

    $(I^{h=1\frac{1}{2}} + II^{h=-2\frac{1}{2}})$ $Jh\Sigma = -1;$ $I^{h=-1}_{\dots\dots} + III$

Obs.—Stated in this way, the formulas show that the real and imaginary voices must agree. But the same problem can be solved by a similar method, with the aid of all three formulas, because of the fact that the voice entries fall definitely into three divisions: (1) from the beginning to measure 6; (2) from the entries of the voices after the rests in measures 6-8 up to measure 10; and (3) from the new entry of the outer voices in measures 11-12. These divisions may be written as three different problems. But in this case the measures where the divisions coincide would have to be written without the corresponding formula, then compared with the derivative in order to avoid inaccuracies.

(b) Derivative (without rests)

§ 494. Compositions featuring this kind of counterpoint—"with and without rests"—are little more than historical curiosities. On the contrary, more freedom in using counterpoint admitting of horizontal shifts, as one of the resources of thematic development, is of much greater scope, as is proved by the numerous shifts in the examples quoted. This counterpoint was known to the composers of the Flemish Schools. Passed on to the old Italian and German composers, it was extensively used at the time and is still a resource of contemporary music (cf. Ex. 244, from Glazounow). These facts should have aroused the interest of theorists and led them to an investigation of this counterpoint—to study its characteristics and to establish its place in the other categories of complex counterpoint, and if only in a general way to explain how such contrapuntal combinations are brought about. What light does present music theory throw on this matter?

§ 495. The earliest known examples of this counterpoint in theoretical literature are found in Vicentino's *L'Antica musica,* published in 1555, three years before the publication of Zarlino's treatise. These examples illustrate double-shifting counterpoint. Following the terminology of his time, the author calls his counterpoint "with and without rests;" he bases his treatment on a common characteristic of double counterpoint (the inverse shift) and disregards the other characteristics by which the horizontal shift is defined, thereby referring his examples to the province of double counterpoint, to which he devotes a chapter. Vicentino uses the term "double counterpoint" in the same sense in which "complex counterpoint" is here employed; he divides the entire domain of counterpoint into two categories: simple and double, a classification still found in the latest works.* Vicentino's examples are chiefly of historical interest—they can not be regarded as models to imitate. Observe in both derivative combinations the proximity of fifths and the hidden fifth at the beginning of Ex. 259, evidences that the author had not fully mastered the limitations inherent in the problem.

Ex. 258   Vicentino

Ex. 259

Irreproachable as to technique is the question from Berardi, Ex. 257, which as already stated is the only three-voice specimen of this counterpoint found thus far in theoretical literature. It dates from the late seventeenth century (*Documenti armonici,* published in 1687). This example proves that the traditions of the Flemish composers regarding the resources of complex counterpoint were not yet lost. The length of this example—fifteen measures—precludes any idea that the horizontal shift of three voices may have been a mere coincidence. The writer could not have been unacquainted with

---

*It is hardly necessary to dwell on the fallacy of such a classification. Since the characteristics of double counterpoint are represented in the inverse shift, cases where the shift is direct would be excluded from the domain of both simple and double counterpoint.

the methods that yield such combinations. Had his skill been of a purely empirical nature it would have been concerned with problems of a single definite form, or would even have generalized to a greater extent, but no light is thrown on these questions in his text. The author limits himself to the statement that he could have quoted other compositions of no less interest than this (he does not say that the example is by himself); in his own words such examples prove that "musica est res profunda", but as to how they are written he is silent. No doubt this is an illustration of a fact often mentioned in music histories—that the old contrapuntists kept their knowledge secret, passing it on to the elect only verbally. Certain expressions used by Berardi in reference to the example quoted seem to confirm this supposition, for instance: "per dare un poco di lune, come si devono comporre simile artificii . . ." If this was the attitude of the old contrapuntists their efforts were certainly crowned with sucess as far as horizontal-shifting counterpoint was concerned. That this was the state of contrapuntal study in the eighteenth century is clearly shown by the fact that one of the best-known theorists, Kirnberger,* in combining two melodies in double counterpoint, included, among other shifts, the following combinations in double-shifting counterpoint:

Ex. 260   Kirnberger

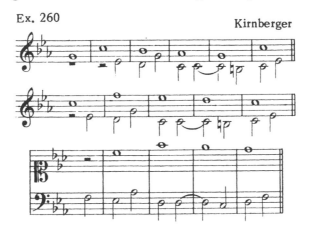

He places these examples in the division entitled "Von dem doppelten Kontrapunkt", but did not accompany them with any remarks nor did he say anything about horizontal shifting. If Vicentino, the sixteenth-century theorist, incorrectly referred horizontal shifting to the category of double counterpoint he at least classified such examples, calling them "counterpoint with and without rests." Even the eighteenth-century theorists took no notice of the horizontal shift when it appeared among other shifts and apparently gave no examples from which to quote.

Of the theoretical literature of the nineteenth century, Habert's work on imitation is worthy of notice. In analysing the imitations of Palestrina Habert does not pay enough attention to the numerous cases of horizontal shifting where two subjects are concerned. Referring to these cases he says that at first glance they seem to be in double counterpoint, whereas in fact they are not.** In this quite correct observation is seen the first

---

*J. Ph. Kirnberger: "Die Kunst des reinen Satzes," II Theil, II Abtheilung (1777), S. 177-81. 5-ter Abschnill, "Von dem doppelten Kontrapunkt."

**"It would appear that double counterpoint were present, but such is not the case," Habert, "Die Lehre von der Nachamung, 1899, S. 208.

step in advance since the time of Vicentino in the study of horizontal-shifting counter-point. Habert treats this feature of horizontal shifting as an accident peculiar to the combination given; he advises to continue horizontal shifting only as far as it forms counterpoint with the other voices (p. 208), but he gives no indications as to how shifting the subjects horizontally gives a contrapuntal combination.*

If it is added that Riemann called attention to the horizontal shift in contrary motion in two of the fugues from *The Well-Tempered Clavichord,* as also did Prout to the shifting of the two subjects in the E♭ organ fugue of Bach (Ex. 243), it is clearly seen that more than three centuries have elapsed before any material advance has been made in the study of horizontal-shifting counterpoint. It may be asserted without exaggeration that the questions brought up in Part Two of this work have hitherto not only remained unsolved but have not even been stated, and that the study of them as here presented is the first of its kind.

---

*And this same policy of evading an important issue is still prevalent in the twentieth century. The statements of at least two eminent writers confirm this. Dr. Percy Goetschius ("Applied Counterpoint," 1902, pp. 277-8) quotes two examples in horizontal-shifting counterpoint and refers to two more in a footnote. In the text he says (p. 277): "These are purely experimental, and cannot be obtained by any method of calculation." Also Dr. Donald Tovey, referring to a case of the horizontal shift in Contrapunctus VIII of Bach's "The Art of Fugue," says: "The abnor-mality in this relation . . . consists in the fact that it is not only at a different pitch, which in itself would mean inversion in a double counterpoint other than in the 8ve, but that it combines at a different point, a device for which the books have no name" ("A Companion to The Art of Fugue," pp. 19-20). The place he refers to is m. 125, cf with m. 39. —Tr.

CHAPTER XXV

CONCLUSION

§ 496. The study of shifting counterpoint is a most important and extensive phase of complex counterpoint. Closely associated with it in the present work is counterpoint that admits of duplication in imperfect consonances. In discussing the functions of the basic version the method for obtaining derivative combinations with altered note-values and other changes of form was indicated (§§ 338-9), cases that also refer to the province of complex counterpoint.

A summary of its divisions was given in the Introduction, and of these only one is absent from this work: metamorphosed counterpoint. This phase of the subject, found in the older textbooks (Vicentino, Zarlino), also in later ones, is applied—among others—by Bach, in two of the fugues from *The Art of Fugue*. It can be explained very concisely and a sufficient mastery of it should take only a comparatively short time. Best of all, it can be studied in Marpurg's *Abhandlung von der Fuge*.* With the exception of metamorphosed counterpoint all other kinds of complex counterpoint are represented in this book.

§ 497. Since multi-voice counterpoint in the strict style, both simple and with certain changes that have already been dealt with in the study of three-voice counterpoint, there would be no purpose in explaining the theory of shifting counterpoint for a larger number of voices. Such a theory would present nothing new, and the difficulty of working out problems would increase to such an extent that although they might be theoretically possible they would often prove incapable of solution. At the beginning of the study of shifting counterpoint attention should be concentrated on two-voice counterpoint (Divisions A and C, especially the former). These divisions may be studied independently, in succession, or concurrently. As to specific instructions, see Chapter VIII, also § 275, and the observations to §§ 290, 340, 423 and 482.

§ 498. In passing from strict to free counterpoint it is necessary to have a good command of harmony. The harmonic attitude toward music, which coincides with the beginning of the seventeenth century (rise of opera, the homophonic style, figured bass), appeared as the exact antihesis of strict counterpoint. Multi-voice music was not the result of combined melodies, but that of harmonies (chords) in succession. Instead of all voices sharing equally in the texture of a composition, one principal voice predominated, accompanied by chords—the system of ecclesiastical modes was superseded by the present tonal system. The synthesis of these opposing forces resulted in free counterpoint. The ideal relationship of these elements—counterpoint and harmony—is that by the union of voices that move freely and independently harmonies arise that satisfy all the requirements of tonality and modulation.

In the free style the use of intervals is entirely different from that in the strict, and varies according to the harmonic context. At times their use is in agreement with the strict style, at others there is more or less departure, finally all connection with the strict style is broken, as harmonic function takes control.

---

*Part II, Chapters 3 and 4. [See also the articles Augmentation, Cancrizans, Diminution, Recte et recto, Rovescio, in Grove's "Dictionary." —Tr.]

But the possible effects of the strict style on the free is not abrogated; dissonant intervals, for example, that enter into the structure of chord-figuration, can be made to conform to its conditions, so that these effects do not prevent the chords remaining in the tonal system (cf. §§ 232-5).

The general features of the strict style, penetrating in some form or another the free style, exert on the latter the most salutary influence. The result of this influence is logic and consistency, and a good harmonic basis is secured for both instrumental and vocal music, especially vocal.

The variable conditions of using intervals that are not subject to exact control prevents in the free style the statement of rules for vertical-shifting counterpoint in the simple and definite form that the strict style renders possible. It may be said that an independent theory for shifting counterpoint does not exist in the free style. Certain features common to both the strict and free styles may serve as guides, for instance in double counterpoint, where the practical application of the strict rules are of value, as in the establishing of limiting intervals, the forbidding of similar motion at indices of the second group, etc., often the rules of harmony apply. The strict rules offer something tangible and permanent, those of the free style vary according to the opinions of different theorists.

The dependence of contrapuntal textures on a harmonic basis which explains and justifies it and which requires constant control from the harmonic standpoint for both original and derivative combinations, gives the exercises in complex counterpoint of the free style an original character that distinguishes them sharply from the analogous exercises in strict counterpoint. The assimilation of the new possibilities available in shifting counterpoint of the free style should not be so much a theoretical consideration as a matter of practice and skill, acquired by empirical methods. As for horizontal-shifting counterpoint, the rules are the same for both the strict and free styles.

§ 499. Skill in the handling of counterpoint is of such advantage in composition that the beginner should devote part of his time to its study. The object will be attained with the least expenditure of time and labor by following the methods given in this book; the result will be greater assurance and freedom in part-writing, skill in improving the musical content of the individual voices, the development—of special value in thematic work—of the ability to extract derivative combinations, the profit to be gained by acquaintance with an infinite variety of contrapuntal forms as means of artistic expression, and the subordination of the whole realm of tonal material to the creative imagination. Quoting Goethe:

> Wer sie nicht kennte,
> Die Elemente,
> Ihre Krafte
> Und Eigenschaft,
> Ware kein Meister
> Ueber die Geister.

["Those who do not know the elements and technique of their craft can never be master over its spirit." —Faust, Part I]

The old masters did not scorn exercises in counterpoint. If their custom of giving each other puzzle-canons to solve evokes a smile, the time and work spent on the solution of such problems is not entirely to be regretted. Though the secrets of this skill were jealously guarded it must be admitted that at the basis of such feats was a real understanding of the importance that they had for the development of contrapuntal technique. Therefore the composers of former times were able to write the most com- licated scores rapidly, easily solving technical problems that were beyond the powers of later musicians. Amid this atmosphere of contrapuntal research, with its experimenting with new and intricate interweaving of voices, arose the majestic figure of Johann Sebastian Bach, who reached the furthest limits in his use of complex counterpoint as the means of realizing a high artistic purpose.

§ 500. The object of the present work is not to analyse and classify examples from musical literature but to develop the deductive faculty. The points of departure are: The concept of voice-shifting and the principle that in complex counterpoint both the original and the derivative combinations must satisfy the requirements of simple counterpoint. The analysis of the concept of shifting governs the general plan of the book and it includes in its scope shifting counterpoint in all of its many phases, where each form has a definite place, irrespective of whether or not it is used. The consistent application of these principles gives the system of rules for shifting counterpoint.

The deductive method can be applied without difficulty in a given case, owing to the fact that these same fundamental qualities of voices—their capacity to shift, and the resulting relationship—are completely subject to mathematical treatment. Basing the study of shifting counterpoint on elementary algebra renders possible exhaustive state- ment together with a conciseness otherwise unobtainable. A cursory view of the program of shifting counterpoint leads to the conclusion that musical literature uses only a few of the resources available. Evidence of this is that many of the examples quoted (most of them in Division B and nearly all in Division D), both in the text and in the appen- dices, refer to forms of shifting counterpoint never before actualized in music.

It is believed that the study of this book will lead to the conviction that only on the basis of mathematics can be built a clear and rational theory of shifting counterpoint; that it is no longer possible to revert to the redundant, vague, inaccurate and confused explanations of former times, and that only the method of mathematics can rend the veil of semi-mystical secrecy that for such a long time has obscured the study of convertible counterpoint.

APPENDIX A

Thirty-Two Two-Voice Examples at all Indices from

$Jv=1$ to $Jv=6$ and from $Jv=-1$ to $Jv=-13$ Inclusive

$^2\,\mathrm{J}v{=}1$

$(I^{v=1}+II)_{Jv=1}$

With reference to this table and to those of the succeeding JJv, cf. Obs., § 154

Original

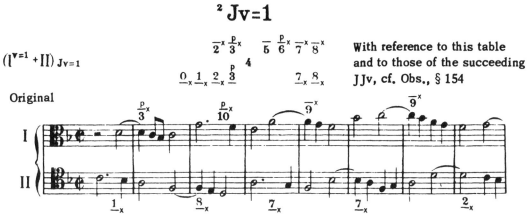

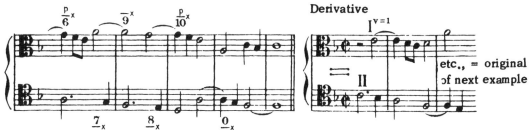

Derivative

etc., = original of next example

$^2\,\mathrm{J}v{=}{-}1$

$I^{d=2}+II,\ I+II^{d=2}$ (§ 204)

$(I+II)_{Jv=-1}$ admits of shift at $Jv=6$ (§ 56)

Interchange of Original and Derivative (§ 68, [1]): $(I^{v=-1}+II)_{Jv=-1}$

Original

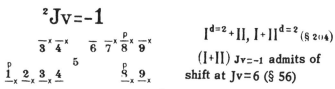

Derivative

etc., = original of preceding example

$$^2\text{Jv}=2$$

$(I^{v=2}+II)$ Jv=2 $\quad\quad\quad\quad\quad\quad\quad\quad$ $I^{d=2}+II$ (§ 196, [1])

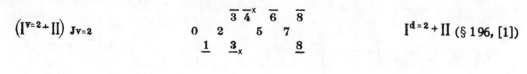

Original

Derivative
$I^{v=2}$

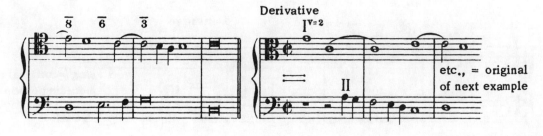

etc., = original
of next example

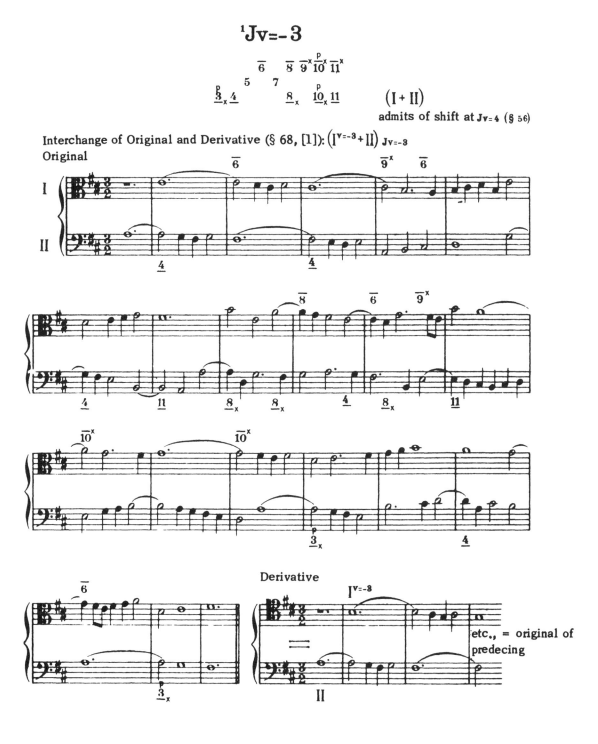

308

Interchange of Original and Derivative (§ 68, [1]): $\left(I^{v=-4}+II\right)$ Jv=-4

Original

Derivative

etc., = original of preceding example

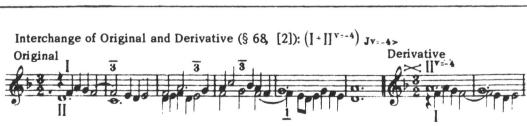

Interchange of Original and Derivative (§ 68, [2]): $\left(I+II^{v=-4}\right)$ Jv=-4>

Original

Derivative

310

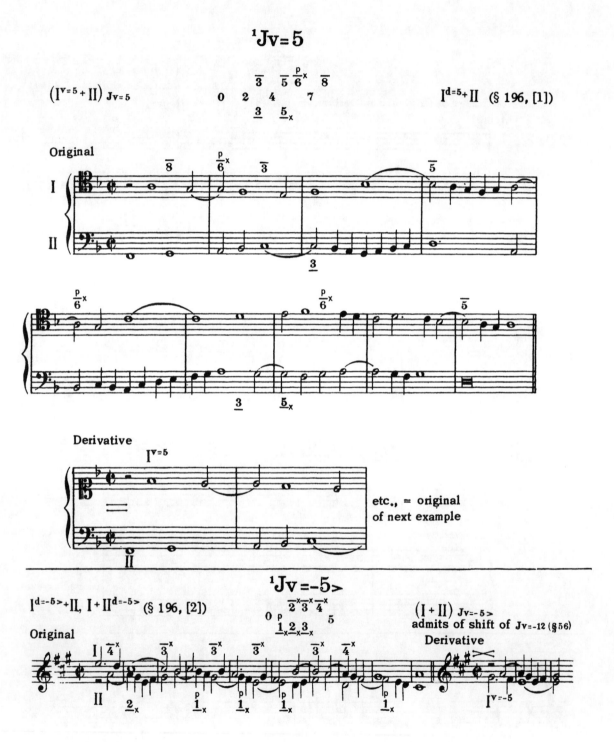

$$^{1}\mathrm{J}v=-5<$$

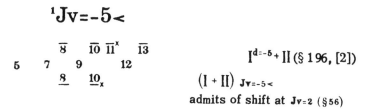

$$\mathrm{I}^{d=-5}+\mathrm{II}\ (\S\,196,\,[2])$$

$$\left(\mathrm{I}+\mathrm{II}\right)\ \mathbf{J_{v=-5<}}$$

admits of shift at $\mathbf{J_{v=2}}$ $(\S\,56)$

Interchange of Original and Derivative ($\S\,68,\,[1]$): $\left(\mathrm{I}^{v=-5}+\mathrm{II}\right)\ \mathbf{J_{v=-5<}}$

Original

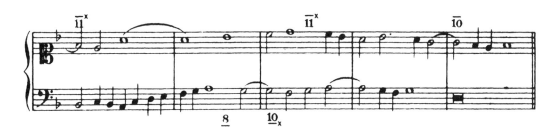

Derivative

etc., = original of preceding example

$$\mathrm{I}^{d=-5>}+\mathrm{II},\ \mathrm{I}+\mathrm{II}^{d=-5>}(\S\,196,\,[2])$$

Interchange of Original and Derivative ($\S\,68,\,[2]$): $\left(\mathrm{I}+\mathrm{II}^{v=-5}\right)\ \mathbf{J_{v=-5>}}$

Original

Derivative

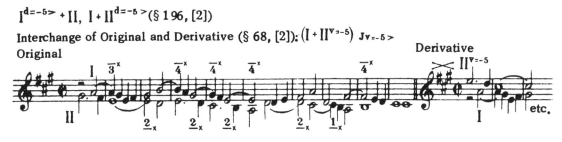

312

$${}^{2}J\mathbf{v}{=}{-}6{<}$$

$$\overline{8}{}^{x}\overline{9}{}^{x}\overset{p}{\overline{10}}{}^{x} \quad \overline{12}\ \overline{13}{}^{x}\overline{14}{}^{x}$$

$$\underline{7}{}_{x}\underline{8}{}_{x}\underline{9}{}_{x}\overset{p}{\underline{10}} \quad \overset{p}{\underline{11}} \qquad \underline{14}{}_{x} \qquad (\mathrm{I}+\mathrm{II})\ \mathbf{J\mathbf{v}{=}{-}6{<}}$$

admits of shift of $\mathbf{J\mathbf{v}{=}1}$ (§56)

Interchange of Original and Derivative (§ 68, [1]): $\left(\mathrm{I}^{\mathbf{v}{=}{-}6}+\mathrm{II}\right)\ \mathbf{J\mathbf{v}{=}{-}6{<}}$
Original

Derivative

etc., = original of
preceding example

Interchange of Original and Derivative (§ 68, [2]): $\left(\mathrm{I}+\mathrm{II}^{\mathbf{v}{=}{-}6}\right)\ \mathbf{J\mathbf{v}{=}{-}6{>}}$
Original

Derivative

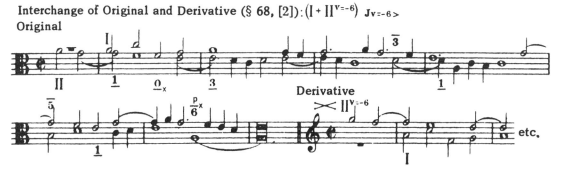

etc.

^{1}Jv=-7

Interchange of Original and Derivative (§ 68, [2]): $\left(I^{v=-7}+II\right)$ Jv=-7
Original

Derivative

etc., = original of
preceding example

316

$$^{2}J_V = -8$$

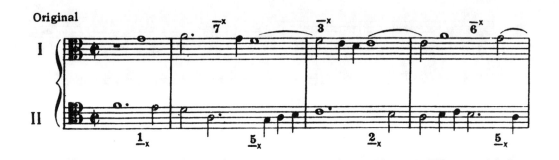

Derivative

etc., = original
of next example

Interchange of Original and Derivative (§ 68, [2]): $(I+II^{v=-8})$ $J_{v=-8}$
Original

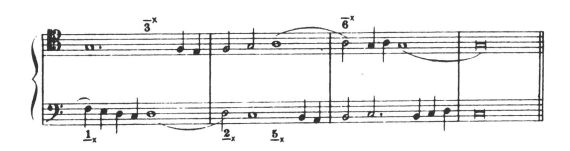

Derivative

etc., = original of
preceding example

$$^2\mathrm{Jv}=-9$$

$(\mathrm{I}+\mathrm{II}^{\mathrm{v}=-9})\,\mathrm{Jv}=-9$ 0 2 4 5 $\overline{6}$ 7 $\overline{8}$ 9   With $\genfrac{}{}{0pt}{}{8}{1}$ possible $\mathrm{I}^{\mathrm{d}=-9}+\mathrm{II}$ (§ 198)

$\underline{1}$ $\underline{3}$ " $\genfrac{}{}{0pt}{}{1}{1}$ " $\mathrm{I}+\mathrm{II}^{\mathrm{d}=-9}$ (§ 200, [2])

Original

etc., = original
of next example

Interchange of Original and Derivative (§ 68, [2]): $\left(I^{v=-9}+II\right)$ Jv=-9
Original

etc., = original of preceding example

Interchange of Original and Derivative (§ 68, [2]): $\left(I + II^{\triangledown=-10}\right)$ $J_{\triangledown=-10}$

Original

etc., = original of
preceding example

322

$${}^{1}Jv{=}{-}11$$

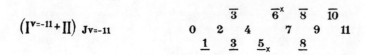

Original

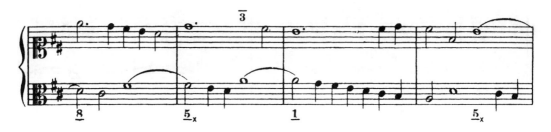

Derivative

etc., = original
of next example

Interchange of Original and Derivative (§ 68, [2]): $\left(I + II^{v=-11}\right) J_{v=-11}$
Original

Derivative

etc., = original of
preceding example

Interchange of Original and Derivative (§ 68, [2]): $\left(I + II^{v=-12}\right)$ $J_{v=-12}$
Original

etc., = original of
preceding example

Interchange of Original and Derivative (§ 68, [2]): $\left(I + II^{v=-13}\right)$ $J_{v=-13}$
Original

Derivative

etc., = original of
preceding example

APPENDIX B

TO PART ONE, DIVISION B

Twelve Examples in Three-Voice Vertical-Shifting Counterpoint,

Two to Each Diagram

$Jv =$ 0,   No. 5 (Jv'), Nos. 3, 6 ($Jv\Sigma$)

$Jv =$ 1,   No. 10 (Jv'')

$Jv = -1$,   No. 8 (Jv')

$Jv =$ 2,   No. 1 ($Jv\Sigma$)

$Jv = -2$,   No. 2 (Jv' and $Jv\Sigma$), No. 9 (Jv'')

$Jv =$ 3,   No. 4 (Jv'')

$Jv = -3$,   No. 1 (Jv')

$Jv =$ 4,   No. 6 ($Jv' = 11$), No. 2 (Jv'')

$Jv = -4<$, No. 7 (Jv')

$Jv =$ 5,   No. 1 (Jv'')

$Jv = -5>$, No. 5 (Jv'')

$Jv = -5<$, No. 5 ($Jv\Sigma$)

$Jv =$ 6,   No. 3 (Jv'')

$Jv =$ $-6>$, No. 3 (Jv')

$Jv =$ $-7>$, No. 10 ($Jv' = -14$), No. 8 ($Jv'' = -14$)

$Jv =$ $-7<$, No. 4 ($Jv\Sigma$)

$Jv =$ -8,   Nos. 7, 8 ($Jv\Sigma = -15$)

$Jv =$ -9,   No. 9 ($Jv' = -16$), No. 11 (Jv, Jv''),, No. 12 ($Jv\Sigma = -23$)

$Jv = -10$, No. 4 (Jv')

$Jv = -11$, No. 12 (Jv'), Nos. 6, 7 (Jv''), Nos. 9, 11 ($Jv\Sigma = -18$)

$Jv = -12$, No. 12 (Jv'')

$Jv = -13$, No. 10 ($Jv\Sigma$)

$Jv = -14$, No. 10 (Jv'), No 8 (Jv'')

№ 1.

332

334

№ 6.

XI I + II$^{v=±11}$ + III

$Jv' = 11$ $(Jv=4)$
$\underline{Jv'' = -11}$
$Jv\Sigma = 0$

(t)
  (§§ 267-8)

Original

Derivative

№ 7.

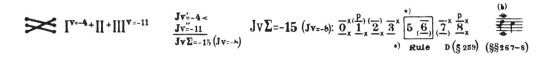

Original

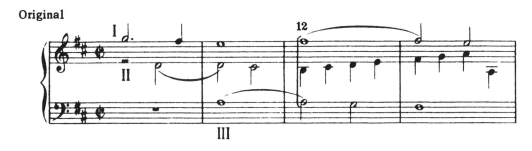

Derivative

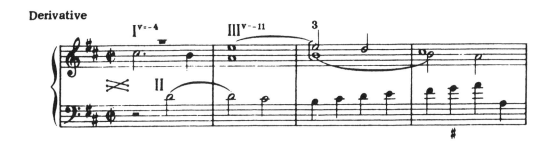

336

№ 9.

№ 10.

338

APPENDIX C

TO PART TWO, DIVISION C

Eight Two-Voice Examples:

Nos. 1-5, Horizontal-Shifting Counterpoint;

Nos. 6-8, Double-Shifting

344

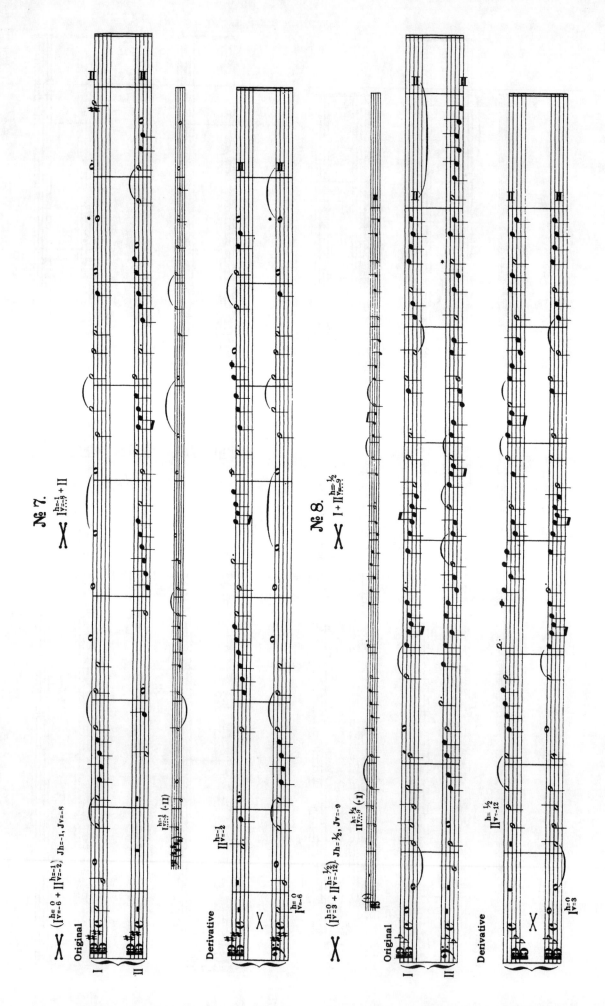

APPENDIX D

TO PART TWO, DIVISION D

Six Examples in Three-Voice Double-Shifting Counterpoint

One to Each Diagram

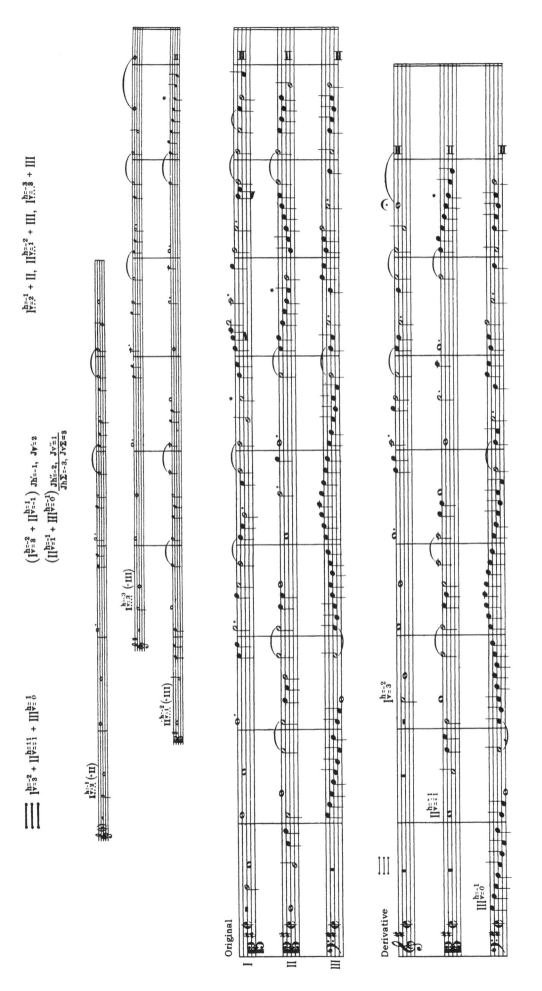

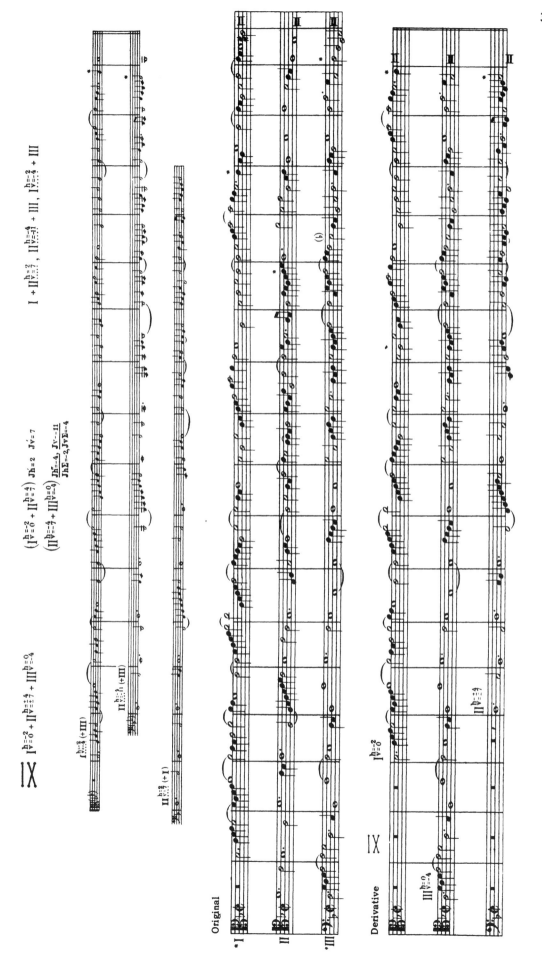

№ 4.

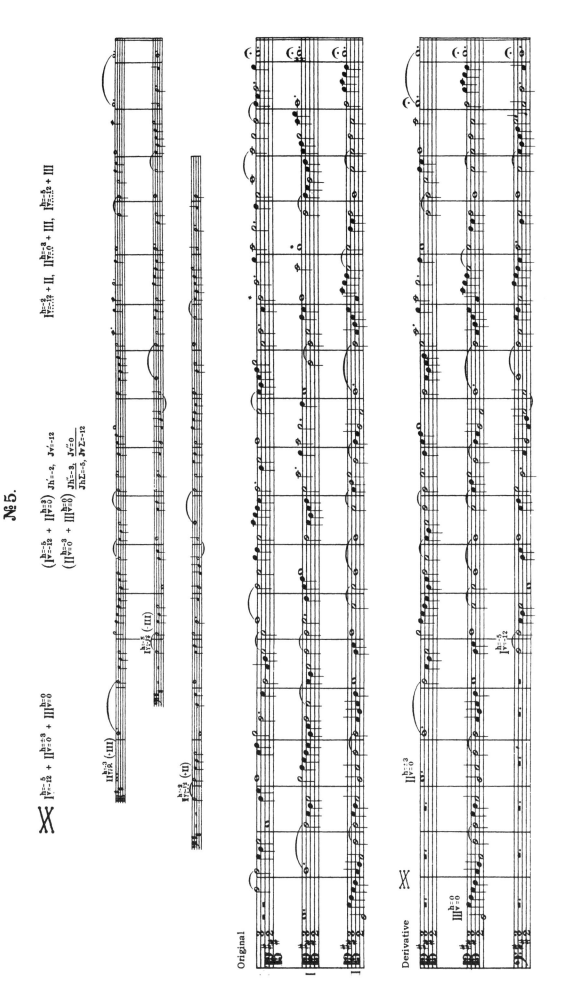

№ 6.

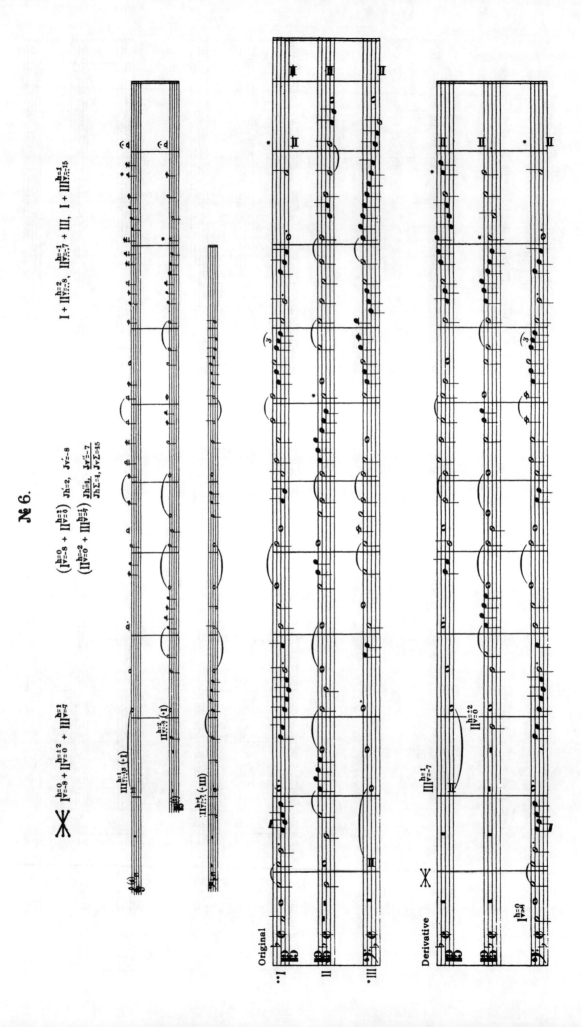

INDEX
(Numbers refer to paragraphs)